# DEADLY
# GAME

# MICHAEL CAINE

# DEADLY GAME

HODDER &
STOUGHTON

First published in Great Britain in 2023 by Hodder & Stoughton
An Hachette UK company

1

Copyright © Michael Caine 2023

The right of Michael Caine to be identified as the
Author of the Work has been asserted by him in accordance
with the Copyright, Designs and Patents Act 1988.

A CIP catalogue record for this title is available from the British Library

Hardback ISBN 978 1 399 70250 8
Trade Paperback ISBN 978 1 399 70251 5
ebook ISBN 978 1 399 70253 9

Typeset in Plantin Light by Palimpsest Book Production Ltd, Falkirk, Stirlingshire

Printed and bound in Great Britain by Clays Ltd, Elcograf S.p.A.

Hodder & Stoughton policy is to use papers that are natural, renewable
and recyclable products and made from wood grown in sustainable forests.
The logging and manufacturing processes are expected to conform
to the environmental regulations of the country of origin.

Hodder & Stoughton Ltd
Carmelite House
50 Victoria Embankment
London EC4Y ODZ

www.hodder.co.uk

For Shakira, Niki, Natasha, Taylor,
Allegra and Miles.

# I

When Dave looked back and remembered seeing the box for the first time, he could have sworn it had been glowing. Well, he couldn't be sure. He was a bit hazy about the whole thing, truth be told, what with the concussion, the general commotion that had rumbled around him for what seemed like hours, and the state of his nerves in general. But that's what his memory told him, or started to tell him, days after it happened: a sort of low glimmering around the edges of the black metal.

Even now, in a lumpy hospital bed, waiting for the X-ray and the results of the other tests that the doctors were a bit vaguer about, he couldn't quite piece it together. The whole thing made next to no sense, especially the speed – and the violence – with which it had all happened. One minute, he was making a phone call. The next, he was being woken up by half of uniformed London, asking him again and again if he was OK and could he tell them, just *once more*, please, sir, what exactly he had found and how.

Dave looked down at the frayed gown they had put him in: the usual embarrassing hospital uniform; the drab spotted pattern barely visible in the grey-white fabric. There was a cannula in the back of his hand, and a bunch of drips at the bedside: 'Just till we've got you back on your feet,' the nurse had assured him. Where were his clothes and boots? His phone? Had they told Jess, like he'd asked? She and the kids would be sick to death with worry. But every time he tried to get an answer or pull himself together, the dull haze of clinical shock reasserted itself. All he knew for certain was that somebody, somehow, was using a hammer drill inside his skull – or at least that's what it felt like – and that, whatever he and Terry had stumbled into that morning was, somehow or other, for someone somewhere, very bad news indeed.

As Dave had told any number of coppers – uniformed at first, then in hazmat gear, and finally in suits – it had been a day like any other, until it had stopped being that in any shape or form, if they caught his meaning.

He had arrived at the hut at eight o'clock as usual, got a brew on, and waited for Terry, who always turned up at ten past eight on the dot. In his hi-vis jacket, T-shirt, paint-spattered jeans and weathered Doc Martens, Terry was the tougher looking of the two, though Dave was, they both knew, stronger. When it came to hauling a beam of timber or a loose headboard off the back of an open truck, it was always Dave who took the lead.

Most of the job was lifting and sorting. Heaving stuff from open-backed lorries and Transits into the dump and then – after a fashion – putting everything into the right pile, ready for 'recycling'. This was what the council rules required, though Dave had never seen much evidence of the half-hearted sifting and categorising making any difference. The piles got bigger, the world turned, and nothing much changed.

The dump was five minutes' walk from Stepney High Street and surrounded on three sides by old warehouses, two of which were being converted for office use. The other side, next to the road, was hemmed in by a twenty-foot-high chicken wire fence, with a gate big enough to allow vehicles to reverse, and a few fake CCTV cameras to put off tramps and druggies. Very occasionally, somebody made it over the top and was found sleeping their previous evening off on a decaying Chesterfield sofa under a tarpaulin. But the odds were seriously against anyone who needed that kind of accommodation that badly being able to scale the fence in the first place.

Terry had once found one of the local street girls and her john passed out on a mattress balanced on top of one of the rubbish heaps. He wasn't sure whether to compliment them on their athleticism – even if they'd been turbocharged by ket or speed, that was a proper climb – or to read them the Riot Act (which he knew he was supposed to). Instead, he'd just told them wearily to sling their hook. As he'd said to Dave later, he'd rarely seen a hook slung faster.

More often, they found stuff that had been hurled over the top in the night. Fly-tipping. Big sacks of noxious garbage. Smaller items of furniture or household tat. Rotten meat, fish, fruit and veg dumped by market-stall traders or restaurant staff on their way home. On those days, you really needed your face mask. Sometimes, the morning catch was plain weird: a big box of wigs – that had been a good one – and a medical teaching skeleton, slumped by the gate when Dave arrived.

Anyway, one of them always did the rounds first thing and checked it off on the clipboard. It was part of the routine and required by council by-laws. 'Health and safety', like almost everything else that shaped their day. Just another box to tick before the scheduled morning deliveries from around the borough began around nine o'clock.

That morning, Dave set off on his quick tour of the site, leaving Terry engrossed by a row on talkSPORT between

Laura Woods and Ally McCoist about Spurs. Stepping out of the hut, Dave was struck by what a lovely morning it was turning out to be: the sky cloudless and resolutely blue, but with a nice breeze cooling his brow as he trudged through the rubble, rust and ruin.

There was a football by the furniture pile – not for the first time, it must have been accidentally kicked into the dump by kids playing in the street the previous evening. He took a run-up, aiming for a beige leather armchair about twenty metres away, and caught the ball with just the right part of his boot. Goal! He raised a fist in celebration. A good omen for the day, surely?

Or maybe not. Over by what amounted to the site's compost heap – a hillock of soil, decaying plants and vegetation that stunk to high heaven in the summer – was a metal box. That was definitely a fresh arrival, and an odd overnight discovery on several levels.

First, there was its size: a big suitcase, or a small packing case, depending upon your point of view. It looked like it was made of black steel, or something similar; scuffed, as if it had been on a bit of a journey. Heavy-looking, anyway. Much too heavy to have been chucked over the fence and reached this far into the site. So, Dave reasoned, it had been left where it was for a purpose. Which made no sense at all.

Second: when he took a closer look, he could see that much of the metal was covered in rows of letters, numbers, and what he could only assume were coded symbols of some kind. Not the alphabet, anyhow. Every edge was plastered with circular markings that indicated some kind of warning – toxic? Poisonous? None of it added up. They had special places for this sort of stuff, didn't they? Like 600 feet underground.

And third: it was completely sealed. If there was an

opening latch, Dave couldn't see it. He tried flipping it over onto the other side, and was surprised by its sheer weight as it tumbled with a menacing thump to the ground. No, not the slightest indication of an opening mechanism or anything similar. Not by or inside the handles, or, as far as he could see, along the hinge. Whatever was inside – if anything was inside – was not meant to be easily accessible, to say the least. Dave ran his finger around the criss-cross of indecipherable alphanumerics. What could it possibly be? No bloody idea. None at all.

'Tel!'

No response. His co-worker must have still been absorbed by the row on the radio.

'Tel!' This time, he was louder, and Terry heard him, poking his head out the door of the hut.

'What?' He sounded mildly exasperated, as if his morning somehow had been fatally disrupted.

'Come and take a look at this!' Then, more quietly. 'For Christ's sake.'

Terry never rushed anywhere and was certainly not going to break the habit of a lifetime early on a Thursday morning. Sauntering towards Dave, he said, 'What you found, a winning lottery ticket?'

'Shut it, Tel. Here, take a look at that.' He gestured towards the big black case.

Terry surveyed it, then knelt down to get a closer look. 'Bloody hell,' he said. 'What the fuck is it?'

'That's what I'm wondering, muppet.'

Terry tried to lift it and was barely able to shift it from its prone position. 'Christ, it's heavy and all, isn't it? Something that definitely isn't normal junk in there.'

'Exactly,' said Dave. 'And how did it get there? That's what I'd like to know.' He rubbed his hands together nervously, out of habit. 'It's like it was left for someone to pick up.' He paused again. 'Which is pretty strange. But, anyhow, they didn't collect it, did they?'

Terry ignored the question. 'All these numbers and stuff. It looks . . . I don't know. Official? Like government or corporate or something? Fucking weird.' He stood up. 'Never seen anything like it in three years here. You?'

Dave shook his head. 'No. And I've done almost six. I gotta say, I don't much like it, Tel. Let's call it in.' He looked at the box again. 'I look at that thing, and my strongest feeling is, let's make it someone else's problem. Soon as. Sweet?'

Terry nodded. 'Took the words right out of my mouth, David, sir.' Then he said, 'Got your phone? Mine's bust.'

'Charging on the desk,' said Dave.

They stomped back to the hut, in lockstep, matching their shared determination to be rid of whatever that thing was as soon as humanly possible.

Inside, Dave opened a drawer and handed Terry a form. 'Fill that in, would you? It's standard when we involve a non-council authority.'

Tel shrugged. 'Will do. I guess. Jesus, more effing paperwork.'

'Hello? . . . Yes. Police. Thank you.' He waited to be connected. 'Yes, hello, police? Hello, my name's Drayton. David Drayton. I work at Stepney dump . . . Yes, that's right . . . Sorry? . . . D-R-A-Y-T-O-N . . . Yes, this number.' He waited again. 'My colleague and myself have located an item on the site that is, well, not on any inventory or accounted for by either of us. Or by the local authority. We're a bit concerned by its presence, to be honest. No, no idea. Looks like it might be a bit . . . scientific, or whatever. What does it look like? Well . . .'

Dave did his best to describe the case, and why it struck

the two of them as odd. He feared for a moment that he was getting nowhere. '*Why* am I concerned? Listen, we see all sorts here, trust me, mate. But this is not your ordinary East London silly-o'clock fly-tipping, believe me. It's . . . well, it looks like it might be dangerous, I suppose . . . What? No, neither of us are feeling unwell. Hold on, I'll ask my colleague. Tel?' Terry shook his head silently. 'No, he's fine, too. Yep, good as gold. We just both reckon— Oh, great, so you'll send a squad car. When might that be? Really? OK, well, the sooner the better. Thanks. Thanks very much. Bye.'

Terry looked at him inquiringly. In return, Dave could only muster a frown. 'Didn't sound like it was exactly high on their list. But then, I guess it wouldn't be round here, would it? Thieving, gear . . . they've got bigger fish to fry, haven't they? All the same. I'd like to get rid of that . . . thing' – he pointed out of the grease-stained window of the hut – 'as soon as we can. One thing I've learned in this job is when something is above your pay grade, you don't want anything to do with it. And whatever is in that box, definitely passes that test.'

Terry looked over his shoulder at the dump. 'I told you, it looks government. Medical. Probably full of some godawful new virus, you know? They're always working on the new ones, aren't they? In their labs? And we know all too bloody well that accidents can happen. Don't we? You hearing me, Dave?'

Now it was Dave's turn to play it cool. 'Oh, what are you bangin' on about? *Viruses?* Gawd, that last booster jab really has done your head in, hasn't it?'

'Yeah, well it's easy to be snarky, but look at what we all went through last time. They said it come from a market, or a bat, or something, but it just happened to turn up in the city where they had all them deep-cover labs. And we know that was at the mild end, compared to some of the horrors—'

'Oh, listen to yourself. You find a dodgy box in the middle of a dump in a Stepney and suddenly you're seeing biological warfare breaking out? *Pandemic: The Sequel.* You *do* have a vivid imagination, Terence, my son. Let's calm down and wait for Old Bill to come and sort it all out, shall we?'

He could see that Terry was mildly peeved by the piss-take. 'Look, let's have another cuppa and just wait it out, eh?' He got up from his chair and went over to the sink to turn the kettle on. 'Then we can go for an early liquid lunch at the Carpenters' and celebrate our exciting morning. I'm buying.'

At this prospect, Terry cheered up. 'Be rude not to, wouldn't it?'

'Exactly.'

They sat in silence as the kettle boiled, listening to the traffic outside, the noise of kids on their way to school and the distant rumble of a sound system being tested in one of the fashionable galleries that had clustered a few blocks away.

What happened next mostly eluded Dave as he lay on his hospital bed and tried to remember. They were still gossiping, that much he recalled, and sipping their teas. And then, in his peripheral vision, something outside, a blur – fast, determined, heading towards them pitilessly. Next, the hut door smashed open and there was a flurry of violent activity.

He did remember a figure in a black balaclava hitting Terry hard on the head, interrupting the protest that was forming in his throat, and Terry slumping instantly to the ground. And just as Dave was himself saying: 'What the fu—?', an arm came around his neck and a ferocious blow struck his

temple that was both intensely painful and completely disorienting. But before he could absorb and think about how
painful and disorienting it was, much less ask whoever was
doing this to stop, another haymaker hit its mark. Then
everything was blackness.

# 2

Harry Taylor was trying to have a lie-in for (he reckoned) the first time in six weeks. Not that he felt he'd earned it.

If there was one thing he hated, it was unfinished business. And last night definitely qualified for that bloody annoying category – and then some. It made his bad leg ache.

Every time he closed his eyes, he heard the whistle of bullets and the hiss of smoke grenades. The shouting of angry and wounded men, and the whine of an SUV speeding away. Chaos. A fucked-up operation, in short.

For almost a year, he and his team had been chasing a seriously high-value target: the Crick Syndicate. The third-generation London villains ran a decent slice of protection, prostitution and narcotics in the capital. Two brothers, Lionel and 'Sweety' Ray, and a younger sister, Bren, had turned the old-fashioned cockney firm into an international going concern that you could probably list on the stock exchange. But, after God knows how many arrests over the years, not one of the three had been charged, much less sent down.

True, a few of their lieutenants, well down the food chain, were already doing time at His Majesty's pleasure, some for decent stretches. But not one had flipped on the Cricks – understandably fearful of what would happen to their families if they did. Murder, assault, human trafficking, embezzlement, breaking and entering, conspiracy to defraud . . . the list went on. But an organisation like the

Cricks' could afford to lose a few junior bosses now and then, as long as they didn't squeal. Which they never did.

And that, as Harry had told his superiors at New Scotland Yard time and time again, was no bloody good. His years as a soldier had taught him that to kill a target – a gang, a team of assassins, a rogue state – you had to aim for the head. Clean decapitation. Remove the leadership, wherever it was (and, often enough, it was lurking in the shadows). Which, in this case, meant Lionel, Sweety, Bren and a handful of top-dollar members of their inner circle, all of whom were now domiciled in Monaco, though they often flitted back to the city of their birth to keep an eye on operations. Until the first team was taken off the streets, the syndicate would continue to thrive.

The top brass, having spoken to their political masters, had finally given Harry the green light. The Crick temple was to be brought crashing to the ground, by all and any legal means available. 'Clean the stables, DCI Taylor,' said one assistant commissioner with an eye on a headline, not to mention the top job at the Met.

Easier said than done, of course. The operation had involved many, many months of round-the-clock surveillance (both real-world and digital), as well as hours of painstaking trawling of documents and databases. For sure, Harry was happy to use all the mod cons the Met had to offer; nothing wrong with a laptop, he'd always said, to make life easier, as long as you didn't expect it to restrain and handcuff a psychopath. And, yes, they'd used plenty of SIGINT – signals intelligence, some from overseas – and been happy for any help that the spooks had to offer which, in a couple of cases, had been considerable. But it was undercover work, the boots-on-the-ground, old-fashioned police work on the streets, stake-outs and the shaking down of informants – or 'persuasive discussions' as Harry described it in his reports to his superiors – that, in the end, had delivered the leads they needed. It was coppers, not algorithms, that had got them a shot at swooping down like hawks on the Crick's top team.

Three strands had converged: a tip that a helicopter and private jet had been chartered, very discreetly, at the last minute, to take a group from 'Furnival Commodities' from Monaco to Nice, and then on to London City. Furnival, it transpired, was a shell company formally owned by two Parisian lawyers but, in reality, according to Five, a front for Crick operations.

Second, the National Crime Agency (NCA) had mid-grade intelligence that there was going to be some sort of auction in London, with interested parties from the underworld, or their most-trusted representatives, allegedly converging upon the capital to inspect the lot, whatever it was, and bid for it. No further information on what 'it' was, or who was coming, but it made the Cricks' apparent snap visit to town more interesting. What were they after, and who might they be bidding against?

And third, a corrupt customs officer had spilled the beans about a large shipment of high-quality heroin due to be shipped in a container to Dover the following day. He was in on the deal for fifty thousand pounds – to clear his gambling debts – in return for which he had to do everything in his power to get the goods off the boat and across the border.

Which led Harry and his team to the customs officer's contact, known only as 'Jericho' – a mid-level drug dealer who was lying low in Folkestone awaiting orders. He was also a vicious pimp, with a rap sheet the length of his arm. But, more to the point, he was a junkie, supposedly clean for two years, but who'd recently relapsed and was desperately in need of a fix when Harry's two closest lieutenants, DI John Williams and DS Iris Davies got to him.

At last, they had a weak link, and knew something that the Cricks obviously didn't. There was a pressure point to which they could apply – well, *pressure*.

After three years with Harry – first as a sergeant, before making DI – John appeared to have grown used to the famed 'Taylor Temper' and the outbursts of rage that were provoked by anything that seemed sloppy, second-rate or negligent. Despite what it looked like to outsiders, it was all part of Harry's MO, his way of managing the task in hand, as well as the people he was responsible for. When, the year before, John's wife had decided that life with a well-heeled chartered accountant might be more fulfilling than living with a mostly absent copper and had taken the kids with her, Harry had said nothing, but slapped his DI reassuringly on the back and kept him on an even keel, checking in on John regularly and dragging him along to Stamford Bridge for a home game or boxing nights at York Hall in Bethnal Green.

If John had ever been stupid enough to accuse his boss of being 'emotionally intelligent', his reward would have been a fat lip. Harry hated psychobabble, self-indulgence and (worst of all) any mention of 'wellness' almost much as he loathed criminals. But he had a heart – not that you'd ever guess it from his regular manner.

Harry had always known that John would make it to the other side of the Crick case, as exhausting and nerve-racking as it undoubtedly had been. But for Sergeant Iris Davies, it had been a test of a different order.

Still only thirty-two – six or seven years younger than John – she had been with Harry's team only a year, promoted to the Met after rolling up an extortion racket case in the West Midlands. She had incredible promise and Harry didn't doubt for a second that she'd one day make assistant commissioner without breaking sweat – and maybe rise higher. But he had hoped that her pen-pushing years wouldn't start too soon, because her talents as a police officer were certain, in his strong opinion, to be wasted behind a desk.

She was a trained sniper, too. A natural on the ranges, her instructors said. Capable of concentrating totally for ten hours in a field-op nest while awaiting a 'go' (or not) in her earpiece. What use would all that be in a seminar on community policing, or at a London Assembly committee hearing?

Despite this, Harry hadn't been certain that she'd be ready for the final punishing months of the Crick operation. But, when it came to it, she had exceeded all expectations, including perhaps her own. On night after night of stakeouts, over sleepless weekends poring over crooked accounts with the finance bods and, during one interrogation, when she had punched a long-time Crick associate hard in the face after he made a crack about 'Afghan bitches dying in containers' while he was out on bail, she had shown Harry that she had what it took to be first-rank copper – on the street, as well as in the conference room, or at a bank of computer screens. She was, if he was honest, quite something. And, though he could barely admit it to himself, he found himself enjoying her company more and more.

As it turned out, Jericho broke in less than half an hour, which, John noted at the time, was probably a record, even for Harry. ('You didn't even have to tickle him, guv.') Under a naked light bulb, in his own basement, sweating and shaking from dope sickness, Jericho had told them all they needed to know.

Yes, the Crick siblings were headed to London. He didn't know which of them, though. Yes, their two top men – Barry Sayles and 'Long' Charlie Watkins – would peel off to

Folkestone to examine the shipment and, assuming it was up to snuff, authorise the transfer of however many millions to whoever was selling the gear.

Harry got up and stretched. Touched his toes with gratifying ease and checked the state of play in the mirror by the bed. Not too bad, all things considered. A bit green round the gills, a body bearing a bunch of scars that told a whole book of stories, but, all things considered, still in decent shape. Especially considering what had happened the night before.

He had turned forty-five a month before and, though he admitted this to nobody, he was starting to feel it. Not exactly losing a pace just yet, he sensed nonetheless that he might do so quite soon. The aches and pains of the job were taking just a little longer to get over than they used to.

Even so, he could still get by just fine on three or four hours a night: exactly as he had when it was his turn to grab some kip during an op in Helmand. Though he'd never slept properly when he was in Afghanistan. Not really. If you knew what was good for you, you kept one eye open for the Taliban blade that would – and did – come flashing in the night.

No room for mistakes against that lot. And no room for mistakes when your adversaries were as practised and brutal as the Cricks.

And yet, that had him wondering. Were the mistakes of the night before his fault?

Harry had thought he had it taped. From a temporary command post at Shorncliffe Army Camp, he had watched on a live feed as the Bombardier Challenger 350 had landed at City airport, and – bullseye – all the Crick siblings, Sayles, Watkins and three heavies had disembarked, split into three groups and been whisked away in black Bentley Bentaygas at 1.10 a.m. precisely.

'Eyes on all vehicles, sir,' Harry had heard in his earpiece.

'All right, Dasher,' Harry said. 'Follow all three and radio in anything interesting. Hang back but don't lose them.' Bill 'Dasher' Brown was a surveillance chief back at New Scotland Yard, and had known Harry for years. It had been good to have him on their team, on that night of all nights.

John looked up from the laptop: 'The helos need to steer clear, Harry. We've got eight vehicles down there. If they see they're being watched—'

'Don't worry,' he said. 'Dasher won't let us down.'

'Alpha Team,' said the voice in his ear.

'What's the latest?'

'Looks like Vehicles One and Two are heading for the Embankment.'

'Makes sense,' said Harry. 'The Cricks have a penthouse near Lambeth Palace. Probably their first stop of the night. Pick up some hairspray.'

'We'll have eyes on them all the way. Vehicle Three is heading east. Towards you.'

'That'll be Sayles and Watkins. Roger that, Dasher.'

He turned to Iris. 'Any joy from the Hackers?'

She checked her screen. The Hackers were a strange group of spotty kids, barely in their twenties, who occupied a fetid room on the third floor at Thames House and tried to hack into whatever system they were told to. Anything, really. From a bank in Moscow to a TikTok account in Cardiff. But in this case, the GPS systems of three luxury SUVs.

'Not yet,' she said. 'Oh, hold on. Vehicle Three. The teen geniuses have just intercepted the coordinates. Where are those bastards heading? Wait a second, guv . . . There it is. East Cliff and Warren Country Park. Very nice, too.'

She showed Harry pictures of the location. Idyllic woodlands, country trails, wildlife, and picnic spots for family visits.

'Plenty of cover,' he said. 'Makes sense for a rendezvous.'

'Only ten minutes away from here,' she said.

'John, you've got the comms,' Harry said. 'Iris and I will head there now. Get us backup lickety-split, OK? We need full tactical, as predicted. This might get quite busy. I don't think this lot will crumble in the face of harsh language.'

Harry and Iris were already wearing body armour, and she was strapped with a Heckler & Koch G36. He had a Glock 26 in his holster. There was every chance that they might need them. Sayles and Watkins would not give up without a fight, and as to the people they were meeting – well, that was a known unknown, dangerously so.

'Any update on the auction, John?' Harry asked.

'All quiet. Could be dud steer, you know. I mean, "auctioning" what? It's hardly fucking Sotheby's.'

'We'll see. Keep it tight here and loop us in on anything – anything at all. This is our night, John. We get to take these scumbags down at last. Right?'

'Roger that,' said John and turned back to the bank of screens in which the three Bentleys and a series of locations flashed into view.

Two guards from the Gurkha Second Battalion had stood outside the hut, silent and unflinching. Harry and Iris had climbed into their unmarked police Range Rover and sped off, slowing down only to be let out at the exit checkpoint, where crash barriers and multiple gates kept the menacing world at bay. Gurkhas, Harry knew, left nothing to chance.

'The rendezvous is a small lay-by with a shelter, gravel parking area – looks like it might be a café during the day,' said John on the comms. 'Crick Vehicle Three is twenty-five to thirty minutes away'.

'Any activity nearby?' Harry asked.

'Nothing yet. Dasher has a unit patrolling in the neighbourhood that will do a run past and send images. Cheltenham satellites say nothing to report.'

'Roger that.'

The park was indeed only ten minutes from the camp and they ditched the Range Rover off-road, near a large Victorian building that looked like a small research centre or small corporate branch. Harry and Iris walked the last hundred yards, flashlights off, hugging the treeline on the other side of the road.

'Tactical in place,' said John over the radio. 'Three units within a minute away from the site. Fourth unit, two minutes out. Plenty more if you need it.'

'Roger that.'

Harry and Iris found a small shed with a brick wall and took cover.

'Well, hello,' John said. 'Got a bloody motorcade heading your way from the east.'

'From Dover? Where from?' said Harry. 'Can you retrace its steps on CCTV?'

'Doing that. Running the plates through now . . . No, this lot came from a headland not a port. Looks like they started their journey about eight miles west of Dover. Doesn't tell us where the package arrived initially, of course.'

'Leave that till later, John. Focus on the meet, and who's heading towards us.'

'Crick Vehicle Three is very warm indeed now. A quarter click from you.'

'Standing by,' said Harry. 'All units on standby. Ready on my command.'

He and Iris remained crouched behind the wall, Harry's pulse throbbing in his temples. This was it, after all these years. The chance to bring down one of the last great home-grown London gangs and make the city – the whole country – just that little bit safer. But he couldn't let that dream distract him. For now, Harry needed to stay frostier than Olaf's arse.

Two a.m. The lay-by was suddenly bathed in light as three identical black BMW X SUVs swung into the gravelled parking bay. Before Harry and Iris could check plates, the darkness returned – and the silence became deafening.

Iris pulled down her night-vision goggles. 'I can make out two plates. I think . . . yes, UK, 2022 reg. I'll send to John now.'

'Crick Vehicle Three approaching,' said John in their earpieces.

'Roger that,' said Harry. 'All units await my go.'

The Bentley purred into the woodland clearing and across their line of sight. For what seemed like an eternity – but was no more than a minute – the occupants of the four vehicles hung tight.

Then, as if they could bear the suspense no longer, the driver and front passenger of the first BMW got out and walked towards the brick building. They were tall, wearing leather jackets and jeans, dark-haired and seemed younger than he had expected. They had the bearing of trusted middlemen, rather than of an underboss or consigliere.

In response, the Bentley disgorged all four of its passengers. Harry immediately recognised Long Charlie Watkins from his lumbering silhouette: suited and booted, as always, a rich man in his own right these days, though still quite happy, when the job required it, to pull out a few fingernails for old time's sake.

'I have eyes on Watkins,' said Harry. 'And – fuck me – there's his other half. Barry Sayles. Well, well. He's a sight for sore eyes.'

Sayles was wiry, sly, edgy. Smaller than Watkins but no less deadly. Electrodes had been his specialty back in the day.

Legend had it that he would play Charlie Parker on full blast to drown out the screams of his victims.

The two sides strode towards one another and exchanged some sort of greeting. But it was all business, no bonhomie. By their body language, Long Charlie and Barry didn't like being out in the open one bit. They wanted to do the necessary and get away as fast as humanly possible. But their very presence showed how important this meeting was.

Sayles and Watkins followed the two mystery men towards the first BMW and waited as they opened the boot. Charlie raised a gloved finger to beckon one of his hooded heavies to join him. After a brief pause, the hood took something in his hand and headed back to the Bentley.

'He's testing the gear,' said Harry. 'This should be fun.'

'How do you know?' said Iris.

'I don't. Not for sure. But I bet I'm right.' He breathed deeply. 'OK. On my mark. If they give any sort of go-ahead, all units to move in. Arrest all present. Assume all suspects are armed. Extreme vigilance.'

His task, whatever it was, now complete, the Crick hood stepped back out of the Bentley and gave a thumbs up to Sayles and Watkins.

This was it.

'All units go!' said Harry.

The few minutes that followed that pivotal moment had already become a blur in Harry's memory as he sat on the edge of the bed the following morning. The lay-by had suddenly been flooded in light by the tactical team. A warning through a megaphone ordered the crooks to hit the deck and wait to be cuffed. Shots were fired immediately, first from the BMWs, then by the Crick heavies.

Iris took both of them out in the first thirty seconds. They fell like twisted mannequins, riddled with bullets.

Sayles made a run for it, but Harry got him in the leg and, recklessly he knew, ran out to grab him and drag him back to their cover. *No,* Harry had thought, *you're one little rat that's definitely going to live in a cage from now on.*

He heard the distinctive pop of a smoke grenade, hurled from God knows where. 'Cover up!' he yelled to Iris. She pulled up her mask. Sayles began to cough. 'And you can shut up and all!' Harry yelled at him.

The lay-by, so still only seconds previously, had become a scene of bedlam. The comms feed was jammed with updates, some conflicting. Harry could feel the bullets slicing through the air. This was not how he had wanted it to go. Not even close.

'I have Sayles!' Harry shouted. 'All units report on status!'

'Unit Bravo here. We have one officer down. Two of theirs also down, I think. Their Beemers are revving up to go. Counting four hostiles inside, plus Watkins still unaccounted for.'

'Tell Unit Charlie to pursue,' Harry said. 'John, scramble more backup, stat!'

With a screech, three of the BMWs raced into the night, kicking up dust in their wake. The air was thick, and it took a few minutes for the smoke and dust to clear enough to reveal the aftermath of the battle.

Two of the BMW squad were indeed dead. Harry cursed as the scene revealed another body. Watkins. Apparently shot at close range, which suggested that his new business partners suspected a double-cross.

To Harry's fury, the BMWs lost the police tail about four miles out. The vehicles turned up in a Folkestone NCP the next morning and were towed away by SCD4, the Met's forensic services team. Harry doubted they would find much. Some DNA perhaps? Even that wasn't a slam dunk.

Professional criminals were so careful these days. And only a relatively small percentage of them were on the DNA database.

Yes, they had Sayles. He would go down for a long time, thanks to the impressively pure heroin sample still in the bloodstream of his unidentified colleague's dead body – proof enough that this had been a big smack deal. But he would never talk. He had two daughters, one of whom ran an upmarket florist in Chelsea, while the other was studying English at St Andrews. If he so much as breathed a word about the Cricks, both girls would be dead in twenty-four hours. Nothing his interrogators said to him about protecting them moved him in the slightest. Not yet charged, he already had the countenance of a man who knew he was going to die in prison.

And the three Crick siblings? They were indeed in their Embankment penthouse, vexed to be visited by detectives at such a late hour. Though they were still up at 3 a.m., and, curiously enough, accompanied in the middle of the night by two of their lawyers.

Questioned under caution, Lionel, Sweety and Bren denied all knowledge of the Folkestone deal. Yes, they employed the late Mr Watkins and the unfortunate Mr Sayles as part of their security team. But they were, they all said, *shocked* to hear of this alleged connection with the narcotics trade – which they found hard to believe, but of course deplored.

They themselves were in London to see some properties they were thinking of adding to their family portfolio (hence, they said, the presence of their lawyers, who had worked late and stayed for some food and a glass of champagne). And the three of them hoped to attend a niece's birthday party in Chiswick the next day. A marquee, and all the trimmings.

An 'auction'? No, they knew nothing about that either. An auction of what exactly? Yes, it was true that they had started to dip their toe in the art market but that was all managed by an experienced agent who did most of his business in Paris.

The mask slipped only once, at the very end of the interview. Shown to the door by Bren, the two detectives – through gritted teeth – wished them goodnight. Lionel finally snarled: 'Why don't you just *fuck off* out of our home, you *filthy fucking coppers?*'

By then, Harry was at home, trying to get some sleep before the morning debrief. He knew that the Yard would already be spinning the whole thing as a triumph: the interception of a top-level gangland meeting after months of surveillance; the arrest of a senior mobster, now facing multiple life sentences; the gunning down of Long Charlie, a legendary villain, ideal for lurid profiles in the red tops, and two as-yet-unidentified criminal associates (believed to be Albanian); and, to give emotional depth to the story, the death in the line of duty of a brave tactical officer – now named as twenty-five-year-old Constable Jai Bahri.

As Harry sat on his bed the following morning, he saw only failure. Watkins dead: what use was that? All three Cricks still at large and unlikely to stick their head above the parapet again anytime soon. And a young copper taken out in a messy firefight. Sure, Sayles would do his time, God rot him. But it had not been the night he had been hoping for. The stables had not been cleaned. It was a fucking mess, and that was on him.

His phone rang at 10 a.m., and he immediately recognised the voice on the other end of the line.

'All right, sleeping beauty?' said DCS Bill Robinson at the end of the line. 'Thought you might have a cushy one today, did you?'

'It had crossed my mind, guv, yes.' Harry mumbled.

'Well, forget it. Get your arse into work now.' He was about to ring off but added, 'Oh, and Harry?'

'Yeah?'

'It might be an idea to check the news on your way in.'

# 3

Most of Harry's colleagues couldn't believe he still drove an XJS. Jaguar had stopped making these beautiful beasts in 1996, and they guzzled about a gallon of petrol a mile. They were hardly the most practical of motors for police work, either – try squeezing a six-foot-six coke dealer into a coupé – which meant that Harry often had to use a police pool car when he was on the job. And – as far as the younger members of staff were concerned – the ownership of such a motor in the first place was as close as you could get to announcing 'I don't give a toss about climate change', short of plastering a sticker across the bumper reading, *I hate Greta Thunberg.*

Harry didn't hate Greta Thunberg, but he did like classic cars, and he'd be damned if anyone was going to tell him what he could or couldn't drive. Though he was bracing himself for the painful inevitable when, as the new laws on what cars you could and couldn't use on the road took hold, there might come a time when he would have to arrest himself. Until then, the XJS was one of the few unambiguous luxuries in which he indulged.

It made for good camouflage, too. Cops in the 2020s weren't supposed to drive flash motors. They weren't supposed to do much, when he thought about it. Stick to a set of rules that hemmed them in more and more every year. Wear body cameras at all times, mug up on the

Equality Act, think twice before saying anything lest a suspect report a 'hate incident' to their superiors. In all the new clobber and with all the regulations, they weren't really coppers any more: half robots, half bureaucrats – at least in Harry's book.

Not that he had any time for the real dinosaurs. He hated bent police officers and racist or sexist talk in the canteen. But he also hated being treated like a kid by people who had never felt a bullet brush half an inch past their ear, or taken cover from mortar fire – as he'd done for ten hours straight in Tora Bora. Two of his mates had died that day.

Another thing Harry hated was the phrase 'old-school copper' – especially when applied to him, as it often was round the Met. Yes, he liked to get the job done. Yes, he could throw a punch as well as take one. And no, he didn't think police officers were social workers or local politicians. Their job was law enforcement: pure and simple. Not therapy.

All the same: he wasn't Dixon of Dock Green, for Christ's sake. Or John Thaw in *The Sweeney*. Harry had grown up during the eighties and knew all about social strife and what it was like to see poor, powerless people treated badly by the authorities. It was vile. He had only been three when his neighbourhood was traumatised by the New Cross fire of 1981, in which thirteen young Black people had been killed – and nobody had been charged, much less prosecuted. He had seen the British Movement marching and felt his stomach turn at the hatred they were spreading.

More than a lot of the middle-class people who came to the Met to teach courses on this 'ism' or that 'bias', he had seen the ugly side of life close up and had nothing but contempt for those who fanned the flames of bigotry. He didn't need a special course to coach him on what he had already learned first-hand.

In fact, he'd only ended up in the police service by accident. Enlisting in the army as soon as he left school, he was talent-spotted in the ranks of the Irish Guards after four years and encouraged to apply for recruitment to the SAS: a test of endurance and grit like no other he had ever experienced, and one that, when he had passed, he was determined never to subject himself to again.

Some chance, of course. Life in a brown beret in Hereford was a combination of anxious waiting and bursts of unbelievable activity – most of which never reached the public domain at all, much less the newspapers or TV bulletins. In Helmand and Colombia, Georgia and Myanmar, he had served Queen and country in operations that ranged from exfiltration – how had that stupid diplomat got himself kidnapped in the jungle? – to lightning strikes on terrorist encampments, acting on human intelligence that, he and his troop-mates knew, had been gathered by assets risking their very lives, and would be actionable for only a few hours. He'd put field dressings on plenty of wounds, helped to airlift civilians out of disaster zones and watched too many of his comrades die in action. Yes, Harry Taylor had seen the world, all right.

And then, one blazing day at Camp Bastion, the sun starting to set but still doing its work, he had been properly crocked on the right knee by one of his best mates, Sergeant Jim 'Jawbone' Jackson. Well and truly floored. In a game of five-a-side, for Christ's sake. Jawbone had laughed when Harry first hit the deck, swearing blue murder. But had stopped pretty sharpish when he realised that his friend couldn't stand – and that, the medic had quickly warned, the damage to the knee would put Harry out of commission for 'a fair bit'.

Two surgeries later – one back at a specialist hospital in

London – 'a fair bit' had turned into 'indefinitely'. Although, the knee would heal just fine – he was still a young man – it might also give way at any time, which was a possibility that he knew the regiment could never countenance. Nor could he, to be fair.

And so Harry was faced with a grim choice, one of the decisions that was part and parcel of the life he had chosen. What were his options? What future faced Harry Taylor as he picked at the plaster cast encasing his leg, on which his mates had scrawled obscenities and *Get well soon, you prick* messages? He would never be passed as fit for a troop op, that much was clear. He could stay a soldier but return to his original regiment and accept a desk job, with no prospect of getting back in the field. Or he could leave the army and see what Civvy Street had to offer a man who had – literally – been kicked out of the special forces. As he said at his Bastion leaving do: 'It was a tackle that got me, not the Taliban.'

And that was that. He left soldiering behind and, as he healed and recovered his fitness – he was back to running half-marathons within six months of his return to the UK – wondered what to do with the rest of his life. What did he have to show for his thirty years on Earth? A few medals. Some seriously classified memories. And a bit of money put away for a deposit on a flat (You don't spend much of your salary when you're dodging bullets in the desert).

But no wife or kids, and none in prospect. Women passed through his life from time to time, usually departing on amicable terms, but always making clear on the way out that they had wanted more of him, more commitment. Though not exactly film-star handsome, he was a lean six foot two, with a shock of thick, dark hair and strong features that girlfriends had described (variously) as 'Roman', 'hawkish' and (in the words of DeeDee, the hairdresser from Peckham) 'fucking fit'. He went on dates, enjoyed the company of women, but never seemed to make it to the next stage – or anything like a life partnership. They said he was married to the job.

And they were right, weren't they? Because in what his old man called 'one of your frying-pan-to-fire manoeuvres', he had applied to join the police three months after getting back from Afghanistan and signing off in Hereford. What else was he going to do? Work in sales? Sing and dance? For a man with his CV, there were always those dodgy security firms with anonymous offices in Mayfair; outfits run by public schoolboys that, describing themselves as 'contractors', provided all manner of wicked services all over the world – for a price. Harry was proud to have been a soldier. But he knew the difference between a soldier and a mercenary.

Come to think of it, he'd always known – if only subconsciously – that he would end up as a copper if, for whatever reason, he left the army. In his first months back home, he was badly afflicted by insomnia. So badly that he went to a doctor, who said it was common enough in veterans and prescribed sleeping pills, and those just made Harry feel groggy most of the time, which was not the idea at all. It was only after he flushed the pills down the loo and thought about his predicament that he realised he had the problem the wrong way around. He wasn't suffering from a surfeit of adrenaline. He missed it.

The next day, he had filed an application to join the police service. The best decision he had ever made, he freely admitted to anyone who would listen, because, for all its frustrations, his second career had spared him from living forever in the shadow of his first. And he had prospered as a copper, thanks in no small part to the guidance and patronage of the man he was on his way to see now: Detective Chief Superintendent Bill Robinson.

As the car glided out of the garage and he turned right into Borough High Street, he switched on the radio. The LBC presenter was speaking with a breathless reporter on location somewhere.

'*And that's all we know so far, is it, Ben?*'

'*Yes, that's what we've been told so far, though we're expecting a press conference later in the day, possibly with Met Commissioner Sir Muhammad Baqri.*'

'*How many people have been evacuated?*'

'*Well, we don't have an exact number yet, Gavin, but my sources tell me it's between sixty and one hundred. Most of the blocks that have been sealed off are unoccupied or would have been full of construction teams, all of which have obviously been stood down for the day, pending clearance from the police.*'

'*Just to reassure listeners, Ben, there hasn't been an* incident *as such.*'

'*No, not as far as we know. There were reports about an hour ago of a bomb disposal unit using a remote robotic rig, but these, I'd stress, are unconfirmed. Also, plenty of police officers in hazmat suits – and I've seen them myself – moving in and out of the area.*'

'*Tell us what that means, Ben.*'

The reporter paused for a beat. '*Well, I'd emphasise that I'm speculating here, Gavin, as we really need to wait for the Met's briefing, but such suits can indicate concern about some sort of chemical or toxic waste spill. That's one scenario. But I'd really underline that this is only hypothesis right now.*'

'*What is the mood like down in Stepney?*'

*'Well, half an hour ago it was pandemonium. I counted fifteen fire engines and a similar number of ambulances. Crowds being dispersed. The Tube station is still closed, and there are plenty of pedestrians and traffic being rerouted out of the sealed-off zone. I'd say that, whatever it is, the relevant agencies have some idea of what they're up against and are trying to reduce the number of people in the area as they get on with – whatever they're getting on with.'*

*'Do we know if there's going to be a COBRA meeting today—?'*

Having had enough of Gavin and Ben for the time being, Harry turned off the car radio, checked the regular police frequencies on his in-vehicle comms and then his phone. No further units were now being despatched to Stepney, which meant that the relevant specialist teams and agencies were already on the case – and made it slightly odd that Robinson should be calling him in at all.

As the lights at the next junction turned red, he skimmed some of the news sites. *Breaking: six blocks of East London sealed off by police* was the BBC's lead headline, while *The Times* had: *Met briefing on East End closure imminent. PM receiving regular updates.* The *Sun* app had stuck with a supposedly big scoop about a *Strictly* love rat scandal.

Harry had worked out some of it already. Sealing off an area was much more commonplace than people imagined – especially in a big city. Most went unreported, not because they were secret but because the closure came and went so quickly. He had been involved in a drill himself two years before in which a neighbourhood in Manchester was closed down for an hour – to permit a pretty half-hearted exercise in preparation for a local outburst of civil conflict. The residents and community leaders had been warned to expect a spot of disruption of their Wednesday afternoon – low-flying helos, reconnaissance vehicles and police support units for

riot control – but most just gawped at the spectacle which
was all over in forty-five minutes.

In any case: whatever was happening in Stepney was definitely not a drill. It had already been briefed to the media,
which meant that whoever was running gold command was
trying to get out ahead of the story before what the suits
called 'an unhelpful narrative' got a grip on social media.
Twitter, Facebook and Gettr would already be fizzing with
conspiracy theories and wild claims – but, in such situations,
the majority of the public still took their cue from mainstream
channels and would be watching and listening to regular news
for updates. Those outlets had clearly been told to stand by
for more information and (it seemed) nudged slightly towards
the idea of a toxic spill that would keep disaster tourists at
bay, at least for the time being.

It was serious, that much was clear. But not so serious,
Harry noted, that a news blackout had been imposed; or, at
the other extreme, that a snap emergency statement had been
made, explicitly instructing people to keep away at all costs
and to expect worse to come. Instead, there was just enough
coquettish menace in the toxic-spill line – wherever that came
from – to make the public take it seriously, but not so much
that London would descend into panic. Yes: serious but
manageable, he would say.

He drove down St George's Road, past the sunken majesty
of the cathedral and Lambeth North station (where he had
once headbutted a suspect into unconsciousness) and up past
the Park Plaza hotel where the politicians stayed during elec-
tion campaign season (protection officers with them), over
Westminster Bridge, before turning sharp right and cruising
towards his destination: New Scotland Yard.

SO22 had its base on the sixth floor, just by the lift
waiting area. When Robinson had announced, four years

before, that the new unit was to be located in such a prominent part of the Met's HQ, Harry had immediately objected. The whole point, he said, of the new SO team – one whose existence would not be secret but would certainly not be loudly advertised – was to stay on the down-low, keep a modest profile, away from the office gossips and the politics. Why not make a den for the new team in the vacant Tobacco Dock premises that the Commissioner was talking about putting on the commercial market? It would be perfect for what the architects of SO22 – Harry among them – had in mind.

'You know what your problem is?' Robinson had replied. 'Correction – *one* of your problems?'

'I've a horrible feeling you're going to tell me,' Harry said.

'Too right. Your instincts always did serve you well. All those patrols in the jungle. One of your problems, Harry, is that you lack imagination.'

Harry was having no trouble imagining giving Robinson a smack, as it happened, but he decided not to clarify the point.

'Right, guv. How's that, may I ask?'

'Well, here's the thing. We could hide away in a sweet little spot, all on our own, miles from here. All the flash stuff, new glass walls, brand new tech, no distractions, just the business of stopping villains. We *could* do that. But do you know why that would be the prat move to make?'

'Again, I have a weird premonition that you're going to bring me up to speed.'

Robinson spun round on his chair, his not-quite-nice suit bulging around a gut that showed a bit too openly how many years had passed since he had been active in the field (although – fair play to the man – he'd been an operational legend at his peak). 'I certainly am. Here's the reality: what we're doing here is being badged as an "ancillary unit" or a "wild-card elite team for special projects" . . . Something *additional* to all the specialist units that already exist. Right? Not a threat to them?'

Harry nodded.

'But you and I both know that's absolute fucking bollocks. SO22 came into being because a few of us, from ministerial level down – including you from the earliest stages, I might add – were fed up with a Met that had lost its balls, lost its focus and was too busy covering its arse to make the calls that get proper bad guys behind bars. With me so far?'

'Think I'm just about following.'

'And the very decision to call into being such a unit,' Robinson said, 'was a reproach – no, more like a "fuck you" – to at least half of the other units in this building. Even using the old-school "SO" handle. It sent a message. It was the Commissioner's way of saying – the Prime Minister's way of saying, for that matter – that there had to be a new elite unit to do what the other teams patently couldn't quite manage and, in particular circumstances, to get the job done when others were blethering on about how hard it all was. Everyone knows that the very *existence* of SO22 is a rebuke to most of the people working in this building.'

'And so?' said Harry.

'And so those people hate our guts on principle. Before we've even started. They're longing for SO22 to fail, and the more spectacular the failure, the better.' He paused. 'And we won't always get it right, will we?'

Harry shrugged. 'I suppose not.'

'Which is why I need us to be here, in the thick of it, protecting our people and making sure the sharks don't get what they want. And so do you, Harry. I know you'd rather be away from all the suits and the meetings and the procrastination. I get that and, believe me, I feel your pain. You're a great copper and one of the things that makes you great is that you hate to waste time on all that, when you could be chasing villains. But – trust me – we need to be here, in the nest of the vipers.' He pointed up to the floors above. 'Or we'll wake up one morning and find we've all been bitten in the arse. Capeesh?'

Again, as he now recalled, Harry had nodded. As infuriating as it was to admit, Robinson was absolutely right. To stand a chance of making a difference, SO22 needed to stay close to all the people that weren't doing so; the people for whom a career in the police was all about backstabbing and plotting and positioning yourself for the next big desk job.

So – against all operational logic – the new unit was based in New Scotland Yard, surrounded by sceptics and outright internal foes, shoe-horned into a space that was much too small for its needs. During the final stages of the Crick investigation, the much-expanded team had been forced to requisition a large meeting room on the seventh floor.

It was to DCS Robinson's office rather than his own that Harry made his way first that morning. As usual, he was decked out in pressed black Levi 501s, a button-down Lauren shirt and a vintage leather jacket that he had owned since his service days. Robinson was at his desk, frowning as he scrolled down a screen of what Harry could only assume were the latest need-to-know postings from gold command in East London.

'Morning, chief,' said Harry.

'Barely,' Robinson replied.

'Still only eleven thirty. What's wrong with that?'

'You've got a busy day ahead, my son.'

'I had a busy night. And a crappy one, too. We need to talk about it. This isn't how SO22 should work.'

Robinson paused. 'Listen. I know you wanted a full house last night. But you got Sayles. You stopped a big drug deal. You put Watkins in the ground, where he belongs. And you put the Cricks on notice that they're dead meat if they put a foot wrong.'

'That's bollocks. They'll feel they can get away with more than ever now. We fucked up. *I* fucked up.'

'I disagree, Harry. Not every op goes even half to plan. It's the nature of what we do.'

'And Constable Jai Bahri? What about his family?'

'I spoke to his wife and parents this morning. It's tragic. Two kids left without a father. But Harry . . . that's the nature of what we do, too. We've both lost plenty of people over the years. I've got a funeral of another young constable to attend later.'

That explained the full dress uniform.

Robinson sighed. 'It never gets easier. But it wasn't your fault.'

Harry frowned. 'What about the two dealers? Who were they?'

'I know the gossip is Albanian. That seems to be their nationality, yes. But I'd place a side bet that they were working for Xavier Ramirez.'

Harry prided himself on keeping his ear to the ground about the general rumblings in the criminal underworld, but this name hadn't crossed his radar. 'Who the hell is that?'

'The new king of Juarez, that's who. Mexican cartel nobility. Son of Diego Ramirez who shot a judge at point-blank range. No proof yet, but there's a lot of static in the air about his new ambitions to expand operations to Europe. Fancies himself as the new king of the world.'

'Bit of a stretch, isn't it? A cartel king hooking up with old East End villains?'

Robinson looked out of the window. 'It's just a hunch. We'll leave it for now.'

'*Leave it?*' said Harry. 'Are you kidding? We need to clear this mess up. This is not even close to being finished. We've got to chase the smack, maybe take another run at the Cricks, and—'

'And we will. Believe me. But not today, Harry.'

'Why the fuck not? Are we giving them a head start, you know, just to be *fair?*'

Robinson's cheeks were turning a dangerous crimson. 'Will you just *shut it* for a second, DCI Taylor?'

Harry relented. For now; he wasn't anywhere near finished. He folded his arms and waited to be enlightened.

Robinson acknowledged the gesture. 'Thank you. Now, I need you to shift your focus entirely. File the Cricks away. I know it's hard. But believe me, this is more important. Did you catch the news on your way here?'

This did surprise Harry. It was natural enough that Robinson should want to chew the fat over what was clearly a significant London incident. But there was nothing he had yet heard that made him think that the Stepney situation was really SO22 territory.

Harry nodded. 'All right, then,' said Robinson, gesturing for him to sit in one of the chairs by his desk while checking his screen. 'What have you picked up about Stepney?'

Harry recited the sketchy story he had heard so far, freely admitting that it was all from public sources. 'I assume it's serious? Counter Terrorism? Or SCD4 Forensics?'

'Both. Neither. I mean, every agency in the British criminal justice system is down there right now, checking every possible angle – or acting like they are. Five, the NCA, military intelligence, even some stiff from the National Security Council making a nuisance of himself, apparently. Nobody knows exactly what the nature of the problem is – which is the problem.'

'Well, all right. Go on. What *do* we know?'

'Two blokes who manage the local tip, apparently, they call in anything weird that turns up. Normal procedure. Course, it mostly turns out to be a false alarm, very occasionally something drug-related. This morning, though, they find a black metal box that wasn't there the night before. Covered in markings they can't make head nor tail of, and very tightly shut. They don't have a clue what it is, or, more to the point, where it came from.'

'But the local nick goes down, right?' Harry said.

'Yeah, two uniforms from Bethnal Green. Expecting to find – well, who knows what they were expecting. When they got there, round nine thirty, the two workmen were spark out in their hut, on the floor, bound and gagged, and the box had gone. Straightforward heist. And only minutes after one of the blokes had called it in.'

'How many were involved?'

'They think two men, three at most. Masked. Thumped them both good and proper and then – we can only assume – made a bolt for it.'

'Assume?'

'No CCTV. All cameras fake. I can't help but wonder if that was why the location was selected for whatever kind of drop this originally was. Hard to say. Was it just somebody dumping something they didn't want on their hands? Or was it due to be picked up later? First two of a million questions, Harry.'

'Hang on, though – whoever did the heist must have known what they were looking for. Picking it up, as per an existing plan. Or they'd been listening in to the lines at Bethnal Green nick, or tipped off, which is—'

'Much more common than we'd like. But I agree. It was a very fast turnaround.'

Harry absorbed this. 'So what was in the box, do you think?'

'I'm not positive, but I've got a pretty good hunch and so do all the other agencies hovering over this.'

'Based on? I mean, there's no evidence, is there?'

'Not directly. But one of the guys, once he was more or less compos, remembered some of the alphanumerics on the box.' Robinson paused, as if weighed down by something he would really rather not know. 'Are you aware what "U-235" stands for?'

It rang a bell, but before Harry could answer, his boss jumped in.

'Uranium-235, that's what. Which, as you know, is the main ingredient in atomic fission – well, that or plutonium.'

Harry took in what Robinson was saying to him. Weighed it up. Then pushed back. 'Oh, *come on*. Enriched uranium left lying around in Stepney? Stroll on. A metal box full of the stuff? Hardly likely, is it? I mean, guns and gear and poor bastards trafficked in from God knows where to pay off what they owe in stinking massage parlours . . . All that, yeah, I can see. But the fixings of a mushroom cloud, in E1? Bit fucking incongruous, isn't it?'

Robinson stood up and gazed out of his window. 'Ever heard of "Dragonfire", Harry?'

'Nope. Should I?'

'Not many people have. But – yes, as it happens – they should.' He sat down again. 'It's a bit of history, actually. Exactly one month after 9/11, the CIA briefed Bush that an agent codenamed Dragonfire had reported that bin Laden had a nuclear weapon, smack in the heart of New York City. Not a full-blown, dropped-from-a-plane bomb; more of a suitcase job. But enough to open the gates of hell, in a city that had just suffered three thousand deaths. For a few hours, the White House umm-ed and ahh-ed about what to do with this intelligence – which they knew would cause mass panic and overturn the global markets if it became public, even before you got to the explosion bit.'

'Which obviously we didn't,' Harry said.

'No. Exactly. Nothing happened. But the point is that, for a few hours, it all added up. Every piece of the puzzle fitted. It could have been the nightmare follow-up to 9/11, only much, much worse. Biblical escalation. On this occasion, it wasn't. Why not? Above my pay grade, but the big point is this: we all tend to forget stuff too quickly these days. People – even some senior coppers – think that all nuclear material is basically under lock and key and that it's just not something they have to worry about day to day. I mean, since the Iraq fiasco, anyone who talks about weapons of mass destruction gets labelled a crank, right? It just doesn't get mentioned much, if at all. So even the spooks tend to be very careful about getting people too alarmed.'

'But are you saying they should be?'

'What I'm saying is that it's still a clear and present danger, and every law enforcement agency should treat it as such. I mean, it's public domain that the US admits that it can't account for more than five thousand pounds of weapons-usable nuclear material. Stuff it put into play in the old Cold War sandpit and can't locate now. Which means that the real figure of lost property is probably a fair bit higher – and that doesn't even start to take account of the other countries that are capable of producing the stuff and have experienced thefts, losses, inventories that don't add up. Basic failures. Reported or otherwise.'

Again, Harry let what Robinson was saying sink in. 'Yeah,

OK. But since when have SO22 been experts in all this, anyway? We chase drug lords, human traffickers, gunrunners, the scum of the earth. We chase them hard. But nukes? I never had that down as one of your specialties, Bill.' He rarely used his boss's first name, and it was a sign of his seriousness that he did so.

'Not really a specialty. More of a lurking dread. I had a hunch that this day would come when I persuaded the Commissioner and the Home Secretary to authorise and fund SO22. One day there'd be a moment like this.'

'How do you mean?'

'Listen. When you and I were kids, this kind of kit was strictly military, right? I mean, your average IRA quarter-master or PLO bomb maker – they wouldn't have even thought of this. Way out of their league. But now . . . you've got a world full of separatists, far-right, jihadis, militiamen in the Appalachians, not to mention good old-fashioned villains, all trying to be top dog and get one over each other. No rule book any more. That's what I'm saying, Harry. If you ask, who might be after this box, the answer is: *anyone.*'

'All right, fair enough. Remember, I saw those jihadis up close and personal in Afghanistan . . . I believe you when you say they'll look for the nastiest weapon they can possibly get hold of and use it to kill the maximum number of people. But you still haven't answered my question. What's all this got to do with us? Surely it runs much higher up the mast? I mean . . . uranium, for Christ's sake. That's national security. It's transatlantic calls between the PM and President Whatshisname. Chief of the Defence Staff doing his nut. Panic at Vauxhall, spooks dashing around Whitehall. Realistically, what do they need coppers like us for?'

'Plenty,' Robinson replied. 'I mean, you're right, Harry. All the posh lot will be running around like blue-arsed flies – they already are, as I'm sure you've gathered. And the first thing they'll be asking is: How could this have happened?'

'Good question.'

'Very fucking good question. But not the *first* question. We *know* that this stuff is on the market. The oddity is that it hasn't turned up on British soil before.'

'That's true.'

'And I'm beginning to wonder, with respect, whether the story of last night really was the drug deal in Folkestone.'

'How do you mean?' said Harry.

'Well, what if that was a secondary operation? And the main business of the night was that "auction" we heard about.'

'That was never confirmed. Conjecture from the NCA. We didn't hear anything about it all night. Feels like it went cold.'

'And yet there were the three Cricks, still wide-awake at three a.m. And then this morning . . . that box turns up in Stepney. Doesn't that sound like an entirely different fuck-up? Like a snatch gone wrong, the package ditched somewhere it would be safe for a few hours, in plain sight but where nobody goes.'

Harry reflected. 'I see where you're heading. You think Folkestone was a diversionary tactic?'

'Not a diversion – I'm sure they wanted the smack. More of the supporting feature on the bill. The main event was – well, it ended up in Stepney.' He paused. 'But what really matters now is not an inquest into where it came from, but the rather more urgent question of where it is *right now.*'

'And that's where we come in. That's what you're saying.'

'What I'm saying, DCI Taylor, is that twenty minutes before you arrived, I received a direct call on the most secure line on this desk from the Cabinet Office. And someone I won't name – let's just say, a very senior member of this government – tasked us, and tasked us directly, with getting it back.'

'But why? There must be a task force of over a hundred officers on this already.'

'There is. And, looking at the chatter on my screen, five commanders are already arguing with each other about who does what, when and in what order. They've got resources. But you know as well as I do, Harry, that speed is what counts in a case like this. A bit of agility, a bit of nous. Whoever snatched the box, they'll already have put it back on the market, or be trying to, assuming they don't want to keep it for themselves. Highest bidder. And while the official team two floors down is deciding what colour their document folders should be, the trade will be made and the hot stuff could already heading to another country. Or, worse still, staying in this one.'

Harry leant back and ran his fingers through his hair distractedly. 'All right. All right.' He nodded towards Robinson's main computer screen. 'What leads have we got so far? If any?'

'I've sent the prelim debrief doc to your phone. That's got the basics on what the two tip workers could remember, though they're still pretty out of it, so it's not much. Plus some general stuff on potential buyers for the box, active traders in the past twelve months. A few faces who might have an interest. To be honest, that list is too long to be much use. But it's good background.'

'OK, thanks,' Harry said. 'Listen. Just rewind. What does your gut tell you? I mean, who the hell leaves a box full of weapons-grade uranium on a rubbish tip in the dead of night? Was it a drop for a pickup that went wrong? Or something else?'

Robinson stood, stretched, frowned. 'If I had to guess right now, I'd say the goods were snatched and whoever did the snatching got rattled or was found out, and ditched the package as soon as they could. Somewhere. Anywhere. Because the thugs that turned up to grab it this morning obviously *knew* it was on the loose – or that something valuable was, anyway – and must have been tipped off by someone on the inside at Bethnal Green nick. Or been tasked already to make the pick-up. Because they worked bloody fast.'

Harry nodded. 'Yeah. If it was a tip-off, they might even be local. Seeing an opportunity, taking it – by force. And now . . .'

'And now they have to work out what to do with it.' Robinson finished Harry's thought.

'Yeah,' said Harry. 'Exactly.'

'Oh, and as far as anyone else is concerned, we're riding strictly shotgun on this. I've had the investigation classified as "Special Supplementary".'

'What does that mean when it's at home?'

'Anything I damn well want it to mean. But – officially – you and your team are tidying the edges of the lawn with your dainty little strimmers, if you catch my meaning. I'll make sure you get any intel that will be useful. But the whole point is to work in the shadows. Get the job done, get the box back. And try not to ruffle too many feathers, at least on our side. Got it?'

'Got it.'

'Oh, and Harry?'

'Yes, guv.'

'Don't punch anyone you don't have to. Pretty please.'

Harry's reply was interrupted by a familiar voice at the door.

'Morning, guv. Sir. Just told a journalist poking around the

Crick case to piss off. After last night, I'm having a sense of humour failure. What did I miss?'

Harry Taylor and Bill Robinson looked at one another, wondering which of them should bring Sergeant Iris Davies up to speed.

# 4

In the bar of The Ritz-Carlton hotel in Cancún, the Trader nursed his first dirty martini of the evening. There were so many decent places to stay in the city these days, but this hotel had a terrific bartender who knew how to mix a perfect cocktail and, correctly, loathed his more pretentious colleagues who insisted on calling themselves 'mixologists'. The drink was excellent: sour, bracing, with a mule's kick that made you feel alive in every pore of your skin.

It had been a good day. As a favour to his principal client, the Trader had paid his respects to the local jefe, who had given him a verbal account of business, which was excellent – all of which could now be reported up the hierarchy in person. On the whole, the Trader disliked these errands, which seemed to him to be outside the scope of his core business on the markets. But trust was trust, and a favour was a favour. And the client in question was not a man you said no to. Not twice, anyway.

The beachfront villa to which he had driven that afternoon was a tasteful blend of modern elegance and Mayan embellishment, its red clay offset by sunflowers, Virginia creepers and lime trees. The jefe himself had greeted the Trader in the porticoed entrance – all smiles and warm embraces – and steered him straight to a large study on the ground floor, deep within the building. Outside the door, a sinewy *sicario* stood guard, his Uzi barely visible under his loose-fitting black jacket. He stared straight ahead as the two men walked in.

The jefe had promised the Trader that he would not detain him long, as he knew he was only in Cancún for the day and thanked him effusively for making the journey to his home. On the desk, a range of screens, including a Bloomberg terminal, displayed rolling news and market information. *Yes,* remembered the Trader, *you're an ambitious one, not content with cash, girls and muscle. Which means, a year from now, you'll either be on top, or dead.*

To the right of his host, four lower-tech black-and-white screens blinked with soundless CCTV. Three of them were trailing panoramic sections of the compound. A fourth – beamed from God knows where – showed images from a fixed ceiling camera of what looked like a cell. No windows, or natural light. Three men standing, one seated and bound to a chair. His head was in a plastic bag, held tight by one of his captors, and his body strained desperately against the ropes. When the bag was pulled off, the man gulped in air with desperation and – against all physical logic – seemed to be coughing simultaneously. But before he could get his breath back, a second captor pushed something up his nose – pepper spray, the Trader assumed – and his body went into convulsions of tormented agony. There was a time, years ago, when such a sight would have made the Trader physically sick. Now it was just part of the scenery of his work; a part with which he was glad not to be directly involved but which he knew was never far away.

He sipped his drink. He would report all that the jefe had told him during a scheduled call with Juarez later that evening, using his most secure, heavily modified and encrypted laptop. For now, sitting at the hotel bar, he scrolled through the emails on his iPad and, as part of the day's routine, checked a Reddit page that he and those his profession frequented for coded market tips, gossip and person-to-person messages that, in his case, only two people in the world could understand.

What he saw almost made him drop his martini glass.

There, in a simple if eccentric cipher that he and one of his best contacts used, was a message that he had, frankly, never expected to receive – from this particular contact, or from anyone, for that matter.

He jotted down the original characters on a napkin and, using the rough-and-ready system they had developed, transposed them into English. Yes, he had read it right: *HOT PACKAGE IN PLAY.* Then a GPS location, which he would soon identify. And finally: *ADVISE ACTION.*

What now? A call to Juarez. And immediately. So the Trader did something that he had never done before. He left a dirty martini unfinished.

# 5

They were passing Tower Bridge before Iris paused long enough for Harry to give her a proper answer to any of her questions.

'Is John in the loop yet?' she asked.

'Not yet. He stayed up all night cleaning the scene at Shorncliffe. Had his breakfast with the new mates, the Gurkhas. I said we'd brief him when we got back. Robinson has apparently requisitioned a room on the fifth floor for us to work from.'

He wondered how disappointed John would be by the Crick operation. He was certainly resilient: a third-dan judo black belt, a guy whose idea of recovery was a couple of hours of intense training at his club in Fulham to sweat it off. Which was good, because Harry would need all of John's skills if he was to get anywhere with this latest peach of a case.

Iris's skills, too. For the first time in a long while, he was hurtling into an op more or less blind. Starter for ten: How do you stop an atomic explosion? Or the threat of one? Or the threat of several? What prepares you for a task like that? Harry loved a challenge, it was true; that was the fun of SO22, he always said. And the stakes were often high: life or death. But he had never chased a beast with a bite like this one.

Iris tried and failed to stretch out in the passenger seat. 'Christ, guv. Why don't you get a car for human beings?

People were smaller in the fifties, I get it. Before colour TV. But honestly—'

'Reach under and push it back. And stop moaning.' They turned left, away from the bridge and up towards Whitechapel.

She ignored him. 'What I don't get—'

'Is the whole thing, like the rest of us. Please, Iris. This one is going to make the Crick op look like a first-year test paper at Hendon.'

'No, what I don't get is what kind of idiot leaves a box of fissile material on a rubbish tip. I mean, there's careless, and there's . . . well, this.'

'Robinson thinks it was someone running scared, maybe connected with the auction – assuming it actually happened. I reckon he's right. Someone realising they are seriously out of their depth, that they've taken something that they really shouldn't have, and not even stopping to think before dumping it. I mean, short of leaving it in the middle of the bloody road.'

She laughed. 'I once worked an op where we found three kilos of smack just lying around in a holdall in Yardley. Just sitting there, plain as day. In a playground, too. Couldn't believe it. The bag was covered in dabs, too. We had them in custody inside two hours.' Iris smiled at the memory. 'I was stationed as the lead shooter on the roof of a tower block, a good five hundred metres from their flat. In case they took it personally, you know?'

'Yeah,' said Harry, spinning the car left into Jubilee Street. 'Tempers fray when you lose stuff with a street value of – what? Quarter of a million?'

'More like three hundred grand and change,' Iris corrected him. 'It was pretty pure gear. And, sure, they were seething. But mainly because they had panicked and dumped the dope. Thus buying themselves nothing more exciting than a twenty-stretch, serving a minimum of ten. A deal gone wrong. It happens.'

'It does,' Harry agreed. 'Though not usually with nuclear weapons.'

Iris fell silent. Finally, she said, 'Are we being set up, guv?'

Harry had not expected this. 'How do you mean? Set up by whom?'

'Well, just that it feels like a test. I mean, this is a nightmare, right? I mean, the fact that it's a nightmare is surely common ground?'

Harry hated this kind of question. But eventually conceded: 'Yes.'

They were doing fifty down Stepney Way now, the park flashing past to their left.

'So,' Iris continued, 'the one thing we know about night-mares and the Yard is that they love nothing more than the hospital pass. Hand it to Bill and Harry, and if it all goes wrong . . .'

'Possible,' Harry agreed. 'Anything is possible in that joint. But if that's part of the story, I don't think it's the main plot. Robinson says this is political. Big wheels worried that all the agencies will fall over each other's laces in the scrum. I think they want at least one team that does its own dirty work and has an old-fashioned preoccupation with getting the job done.'

As they approached the junction with Stepney High Street, the officers at the first cordon – armed, of course – braced visibly.

'Here we go,' said Harry.

He lowered the window as the first – all moustache and stony features – marched over to the Jag.

'Afternoon, sir,' he said. 'Area is off limits.' He gestured to the sky where a lone police helicopter still circled.

Without speaking, Harry flashed his badge and caught the unmistakable change of expression on the face of a checkpoint charlie who knew he'd been trumped.

Rather lamely, Harry thought, he tapped the bonnet of the Jag – as if doing him a favour. 'That'll do it, sir,' he said. 'Carry on through.'

There was a second, less conspicuous cordon on Stepney High Street. More of a wave-down, it turned out.

'Oh, look,' said Harry. 'It's Gordon.'

'Gordon?' said Iris.

'Five. Usually one of their first responders if there's a whiff of terrorism in the air. They'll be having kittens in Thames House.'

Gordon Neary was almost exactly Harry's age but you would never have guessed it. You'd also never had guessed he worked for the security service. He always looked like a harried middle-aged father sent out on a shopping trip that was far beyond his capabilities. Pale gabardine summer coat, suit, tie loosened at the collar and hair matted with sweat; not a man who put in many hours at the gym. Good with a PowerPoint, Harry always thought, but less useful in a pavement straightener.

'Hello, Gordon,' said Harry. 'Are you going to make us sign the Official Secrets Act?'

'Oh, shut up, Taylor. You're not funny, you know.'

'Hear that, Iris? The world's come to something if a spook accuses you of being humourless.'

'Anyway,' Gordon said, straightening up. 'What the hell are you doing here? This is not SO22 terrain, and you know it.'

'Excuse me, Mr Bond, but you'll have read the updates on your fancy Five phone – so you'll know that is, pardon my Brexit, a load of crap. SO22 is here on a "special supplementary" basis, no less, to observe and assist. All signed off by posh fellas in crisply ironed white shirts and shiny epaulettes. We're at the sidelines, while all you dashing heroes do the running.'

Iris was trying not to laugh – and failing. Neary looked pained, as if Harry had just passed him a bill or a summons. Or promised him an endoscopy.

'Take it easy, Gordon,' Harry said. 'We'll be out of your hair in no time. They've thrown the kitchen sink at this one, so we were bound to turn up sooner or later. We're just taking a peek.'

'It's a mess, I'll tell you that much, Harry.'

'Yeah,' he said. 'Any leads at the dump?' Harry knew there weren't any but wanted to gauge the extent to which Gordon was being open with him and might be willing to help later on.

'Nope. Not yet. They've narrowed the formal seal to two blocks. Under a bit of pressure from on high to decrease the temperature generally. Specialist forensics from the Yard and our lot are combing the site now. Nothing useful from the dump workers yet. They're still under observation at the Royal London. I'd be surprised if there's any more to come, even when their heads clear properly.'

'Could they be in on it?' asked Iris.

Gordon shrugged. 'I doubt it. They both have pretty clean records. Nothing unusual in their phone activity for the past fortnight. All looks kosher. I think they were just in the wrong place at the wrong time.'

'I'll say.'

'Anyway, the Commissioner's doing a press conference at three. He's going to say that it was a drug heist gone wrong – that the dump managers were attacked by unknown parties apparently seeking narcotics that weren't even there, blah,

blah, blah, investigations proceed, blah, blah, will be brought to justice. Blah, blah.'

'And when the BBC guy in the front asks about pandemics, and biological warfare, and rumours of the new Stepney Variant already infecting thousands?'

'We'll tell him to . . .' Neary straightened up, doing his best to conceal his stress. 'We'll tell him that the investigation remains open, but that there is no reason for public alarm.'

'Which is a bit of a porky, really.'

Gordon seemed to sag. 'Yeah. Just a bit.'

'What do you reckon though, Gordon?' Harry said.

The spook massaged his stomach, as if consulting it for wisdom, then grimaced. 'I reckon I'm going to miss my day at Lord's on Saturday. That's what.'

Harry smiled at the bedraggled intelligence officer and pulled away from the kerb.

The shops on the high street were all still shut and the only vehicles were a couple of police cars, a lone fire engine and a flotilla of unmarked vans that probably belonged to the forensic teams now hunched over piles of unholy rubbish. The area close to the yellow-and-black tape swarmed with uniformed coppers, officers in hazmat suits and plain-clothes personnel doing their best to act like they knew what they were doing. Harry was well aware of what barely suppressed group panic looked like when he saw it, and he was looking at it right now.

As Gordon had said, the cordon had obviously got smaller, which meant that the dump was not radioactive and – no less important to the top brass – the order had indeed been given to let the steam out of the incident as quickly as possible. Nobody wanted a scene. Minimum fuss. Smooth surfaces, please. That was always the way when the people in charge wanted to be left alone with a problem which they had no idea how to solve.

'What do you make of all that?' Iris asked Harry, as they pulled into a parking space by a kebab shop.

'What Gordon said? I don't think anyone knows anything yet. Didn't get the feeling that he was holding anything back, or not much. Spooks *hate* this sort of thing.'

'What?'

'Something which is genuinely out of the blue. No chatter, or online warnings of 'fire from Allah' or 'hail to the new Aryan Reich'. Or whatever. No context. It gives them vertigo.'

'Can't say I blame them. I mean, it *is* an odd one, guv. Isn't it?'

'Yeah. Except that lots of things are odd – until they aren't. You never know when something that looks like a hot mess is suddenly going to change into clear lines and all make complete sense.' He turned his head to her. 'You just have to be patient.'

'Understood.' Iris looked across the street at the growing stream of civilians mingling with law enforcement officers as the rest of the neighbourhood began its journey back to some sort of normality. An elderly woman with a shopping trolley was giving one of the uniforms, who towered over her, a serious ear bashing, pointing a gloved finger into the yellow polyester of his hi-vis jacket.

'How are you going to play it?' she asked Harry.

'The burnt Fool's finger,' he said – more to himself than to Iris.

'Cryptic. Meaningless, actually.' She waited. 'All right, I'll bite. What are you on about?'

'Bit of Kipling from my occasional, very accidental collisions with education. "The burnt Fool's bandaged finger goes wabbling back to the Fire". Meaning that some people can't help going back to the scene of the crime. And they really can't.'

Iris could not disguise her scepticism. 'You're joking, aren't you? Come on, guv. A couple of heavies – maybe three – storm the place, smash the shit out of the two workmen, grab the box and get the fuck out of here. No CCTV, no nothing. And one of them's going to come back?'

Harry shook his head. 'No, not them. *They* won't be back. But a lot of people hang around these streets at night. Remind me. Where were you a beat cop? I mean, I know it wasn't for long–'

'Birmingham city centre and Walsall for a bit,' she said. 'You were round here, weren't you?'

He nodded. 'Yes. And the City of London itself, as it happens. So anyway, I don't know about you, but one thing I learned on the beat is that walls have eyes as well as ears. I mean, take a place like this.'

He pointed out, over the bonnet: a twenty-first-century urban landscape of flats above shops; graffiti tags of varying quality; bus stops; wheely bins with the lids ripped off; a tiny mosque sandwiched between a dry cleaner and a coffee shop; a long stretch of blacked-out windows, probably a club of some sort; a bookies that looked like an entrance to the underworld; a twenty-four-hour mart that advertised halal food; a chicken joint optimistically called 'Cluck Luck'; fast-food cartons on the pavement; a charity shop, outside which had grown a pile of people's junk in black bin liners; a brightly coloured mural with what looked like the faces of Bob Marley, Malcolm X and George Floyd. London, in other words.

'I don't know what it was like in Brum,' Harry continued, 'but, round here, however late it gets, or early, *someone* is there. Someone sees *something*. Or thinks that what's up involves them in some way. They *hover*. They come back. Like they can't really help themselves.' He tapped his head.

'I expect there's a fancy psychological word for it, but it's real, whatever it's called.'

'So, what?' asked Iris. 'We just wait until someone with *WITNESS* tattooed on their forehead walks past us?'

'You know, Iris,' said Harry, 'one day that sharp tongue of yours will get you in serious trouble.'

She smiled. 'Sorry. But you know what I mean.'

'Sure. But – trust me – we're better off holding back while all this craziness fades away. See what happens. Who turns up.'

So they did. As the melee of uniforms, plain-clothes officers and forensic scientists began to thin, so it became progressively easier to spot the civilians that were lingering; or trying to. A bunch of kids on their way back from school gawping over the tape and being hurried on. A white-haired man in his mobility scooter slowing down for a closer look. Lads in Champion parkas and box-fresh trainers scoping out any action they could find. A worried-looking vicar with a beard who consulted a police officer for reassurance and nodded gravely as he was brought up to speed. A steady stream of journalists, some with crews; a handful recording pieces to camera for later bulletins. A food-delivery driver who had obviously been denied access to the street and wanted to know when the hell he could get in. A delegation of town hall officials making a nuisance of themselves, then leaving with their tails firmly between their legs. A middle-aged guy in purple dungarees with green hair, yelling at the cops that they were the servants of Satan, and Bill Gates, and the Illuminati, and the globalists, and 5G, and big pharma, and other supposedly evil forces whose names Harry couldn't quite catch. A woman pushing a keg of beer towards the pub on the corner and stopping to see what was going on.

A couple of hours passed and, seeing that the coffee shop had reopened, Iris went to sort out sandwiches and tea.

As she got back into the Jag, setting down the cups and paper bag, Harry said quietly: 'Him.'

'Who?'

'One o'clock. White male. Eighteen to twenty. Slim build. Grey hoodie. Unhealthy pallor. Possibly close to death, in fact.'

'Got him.'

'That's his third time passing by.'

'What, since—?'

'Since we've been parked here. Three times. That's not just curiosity.'

'Maybe he's just bored.'

'Only one way to find out.'

Harry got out of the Jag and strode across the street. In his hand, his badge, in case the uniforms tried to intervene. He heard the passenger door close behind him as Iris followed. The kid had his back to them as he peered down the street towards the tip. But he was edgy, visibly so, twitching with nerves. He turned around and saw Harry heading towards him. Eye contact was enough to make him start walking away immediately. Walk, not run. *So,* thought Harry, *you don't want to talk to me, but you also don't want to draw attention to yourself. You're hoping quite badly that I'm not after you. Bad luck, sunshine. I* am *after you.*

He could see that Iris was also on the case now and making her way ahead of the boy to cut him off at the pass. She moved with real steel and precision, Harry noted with admiration: a properly effective copper who knew exactly how to hunt her prey. Only a few hours before, she had been strafing villains with bullets in a Kentish bloodbath. But she was not fazed in the slightest.

Now on the pavement, Harry followed the kid, who was loping a little faster. Iris slipstreamed behind him, and the trio carried on their odd little march through Stepney for another hundred metres or so.

Then the kid stopped. Turned round. Clocked Harry, and possibly Iris. And, losing his cool completely, started to run. As fast as he could. No athlete, Harry thought, as he watched the young man's arms fly in all directions, but seriously scared. For whatever reason, or reasons, he was running for his life.

Iris yelled, 'Stop! Police!'

The kid took no notice and continued his flailing sprint, his head back as he gulped down air. And then – unceremoniously – he was grounded as Iris grabbed his hood and, with a single sharp tug, pulled him to the pavement.

Harry checked back to see if the commotion had drawn any attention at the barrier, now well behind them in the middle distance. Nope. This party belonged to him and Iris.

The kid was squirming face down as Iris held his arms in what Harry imagined to be one of her less painful locks.

'Jesus!' he shouted. 'Get off me! I ain't fucking doing nothing.'

'Shut up,' Iris said. 'If you're not doing anything, why did you run?'

'I'm just taking a look, Fed. These are my yards, right? Wanted to see what all the fuss was. Free country, innit?'

'Not today,' said Harry.

# 6

In all honesty, the Extra Cup Café could not be described as one of East London's unmissable destinations. It lacked the authenticity of a proper greasy spoon but nor had it made the leap to full barista-led, artisan-bean gentrification. The walls were, rather desperately, decorated with black-and-white stills of Frank Sinatra, Muhammad Ali and other legends who had definitely not visited it. Or coughed up three quid for a tepid cappuccino.

Still, thought Harry, needs must. It would do for the conversation they wanted to have with this kid, who was sitting opposite him, running his fingers nervously through a blond crop with a black stripe. He looked as if he hadn't eaten a square meal in days, and smelt as if he hadn't showered for a while, either. His hoodie sleeves reached well past his wrists, as if he didn't want anyone to see his forearms. Which told Harry one thing, and one thing alone: dope fiend.

Adrian 'Adey' Foreman. Nineteen years old. Multiple arrests, charged twice on possession and sale of class A drugs. Acquitted on technicalities in both cases but recently released from the Scrubs, having served six months for a breaking and entering in Stratford.

The kid twitched as if really bad things were about to happen. Which, for all he knew, they might do.

'Listen, Adrian,' said Iris, sitting on the green plastic seat to the boy's left to deter him from running off. 'Adey, is it?

We could have nicked you already. You ran, which is a bad look on a day like this. And a bad look any day, for a boy on parole.'

'Ain't got anything to say.'

'That's a shame,' she continued. 'Because we think you do, and, unfortunately for you, what we think is all that matters right now.'

'This is harassment. I know my fucking rights.'

'No, you don't, son,' said Harry. 'You don't know your arse from your uncle. But you've seen the inside of enough cells to know that you'll be heading for another one today if you don't cooperate. And sharpish.' He tossed the bag of weed they had found in Adey's back pocket on to the chipboard table. 'Not exactly Scarface, are you?' Harry chuckled. 'But there's enough there to send you straight back inside if I make one call to your parole officer.'

'You fucking wouldn't. Pigs!'

Iris cuffed him round the head. Not a slap or a punch, Harry noticed, impressed again by her control of the situation. A *cuff*. Technically police brutality, no doubt – which, these days, covered anything more severe than massaging a suspect – but nobody in the café was taking any notice. And Adey was not going to complain to anyone, under the circumstances.

'Let's dial it down a bit, eh?' she said. 'Bit less with the insults, bit more polite conversation. How does that sound, Adey?'

'All right.' He rubbed his head. 'Fuck. All right. What do you want?'

Harry spread his hands out on the table.

'So listen, Adey. We clocked you hovering around the dump three times. Which means you are interested in what happened there. Doesn't mean you're involved, or not directly at least. But you couldn't stop yourself, could you?'

Adey shrugged, sniffled. 'I dunno. I just wanted to see if Tel was all right.'

Iris chipped in. 'Tel?' She checked her iPhone screen. 'You mean Terry Stanhope? One of the guys from the tip, isn't he?'

'Yeah. That's 'im.'

'Well, he's fine, if you're worried,' said Harry. 'Bit of a lump on his loaf. But otherwise – no harm done. What's your interest in our Mr Stanhope?'

'Nothing. He's a mate.'

'A mate?' said Iris. 'Adey, don't take this the wrong way, but blokes like you don't have many *mates*. And certainly not people who manage rubbish dumps. What's the connection?'

Silence. Adey stared at his cooling tea.

'Come on,' she said. 'Don't force DCI Taylor here to make a phone call he'd rather not make. We just want to know what you know. And then you can be on your way. Wherever that might be.'

Harry scrutinised Adey. His face was screwed up in mock defiance, but it did absolutely nothing to hide the despair and fear he was obviously feeling. Iris had handled this just fine. There'd be no need to turn up the heat, or to take the kid for one of Harry's notorious little drives to jog his memory.

Adey sighed. 'Look,' he said. 'Is this on the record?'

'Do you see us taking notes?' Iris said.

'I don't *know* what 'appened at the dump today. I only 'eard on the estate that there was about a million coppers down there.'

'Which would be a good reason for a boy on parole to keep clear,' she said.

'She's got you there,' said Harry.

Adey bowed his head. 'Look, I buy and sell weed from Tel.

Small-time. It's his side hustle. Nothing much. He smokes a bit, sells a bit. You know, a bit of personal, a bit of extra.'

'Jesus,' said Harry. 'Bloody Scarface *and* Escobar now.'

'It's all a big joke to you feds, innit? Everything's just a joke. I was worried about my mate. That's all.'

Iris clasped his shoulder in warning. 'No, you weren't.' Her grip tightened. 'You *lying little junkie*. Now – final warning – tell us why you were there.'

'I know why you were there, Adey,' said Harry. 'You were worried that Stanhope – sorry, your mate "Tel" – might shop you. You wanted to get to him to find out what was what. Which was, all things considered, extremely bloody stupid.'

'Why's that?'

Harry laughed. 'Because you shopped *yourself* by hanging around with about three hundred coppers. I don't know what rubbish you're injecting into your veins, son, but I don't think it's doing your cognitive abilities any favours.'

Adey scowled. 'Are we done, then? I mean, what more do you want? Or do you just wanna take the piss a bit more?'

'Well, I'd say yes if we had time,' said Harry. 'I had a bit of a rough night and could do with some light entertainment. But, seeing as we're rather busy, a spot of local knowledge should do the trick. And then you can be on your way.'

Adey just scrunched his face tighter.

'Listen,' said Harry. 'If I say the word "hypothetical", will what's left of your brain explode?'

'You what?'

'Never mind. Let's just call it a game, shall we?'

'Whatever.'

'Let's just say, for the sake of argument, that Tel had come across something he shouldn't have. Nothing to do with weed or everyday gear, you understand. I mean, by accident. Something possibly worth a bit.'

'What? Like stones? Or class A?'

'Yeah, something like that. Maybe even a bit more valuable.'

Adey shook his head. 'Class A's already *way* out of Tel's league. He'd have nothing to do with that. He tries to convince me not to score, you know. Playing the big brother figure, an' all.'

'Oh, I'm sure he does,' said Harry. 'But my question to you, Adey, is this. If this stuff wouldn't be in Tel's league – and it definitely wouldn't be in *your* league, given that you're a scruffy little arsehole – well, then, *whose* league, exactly, might it be in?'

Confusion crossed Adey's face. He was probably worrying about his next fix – Harry remembered Jericho – and was certainly struggling to keep up with the conversation.

Iris intervened. 'What the DCI is asking, Adey, is who round here deals with the really high-end stuff – you know, top-level – when it comes on the market? Or might be *taken* from the market, if you catch my meaning. Who finds out there's a prize on their manor and sends a couple of thugs out to get it?'

'A prize?' Adey's eyes glimmered for a moment.

'Yes, Adey. A *prize*. But, seriously, it's not the sort of prize a spotty little herbert like you wants to know about, believe me.'

Adey shut his eyes, grimacing in the way that Harry had seen countless times before. The way someone looks when they're about to cough to something they'd really rather not.

'Devereux,' he murmured.

'Pete Devereux?' said Harry. 'Old "Pliers" Pete? Come on, Adey. He's old news. Or dead, more likely. You'll have to do better than that.'

'No, not Pete. And you call yourselves coppers?' Adey scoffed. 'No. His nephew. Phil. Much more – what's the word? – *discreet*. Much more, you know, ambitious.'

'Ambitious?' Iris asked.

'Nothing worth fencing gets fenced round 'ere unless it's by Devereux. Or else he gets a tasty slice of the action.'

'His uncle was a nasty piece of work, I'll tell you that for nothing,' said Harry. 'I remember cleaning up the mess he left behind him more than once.'

'He passed, like, five years ago or somethin',' Adey said. 'Phil runs the store now. Had already been for a while. Slick, like, you know? Connected. Me, I pay my taxes to his people and stay well clear the rest of the time.'

'And where would my colleague and I find Mr Devereux on a nice summer's day like today?'

Adey looked at Harry as if he were insane. 'Are you *kidding*? Mate, if he or anyone around him knew I was even *talking* to the feds . . . I'd be dead. No questions, no appeals. A cap in my head, one in the throat. Next thing they'd find on that dump would be my body.' He shuddered.

Harry sat up, shoulders back. This had gone on long enough. 'Like that, is it? Well, I guess I'll just have to make that call, then. What's his name, Sergeant Davies?'

'Adey's PO? Mr Dwayne Green. The number is 0777—'

'OK!' said Adey. 'OK. Jesus, man. All right. All I know is – the Cube.'

'Oh, for Christ's sake,' said Harry. 'Speak English. You know a cube? What the hell does that mean?'

'The Cool Cube. It's a club. Round Brick Lane. Techno, most nights. And trap, some Afrobeats. Good sounds. Pricey, though. Anyway, the whole gaff belongs to the Devereux firm. They've got a separate team operates it, course, but it's theirs. That's where I go when I pay my weekly dues and that. And I don't 'ang about.'

'Right,' said Harry. 'Helpful.'

'Can I go now?' said Adey.

'Not just yet.'

'Why not?'

'Slow down,' said Iris. 'Just listen to DCI Taylor.'

'I know you, Adey. By which I mean, I don't know *you*, but I've known kids like you since I was a kid myself,' said Harry before Adey could get in a smart comment. 'And the minute you leave, there's going to be part of you tempted to score a few quid by phoning somebody up and telling them that Sergeant Davies and myself have been asking questions. Telling that same somebody what we look like and all the rest of it. Probably earn yourself enough for a couple of baggies in five minutes. Or so I'd imagine.'

'You're kidding! The last thing—'

'Don't interrupt. It's bad manners and upsets me.' Harry put a large hand down on Adey's. The kid achieved the impossible, which was to turn even paler. 'All I'm saying is, if you tell anyone about this, I will find out. It's the kind of thing I hear, you see. And next time I see you – well, I might not be so . . . *patient.* Isn't that right, Sergeant Davies?'

'Absolutely right, guv. It would be a very different sort of chat. A bit livelier, I'd imagine.'

Harry lifted his hand off the kid's. Adey scratched the back of it, as if all the stress had compounded the deeper itch within for chemical relief.

He waited a few seconds for a formal dismissal. When none was forthcoming, he left like a man in fear of his life – which, Harry guessed, he probably was, much of the time. Before he could turn round, the bell on the door rang as Adrian Foreman put as much distance between himself and the two coppers with as much speed as he could possibly muster.

They were both silent for a moment. Then Iris said: 'Next stop the Cool Cube, I guess?'

'Next but one. Just seen that Robinson wants us back at the office.'

She nodded. 'Did you buy all that, then?'

'As far as it goes. Kid didn't have it in him to fabricate. He's barely a cog in the machine round here. But at least we know a little bit more about the machine now.'

'He was certainly scared out of his brains.'

'Charming bloke,' said Harry, draining his coffee cup. 'Told you, didn't I? The burnt fool always comes back.'

# 7

In the view of some connoisseurs – a select group, it must be said – the Dassault Falcon 10X is the finest private jet money can buy. It can fly you non-stop from New York to Shanghai, Los Angeles to Sydney, Hong Kong to New York, or Paris to Santiago, cruising at up to 12,500 metres. But its admirers tend to be drawn by the sheer spaciousness of its cabin, and the consequent scope for bespoke luxury. Though, for seventy-five million dollars, that is the least they would expect.

The man who owned this particular jet was much less interested in its interior features than his handful of passengers. And he had just abruptly waved away a Latina server asking if he wanted a drink or other refreshment. His most secure phone was buzzing on the table in front of him.

For those around him who could hear, what followed was a staccato utterance at whose full meaning they could only guess.

'Yes? Why this line?' Beat. 'Where? Yes, immediately. Any means. No object. Report back. Don't fail.'

The man settled back. The server thought she saw the merest hint of a smile cross his face. But she did not want him to see her observing and resumed what she was doing at the bar with even greater application.

# 8

DI John Williams met Harry and Iris in the lobby of the Yard. An inch taller than Harry and kitted out in a suit doing its best to look stylish rather than flash, Williams did not resemble a man who had not been to bed. In fact, Harry would bet twenty quid that John had made a stubborn point of going for a five-mile run after they had spoken on the phone that morning about what was now being referred to by everyone in British law enforcement as 'Stepney'.

'Got hold of my old guv'nor at NCA,' Williams said, his fair hair brushing against the fronds of a tall African fig as the three of them huddled away from the throng passing through the atrium.

'Oh, yeah?' said Harry. 'What did his nibs have to say?'

'There's a bit of chatter from terror groups out there now, of course. But it seems like mostly a response to the news, rather than any authentic claim of ownership or involvement.'

'Like who?' said Iris.

'Oh, a few extreme Islamist posts. Vague stuff about "the plague that will finally vanquish Great Satan", meaning they think it's biological stuff. Which suggests they're just guessing.'

'Or misdirecting,' said Harry.

'NCA likes ISIS or one of its newer affiliates for this one. Claims it "fits the handwriting" or something. That's what old Grant said, anyhow.'

Harry snorted. 'Confirmation bias doing its bit. They want it to be Islamist, so they're saying it fits the bill.'

'Which,' said Iris, 'it doesn't necessarily. Does ISIS have form when it comes to snatching fissile material off a rubbish dump? They're reaching, aren't they?'

'Yes,' said Harry. 'Which, unfortunately, doesn't mean we can rule out the possibility that they might be right. Open minds on this one, folks.'

John checked his phone. 'What does Robinson want? Think he knows something?'

'Bill always knows something,' said Harry. 'That's why SO22 exists. He fills in the gaps. I called him on the way back about the possible Devereux link and he just said he wanted us in for a briefing before we chased that up. Wouldn't talk details over the phone.'

'Loves a bit of mystery, Bill, doesn't he?' said Iris.

'Always has,' said Harry.

They made their way up to Robinson's office in the lift.

Outside of Robinson's office, a tall young Black woman was sitting on the small sofa, elegant in a trouser suit with an expensive-looking valise. She smiled at the trio as they walked in. Harry nodded politely. *Wonder what she's here for?*

'Ah,' said Robinson through the door, waving them in without looking up. 'The Three Amigos.'

'Present and correct,' Harry said. 'What are we here for, sir?'

'A bit of education.'

'Not following, sir,' Williams said.

'Didn't expect you to, John,' said Robinson. 'You can take the boy out of NCA, but you can't take NCA out of the boy.'

'Harsh,' Williams said.

'But fair,' Iris observed.

Robinson ushered them over to the small round table with

which the senior members of SO22 had to make do for most of their team meetings. 'We'll be getting a large cupboard as an ops room by close of play,' he said. 'Meanwhile, I'm delighted to announce that the core squad is expanding for the duration of this . . . er, "special supplementary". Some extra resources to help us and keep us on our toes.'

'Expanding?' asked Harry. 'We don't need more manpower yet, do we, guv?'

'Manpower, possibly not. But womanpower – definitely.'

'I'm not following,' Harry said.

'That's usually my line.' John chuckled.

'Come on in, Carol,' said Robinson. 'People, please meet Inspector Carol Walker, generously seconded to us by our colleagues at SCD4.'

The woman who'd been waiting outside strode into the office and towards the awaiting officers. The team shook her proffered hand in turn.

'Forensics?' said Harry. 'Nice to meet you, Inspector.'

'And you, DCI Taylor. Heard a lot about you.'

'Oh, really? All of it bad, no doubt.'

'No – not quite all of it.'

'I've asked Inspector Walker to join us for two reasons,' Robinson interrupted. 'First, she's worked NBC – nuclear, biological, chemical – for five years. So, this is her terrain. And – apologies for my candour, Carol – because her father is Otis Walker, who you may or may not have heard of. You should have, anyway.'

'Professor at King's College London? That Otis Walker?' John chipped in.

Carol smiled. 'The very same. Professor of nuclear physics.'

'And,' said Robinson, 'sparing your blushes, Carol, the country's leading expert on the practical applications of atomic fission in modern industry – and warfare.' He paused. 'I could be polite and say that this didn't influence my request for secondment, but it did, and I don't have time to pretend otherwise. With Carol, we get her own front-rank experience and instant access to her father's. I've already spoken to him, incidentally.'

'The apple didn't fall far from the tree, then?' Harry asked.

'Not in this instance, no,' she said. 'Though I think Dad would have preferred it if I'd stayed in academic research, rather than become a copper.'

'I heard him give a talk once,' said John. 'At an off-site day, when NBC and nuclear markets were flavour of the month again, briefly. Very impressive. Very technical. I reckon I followed about half of it.'

'You did well,' she said. 'Dad can get very . . . intricate. Carried away by the maths and the physics. I'll try to be more practical. And when I can't answer a question . . . well, we know who to call, I guess.'

Iris said. 'What can you tell us, Inspector? I mean, right now? On the basis of what little we know.'

Carol opened her valise and removed a laptop, which she opened up, before clicking on a tab that filled the screen with an image of a simple atomic device.

'What we know is that this is what we could be facing,' she said. 'And pretty soon.'

'It looks alarmingly simple,' said Harry, pointing at the schematic on the screen.

'It is,' she said. 'That's the whole point, I suppose. And why we're here. A basic fission atomic device that uses an isotope like uranium-235 – apart from the isotope itself – there's nothing complex about it at all. You need hard metal casing, conventional explosive to start the chain reaction, a few more odds and ends. Basically, you construct a gun to fire what's called "subcritical material" at the unstable material. That starts the chain reaction, which leads to . . .'

She didn't need to finish the sentence.

Breaking the silence, Carol continued. 'Just to be a little bit more scientific, the nucleus of a U-235 atom has one hundred and forty-three particles called neutrons. When a free one of those bashes into the atom, it splits the nucleus. That spins off additional neurons, which hit the nuclei of other nearby U-235 atoms – and that creates nuclear fission.'

John was the first to respond. 'How much of the stuff do you need for a bomb?'

Carol pointed at the core of the on-screen device. 'Let's say you had fifteen kilograms of decently enriched uranium. Assuming the device has been well put together by a reasonably well-qualified professional – and the level of expertise needed isn't that great, it really isn't – then you're looking at about fifteen kilotons of damage.'

'What does that mean in real terms?' asked Harry.

She fixed him with her gaze. 'It means something a bit like Hiroshima.'

# 9

The mezzanine was where most of the action seemed to be going on. Which is to say: that was where the VIP section of the Cool Cube was located. From the main dance floor and the booths that lined the ground floor, you could see the glow of freshly laundered white shirts in the lights and the shimmer of sparkling black dresses, jewellery and make-up above. On the low tables were ice buckets and tall cocktails and you could just make out the faces of the club's more favoured patrons. And, as if to emphasise the point, there were two red ropes that separated them from the main body of the club: one at the top of the stairs, and one at the bottom. You were left in no doubt that – on its own terms, anyway – the Cube, as Adey had called it, had its aristocrats and plebs.

Harry and Iris had queued and paid to get in, not wanting to draw attention to themselves as cops. If this really was a Devereux venue – and a quick Land Registry check did link the property to one of the shell companies associated with the family – then the staff would be briefed to sound the alert if anyone even slightly connected with the law swung by for the evening. Their little visit had to be strictly incognito.

It helped, thought Harry, that Iris looked as amazing as she did. He'd never really clocked her sheer glamour before; not that he had been looking nor had there been many opportunities through her SO22 work to dress up. But, in her little black dress and heels, with her blonde hair up and just the right amount of make-up, she looked a million dollars. Not just at home in the club, but the sort of customer that it would be positively enthusiastic to attract. Harry had noticed how swiftly they had been moved through the queue by the bouncers; he doubted that it was anything to do with him.

Sure, he'd done his best not to look like an off-duty specialist police officer visiting a club he would normally avoid like the plague. So, out came his smartest blue Armani jacket, navy chinos and a pair of loafers that rarely saw action. All of which was fine. But – as girlfriends had told him in the past – he would never be fashionable: not ever. Not even if a team of stylists from *Vogue* had spent a day trying to make him look edgy and contemporary. He knew that people in the club would look at him and Iris and think, 'What is *she* doing with that tall stiff?' Which, to his great surprise, bugged him ever so slightly. Not much, but the feeling was definitely there.

Adey had been right about the buzz in the Cool Cube. A dazzling light show made the dance floor a riot of colours, and dry ice occasionally emerged from an outlet below the DJ's booth to add to the atmosphere. The crowd was mixed: some local, young and hip; some slightly older, probably from outside the East End, but drawn by the energy and panache of the club. The music was overwhelming in its combination of heavy beats, hard rap and occasional breaks into Afropop and old-school disco. Iris was entranced and began dancing as soon as they were through the doors. Harry did his best – knowing there was little point in approaching the DJ and asking if he had any Miles Davis or Thelonious Monk.

Harry, finally accepting that his moves were fooling no

one, found them a booth and, raising his voice, asked Iris if
she wanted a drink.

'Inner locket freeze!' she yelled – or seemed to.

'What? Never heard of that!'

She tried again. 'Gin and tonic please! Bombay Sapphire!'

That made more sense. *Christ*, he thought, *I'm out of my
depth here*. Still, there were worse ways of spending a Thursday
evening in the line of duty, it had to be admitted.

Harry made his way to the bar and used his well-sharpened
elbows to get to the front. To his side, a couple of young
guys were having a heated discussion; about what, Harry
wasn't quite clear.

'No way, fam!' said the first. 'He be fuckin' messing with you.'

'For real,' said the second. 'I told him: I brag different, like
the man sing. Tense, like. I said: "Y'all be safe."'

'You're the real G. Facts is facts.'

Maybe they were, thought Harry, but how would he know?
The world was changing, and it was hard to keep up with
the truth sometimes, and the way people talked about it. Not
that he was against change itself. But he was definitely against
being made to feel Jurassic.

'What'll it be?' asked the barman, standing in front of a
dizzying array of optics and cocktails illuminated by their
own light panels, flashing pink, green and orange. 'Want to
try one of our special cocktails?'

'No, thanks,' bellowed Harry. 'Two large G and Ts. Bombay
Sapphire. Ice and lime, please.'

The barman nodded and dug a trowel into the icebox to
begin his work.

Harry considered starting a tab, but thought better of it
and headed back to Iris.

'Thanks,' she said, taking a healthy slug from her drink.
'Oh, that's great.'

'Out two nights in a row,' he said. 'Never known anything like it.'

'I tell you, it's odd for me, too. My ex-husband said I never went anywhere with him. Too exhausted. Head too full of the job.'

*Yes*, thought Harry. *All our heads too full of the job.* No time for anything – or anyone – else. All of us single or divorced. SO22: the divorce machine. The homewrecker.

She smiled – with, he thought, genuine happiness – and nudged him playfully. She had warm eyes. Yes, he could definitely get used to this. Or, at least, he could in another life.

Iris said, 'That VIP area . . .'

'Yeah,' he replied. 'We need to get up there, don't we?'

'Definitely. If Devereux's mates are going to be anywhere, it won't be down here, will it?'

'Depends what you mean by "mates". Man like Devereux has hundreds of people like Adey who pay him weekly – I bet you Adey's never been up there in his life. He might not even make it into the club itself. You can imagine him being shown to the tradesmen's entrance, can't you? Some seedy back room where they count out the bills and smack those who come in short.'

'Definitely.'

'So then I guess that bit' – he nodded up at the mezzanine – 'is where Devereux or his top people take anyone they want to impress. Anyone who's a face. Assuming, that is, that they ever come here.'

She smiled and – very naturally – took his hand. 'Come on. Drink up. Let's go and see.'

They drained their G & Ts and forged a path through the sweat of the dance floor to the rope at the bottom of the stairs where a bouncer in a suit stood sentry. He looked, thought Harry, like a WWE wrestler on his wedding day.

Iris placed a gentle palm on Harry's chest. 'Leave this to me. Not to throw shade, but I think I might be able to speed this up.'

No point in denying the truth. 'I think you're right,' he said.

Iris sashayed towards the WWE gatekeeper, leant up to whisper something in his ear and – open sesame – the brute was laughing his head off, unclipping the rope and ushering Harry forwards to follow Iris up the stairs. At the top, Brute Number Two needed no further persuasion and repeated the procedure.

A greeter in a short black suit welcomed them. 'Just two this evening?' she said.

Iris nodded, and they walked over to an old-fashioned gold art deco table with two stools.

'Champagne?' she asked. 'Or something else? We have all kinds of . . . refreshment available. We like to accommodate all our most important guests' needs.'

'Champagne is great,' Iris said. 'Moët. Two glasses.'

The greeter smiled. 'Very good. With you shortly.'

'Christ almighty,' said Harry. 'How the other half live, eh?'

'Don't worry,' she said. 'I've a feeling that we won't be in character much longer.'

'Yeah,' he said, privately disappointed; he was starting to enjoy their masquerade more than he knew he should. 'Can't help feeling that the real business – assuming Adey wasn't sending us off on a wild goose chase – takes place backstage.'

Iris nodded. Their drinks arrived and she lifted her glass, toasting him. He reciprocated and relished the ice-cold sweetness and bite of the champagne. No doubt about it, he could definitely get used to this; or at least, if he was honest, to the company.

His reverie was broken by a noise from downstairs, almost

loud enough to cut through the thumping music. At the bar, the two men whose conversation he had overheard were now taking chunks out of each other. The larger one had the other on the ground and was about to start pummelling him – his visible fury driving away the crowd that, only a few seconds before, had surrounded them. *Oh fuck*, thought Harry, *am I really going to have to go down and be a boring copper and break up a fight? So much for our sort-of-undercover night out.*

He needn't have worried. Even before the young man had landed his first punch, he was being restrained by four security guys – their earpieces giving away their function – who physically lifted him to waist height and carried him towards the door of the club, which opened as if by magic, so he could be unceremoniously dumped on the pavement. His victim, shaken but not badly hurt, was frogmarched behind him by two more security personnel, who shoved him out the door too, shouting some indecipherable warning at him as they did so.

As he looked down, Harry noticed something else. He had clocked it earlier, but not seen it for what it was. There was a decent number of men heading for the gents: well, nothing odd about that in a place where most of the punters were drinking heavily. The odd bit was that a good half of them were turning left at the archway – which was not where the loos were. Where were they going?

'Hey,' he said, grabbing Iris by the wrist. 'We're in the wrong place.'

'What do you mean? We've only just arrived—'

'I know. Trust me. We won't find anything interesting up here. Apart from the size of the bill.'

They headed downstairs, murmuring confected excuses to the bouncers, and made their way back across the dance floor to where Harry had been looking. Just ahead of them, one guy turned right, in the direction of the gents. Another turned left, heading somewhere else. They followed the second.

Without knowing it, he led them through a black door into a long corridor that, in its cold, dingy bareness, was a shock to the system after the sensory bombardment of the main clubroom. There were chalk marks on the bare concrete walls, a couple of stray shopping trolleys and a few doors leading God knows where. But their unwitting guide was heading all the way to the end, towards a fire exit. At times, they could barely make him out in the gloom.

When the man pressed the bar and opened the door, Harry and Iris could see that it led into an alleyway. It closed behind him with a nerve-jangling crash. Harry looked at Iris and put his finger to his lips. They were about fifty paces behind but didn't want to seem as if they'd been following the man. Harry counted out thirty seconds and then led them on.

# 10

He was in bed, enjoying, as he always did, the Frette linen that he absolutely insisted upon. Nothing came close, he believed, to its Egyptian cotton or Italian manufacture. How should a man like him know about such things? Nobody would ever ask him a question like that because they knew the response would be an uncomfortable one-way journey in the boot of a car. Without their head.

In the corner, a state-of-the-art air purifier purred almost inaudibly, doing its work. For a while, when sleep had eluded him in the past, he had streamed ASMR audio into his room at night to help him drift off. But his normal patterns had soon reasserted themselves and he now felt able to let nature take its course, only occasionally, taking a melatonin tablet to seal the deal. At any rate, sleep mattered to him very much.

So he was enraged – reflexively so, in fight-or-flight mode – when his phone buzzed at his bedside. He sat bolt upright, suddenly murderous and unable to think of an immediate target for his fury. It buzzed again. He lashed out, sending a glass of water on his nightstand smashing into the wall. Then, on the third buzz, he reached for the phone.

It was a Telegram message and consisted of a single word: *Secured.*

He put the phone back where it had been and fell back into a deep slumber.

# 11

The alleyway was, as Harry muttered under his breath, 'A bloody boulevard of scumbags.' He had never seen so much open drug dealing in his life, or such flagrant using for that matter. The hum of bartering – prices, quantities, street brand names – was interrupted occasionally by the noisy sneezes of the coke snorters or the coughing of the skunk smokers, the fumes of which curled to the sky from tinfoil heated by lighters as smackheads got their late-evening fix. What a hellhole. Was there no decency left?

This wasn't just a single dealer operating on the quiet in a night spot. It was its own tidy bazaar of criminality, operating right behind a supposedly legitimate club, and treated, it seemed, as a perfectly normal facility by sellers and punters alike. Which meant, he concluded bitterly, that the local nick knew all about it and had either agreed to leave it be in return for information or – more likely – for a slice of the take.

Under any other circumstances, this would have been a no-brainer: call for backup and then arrest everybody. Scarcely a prize on a par with the Cricks, but Harry reckoned he was looking at between ten and fifteen hardcore dealers, all of them carrying class A narcotics in reasonable quantities, all of them looking at serious jail time.

And the users? At the very least, they could be squeezed for information in the interview rooms: names, places, details. Some of them would get off with a caution, but others would be looking at charges. All in all, there were a few hundred years of imprisonment just waiting to be scooped up in this rank alleyway.

But that wasn't going to happen tonight, was it? There was a much bigger task at hand for him and Iris, and the tribe of bottom feeders before them, just waiting to be pinched and slung behind bars, were going to escape justice – at least for now – because, as Robinson had often warned him, half of police work is a matter of priorities. Psychedelic mushrooms versus mushroom clouds? In the end, there wasn't really a choice.

Although that wasn't strictly true. What Harry realised was that he had a tricky judgement to make, and quickly. Namely, which of these grisly lowlifes to pick on? All this was going on under the protection of the Devereux firm. Which meant that every single one of the dealers would have something to say, if pressed, about where, exactly, he and Iris should be looking.

It was already midnight. Good. Time to warn someone that he faced a pretty simple choice: tell them what they needed to know or end up looking like a squashed pumpkin. He could already imagine an inquiry, at some date in the future, when the words 'unreasonable force' would be used in direct reference to his methods. And maybe they would have a point, in the abstract. But he couldn't help feeling that this would be a better outcome than a very different kind of inquiry: into an atomic blast that devastated a large portion of London. Or of Birmingham. Or of anywhere. This was no time to be squeamish, even if he had to pay a price further down the line.

Looking down the alley, he spotted his man quickly and beckoned Iris to follow him.

'Come on,' he said. 'We're going to make a trade.'

'Are you kidding?' she said.

'Not entirely.'

His target was near the end of the line-up and looked like a more muscular, upgraded version of Adey – taller, healthier, without the telltale wrecked skin of the habitual user. He bounced from foot to foot in his cashmere hoodie, rubbing his hands together, full of salesman's brio.

'Evenin', evenin', folks. What you looking for?' was his opening line. 'I got H, charlie, ket, speed, vally, xannie, acid . . . anything. I can get you a nice girl. Oh! You got one already. Sorry, miss. Forgetting me manners.'

'Well,' said Harry. 'I must say that's an impressive bill of fare.'

'Best deals, come to Roy. That's what all my customers say. Nobody has trampled on Roy's gear. It's the *best*.'

'Thing is, Roy. I'm not actually looking for drugs tonight.'

Roy burst out laughing, slapping Harry on the back with ill-judged mirth. 'Oh, I like you already! We good, we good!' He calmed a little. 'So, anyway. What can I be getting you, boss?'

'I just want a little information.'

Roy was still smiling, a single gold tooth flashing. But he had stiffened a little. '*Information?* Oh, well. Depends on what you mean by that, innit?'

'I mean, you *prancing tosser*, tell us where to find Mr Devereux or his close associates. Or, better still, both.'

Roy's smile vanished, and he threw his cigarette stub at Harry's chest in disbelief.

'You some sort of fucking maniac?' he hissed. 'Come down *this* row, asking a question like *that*? You want to get yourself rubbed out? Fool!'

Before Roy uttered the L of 'fool' he had been lifted bodily by Harry and slammed against the fence, both arms pinned at his sides. Even as he squawked protest, Harry calmly asked Iris to remove her badge – *discreetly* – from her clutch, so that Roy could see it, but so that nobody else on the drug-dealing drag would be any the wiser.

'Clock that?' he said.

Roy nodded.

'That means, sunshine, that you've got a big decision to make in the next ten seconds: prison, or verbals.' He waited, but not for long. 'Well?'

Roy scowled. 'Not here,' he said.

'Lead on,' said Harry. 'And there better not be a gang of your mates waiting for us. Or my colleague here could lose her temper. And then you really will be fucking sorry.'

The brief fracas hadn't attracted much attention; Harry assumed that Roy and his fellow dealers were routinely involved in minor tussles with customers, not to mention with one another. Roy beckoned them towards the end of the alley, where an old wooden door, studded with rusty metal, led out into a patch of rough land. A hundred metres further on, a warehouse twinkled with lights.

Roy pulled his hoodie tight around him, like makeshift armour. 'Make it quick, copper. I don't want no aggro. You shouldn't be here – either of you. This place is meant to be . . . you feds are supposed to stay clear. That's been the arrangement for years. No fucking respect.'

'Yeah, I'd worked that one out for myself,' Harry said. 'But we're not ordinary . . . "feds". We don't do deals with toerags like you. We don't do deals, full stop. We chase villains and send them to prison for as long as humanly possible. Which is exactly what I'd like to do to you for selling all that *filth*.'

'Wait a minute—'

'So,' said Iris. 'If you'd like to avoid . . . What do you reckon, guv? Ten, at least? Maybe fifteen?'

'Yeah,' Harry said. 'At least, depending on the judge. And the prosecution. And, of course, us.'

'If you'd like to avoid that,' Iris continued, 'you just have to behave yourself, stop whining and answer the bloody questions.'

Roy looked up at the night sky, as if seeking divine guidance. 'Christ. All right. What do you want to know? As if I fucking know anything—'

'Man like you?' scoffed Harry. 'A *player* like you? I'll bet you know plenty.'

Roy shrugged. 'You're tripping, fool.'

'I'm not. Are you going to do us all a favour and start cooperating?'

'I'm here, aren't I?'

'You are,' said Iris. 'And you can stay here as long as you like and ply your disgusting trade if you just tell us one simple thing: Where do we find Devereux?'

Harry could see a truly wretched calculation flicker across Roy's face. If he talked, he would be risking death. Then again, if he didn't, he would definitely be doing a long stretch inside. And he didn't look like the kind of guy who would cope well with life in prison.

'Listen,' he said. 'Nobody knows where Top Man – Mr Devereux, I mean – where he is, you know? At any one time. Know what I'm saying? He moves around all his gaffs, always on the move. And nobody with half a brain would ask, either.'

Harry shoved Roy hard in the shoulder. 'You're testing my patience, Roy. I don't have the time for this crap.'

'Even if you don't know where Devereux – sorry, the *Top Man* – is, you know where his people are,' Iris said. 'Don't pretend you don't. We'll nick you right now if you do.'

Roy laughed quietly. Harry rested a menacing hand on his

shoulder: 'You think what Sergeant Davies is saying is funny, do you? I'd say that was pretty bloody foolish, myself.'

'Not funny,' said Roy. 'It's just' – he pointed at the warehouse behind them – 'you're already *there*.'

'That ratty old building?' asked Iris. '*That*'s where the Devereux crew hangs out?'

Roy nodded.

'See?' said Harry, removing his hand. 'Wasn't so difficult, was it?'

He dismissed Roy with the merest tilt of his head. 'Iris?' he said.

'Yes?'

'Time to call for backup.'

# 12

The interior of the warehouse was unexpected. It was more like a set of Russian dolls than a large single space, with a warren of rooms under the same roof. There was an outer corridor that wrapped itself round the building, then an inner ring of grim-looking offices, some with desktop Macs, others full of files and packing detritus. Neon lighting flickered above them, illuminating brick walls of unremitting bleakness.

On the east side, there was what looked like a vault or an armoury. Iris had been able to pick the padlock on a side entrance to the building, but the lock on the vault would need specialist skills – cutting tools, cryptographers if the lock was coded, or good old-fashioned C-4. They would leave that to the backup and forensic teams.

What troubled Harry was the silence. He'd broken into a fair few lairs of villainy in his time – sometimes with a warrant, sometimes more creatively – and had come to recognise the noises you encountered within. Usually the distinctive rumble of male conversation, the beat of music, zapping sounds from computer games, occasionally the cries of somebody held hostage or facing the wrath of the boss. Drug factories, trafficking dens, counterfeit plants, edge-of-town hideouts: he'd seen them all and he knew what they were like. But this was different. All he could hear was the sound of their own footfall, the distant thump from the club and traffic from the other side of the warehouse. It was as if the whole premises had been deserted, a ghost town abandoned by its lawless inhabitants. It didn't add up. The lights were on, but nobody was home.

'This way,' said Iris, pointing to a corridor on the left. She had ditched her heels, Harry noticed and was padding quietly in her stockinged feet.

He nodded. 'Backup?'

'Four units, three minutes away. Armed response and uniforms. Forensics will follow.'

The corridor was short and the frosted glass above the door indicated a well-lit interior. Here, perhaps, was the inner sanctum of the Devereux gang.

Harry put his ear to the door. He could hear voices but realised quickly that it was the sound from a television, possibly football commentary. Nothing more. No laughter, or argument, or even the grunts you would expect to hear exchanged late at night between members of a crew in their headquarters.

He whispered to Iris. 'I'm going in.'

'Don't be soft, guv. They're bound to be strapped. You'll catch them off guard and they won't ask any questions. You'll up end up looking like a colander.'

'Don't worry, I'm going to use my trademark charm.'

'Harry!' Using his first name: that was new. 'For Christ's sake. Wait for the shooters.' She looked around. 'We probably should have waited for them before coming in at all.'

He smiled. 'Yeah, but we didn't, did we?'

He put his hand on the door handle. She put her own on top of his, in a last-ditch effort to dissuade him. 'Harry.' But he was already turning it. The door opened easily.

What was he expecting to see? Not this, that's for sure. The first surprise was that the main space led directly to a broad downhill ramp to his right and, he assumed, a subterranean exit for vehicles. Below the overhead floodlighting were parked several Transits, a couple of blacked-out Land Rovers and a red Bentley Continental. A dozen or so tea chests were stacked on one side, alongside a pile of large polystyrene insulating boxes. An Outslayer punching bag hung from the rafters by the door to an inner office – whose walls were covered with maps, calendars and whiteboards. No doubt about it: this was the nerve centre of a business.

What it lacked was people. Except that wasn't quite right, was it? It was the look on Iris's face that tipped him off. Unusual to see her shocked – he wasn't sure if he ever had, in fact – but there was no disguising her horror at the scene they both now beheld.

At the end of the inner space was a makeshift lounge area: a few sofas, battered leather armchairs and a couple of coffee tables, strewn with old copies of the *Sun*, *Racing Post* and the *Ring*. Three nearly empty bottles of Elit vodka, and a forest of shot glasses. There was an ashtray, from which a trail of smoke still rose, and what looked like a box of cigars.

On the sofas were six men. They varied in height, build and age, from the young and athletic – street soldiers, Harry assumed – to the older, burlier duo wearing suits and flashing gold watches and tie pins – probably senior members of the Devereux crew. What they had in common, all six of them, was that their throats had been cut from ear to ear. Some sprawled back, their wounds gaping grotesquely. Another leant forwards as if dozing, except that his trainers were at the centre of a pool of his own blood, and his shirt was soaked with what looked like a vile, outsized scarlet tongue.

There was no discernible sign of struggle or a firefight. Whatever had taken place had been quick, unexpected and pitiless. Had there been a discussion first, before the execution?

It seemed so. Drinks and a convivial smoke, followed by a massacre. In any event, a top London firm had been taken out in a matter of seconds, its men executed in cold blood, no doubt at gunpoint, by a much deadlier outfit that had done its ghastly work – and then got the hell out.

'Well,' said Harry. 'If they had what we're after, they fucking well don't have it now.'

'Christ, what a mess,' Iris said. 'Here.' She passed Harry a pair of forensics gloves from her clutch. 'We'd better wear these.'

On the television, a replay of a match played earlier that evening was just concluding. Harry gestured. 'Still, not a total disaster. At least Chelsea won.'

Before Iris could reply, he said, 'Hello. What's this?'

Clambering between the legs of the dead bodies, some of them slumped, Harry picked up a box of cigars: a limited-edition Arturo Fuente Opus X, which, he knew, was one of the most expensive smokes in the world. What, probably a grand at least for a box like this?

'Here, take a look,' he said, walking back towards her.

'This was a gift when they arrived – whoever "they" were. Or at least presented as a gift. And the classy vodka, too. This was supposed to look like a meet. For an amiable trade. Chummy, you know? But, Jesus, whoever brought the pricey smokes and booze had no intention of paying for anything else. Certainly not for a crateful of uranium. They had a few drinks and then, before they'd finished a single cigar, the visitors slaughtered their hosts – and bloody fast, too.'

Iris looked at the box. 'Why leave that, though?'

Harry shrugged. 'Must have been interrupted. Or, more likely, heard that somebody else was on their way. Us, another crew. I mean, does this look like sloppy work to you in any other respect?'

She shook her head.

'Not a bit of it,' he said. 'They would have cleaned the scene, a crew like this. But something made them leave in a hurry. And leave this behind.'

'Does it tell us anything?'

'Could have some dabs on it. Though I bet you it doesn't. This level of villain, they use acid or superglue or tape to make sure they don't leave recognisable prints anywhere.' He looked at each side of the box. 'Could come from any cigar merchant— Oh, well, well. Take a look.'

The writing was tiny but she could just make it out: *Joe's Cigars, Barbados.*

'Caribbean? You think the snatch squad is from there? Long way to come.'

'Might just be. That's worth us keeping. Here, have you got a polybag?'

'Too late for that, isn't it? If we find anything, we have to hand it over anyway.'

He looked at her. 'That's true. *Technically* speaking. I was just thinking of – what's the word? – *borrowing* something. For a bit.'

He held out his hand for the polybag. With a sigh, Iris handed it over. Harry dropped the cigar box into the bag and handed it back to her. No doubt, she was about to say that if they were found out and put on traffic duty, it would be his fault, when they were startled by the sound of a shot being fired. At them.

By reflex, Harry grabbed Iris and dragged her down behind one of the sofas. That would provide cover for the time being. But not for long.

He squinted round the side. A figure was marching towards them, a tall, dark-haired man in a black jumpsuit. He put a fresh clip in his revolver and unloaded three more shells into the sofa. If he got much closer, it would no longer protect them. Each shot made the upholstery shudder.

'Shit,' said Iris. 'Of all the nights to be unarmed.'

'We're police!' Harry yelled over the sofa. 'Drop your weapon now. You cannot escape and if you shoot us, you will go to prison for-fucking-ever!'

He looked around the sofa – and felt another bullet whistle past his head.

'Big mistake, mate!' he said. Still, the footsteps grew closer.

Then, a much louder shot rang out from their own end of the Devereux lair. A warning shot, as it turned out.

'Armed police! Put down your weapon and hit the deck. *Now!*'

But the other guy was having none of that. He raised his gun once again – and was immediately perforated with bullets, his body twitching like a rag doll as blood suddenly gushed from the entry and exit wounds. He fell dead to the ground, a scarlet pool rapidly growing in size below him.

They heard the screech of tyres somewhere deeper in the building. There must have been others. Two members of the newly arrived firearms unit took off in hot pursuit.

The lead officer walked over to the sofa where they were still crouching and pulled down his mask. 'Fuck me – Harry! Del Farris, SCO19. Remember me?'

Rarely had Harry been so pleased to see a fellow officer. 'Del! Thank fuck it's you. I— wait, this is Sergeant Iris Davies. She's SO22 too. We worked on the Selfridges plot, me and Del, just after lockdown.'

'That's the one. How you doing?'

Harry laughed. 'Well, glad to see you, that's for bloody sure. It's like a morgue in here. And we didn't spot Laughing Boy on the ground over there. He must have heard us and come back.'

'So I see,' said Farris. 'Fucking hell. Carnage. Any idea how long ago . . .?'

'No, not really. I mean the blood is pretty fresh, so not that long. Looks like they had a little vodka party first before the slaughter began.'

Farris nodded. His team had spread out and were checking the remaining nooks and crannies of the warehouse – not least for booby traps.

'These are all Phil Devereux's boys, right?' he said. 'Or were.'

'Yeah,' said Harry. 'We were hoping for a quiet word with them. Thought they might be doing a spot of fencing we were interested in. They won't be saying much now.'

'Certainly won't. What were they fencing? Is this part of the Crick op? Or are you lot freelancing on Stepney?'

Harry smiled. 'Freelancing? Come off it, Del. You know we don't freelance on anything. Very well-behaved bunch of individuals is SO22. You've seen us in action, after all.'

'Yeah,' said Farris, replacing his helmet. 'And the rest.'

Harry checked on Iris, who seemed relieved rather than shaken. That had been too close for comfort. But they were still alive, which was good enough for now.

Harry looked around, wondering what he might be overlooking, angry that he had missed the lingering member of the death squad and put their lives in danger. Soon the place would be swarming with forensics officers and he wouldn't be able to get near anything or hear himself think.

The ramp leading out of the complex intrigued him. *That* was a nice spot of interior design, ensuring that the Devereux crew – RIP – were able to keep their operations that much more discreet. Or as discreet as anything could be in the digital age. He wondered where the underground exit led: you could be sure it was somewhere off-road. The inside court of a pub or the loading bay of a wholesaler. A location where the comings and goings of vehicles would attract minimal attention. That was smart.

The two tactical boys who had gone after the departing vehicle were heading towards him, breathless after their sprint, and talking into their radios. Maybe an eye in the sky could catch the getaway vehicle. But, then again, maybe not.

He caught Iris's eye and indicated that she should follow him. Her glamour – so alluring earlier in the evening – now looked out of place, and he could tell that she was longing to be back in work clothes. As was he. The jacket was much too flash for a crime scene with corpses and blood everywhere.

'What are you thinking?' she said.

'I'm thinking that we got lucky,' said Harry. 'This was very professional and I should have checked the whole place before coming in. You were right. I'm sorry.'

'Forget about it,' she said. 'I have a feeling this job is going to be full of surprises.'

'Yeah, just a bit. We know there was at least one vehicle, because we heard it. Say just one, for the sake of argument. It was ticking over down there while the killing was going on and the uranium – assuming it was the uranium – was being taken. *That* could have been shifted using one of the trolleys up there.'

She nodded.

'You know what I think?' he said.

'Probably not.'

'I think it's time for a team trip to Barbados.'

# 13

'Barbados?' roared Robinson. 'What the fuck makes you think I'm going to authorise a four-man deployment to Barbados because of a *cigar box*? Do you know what your budget's looking like already this financial year?'

Harry stood his ground, confident he would get his way. 'It's a hunch. Remember those?'

'Don't get fresh with me, Detective Chief Inspector. You'd do well to remember what's at stake here. And what'll happen if either of us fucks up.'

'I imagine we'll be eaten by wild dogs live on TV, sir?'

'Only if granted clemency,' said Robinson. He sat down at his desk with the air of a man well-used to responsibility, upon whose shoulders rested even more than usual. 'Tell me it's not just the cigars. Please, Harry. That's a cute angle, but it's not enough for a pleasure trip.'

Uninvited, Harry sat down too. 'Listen, Bill,' he said. 'I was going through some of the background you sent me and the Barbados angle had actually crossed my mind already.' He paused. 'Remember Voldrev?'

Now he had Robinson's attention. 'Yes. Yes, I do, as a matter of fact. *Vladimir Voldrev*. We liked him for the Calais drug bust last year, didn't we? Didn't nab him, though. Clever bastard, as I recall. Loved to live it large, swagger and bling. But totally legitimate on the surface.'

'Correct. Russian oligarch. Sixty-five or pushing it. Some

legitimate businesses in insurance and investment capital. Never in Putin's inner circle, which, luckily for him, has kept him mostly free of sanctions since Ukraine. Not significantly impaired by any of the measures since the invasion. But active worldwide since the collapse of the Soviet Union and, as we both know, up to his hairy armpits in narcotics for most of that time. But nobody has got close to nailing him. Us, the Yanks, Interpol. He always gives us the slip. Just vanishes into thin air. And none of his Bratva mafia brethren has ever told us a word about him.'

'Yes, got all that. But what links him to Stepney? He's a drug smuggler, not a terrorist warlord or a far-right cult leader. What does he want with uranium-235?'

Harry warmed to his theme. 'I was thinking about what you said about *anyone* being a suspect in a case like this. And then I was also thinking about what Walker told us about the simplicity of atomic weapons. And how being in control of fissile material could give you – well, not just military power, but also – unique *status*.'

'What's your point?'

'That *everybody* wants status. Not just jihadi crazies and skinhead ethnic cleansers. Villains crave it just as much. Not for a cause but because there are only so many yachts and supermodels and football teams that you can buy. Imagine . . . the ultimate oligarch super-toy: an atom bomb.' He sat back. '*Now* you're talking.'

'I suppose,' said Robinson. 'But what do you do with it? I mean why would a character like Voldrev want to re-enact Nagasaki? It makes no sense. Those guys want to own cities, not to blow them up. His business relies on evading attention, not nuclear mayhem.'

'But he wouldn't be blowing up a city,' Harry said. 'Listen, Bill. We always think of atomic weapons in terms of mass destruction, right?'

'Yes,' said Robinson, clearly becoming impatient. 'We do. And with good fucking reason.'

'But that's not necessarily true. After Stepney, I read everything I could on the joint database about uranium. Everything I have clearance for, anyway. And here's the thing: it's not all mushroom-cloud apocalypse.'

'What are you talking about?'

'Look, Carol Walker's right, up to a point. You *could* re-enact Hiroshima with this stuff, if you're a full-blown maniac. But that's not all you can do. Not by a long chalk. There used to be a whole range of tactical weapons – never deployed – before the Cold War ended, meant for much smaller attacks. Battlefield weapons. They were all shut down in the 1990s, or before. Though – surprise, surprise – Trump reopened research into their use.'

'What use are they to someone like Voldrev, though?' asked Robinson.

'I'm not saying they are. All I'm saying is, imagine a man like him who was known to have that firepower at his disposal. Not to destroy a city but – I don't know – someone's coca plantation. Or their fucking bank. Or whatever. That takes a regular common-or-garden oligarch and turns him into an underworld god. The ultimate prestige weapon for the twenty-first-century gangster. It makes you global top dog. *Instantly.*'

'Fair enough. I like your little speech, Harry, don't get me wrong. But everything you just said could also be said of, I don't know, a thousand bad people who are presently living on the planet. Ramirez, for one. The Cricks. You know the list. We're still trying to identify the guy that tried to shoot your head off at the Devereux HQ. No tattoos. Doesn't match any photofits. And could just be a private contractor for all we know. Working for fuck knows who.'

'Listen,' said Harry. 'What you say about a thousand bad

guys is true. Course it is. I'm aware. But not all of them have, for the last five years, spent much of their time in a chateau on a private island just off the coast of Barbados. Have they?'

Robinson scrutinised Harry for what seemed an age. He patted his pen against his palm as if conducting a complex inner calculation. 'All right, DCI Taylor. All right. I see where you're heading with this. I can't say I'm all the way along the path with you yet, but it's worth a scout. Take the trip. But not for too long, mind. I need you back here as soon as possible.'

'Much obliged, Bill. Oh, one more thing. Since we're officially chasing white rabbits this week. Do you remember Julian Smythe?'

'Rings a bell vaguely. Remind me.'

'Again, it was the Calais case.' Harry handed him an iPad. 'When we were trying to get to Voldrev. Nobody had anything approaching a CHIS or asset in his circle, so our intel was pretty shabby. But I remember Five telling us that the quickest way to smoke out our friend Vladimir was to do anything nice for this guy.'

'Julian Smythe.'

'The very same. A proper English toff he is. Eton, Cambridge. His father, the late Sir Roderick Smythe, a top-drawer diplomat, serious great and the good. Royal connections – the father, that is. Old money. But that had only given young Julian a taste for more. An art dealer, officially: modern stuff, very high end. But also, we're as sure as we can be, one of Europe's most effective boutique drug lords. Only does a few deals a year, at least that we know of, but they're worth a fortune.'

'And I'm guessing he shares the Voldrev coating of Teflon?'

'Correct. Always a fair few paces ahead of the law. He must have very expensive informants inside the system,

because as soon as anyone gets a sniff of villainy in his operation, it disappears. The DEA had to pay him substantial
damages a few years back after they intercepted a cargo
landing in Miami and ended up wrecking some Finnish
wanker's carefully packaged installation art, which was on its
way to a private purchaser.'

'Why did they do that?'

'Because they were certain – *certain* – that the crates were
packed with cocaine and that they had Smythe bang to rights.
Which they absolutely did not. He made a real stink, too.
Got his Washington connections involved. Senior agents lost
their jobs over that one. Since then, the politicos on both
sides of the Atlantic have been nervous about anything that
might upset him. Which doesn't make him untouchable. But
as good as.'

Robinson smiled. 'But you want to rattle his cage anyway?'

Harry took the iPad back. 'Not exactly. The reason I'm
mentioning him at all is that he and Voldrev *hate* each other.
I mean serious, kill-his-granny loathing, Bill. It's a legend in
the drug world, really. Not just business, but extremely
personal. A proper blood feud. It came up once or twice on
the margins of the Calais case.'

'Christ, yes,' said Robinson. 'I do remember you mentioning
this at a morning briefing back then. Didn't pan out?'

Harry shook his head. 'Not enough for it to be worth our
time. John took a run at it. But it was all, well, insubstantial.
This upper-crust art dealer and the tough-guy oligarch. It
was hard to imagine them in the same room, let alone
obsessing over destroying each other.'

'What was the original beef, anyway?' asked Robinson. 'I
don't remember the details.'

Harry threw up his hands in mock despair. 'Fuck knows.
Nobody could ever get a straight answer as to why they

despised each other so much. Supposedly, something happened when Smythe's dad was working in St Petersburg, or Leningrad as it still was, and Moscow – Sir Roderick was our top man there for a while. Voldrev was still KGB in those days, so God alone knows what the trouble could have been. Another story I've heard is that Smythe was responsible for the death of the love of Voldrev's life – a younger woman – and was none too subtle about it. It's rumour and counter-rumour. When a cousin of Smythe's killed himself last year, some of the gossips had it that it wasn't suicide at all, but part of Voldrev's blood feud against Julian. Then there was the story that Smythe had put a three-million-dollar contract out on Voldrev. And so on, and so on.'

'So,' said Robinson. 'They really hate each other.'

'Seems so. But how much is true and how much myth? You know what that world is like. It's a fog of fucking legends. You never know how much to believe, what to dismiss. It's part of their strength, these characters. They wrap themselves in rumours like armour.'

'But you think it might be worth poking a stick at Smythe over Voldrev? Just to see if he reacts?'

'Well, why not?' said Harry. 'He might say nothing – he's supposed to be smooth as fuck, so he'll be very much on his guard – but he'll also be intrigued. And you can be sure that, with his network, he'll know more about Stepney than an art dealer should. Also, you know what it's like with his sort.'

'How do you mean?'

'Toffs. They love playing verbal chess with us low-born coppers. It's like grouse shooting or stalking. Or whatever else they get up to in their spare time. Anyway, I just want to throw him a bit of bait. To mix metaphors. And go alone. This is a one-on-one job.'

'Where does he live?'

'Beautiful apartment in Belgravia. He has a duplex in Manhattan, too, and, according to John's trawl, a place in Switzerland that's in the name of one of his mistresses. But Eaton Square is home. Worth at least twenty million, apparently, and the art inside is supposed to be worth five times that.'

Robinson pondered all this. 'He could be out of the country.'

'Don't worry. I sent a squad car to check he was in while we were talking. I can type as well as think, you know.'

Robinson stood up and shook his head, smiling in a moment of rare concession.

'Well, then, Harry,' he said, looking down at a briefing note on his desk. 'Off you trot.'

# 14

In a first-floor room in a Dagenham side-street building, four men sat around an old table, their expressions fixed upon an ashtray at its centre. With their shaven heads and black bomber jackets, they resembled a makeshift family of thugs: heavy-set, tattooed and drenched in testosterone.

None dared speak, though, until the fifth man pacing the room in fury had said what he wanted to say. He was a little older than the quartet, his hair longer, his suit and smart shirt indicating his seniority in the group. All the same, he had the build of a boxer and exuded the menace of barely suppressed violence. His command of the other four was absolutely clear from their paralysed silence.

After what seemed an age, he marched up to the table as if to strike one of them. Two of them flinched visibly, which only compounded his anger.

'For fuck's sake!' he yelled. 'Stop cowering! You should be ashamed of yourselves.' He looked at them all in disgust. 'All of you.'

None of them had anything to say, or at least anything that they dared say.

The older man put his fists on the table and leant in.

'Now, you lot, listen to me and listen good. I *want* it. The other night was a disaster. Do you understand? No "if"'s, no "but"'s. No fucking excuses. This is . . .' He pondered the right phrase. '. . . A defining moment, right? We get this, everything changes. If we don't, we're stuck where we've been for ten years. And that's' – he slammed a fist on the table – '*not enough any more!*'

Another long silence.

'Do you understand? Well, you fucking better. I'm telling you to go and get it. I don't care how, I don't care what you have to do or who you have to hurt.' A pause. 'Because if you don't bring it in, your families are bang in trouble.'

The four men did not need to be told that this was – among much else – a dismissal.

# 15

'Isn't it magnificent?' said Julian Smythe. They were in the hallway of his flat, looking at a large canvas of bright colours, powerful lines and words that didn't make much sense to Harry.

'Basquiat,' explained Smythe. 'Painted the year before he died, which was 1988, if I recall correctly. He was only twenty-seven, you know? A genius, though. African expressionism and graffiti that actually made you *think*. He upstaged his contemporaries, not to mention his mentor, Warhol. Astonishing. Don't you agree?'

'Oh, er,' said Harry. 'Well, I'm not much of an art critic, Mr Smythe. But it's certainly . . . striking.'

'Oh, please, do call me Julian,' said his host. 'As you said, this is only a conversation. Not a formal interview. I'm always glad to assist the police when I can. Usually a case of fraud in the art market – all too common, I regret to say. Shall we go through?'

In person, Smythe looked every inch the reserved aristocrat, even more so than Harry had expected. Tall, broad shouldered but not remotely *physical*. Neatly bearded, with frameless spectacles perched on his nose. He wore a linen jacket, check shirt and battered cords. Nothing to suggest specifically artistic interests, much less a bohemian lifestyle; more the retired hedge funder, perhaps, who devoted himself now to reading biographies of great men and to his arboretum in the country. Only his velvet monogrammed house slippers hinted at the dandyism that, as Harry had discovered, toffs like Smythe revelled in when the occasion was right.

'Very kind of you to spare me the time,' he said to Smythe. 'I know you're a busy man.'

'Oh, not so busy today. I've been dealing with the sale of a few items from my gallery in St James's, but that's it for me. I'm drawing stumps early!'

'Wise decision,' said Harry.

'Oh!' said Smythe, as though he had left something on the stove. 'While you're here – indulge me, please – do take a look at my favourite room.'

*Christ,* thought Harry, *what a performance. Still, better go along with it.*

His host led him down a corridor to the left and opened the first door.

'Let's take a peek, shall we?'

'After you.'

Smythe entered and switched on the lights, revealing what amounted to a shrine. There were no furnishings, other than a small burgundy chaise longue by the window. But the walls were covered from skirting board to architrave with theatrical playbills – old and new, beautifully framed and in immaculate condition.

'Do take a look,' said Smythe, like a toddler in his undisguised glee.

'Thanks very much,' said Harry, who had no interest at all in the collection but knew that he was required to make the right noises.

'I'm the first to admit it's terribly *vulgar*. But the truth is, I have a taste for the dramatic and for the stage that I have indulged quite shamelessly since I was a teenager.'

Harry cast an eye over the right side of the wall. Marlon Brando starring in *A Streetcar Named Desire* at the Ethel Barrymore Theatre in New York, 1947. Olivier as Hamlet, the Old Vic, ten years before. *Blithe Spirit* at the Manchester Opera House, 1941. A whole row of Sondheim productions. *Cabaret* on Broadway in 1966. *Angels in America*, 1993. It was impressive all right, but obsessive, too. As if Smythe was trying to capture lightning in a bottle.

'It's quite something,' Harry said. 'A lot of dedication goes into a room like this.'

'Oh, I'm so glad that you like it! And that you understand. It's an entirely private hobby, you see, but one very dear to my heart.'

'Did you ever want to act or direct yourself?'

'If only. I would have loved to, and I tried my hand here and there at school and university. But I never got much beyond third spear carrier in *Titus Andronicus*! I was no loss to the stage, I fear, but there's a part of me that wishes it had been otherwise. Still, I was lucky to find my niche elsewhere. One shouldn't grumble.'

He ushered Harry out of the small gallery and into the main room.

'Do sit wherever you like, please.'

The drawing room was nothing short of stunning and Harry couldn't help but gaze around him as he perched on one of the sofas. He had expected fussiness and clutter and baroque furniture, but Smythe was clearly absolutely precise when it came to his surroundings. One wall was covered with bookcases and tall volumes, presumably lavish art catalogues. Elsewhere there were imposing modernist paintings, including a triptych of violet abstracts, distinguished only by the different style of brushstrokes in each of the panels. The vast black marble fireplace was flanked

by what looked like two granite minotaurs: simple, compel-
ling, no doubt priceless. Much of the white tiled floor was
covered by an exquisite rug, black again, with the faintest
Eau-de-Nil twill pattern. There were three white sofas, a
long footstool by one of the floor-to-ceiling windows, and
a couple of armchairs. At the centre of the room was an
outsized coffee table – again, apparently fashioned from
black marble – its surface bare apart from a vase full of
simple white tulips, and Harry did not doubt that there
was a huge television screen, sound system and workstation,
all of them concealed somewhere in the room but available
to Smythe at the press of a button. The overall effect was,
he had to admit, impressive. This was the home of a serious,
focused man.

Smythe rang a bell concealed under a console table. 'Now.
What can I offer you? Tea? Coffee? Something stronger?'

'Oh . . . thank you. Just a glass of water would be fine.'

A maid had appeared beside them like a shapeshifter.
'Matilde,' said Smythe. '*Un verre d'eau pour Monsieur Taylor.
Enfin . . . pour moi, peut-être un pot de thé à la menthe? Merci
beaucoup.*'

'So,' said Smythe, settling into one of the sofas, 'now you've
indulged me on my little tour, how can I help?'

'Mr Smythe— sorry, Julian,' Harry began. 'As I said, this
is very much an off-the-record chat. It's actually a request
for help, really. And I'm sorry not to have made a appoint-
ment sooner, but we're working on a very tight timetable.
My team, that is.'

'Not at all,' said Smythe, stretching out his legs as Matilde
brought in the drinks. 'What can I do to assist your inquiries?'

'My team – we operate out of New Scotland Yard. Specialist
unit that takes on particular kinds of cases.'

'Good heavens,' said Smythe, registering, it seemed, real

interest for the first time. He poured himself a mint tea and sipped with relish. 'How *thrilling*. Oh, I shouldn't say that, I know. But, as I said, I do have an appetite for drama. It's a terrible weakness. These are serious matters. But I find myself enthralled by the *spectacle* of it all! You probably think me frightfully lowbrow.'

Was Smythe playing games? Harry wondered. He hadn't had much of a heads-up before Harry had turned up, but a man with the network that John's research had sketched out for him earlier would know all about SO22, quite possibly the names of its most senior officers. Just as he had known who, exactly, to call in Washington to destroy the careers of his DEA adversaries. Harry decided to go along with what he assumed was Smythe's little charade.

'I can't tempt you to a glass of champagne? I have a bottle of Krug 2008 in the fridge that is just asking to be knocked back in agreeable company.'

'You're extremely kind,' said Harry. 'But, no, thank you. On duty and all that.'

'Of course. *Dommage.* Another time, perhaps? Anyway, I'm distracting us, I'm sure, from what you came here to discuss – whatever it is. I'm on the edge of my seat.'

Enough with the preamble. Harry decided to jump straight in. 'So, Vladimir Voldrev. I understand that the name is known to you. The man also, I think.'

Smythe was a cool customer, all right, but even he couldn't conceal his response entirely: Harry caught a slight twitch in his right cheek at the mention of Voldrev. But the true tell was his sudden immobilisation – a revealing change from the animated way in which he had previously spoken.

When he finally broke the silence, it was with a wintry expression. 'Vladimir Voldrev? Ah. Yes, well, I suppose I know a little bit about *that* bloke. Enough for me, that is.'

'Not a fan?' said Harry.

Smythe thought about this. 'Well, I wouldn't say a *fan* exactly, no.'

'Because the word around the campfire is that you really rather dislike him.'

'Indeed. The *campfire*. What an extraordinary place for my opinions of other people to be discussed.'

'Sorry,' said Harry. 'Just a figure of speech.'

'Oh, no, my dear fellow. Not at all. I see what you mean entirely. We all have our . . . sources – I suppose there's no other word.'

'The question is, are our sources right? About you and Voldrev, I mean? Your relationship – so to speak.'

Smythe stood up and replenished Harry's glass with the bottle of iced Badoit that Matilde had left on the table, and returned to his spot on the sofa.

'You know,' he said, 'one of the perks of wealth – oh, one's not supposed to mention it, I know, but it's such a gauche pretence, don't you think? One of the perks is that I don't have to *think* about people I don't much like. So, the honest truth is that I rarely devote a moment of my time to someone like . . . Voldrev.'

'Why, though?' asked Harry. 'I mean, why are you disinclined even to think about him?'

'Well, where to *start*?' Smythe removed a red polka-dot handkerchief from his breast pocket and blew his nose theatrically, as though expelling the very idea of Vladimir Voldrev from his system. 'I mean . . . the man is utterly *ghastly*. The sort of fella you'd set your groundsman on if he got into your estate. If that makes any sense?'

'Oh, yes,' said Harry, wondering how many friends Smythe actually had that didn't own estates. 'Completely.'

'I mean, he's just such an ill-bred sort of chap. The kind

that, if I can speak frankly, are ruining London nowadays. Russians of the very worst sort, coming to this great city and buying up property and anything else they can get their hands on. Sending their beastly children to the best schools. Awful.'

Harry permitted himself a smile. 'And buying art?'

Smythe smiled with a measure of relaxation. 'Touché. It's perfectly true that some of my clients are Russian. They buy art like they buy everything else: entirely as an investment and a status symbol, one supposes. Oh, please understand, I'm not naïve. I understand that all art collectors do that to some extent. But most of them have a measure of aesthetic understanding. The Russians in this town? They buy it because it's fucking expensive and they know it will appreciate, if they take good advice. They wouldn't know Rothko from Rembrandt, though. Philistines.'

'And yet you lived there, didn't you?'

'Well, *yes*. I mean my dear mother – bless her departed soul – was Russian herself. She met my father in Petersburg on his first tour there. A remarkable ballerina, swept off her plié by the dashing Roddy Smythe, rising star of the Foreign Office, and of pretty much everywhere else. At least in his youth. What a hullabaloo their romance caused! Well, you can imagine. A prominent British diplomat, seeing classified documents every single day, and a *Bolshoi dancer*. Unheard of! Both sides had to clear everything in triplicate before they could be wed. As my father told the story, *his* father was visited in the country – our family home in Sussex – by a menacing-looking Russian hood in a leather coat claiming to be lost. Well, I mean. Trust Grandpapa to invite him in for tea and sandwiches and a cosy chat! Anyway, after all the clod-hopping background checks and what have you, the marriage went ahead, and Roddy and Ludmilla were wed at

St Margaret's by Westminster Abbey. Reception at the In and
Out Club. *Le tout Londres* turned up to toast the happy
couple. Pa was stationed back at King Charles Street for a
bit while they decided what to do with him. But we were
back on the road soon enough.'

'Back to the USSR?' said Harry.

'Oh, dear me, no. Not immediately. Paris first. Then
Washington. I was at school for a fair amount of that time
– Eton, hated it – then Cambridge, of course. That was more
pleasurable. Then Papa was posted to Moscow, so I went to
see them from time to time. I suppose, looking back, it was
a pretty tense period; early eighties, Reagan and the Cold
War and so forth. But I remember it as a rather happy time
for the family, you know? I think their marriage was in good
shape and they lived in some splendour, as all top ambassa-
dors did in those days. Nowadays, it's a bit different. Cuts,
and what have you.'

'Did you come across Voldrev then? I mean, he'd have
been – what? – in his twenties. Climbing the KGB greasy
pole, I suppose.'

'And how! Never have you seen such a desperate *climber*.
He was put on my parents, day and night. We quickly came
to recognise him in his fucking GAZ-31013. I remember the
model, after all these years. The car of choice of the KGB
hood in those days, you know. Barely bothered to hide. Just
stayed with them, or near them, all the time. It wasn't surveillance, really. How could it be? There was no attempt to
conceal his presence. Just this ugly brute letting them know
that he was never going to leave them alone.'

'How did that go down?' said Harry.

'Well, you know, stiff upper lip and all – it was never
acknowledged. But Mama started taking pills round about
then, which did her no good at all. Oh, I'm not saying it was

*all* Voldrev's doing. There was plenty else to shred the poor old girl's nerves. Including a king-size identity crisis as a former Bolshoi star who had married into an aristocratic family in a fascist state. She was not always made to feel welcome in the old country, I think. Always kept her poise in public, of course. But, well, it all took its toll.'

'Were you close? You and your mum?'

'Oh, yes. Very. And it was she who introduced me to art. Wherever we were – the Louvre, the Prado, the Pushkin. Always helping to *see* art and to appreciate its beauty.'

'So, you were a young man when they were in Moscow. With all this Voldrev carry-on. Were you ever tempted to confront him?'

Smythe became very still once more. 'I did, but only on one occasion. It was considered *very* poor form at the embassy for civilians to interact with hoods – even if you were the ambassador's son. Even if he was defending his poor ma from the most thuggish . . . I'm sorry, but the memory of it is still rather intense.'

'I can imagine.'

'This was when the embassy was still at Sofiyskaya Embankment, number fourteen, you see – which is now the residency, of course. Beautiful nineteenth-century building. And one day – oh, I must have been twenty-three or twenty-four, something like that. I remember I was taking a spot of leave from the Courtauld to see them, and my mother, in particular, had cheered up a bit because I was able to spend the days with her while Pa was hard at work. Anyway, it was uncommonly sunny, I remember that, and we'd just dropped off Pa, and my mother said, "Julian, why don't we walk?" Which wasn't something you just did in those days, especially if you were a senior diplomat's wife. With her son. But our security chaps were in a good mood and said it should be fine, and why not, so we clambered out of the car and marched with her little dog – she had this appalling little Pekingese called Chekhov, to whom she was mysteriously devoted. But, really, who was I to begrudge her such simple pleasures?'

'Yes,' said Harry. 'I can see that.'

'So we walk to the gate of the embassy, bit of a school outing, but who cares? And then I suddenly realise that my mother has fallen a few paces behind and is standing quite still. And I was about to say something filial and facetious – you know, "Come on, slowcoach", or the like – when I saw what she had seen. Which was the same fucking car, and that fucking brute Voldrev behind the wheel. Just *staring* at us. I suppose I should have raised it with our security chaps first. But, well, you'll know that there are moments in every life when even the most well-brought-up and best-bred among us lose our cool. And I'm rather afraid I did.'

'How so?' said Harry.

Smythe was now time-travelling in his head, transported back to Moscow in the eighties; a son full of seething fury, trying to protect his mother from the horrors of the world. 'I strode out, without asking permission – again, a big no-no – and walked across the road, barely checking for traffic. I went over to Voldrev's car and I rapped my knuckles on his window. Plain as day.'

'What happened?'

'Nothing. Not at first, anyway. He carried on staring ahead, not even acknowledging my presence. Which was, of course, quite deliberate and calculated – correctly, I might add – to infuriate me even more.'

'Weren't your security detail with you by now?'

'Yes,' said Smythe. 'Oh, indeed. Either side of me, actually. And sweating bullets. But I was, I have to admit it, pretty much out of control. They were trying to calm me down, poor chaps – I liked them both, very much. Mike and Raymond, they were called. Salt-of-the-earth types. Last thing they needed was the boss's arty son going tonto on their watch. In retrospect, I felt very sorry for them – I made a point of apologising later, in fact. But in the heat of the moment . . . well, I was shrugging them off, and effing and blinding at Voldrev, threatening all manner of terrible things if he didn't open up.'

'Did he?'

'Quite the opposite. He picked up a *newspaper*, if you please. From the passenger seat. And started to read it. Right in front of me. That smug face, I can see it now. And so I scooped up a rock from the ground – bad luck all round that it was lying there – and I damn well smashed the window. Bang, wallop, crash. Angry-son moment turns into full-blown diplomatic incident.'

'Wait,' said Harry. 'Before we get on to the diplomatic incident, what did Voldrev do when you smashed the window?'

Smythe's face twisted as he remembered. 'That's the thing. He did *nothing*. Didn't even flinch. Brushed the shards of glass from his lap and his coat. But never once turned to look at me. And he waited until I was back across the other side of the road – pretty much manhandled there by poor Mike and Raymond – before he finally drove off.'

'What happened?'

'Oh, bedlam, as you can no doubt imagine. Ma was distraught, Pa was *furious* with me. The press was officially warned not to report the incident – and those were the days when the papers did as they were told by the embassy press attaché. If it happened today, I'd have been all over Twitter in an hour. Maybe less. But – after a real scorcher of a dressing-down from Pa in his office – the spooks warned him that, according to their informants, it would be wise if I left town straight away. Which I did, with full diplomatic protection. Straight out of Dodgeski, tail between my legs, so to speak.'

It was darker outside now, the sky overcast. Smythe tapped on a remote control and spotlights bathed them just sufficiently to prevent the room from becoming gloomy.

'No wonder you dislike him so much.'

'Hmm?' said Smythe, apparently still distracted by his memories.

'I mean, it's only human nature, isn't it? A man wants to protect his old mum. It's instinct as much as anything.'

'I told myself that for years, DCI Taylor. I did. But I also regret embarrassing my parents. And – for that matter – giving that *pig* exactly what he was after. Which was a reaction. A loss of control. The British Ambassador's wife with shattered nerves, the Ambassador distracted. His son packed off on the first flight back to London. No, I gave him *precisely* what he was after. And I'm sure his superiors were *delighted*.'

'I see what you mean.'

'And have we not seen the same pattern of behaviour in the intervening years? It is the great Russian talent. To destabilise. To disorientate the enemy. To make us turn on each other. It was a cruel lesson, of course. But it *was* a lesson. I never made that mistake again.'

'Meaning?'

'I never gave my adversaries what they so obviously wanted. Even if every fibre of my being was screaming at me to do so. I learned restraint that day – albeit the hard way.'

Harry stood and walked over to the closest window. A young mother was playing with her toddler outside, the pair laughing in delight at the other's company.

'And then? You and Voldrev?'

'Oh, well, then, we enter the realm of fantasy and fabrication, I'm afraid,' said Smythe.

'In what way?'

'Well, of course, as we both know, Voldrev has acquired a certain notoriety in other, shall we say, *fields of endeavour* in the intervening years. Not a huge surprise, I suppose. He's always been a gangster, it's just that world-historic circumstances forced him to move from the public sector to the private.'

'Tell me what you know about that,' said Harry. 'If you would.'

Smythe shrugged with distaste. 'Oh, I don't know that much, in all candour. Gossip from my Russian relatives, though there aren't many of them left. Mama had a brother, who's dead now, and there are a few cousins scattered around. In any case, when the Cold War ended and the Soviet Union collapsed, Voldrev did what all the top KGB people did – which was to join in the carve-up of his own motherland and grab whatever he could. A demeaning spectacle, if ever there was one: all those middle-aged men looting the very country they had sworn to protect.'

'But he wasn't middle-aged yet, was he? What did he end up getting?' asked Harry.

Smythe snorted with derision. 'Oh, this is priceless. There were so many goodies on offer, depending on your muscle and your status: steel, aluminium, fossil fuels, gold, and so on. Well, do you know what Vladimir was given by his peers? What his great prize was? *Tropical fruit*. Can you believe it? So demeaning. I'm afraid he is only *half* an oligarch, little Vlad.'

'Well, you say that,' said Harry. 'But he does all right for himself, doesn't he? I mean, I wouldn't be here if his activities were legitimate, but he's an extremely successful businessman, whose principal interest just happens to be the global sale of narcotics.'

Smythe threw his hands up. 'Well, so they say. But I am an ingénu when it comes to such matters. I barely got round to smoking a joint at Cambridge and I certainly haven't indulged since. That world is, in every sense of the word, foreign to me, and I intend to keep it that way. If you tell me that's what Voldrev gets up to now . . . well, I'll take your word for it. It would certainly be in keeping with his character. But I have no independent knowledge of these . . . *transactions.*' He spoke the last word as if it were toxic.

'Fair enough,' said Harry. 'I won't keep you much longer. You've been very generous with your time already, Julian. But let me return to the awkward matter of rumour and gossip.'

'Ah, yes!' said Smythe. 'The campfire!'

'The campfire, yes. It's been said by many informants to many law enforcement agencies that – not to put too fine a point on it – you and Mr Voldrev hate each other's guts. That you've been feuding all these years.'

'Feuding? Hardly. Remember, it's almost forty years since I laid eyes on the man. My ex-wife once saw him in Miami, I believe, at some charity fundraiser or other, and told me about it. She might have been mistaken, of course. She was on the dozy side.'

'When was that?'

'Gosh. Well, it must have been a good ten years ago, because we were divorced not long after. Terribly good friends still, she and I.'

'I see. Because, as you can imagine, we talk to all sorts in my line of work.'

'Part of the job. Why one's so grateful to you. Well, one of the many reasons.'

'And I have to say, a lot of informants over the years have said that there is real animosity between Voldrev and yourself.' He waited a beat. 'The sort of animosity with consequences that are not always pleasant.'

Smythe stayed true to his version of events. 'Oh, really, Chief Inspector! Such yarns people spin. Do I look like the sort of bloke who would be entangled with a man like Vladimir Voldrev? I mean, you're right – there *is* a history, after a fashion. But "history" is the word. Would I invite him round for a cosy dinner here? No, I most certainly would not. Obviously. But I think what you describe is a rather extravagant version of Chinese whispers. Or Russian rumours, if you prefer. The detail of the story that most people miss is that – naturally – it got out soon enough that Roddy Smythe's son had had a confrontation with a KGB hood, and then, in later years, when we both became reasonably prominent in our respective professions – well, people *do* tend to join dots that aren't there. They love to see patterns and connections and feuds where none exist. Don't you agree?'

'Well, rumour is certainly a problem for police officers,' said Harry. 'You can't rely on it, you're quite right. The trouble is . . . you can't ignore it either.'

This was evidently not the answer Smythe had been hoping for or expecting. 'Oh, but you *should*, Chief Inspector. Honestly. So often, "rumour" is a euphemism for lies put about to spread trouble, or set people against one another, or nudge them off the scent. I'm sure that the unlovely fellows you encounter in the drug trade find it very amusing that Voldrev once squared off against a Mayfair art dealer in Moscow. And that bit is perfectly true. But the rest is nonsense.'

'The rest? What do you mean by that, exactly?'

'Well, you tell me! I really have no idea what people say about me and I've learned not to let it bother me.'

'But you do know those rumours exist? I mean, you've heard about them.'

'In the vaguest sense, of course. But, like an actor who is wise enough never to read his reviews, I discourage those who want to pour poison into my ears. About Vladimir Voldrev, or anyone else.'

Harry wondered if he should test Smythe with one of the stories that John had sent him in a second file, which collated the relevant intelligence graded according to the likelihood that the informant was telling the truth.

'Well,' he said. 'Let me trespass upon that rule briefly, just to see if I can jog your memory.'

To Harry's surprise, Smythe reacted as if he had proposed a parlour game. 'Oh, how delicious, Harry! Do, *please!*'

'Let me emphasise that no UK law enforcement agency regards any of this as actionable intelligence.'

'I follow you,' said Smythe.

'So,' Harry continued. 'This is just a pretty speculative allegation, remember – part of a complex case, from a few years back. A puzzle, actually. In 2014, the CIA established that there was a Cessna pilot – Guatemalan, I believe – who was running drugs between Belize and New Orleans. But he had to refuel at Galveston, which was the point of maximum vulnerability. So there was a raid planned to intercept him and the cocaine. DEA-led, but with Interpol involved and a couple of seconded officers from the Yard who had knowledge of the case. Multi-jurisdictional, because the idea was to flip the pilot and unravel the whole network.'

'I'm all agog,' said Smythe, a little too flippantly for Harry's liking.

'Thing is, the team is waiting on the ground at Galveston

– a private airstrip they'd basically commandeered for the day. Snipers in position. Expecting a maximum of three – the pilot plus two. But the expected landing time comes and goes, and nothing happens.'

'No plane?'

'No Cessna. No pilot. No drugs. So they are left with their dicks swinging in the wind. Pardon my language.'

'Not at all,' said Smythe, still smiling. 'It paints a vivid picture.'

'Anyhow, they waited for fresh instructions and finally, a few hours later, they get a call from the Coast Guard to say that a grounded plane has been spotted on Cat Island. You know, in the Gulf of Mexico?'

'I didn't,' said Smythe. 'But thank you.'

'So they arrange air transport and get there. By which time, it's almost dark. But it's their boy, all right. The Cessna is beached. Its hold has been emptied, though there are traces of very pure cocaine.'

'And the pilot? Skedaddled, one assumes?'

'No,' said Harry, in a level voice. 'He is still sitting in the cockpit. Unfortunately for him, his head has been cut off and it's lying in his lap.'

Smythe exhaled. 'My God.'

'Same goes for passenger number one. Head nestling between his feet. One can only assume that passenger number three was an imposter or a traitor, forced them to land and arranged the transfer of the dope – probably to a waiting dinghy. That was the working hypothesis, anyway.'

'Plausible,' agreed Smythe. 'A horrific episode. I fear I would not have the stomach for your line of work, Harry. I really wouldn't.'

'Few people do, Julian.'

'But – forgive me – what does any of this have to do with me?'

'About three weeks later, a mid-level *sicario* was crossing into the States illegally and got busted. He turned state's pretty fast, apparently. They had him for murder one, and a lot more. Coughed up a fair amount of useful information. Among which was the claim that the Cessna flights had been operating without a hitch under the protection of none other than Vladimir Voldrev.'

'Good heavens,' said Smythe. 'He gets everywhere, that man.'

'Indeed. But what the DEA's new informant also revealed was that Voldrev was furious about the heist . . .'

'Which I imagine was no surprise to anyone.'

'Not his fury, no. He's known for his temper, and this was a real blow to his network in the Americas. But what was interesting was that this petrified *sicario*-ex-*sicario*, I suppose I should say – also revealed that Voldrev was sure he knew who was behind it all. His associates told him it was bound to be one of the cartels but Voldrev wouldn't hear of it.'

Smythe's expression did not change. 'So who did little Vlad blame?'

'You.'

'Me?' Smythe permitted himself a true belly laugh. 'Well, that is really – I suppose if a man lives long enough he gets to hear everything! And now I rather feel that I have. But I must say the idea of, well, *me*, involved in such intrigue and murderous conduct? Come on, Chief Inspector. Harry. *Look at me.* Do I strike you as the sort of fellow who arranges for decapitations? I arrange for the transfer of collages by Matisse from Luxembourg to Beijing. Which is more than enough stress for me, I don't mind admitting. Beaches and cocaine and headless corpses . . .? That is well outside my remit, to say the least. Sorry to disappoint the DEA and the cartels and whoever else, but they have a very deluded idea of what kind of man I am. I suppose it would be hilarious if it were not so awful.'

'Yes, I suppose so,' said Harry. 'And, of course, the pay-off was that Voldrev had sworn terrible vengeance. But, as I say, it was a fair few years ago and, well, clearly nothing came of it. I imagine that the Mexican informant now lives in a federal protection programme somewhere in Montana or wherever they put those poor sods. Terrified for his life. Nasty business.'

'Indeed it is. How incredible! One leads a quite boring life, all things considered. And – unbeknownst to oneself – people are saying the most *outlandish* things about me. Can't be helped, I suppose. But it really is the most outrageous tosh.'

As inscrutable as Smythe was, Harry knew full well that he was lying. And – he suspected – the man knew that he knew. Smooth as silk, was Julian. Fastidious in every respect. No wonder he had proved so slippery over the years. The refined English gentleman, the very opposite of the brash gangster that Voldrev had become. A drug lord, with a very impressive front operation as a merchant of the finest art; while the only art Voldrev appreciated was probably on his body. Yes, it made sense. A bit of history, a world of difference, finding themselves competitors in the same dark business. No wonder they loathed each other.

'Well, that's very helpful. Thank you. I'll try not to bother you again.'

'Oh, please do, any time!' said Smythe. 'It's been a genuine pleasure. I'm only sorry I wasn't able to regale you with tales of little Vlad's wickedness. The truth is I lead a very different sort of life to his.'

*Not that different*, thought Harry. He stood to shake Julian Smythe by the hand. 'Thank you again. I'll see myself out.'

He was by the Basquiat in the hallway when he heard Smythe's voice behind him. 'Oh, and do have a safe flight!'

It was only when he was on the pavement and looking for his car keys that Harry remembered: he hadn't mentioned he was going anywhere.

# 16

The plane banked. Iris Davies awoke, more abruptly than usual, and looked out of the window. The sun was ahead of them, a misty tangerine dream that they seemed to be chasing through the sky; through clouds of memories – and nightmares about possible futures.

Voldrev versus Smythe: the two alpha males squaring up to each other once again, but this time for stakes that were inconceivably high. That was how Harry had explained it to them at the Yard after his meeting in Eaton Square.

They had sat round the meeting table in the fifth-floor ops room that had been assigned to them. There were barely enough desks to go round – not that this job looked like it would involve too much desk work; the way Harry told it, they would be in the field until they hunted down their prey. The only snag, as she pointed out more than once, was that they weren't even sure *who* their prey was.

Carol Walker sat beside her, taking copious notes but also doodling. Taking a closer look, Iris saw that the doodles weren't doodles at all, but complex equations. What was their new resident genius trying to work out? She dreaded to think. And she didn't want to ask. That would be unprofessional. Harry was all about focus. And she had never seen him so focused as he was today. Not before the Crick op, not before Calais, not during the Singapore sting.

He was holding it together, holding them together. But she

could tell that it was more of a strain than usual, that the stakes were potentially so high and the picture still too blurry for Harry's liking.

Voldrev. Smythe. Two big swinging dicks of the drug world. Two beasts of the narcotic jungle who – across decades, with many corpses strewn along the way – hated each other's guts. If Voldrev had the uranium, what was he planning? How much did Smythe know? And how would he act upon that knowledge? Tricky fuck.

And who else might be involved in the mix? Xavier Ramirez – the new boy that Harry had also started dropping into conversation? ISIS or whatever form it was now taking? The rising nationalist militias? Nothing could be ruled out.

Harry warned them to assume that all their comms were now compromised by one or other of the drug lords; and by anyone else interested in their operation, for that matter. 'Which almost certainly means people on our side,' he said. 'We're not the only UK agency chasing this one, not by a long chalk. Robinson told me as much when I briefed him on Smythe.'

'So why SO22?' John asked. 'I mean, if Six and NCA and God knows who else are in on the game, we're a bit surplus, aren't we?'

Harry frowned. 'No. No, John. That's the *point*. This is where we come in, where they're relying on us. To be nimble, and fast, and do what needs to be done.'

'And be the fall guy if it goes south, right?' said Iris.

'Definitely,' Harry said. 'If we fuck up in any way, they'll pin us to the wall. That's another one of our unofficial roles in the whole rotten mix. The big lumbering mammoths do what they do, chase their own tails and each other's, and then we get pulled up before the official inquiry if it goes wrong. That's the job.' He paused. 'If any of you aren't up to it, sling your hook now. I'll approve any transfer requests with pleasure.'

Iris settled back in the plush seat – Harry had somehow wangled them upgrades to business class, leaning on his military credentials more than his authority as a copper – and finished off her gin and tonic. She flicked through the in-flight entertainment magazine, and wondered if she could face two hours of Liam Neeson in bandit country, or Scarlett Johansson in yet another superhero saga, or a documentary about the Arctic—

Who was she kidding? She couldn't think of anything but the case. Voldrev. Smythe. Pulling the strings, somehow. But why, and how? Was their hatred for each other really so strong?

She chided herself for even asking the question. If the job had taught her one thing, it was that the hatred that can arise between people was one of the most powerful forces on Earth. Maybe the strongest. It made them do stupid, disproportionate, horribly violent things. It made them let go of whatever rationality they might have left and any sense of collateral damage.

Reflexively, she reached to her right side where, a few years back, a bullet had passed straight through. Not long after her full accreditation as a sniper, in fact. Out all night on a job in Brixton, a nest carefully prepared in an empty flat on the fifth floor of a run-down council housing block. Night-vision goggles, a spotter beside her, command keeping her updated in her earpiece. She cradled the modified Heckler & Koch G3, a weapon she had learned to love during her training. It felt snug and reassuringly weighty, a deadly tool she now knew she could use with extreme precision.

On the grass down below, a cluster of hooded youths puffing on reefers, laughing at each other's banter. 'Not our target,' the word came through. 'Stand by.' That very after-noon, a CHIS had tipped off his contact officer that a local gang leader was going to be 'sliced and diced' by a young pretender to the throne. Ras Ronnie, who dressed like a character from his favourite seventies movie, *The Harder They Come*, had been top of the heap for ten years. But now age was catching up with him, with youth knocking angrily on his door in the form of a kid they called Pablo who had run corners for Ronnie before their falling out. Now, the CHIS said, Pablo was ready to make his move and was going to 'end' his former boss, who was expecting nothing more than truce talks – out in the open, so everyone would feel safe.

The meet between the two gangs was set for 9 p.m. She checked her watch: 8.57. She mopped her brow and got into position. The rules of engagement were clear: she was not to fire *under any circumstances* until given an explicit green by the op commander. Police use of firearms, especially in this area, was, historically, an issue of huge political and social sensitivity. A sniper's bullet that went astray could cause a riot, Iris knew – and she understood why that was so, too. This part of London was a pressure cooker and had been for decades. Misused, even without malice, the rifle in her hands could plunge the whole neighbourhood into darkness, illuminated only by flames.

She checked again: 9.01 p.m. No sign of Ronnie or Pablo, or anyone for that matter; the small, patchy green was deserted now, the kids having moved on in search of entertainment elsewhere. It was dark and unusually balmy for an October evening, but autumnal all right; there was a gathering wind that she would have to take into account. The distance from the nest to the alleged meeting site was not that great: eighty metres at most. But she might, she knew, be dealing with moving targets and a degree of confusion that called for the tightest of preparation and the coolest of nerves.

At 9.15 p.m., the ops commander urged all stations to 'Stand by – awaiting update from CHIS.' No such update was forthcoming for a further forty-give minutes, during which time Iris began to cramp in her left leg and realised she had forgotten to hydrate properly in the previous hour. She was angry with the spotter for failing to remind her – he handed her the water bottle and held it a little timorously as she sucked on the straw – but, really, it was her fault, and her fault alone.

At 10 p.m., they were told to stand down. The human intelligence had 'changed significantly'. *Code for 'it was bollocks in the first place'*, Iris thought irritably. She packed up her rifle, and, with the spotter's help, dismantled the nest, awaiting clearance to exit the premises through a back door where a vehicle was already waiting for them. Another wasted evening. But that, as her instructors had told her on and off the range, was at least 80 per cent of the job. Lying God knows where, for God knows how long; breathing meticulously with the technique she had been taught; handling the cortisol released by stress into her bloodstream. Waiting, and waiting, and waiting – so often, for nothing.

They were halfway down the stairs, using torches as the internal lighting seemed barely to work, when the voice in her earpiece suddenly returned – and this time, with much less confidence. 'At least one group seen headed towards op zone. All units to stand by . . .' Then, she could hear no more of the panicked instructions as they were drowned out by the sound of shots from – where? The bottom of the stairwell? Outside?

No time to unpack the rifle. But she had her 9 mm sidearm and pulled it from its holster. She told the spotter, who had fallen instinctively into the crouch position, to take the kit and find cover immediately.

Iris took the stairs three at a time, trying to reach the ops room on her radio. She asked for revised instructions, as a matter of urgency but received no response. In desperation, she tried her squad commander on her mobile, but his number went straight to answerphone. Not good. Not good at all.

The entrance hall of the building was empty. She called again for backup and, looking out of the chicken-wired windows, saw that a full-blown firefight was now underway in the open ground outside. At two o'clock to her position, three men were leaning against pillars and firing on a similar number – maybe four? – on the other side of the grass. At least one of them had an Uzi, to judge by the distinctive rat-a-tat punctuating the run of single shots. Jesus Christ: this was like a bad night in Gaza, not South London.

Had anyone been hit? She pulled down the night goggles, but her line of sight wasn't clear.

She tried again: 'Command, this is Alpha-Two. Requesting backup and instructions. It's a fucking shitstorm. I can't see any of ours out there!'

Finally, an answer in her earpiece: 'Stand by, Alpha-Two. Armed-response unit in place in one minute.'

'They should be here *now*!'

'Stand by, Alpha-Two. This is *not* your show.'

Well, what kind of 'show' was it? And why were the fire-arms officers sixty seconds away rather than on the scene already? As she raised her pistol, she saw a body fall to the ground about thirty metres from where she stood. It danced in a grotesque series of convulsions as it was struck by further bullets. From somewhere close by, someone bellowed: 'That's a kill! Nice! You gonna burn in hell, boy!' Then: 'Coming for the rest, fuckers!' And another burst of Uzi fire.

No way could she stay where she was.

Remaining in shadow, she saw that there was good cover immediately outside the door – what looked like a brick bunker for storage. As stealthily as she could, she eased the door open and darted out, quickly taking up position behind the strongbox. Where the fuck were armed response?

She heard footfall. At last! Backup had arrived and were readying themselves to overwhelm the scene and impose their authority upon the square. By the sound of the manic gunfire she had been hearing, it would not take them long to force out the combatants and subdue them. This was what gangsters never understood. A trained police officer with thousands of hours on the range and hundreds in the field could always read a location better, use a firearm better and defeat an amateur idiot who thought that buying a hot piece and then carrying it around in his Beemer made him a drug baron. They were all the same . . .

Then, she realised that what she had heard was not the footsteps of the blue cavalry but a single person. Slowly, she rolled over to give herself a limited view of the square. Ten feet away, stood a young man – no more than twenty – clutching the sub-machine to his chest. He was muttering to himself incoherently, furiously, dangerously out of control. But she could tell that he had eyes on a target and was already raising his sights.

'Armed police! Put down your weapon!'

The Uzi man turned on his heel to face her. He could stay alive by putting the gun down. Instead, he pointed it at her.

Iris fired off three rounds to his head, which exploded in an instant spray of bone, brain tissue and a mist of blood. He slumped to his knees, as if in prayer.

Suddenly, the square was floodlit, full of officers, and a number of vehicles screeching to a halt.

'Armed police!' a voice from a megaphone shouted. 'You are surrounded. Put down your weapons and take one step forward, hands in the air.'

There was a moment's silence.

'You will not be harmed if you follow these instructions. Put down your weapons and step out with your hands in the air! Now!'

Slowly, one by one, the surviving members of the two gangs emerged. She could hear the ring of metal hitting concrete as they stepped out, suddenly sheepish, their hands firmly in the air. Again, she couldn't believe how young most of them were, how quickly they had embraced a life that could so easily end with one foolish decision.

Directly in front of her, an SCO19 sergeant stepped up and peered over the brick.

She hissed: 'Sergeant Iris Davies! Alpha-Two on op. My spotter is still in the building.'

'Christ, the sniper,' said the new arrival. 'We thought you'd gone dark.'

'Only since I've been out here. Where have you lot been?'

'Command took—'

It was instinct that made her aim and shoot at the gang member who had suddenly loomed up behind her colleague. This time, it was less exact and the tough guy with the Glock managed to get one away before she could put him down. Again, she had fired three times. Which meant she still had a fair few left in the clip.

'Jesus fuck!' yelled the sergeant. 'Where did he come from?'

'The lodge over there.' She pointed behind him at an estates office that she had been assured was empty just before the firing started as officers ran over to where the two of them were standing.

'Christ,' Iris said. 'That was too close. Were you hit?'

'Negative,' he said. 'The shot must have been way off. Thank—'

He broke off as Iris collapsed to the floor. Running round to where she lay, he called for one of the ambulances that would already be on their way to head to his precise location.

She reached down and felt below her body armour. Yes, she had been hit. Not badly, not fatally – or at least, probably not. But there was blood and plenty of it, which meant that she would bleed out and die if she stayed where she was.

'Fuck, Davies,' said the sergeant, reaching into his pockets for a gauze pad to apply pressure to the wound and limit the bleeding. 'That was the worst fucking luck. The worst. And you saved my fucking life. Christ, thank you.' He pressed harder. 'You'll be OK, though. Definitely. Paramedics are thirty seconds away. Stitch you up in no time. I'm Brian, by the way.'

'Brian,' said Iris. 'I've been shot.'

'Yeah,' he said. 'But you'll be fine.'

'Fucking shot,' she repeated. 'What are the chances?'

'Pretty high tonight, it seems. So much for the big peace talks, eh?'

'Yeah.' Her voice was getting hoarse. 'Not much of a summit, was it?'

Behind them rose the comforting sound of men being read their rights, more police vans arriving and, at last, a paramedic with a body camera – which meant she was a specialist.

'I'm Emma,' she said. 'Sergeant Davies. Iris. Right?' She took over from Brian without asking, applying what Iris could tell was more expertly targeted pressure. 'Just let me take a look. Are you in pain?'

'Well, now that you mention it, yeah, I could handle an aspirin.'

'I'll give you a shot now to help you out' – which she did

– 'and then we'll patch you up and get you fast-tracked at A and E.'

Iris started to feel herself drifting in and out of consciousness. She felt Emma slap her cheek, lightly but with intent. 'Wake up, Iris! Stay with us. Don't want you passing out right now. Sorry to be a bitch.'

And somehow, suddenly, there were at least two more paramedics in hi-vis vests over body armour, helping her out and getting ready for a stretcher. Emma spoke into her radio: 'Yes, this is Four. Female PO, thirties, single bullet wound. Vitals OK, for now. Think entry was clean but significant bleeding and imminent risk of shock. Yes, heading for King's and full exploratory laparotomy. Out.'

She leant down to Iris again. 'OK, Iris. We're going to move you now. Get you to hospital so we can check you out. How's your pain? One to ten?'

'Can't count,' she murmured. 'Hurts too much.'

'Good enough for now. Steve, we're moving.'

And then Iris did pass out.

She was in hospital for five days. Observation, they said. But her doctor admitted quickly enough that they were erring on the side of caution, just in case the wound showed signs of infection or poor healing. She had been fortunate, as Emma had said. No bullet fragments and no organs pierced. A flesh wound, in and out. Pretty lucky, all things considered.

The pain came in waves but was bearable. She had indeed lost a lot of blood and her body was traumatised by what it had been through: she didn't need to be told that it would be a while before she was back on active duty. But she did what the physios told her to, taking regular walks around the ward, first with a Zimmer frame, then a cane and, only four days after her admission, without anything to prop her up.

The shoot-out was all over the news, of course, as was the

story of Ras Ronnie (already charged and on remand) and Pablo (killed in the firefight, apparently, by a stray bullet from his own side). Operation Montezuma was hailed as a triumph for the Met, for community policing and for the war on gangs. Her own fate made headlines, too, which she hated, and the hospital had to devote most of its limited PR resources to enquiries from the press about Sergeant Iris Davies and her condition. In the end, the local nick despatched a uniformed constable to stand guard in the ward, just in case anyone tried to sneak in. What a bloody waste of manpower, she had thought.

She also thought that there was something askew about the glamour and excitement that was being attached to what had happened. All the talk of her 'courage' and 'gallantry' in the line of duty, when, in her own mind, it had all just been an unholy fuck-up and she had simply been on the right side of fortune; this time, anyway. Sergeant Brian Duff looked in to thank her properly and brought flowers and a 'Get Well Soon' card from his squad, which did cheer her up.

What the papers weren't reporting, he told her, was the not inconsiderable stink behind the scenes. Gold command had fucked up royally, that much was clear as day. Falling silent too often, failing to respond to requests in good time, and – worst of all – calling off the op altogether much too early when the original intelligence was judged to be suspect. Commander Bryn Sutton had been quietly moved sideways to a desk job, pending an accelerated retirement. And heads higher up the pecking order might have rolled, too, had the story of a lone officer's bravery not crowded out all the bad stuff and left little appetite in the Met, the Home Office or the media for a serious inquisition.

As Harry had told her since: Nothing disinfects a messy scene like a copper's bravery. Same in the army, he said.

People went weak at the knees for individual acts of courage, and once they were preoccupied by that, they tended to lose interest in the less exciting errors and planning failures that might otherwise have attracted their attention. He was pleased to hear about the commendation Iris had been given a few months after she was discharged from hospital: 'Quite right too,' Harry had said.

But he'd mentioned how it also reminded him of an operation he had been involved in – he would not say where, but it sounded like Libya – where one of his closest mates, Tosh, had been gunned down while saving a kid from terrorist fire and had received the Victoria Cross posthumously. It had been a comfort to his widow, his family and his comrades, but, much less to Harry's liking, it had also helped the MoD close the case considerably sooner than he and many others in the regiment thought was right and proper. Tosh, in Harry's opinion, had been killed by shoddy intelligence as much as enemy bullets. He had died in Harry's arms. And even as he did, Harry had raged inside at the poor information upon which the op had been based – which he and his men had used as they trained meticulously for weeks. When they got to where they were heading, things were not at all as they had been led to expect. The building schematics were different. The hostiles were not where they were supposed to be. Harry would say no more than that. But the story – as fragmentary as it was – was a lesson to Iris about how easy it was to become a pawn in somebody else's shitty chess game; how many arse-coverers there were in their line of work.

She felt a twinge in her side as she remembered and adjusted her position in the airplane seat. Psychosomatic, probably. The wound had healed very well and she had been back on duty in less than four months. Recruited by SO22 six months after that. And now she and the rest of the team were heading to the Caribbean on what? The mission of a lifetime, or the ultimate fool's errand?

She caught the flight attendant's eye and he bustled over (so much more quickly than in economy, she had already noticed).

'Another gin and tonic please,' she said. 'Make it a large one this time.'

Her reverie as she sipped on the drink was interrupted by an announcement from the captain. 'Hello, folks, hope you're having a restful flight. We're about two thousand miles into our journey and making good time for arrival as scheduled at Grantley Adams International. Local time is six fifteen in the morning. For now, just sit back and relax.'

*Some chance*, thought Iris.

Across the aisle, she heard what sounded like an elderly sheepdog gurgling its last. It was Harry Taylor snoring.

# 17

The Bridgetown joint to which Tennyson had sent him was, to say the least, a dump. The neon Coca-Cola sign hanging from the awnings flashed occasionally, but otherwise, the Bar Midnite lived up to its name. It was gloomy, stuffy and distinctly unwelcoming. There were five or six tables inside, each with a couple of unlit candles, ashtrays and men busy with their papers and dominoes. Harry sat on the right-hand side, below the slowly turning ceiling fan, and took a slug from his Banks lager. Christ, it was hot.

Deputy Commissioner Lance Tennyson was an old mate of Robinson's – a guy you could trust, according to the guv'nor. They had worked together many years before on a murder case involving a British banker who had washed up just by the Sandy Lane Hotel and ruined a fair few Christmases of the guests staying there for the festive season. Turned out that the victim had taken a dip from one of his client's offshore accounts in the Caymans, been found out and made a run for it to Barbados. Having no tradecraft to speak of, the banker had been discovered quickly enough, and the aggrieved client – a Belgian steel tycoon with plenty of side interests – had despatched a couple of acquaintances to settle up his account.

When Tennyson's team found the body, it was clear that he had been held captive, tortured and then beaten to death before being dumped in the ocean. Tennyson and Robinson, who flew in the day of the body's discovery, had worked together well and pieced together the story quickly enough. But evidence that would stand up in court? They had next to nothing. As Robinson said, all he got from his only trip to Barbados was sunburn and a friendship with Lance.

Harry could see straightaway why the two men had bonded. Leaving the team at the hotel to wash up and brief themselves, he had taken a taxi to police headquarters in Roebuck Street and spent half an hour with Tennyson in his office. He was not a tall man – five-seven, maybe five-eight? – but, dapper in his uniform of light blue shirt and crisply ironed navy trousers, he had real presence and a winning smile. Trusting Robinson's judgement, Harry had been fairly candid about the purpose of his visit.

'Voldrev?' said Tennyson. 'Don't see him on the main island hardly at all.'

'Really?'

'No.' He offered Harry a Gitane, which he declined. 'There was a time when a guy like him would have made a point of being seen in the swankiest hotels and restaurants. Moored their yachts or their powerboats where they couldn't be missed. Made a bit of a *bella figura*, if you like. But they keep a lower profile now. And not just because of Ukraine, either. They lived it up in public for twenty-five years, but they know that everything has its limits.'

'You say "they", Deputy Commissioner—'

'Please, call me Lance. Any friend of Bill's is a friend of mine.'

'Much obliged, Lance. You say "they" – who do you mean?'

Tennyson sat back in his black swivel chair below a map of the island and its police districts. 'Not just the Russian oligarchs. I mean, all the people that got rich quick in the nineties and then treated the Caribbean as a playground to visit whenever they pleased. Of course' – he took a drag on his smoke – 'it brought lots of money here, and that's always good for jobs and so forth. But it also brings rivalry, tension, trouble. Every rich man had at least twenty working for him who could end up getting up to no good. Do you see what I mean?'

Harry nodded. 'I do indeed. Are Voldrev's crew like that?'

'Not really. He keeps himself to himself. Strikingly so, actually. I think I've seen him in the flesh maybe twice in the past five years. His people are not the usual thugs. He has more lawyers than bodyguards, I sometimes think. Anyway, we keep an eye on his little fortress. He never complains about our patrol boats and always waves to our officers. I honestly don't have anything concrete on him. Of course, I know what you know about his background and his activities, but, on my turf, I've never had cause to give him so much as a speeding ticket.'

'I gather Bill clued you in on why we are interested in him at this particular moment.'

'He did. I can see why you're in a hurry.'

'Exactly. Question is, could Voldrev be our man? I mean, is he a fit?'

Tennyson stood up, deep in thought. 'Honestly? I don't know, Harry. I mean, for the people I serve, and my officers, I bloody hope not. I want Vladimir Voldrev to be like . . . what? Like an ordinary retired tycoon, I guess. Sitting on his laurels in his ridiculous palace, living out his remaining years without getting up to any mischief at all.' He sat down again. 'At the same time, I know what men like him are capable of. That's what this job teaches you. You keep thinking you've reached the limit of human greed and depravity and violence – and then you get a tap on the shoulder from reality. Sometimes more like a slap in the face. It's the worst bit of it all, really.'

'Yeah,' said Harry. 'I know exactly what you mean.'

Tennyson went on to say there was someone he should talk to before doing anything else involving Voldrev. An informant of many years called Pépé, a go-between and middle-level criminal who knew everything and everyone and would certainly be serving thirty years in Dodds Prison were it not for his continued usefulness to the Deputy Commissioner. He could be trusted to the extent that he would know not to do anything that might anger his handler. But, Lance warned, Harry should not be precise about his suspicions regarding Voldrev.

'Also, Harry. Regarding your security while your team is on the island. I've already assigned a couple of beat officers to make sure you're safe. I know you've informed the British High Commission of your presence, though I'd respectfully suggest you avoid getting too entangled with them – you'll spend all day filling out forms. Same applies to your own protection. I could issue you and your officers with firearms under licence, but I'm afraid it would take at least a week to clear the paperwork. The Commissioner is punctilious about such matters and so, as you might expect, are the courts. I wish I could be of more help.'

'Not at all. You've been extremely helpful.'

'On that matter, Harry, given what you might be chasing, perhaps it would be wise to be – how can I put this? – creative.'

Harry nodded. 'Read you loud and clear.'

A few hours later, he was in the Bar Midnite, checking his burner phone for any updates on Pépé. Nothing. Bloody hell. He was sweating heavily in his Fred Perry shirt, irritated that he might be wasting his time. He signalled to the barman to bring him another beer. At least he could refresh himself.

Then, without warning, he had company. The man sitting

opposite him – where had he come from? – was bald, wore Ray-Ban aviators and a white Diadora T-shirt. He grinned, revealing a single diamond-studded tooth among the dazzlingly bleached incisors. A Corona with a slice of lime appeared, unrequested but clearly welcome, at his side. He looked like a man that bullets would slide off.

'Harry? Pépé.'

'Yes. DCI Harry Taylor. I'm a police officer from London. I'm told—'

'We have a mutual friend. A good friend. His friends are my friends. So we can chat a little, maybe? You can tell me all about it.'

'Well, let's not go straight for the heavy petting before we've even shaken hands.'

Pépé laughed. 'That's fair! OK. Let's have a beer like a couple of regular guys on a hot day and see if I can maybe help you out a little bit.'

'That's more like it. How much do you know about why I'm here? I mean, why I've flown nine bloody hours to talk to the likes of you.'

'Not so much. My man told me you want information on one of the big players. He was not specific.'

Harry drained his first Banks and moved on to the second. 'Vladimir Voldrev.'

A pause. 'Uh-huh.'

Pépé had a decent poker face, Harry reckoned. It was hard to tell if he was scared, surprised or simply waiting for more information.

'I assume you've heard of him. I also assume you know how he built up his fortune – not from fucking fruit, I mean. And that you also know he is very good indeed at avoiding hard-working police officers like me, and like our mutual friend.'

'Voldrev?' Pépé whistled. Looked over his shoulder reflexively. 'That's some big fish you're after. But it's not just that. Sure, he lives like a king on his island. But he behaves like the perfect gentleman when he's here. Which is not often. *Very* polite. *Very* correct. So they say, anyway. You'll never catch him out.'

'Nobody has – so far, that is.'

'And why do you think that is, Harry? He's like a ghost, I tell you. Sometimes I wonder if he really exists. Like an apparition, you know? A spirit conjured out of thin air.'

'But he's not a ghost, is he? Unless you're saying that he lives in a fucking haunted house.' Harry felt the frustration starting to get the better of him: a bad cocktail when mixed with the jet lag. 'Look. Let me be honest with you. You're Tennyson's friend, not mine. I need some answers and some details.'

Pépé shrugged. 'I hear you. But details is exactly what nobody has on your man Vlad.'

'Well, think harder. Because details are what I'm after.'

For the first time, Pépé's face registered a measure of alarm. He clearly realised that Harry was perfectly capable of calling Tennyson and telling him how obstructive he had been – which would be very bad news. Tennyson was not a man to embarrass.

'The island. I've never been there, but got close in a boat one night. Guards everywhere. It's something else, man. Fit for a king. For years, everyone assumed he must be hiding his product there, that he must be using it for storage and before despatching the goods around the world, but nobody has ever seen anything come or go. Regular shipments of food and fuel, of course. But they all get checked by the water cops. Nothing suspicious. So far anyway. Unless he's paid them off. He's always ahead of the game, somehow.'

'How does Voldrev live? In style? Does he have parties?'

'They say he used to enjoy life to the full. A proper Studio 54! Maybe that's a myth, I don't know. Anyhow, now it's just him and his entourage. You hear about women going back and forth occasionally, but I don't know about that. You don't even know when he's here. Like I say, he's a ghost.'

'What other stories do people tell?'

Pépé batted the question away. 'Conjecture. Speculation. Tongues loosened by weed, spouting fairy tales.'

'Indulge me.'

'They say Vladimir is racked with tragedy. A woman that he loved and lost – not to another man, but to death.'

'When?'

'Oh, a while – ten years, twenty.'

'Who was she? How did she die?'

'Nobody knows much. They say she was Russian, like him. A civilian. A great beauty. She was ignorant of the darker details of his life, but brought him great joy. And then she got caught in the crossfire of one of his feuds and was killed in an attack on his yacht. Voldrev was unhurt, but she died instantly. They say that the man behind the hit is his deadliest enemy – a master criminal you never see, who pulls the strings – and that the Russian swore on all the saints that he would take revenge and destroy this man and everything he held dear.'

'Do you know the other man's name? Think.'

'No.'

'Was it Julian Smythe?'

'If I knew, I would tell you.'

Harry clenched his fist.

'*Was it Julian Smythe?*'

'Why would I hold back a name, Harry? I don't know. I don't even know if the story is true.'

Silence fell across the table as Harry absorbed what he had just been told. The informant was sweating now, too.

'Did you ever meet him?'

Pépé shook his head. 'Voldrev? You don't *meet* him; he *summons* you. And most people don't want to be summoned by a man like him.'

'Why not, if he's officially such a fucking law-abiding citizen? So clean-living?'

'You know what the fishermen call him? Obeah Man. That's like a bad spirit or a demon. Halfway between the worlds. Brings bad luck. Somebody not to mess with.'

Harry scoffed. 'Oh fuck off, that's just superstition. He's a villain keeping his head down. Let's not get stupid, for Christ's sake.'

'I'm not saying I believe in all that old-time religion shit, I'm just passing on the fact – the fact that he *scares* people just by his presence. They fear him without knowing him. If that's not power, what is?'

'I think it's time to prick this prick's bubble, you know, Pépé. I don't believe in ghosts myself. Personally, I believe in crooks and the way they terrorise people. It's not magic. It's the oldest trick in history, and it's always the poorest that get ripped off most.'

Pépé smiled. 'I like you, Mr Taylor. I can see why our friend told me to cooperate with you. You have seen some battles I think?'

'One or two. Now, more importantly, did you bring the stuff I asked for?'

Pépé nodded to his right to a plain green holdall on the ground that he must have brought in when he arrived. Or had it been there even before that? No matter.

'Good,' said Harry. 'Enough for four grown-ups on holiday for a couple of days. Right?'

'More than enough.'

'You'll find the envelope behind the desk at the Lazy Eye Hotel. It's inside a care package addressed to a Mr Stimson, as agreed.'

Pépé shook his head. 'On the house, Harry. Like I said, our friend told me to look after you. Anything else I can help you with?'

'No. Not right now. But I can get you on that number, right?'

Pépé pulled out his phone. 'This one?' He snapped it in two. 'Afraid not. You won't see me again. Happy holiday, Harry Taylor.'

And then he was gone.

# 18

London was five hours ahead, which made it 6 a.m. back home. Christ, no wonder he was all over the shop. John Williams, shoeless and sleepless, kicked at the sand outside the Mango Beach Resort Hotel and wandered towards the lights of the jetty. It may have been 1 a.m. local time, but he needed air and a chance to stretch his legs.

Harry had left them to it at the hotel for much of the day, chasing down what he called 'the basics'. He'd been in a filthy temper once they'd landed, keen to get going. Why were they staying in a resort hotel? John had asked – and immediately wished he hadn't.

'Because four British coppers stick out like a bulldog's bollocks at the best of times,' Harry had said. 'And that's in *Britain*. We're in fucking Barbados, John. I want us to blend in just a bit. Look less like stiffs and a tiny bit like holiday-makers.'

'Is that our cover?' asked Iris.

'You can shut it, too,' he said. 'Get scrubbed up and we'll meet down here in the lobby for a debrief at five. Read up on the files Robinson sent and work on the assumption that tomorrow is day one of the op proper. I don't want us to waste any time here, beautiful as I am sure Barbados is. This is just a hunch, and a pretty tendentious one at that. If it leads nowhere, I want us back in London sharpish, or Robinson will make me eat my own liver in front of him.'

Later, at the briefing, he had filled them in on the meetings
with Tennyson and Pépé, and told them that he would issue
them with the sidearms – Berettas, for Christ's sake – when
they were back in their rooms.

'You know I've never handled a gun?' said Carol.

'I know. And you won't on this trip, I guarantee it. I'll give
it to you as a total precaution, walk you through the first
principles, and then you can hand it back to me for disposal
before we head back. OK?' said Harry.

'I guess so. Physicists don't usually need to be armed, you
know, Harry.'

'Well,' he said, 'First time for everything. Think of yourself
as Einstein with a shooter. E equals M16.'

'Very funny. I'll try.'

'Funny' was the word. John Williams was an experienced
copper, and he had seen a fair few things in his time. But
there was something different about this op. At times it felt
like they were chasing Armageddon; and, at other times, it
seemed that it was all nonsense on stilts, nothing more than
a collision of rumour, hearsay and scaremongering. Did they
really have a clue what they were looking for and whether their
lead amounted to anything more than a mix of wishful thinking and desperation at the top of the command hierarchy?

Still, John trusted Harry. Like the father he had never had,
really – his own dad having bailed when he was three. He
and Harry were separated by less than a decade in age, but
John saw in his boss a person from a different generation,
carved from a different timber. He knew Harry had his faults
– too much of a loner, too sharp a temper, too certain that
he was right when every other officer at the Yard said that
he was wrong. A stubborn bastard. But with the stubbornness
came integrity, and loyalty and wisdom. John wasn't certain
of very much, but he knew that he loved his kids: Livvy who

was six, and Justin, four. And he knew that he trusted Harry Taylor.

The crescent moon was vivid in the sky, and its reflection shimmered in the water, beyond the multicoloured string lights on a small pier. He could hear the waves lapping against the wood and the occasional thud as one of the moored rowing boats or jet skis bumped into its pilings. He'd walked a fair way from the lights of the resort, and the couple he'd passed walking hand in hand were only dots now, no doubt headed back to their hotel room for a romantic night. The opposite way, the beams of an approaching car at the turn of the cove swept across the night. It was just him and the night air and the smell of the ocean. All in all, blissfully peaceful. And he—

The first blow was ferocious. He felt the sand on his face even before he realised that he had been hit – and with expertise. It was a well-aimed chop to the shoulder, intended to put him down but not to injure him seriously. He gathered his wits and tried to stand up and adopt a fighting stance.

The kick to his stomach, in contrast, was administered by an amateur, and it was certainly meant to cause as much harm as possible. He coughed and then dry-retched, desperately trying to catch his breath, clutching his abdomen, which felt as if it was covered in hot coals. He tried to speak but could manage no more than a feeble moan. This provoked another kick to the stomach – the pain was dreadful now – and another bout of retching.

John Williams knew how to handle himself: he had very nearly made the British judo squad aged twenty-three, missing out only to a long-time rival from Redbridge who went on to win a bronze medal at the European championships. He was still in shape and trained regularly at the Budokwai Club. So, even in his wretched condition, he recognised two things:

first, the two men – at least two – he was up against were no strangers to this particular kind of work. They had crept up on him quietly and effectively. Second: only one of them was trained in martial arts and knew exactly how much force to use to achieve his objectives. But the other was just strong, and therefore more dangerous. If he kicked John in the head with the violence he had used when attacking his stomach, he could easily kill him. A man could die of blunt force trauma to the skull much more easily than the cop shows and crime movies ever showed. In his experience, when it came to deaths on the streets of London, cranial injuries were trumped only by bullets.

Now he was on a beach in Barbados, waiting to find out if he was about to die. His eyes were full of sand and he could see nothing. There were, he thought, two voices – maybe three? – hissing at one another in, what? Spanish? Portuguese? Clearly arguing about what to do with him. He wanted to stand up, but knew that if he tried and only staggered, he would be finished off on the spot.

And then, all was a haze of pain and confusion. He heard further blows – except that these were not raining down on him but, it seemed, on his assailants. The groans were not his own. The sound of a boot connecting with bone was unmistakable.

And then: a sudden burst of gunfire. From where? Shots returned. A scream as someone fell to the sand. Must be nearby as he could smell the metallic scent of oozing blood. The indistinct blaze of what might be a flare. More furious exclamations. Coughing, cursing in – yes, definitely Spanish (*'¡Su puta madre!'*).

Then the orderly sound of four precisely delivered shots. Not warnings. Not covering fire. Executions. Two shots each.

★

Hushed voices. But calm, controlled. Professionals. Was he hallucinating? He thought he could hear the sound of bodies being dragged through the sand. Then the churning noise of an outboard motor, growing quieter as the boat – whoever was in it, wherever it was going – faded across the water, into the distance.

Somehow, he realised, he was still alive. Blinking, he looked at the patches of red nearby and felt himself retch. Christ. A bloodbath.

Finally, he managed to scramble to his knees, checking as best he could that his abdominal wall hadn't been ruptured. Fuck, it hurt. But he was OK. He got to his feet, staggering, his vision still blurry.

His phone. Where was the bloody phone? He reached into the buttoned pocket of his cargo shorts, found the burner Harry had given him and called his boss.

He picked up immediately. 'Yeah?'

John could hardly speak.

Harry tried again. 'Who is this?'

'I . . . it's . . .'

'John. What is it?'

'Beach. Jumped. Fucking . . . kill zone.'

Five minutes later, Harry and Iris were with John, checking him for signs of concussion. They had found a plastic beach chair and had lowered him into it. He was still badly winded and – though he hated to admit it – badly shaken.

Harry looked out to sea: 'You definitely heard a boat?'

'Yeah, no question. Couldn't tell you which direction they were headed . . . It makes no sense. First, two guys attack me. Then . . . then somebody helps me out – you, I assumed at first. But then a proper gunfight, and I reckon three dead . . . The other lot take off. But I didn't see faces.' He blinked. 'Sorry, boss.'

'Forget about it, mate. All that matters is you're still breathing. Mad bastards. What's going on round here?'

'Well,' Iris said. 'Looks like the whole bloody town knows we're here. Do you think your little friend Pépé could be blabbing, boss?'

Harry stroked his chin. 'Possible. But to hear the way Tennyson talked, I'd be very surprised. I mean, the only thing keeping that guy out of spending the rest of his life in a stinking cell is one copper's good will. And he's not going to risk that, is he? At least, not unless somebody's really got to him.'

'How do you mean?'

'Well, I didn't mention this earlier – because I still think I was being paranoid – but on my way back here from the bar I had a feeling that I'd been made.'

'A tail?' Iris asked.

'Yeah. But every time I checked, there was nothing. I mean, no vehicle in the rear-view for too long. It was just – a feeling.'

'Well,' said John, wincing. 'Feeling is all I've got right now. And it ain't nothing like fun.'

'Pépé or not,' Iris said, 'it's officially no longer a secret that we're in Barbados.'

'You can say that again,' said her boss.

'So what's next?'

'I'll call this into Tennyson. See what he thinks. His boys are probably on their way already. He said they'd be keeping a discreet eye on us, or checking in now and then at least. If John was attacked by *sicarios*, he might know who they represent. Thing is, the gangs on the island are mostly small fry. Locals, running numbers, pimping, stuff like that. So, if this is Mexicans or Colombians, then he would know if they have a permanent presence here. A high commission, if you like.'

'Ramirez?' said John. 'Is this a move by Ramirez?'

'Could be,' said Harry. 'He's definitely the wild card in all of this. Man on the make, looking to cross the ocean and take over the European market. In a hurry, and famous mostly for his greed and sadism. I'd be surprised if he wasn't mixed up in all of this. But look, John. Whoever it was, it looks like it was meant to be a snatch. They take you, truss you up somewhere, then deal with us from a position of advantage.'

'What are they after?' said Iris.

'Just what we know. Who we're chasing. Where the rock is – if that's what they're after. It's a bloody risky move, attacking an expat police officer so near a very public hotel. Suggests that they're in a hurry. Under orders to get results, fast.'

'So what you mean is,' said John, 'if the fucking execution squad hadn't shown up – whoever they were – I could be sitting in a cellar right now being asked questions to which I don't the fucking answer by a bunch of cartel hoods with my bollocks wired up to a car battery?'

'Pretty much,' said Harry. He kicked a pebble away.

'Christ almighty.'

The three officers were silent for a while as the significance of what had just happened sunk in. They were no longer just the hunters. They were the prey, too. And somebody wanted to help them; which was possibly good news but inexplicable, too.

Harry looked deep in thought: '"*I'm always glad to assist the police when I can.*"'

'What's that guv?' John asked.

'Nothing, just something Smythe said. Probably nothing. Right, I think we should get you checked out, John boy.'

'Nah. I'll be fine.'

'Concussion is no joke,' said Iris. 'Believe me. I've been there. I bet you have, too.'

'Last time I got concussion was in Fulham. Planted six feet into the mat by a Japanese world champion. Now *that* really hurt. At my own bloody club, too.'

Harry's phone rang. Not his burner, but his regular iPhone. Who the hell would be calling him now? On his official SO22 line? At this time of night?

He frowned at the phone, clearly unsure of the number. 'Taylor,' he answered.

The voice was loud enough for Iris and John to hear above the sharp breezes of the night.

'Detective Chief Inspector. Good evening to you. This is Vladimir Voldrev.'

# 19

The luxury of the motorboat was, as ever, another form of code. As the skipper in his starched whites told Harry and Carol – without being asked – it was a 'specially customised' Ferretti Altura 690, faster than the usual production models, with its guest cabins below deck being compact but completely remodelled by an exclusive Parisian designer.

They drank mineral water with crushed ice and a slice of orange, served to them by a waiter in full uniform, and made the most of the cool spray from the sea, the breeze and the sunshine. The white surfaces on deck were utterly spotless, the music piped through hidden speakers pointedly classical – Bach, maybe? Even when ferrying his guests from shore to island, Voldrev wanted them to be in no doubt that he was not only the daddy, but a very *tasteful* daddy.

Only the ink peeking out from the jacket sleeves of the two burly guards gave the game away. Harry was no expert on the complex language of Russian tattoos and the signals they sent within the underworld, but he had heard that an eight-pointed star signified a master thief and that tattooed rings on fingers were indications of prison sentences. The larger of their two minders – a beast of a man, six-six at least, with short blond hair – had at least three such rings. However much Voldrev wanted the world to see him as a suave and sophisticated man of substance and culture, he was quite happy to surround himself with the dregs of the *Russkaya mafiya*. Blondie caught Harry checking out his hands and stared back with a stillness that, in other circumstances, would have been deeply menacing. In fact, it *was* deeply menacing.

But nobody was getting hurt today. That much had been clear from his conversation on the beach the night before. Harry wished he had recorded it for posterity: apart from some early Interpol interviews with Voldrev, mostly handled by his lawyers, there were very few recordings of his voice and almost nothing that could be described as conversational. Yet his manner with Harry had been positively amiable, his warmth and tone almost sufficient to make you forget who he really was.

He began by apologising for calling Harry *at all*, so late at night. But he had just been informed by two of his employees – on the island to run an errand – that one of Harry's team had been 'apprehended' on the beach. His employees had heard that Detective Inspector Williams (Christ, he even knew John's name) had been in danger of kidnap.

Voldrev did not say that his men had intervened or killed at least two gangsters, Harry noted.

As if to fill the gap, the Russian said that he lived a discreet life in the Caribbean and tried not to get embroiled with what he called 'the business of the state'. Well, that was one way of putting it. At any rate, Voldrev believed that he might be able to shed further light on what had happened to John, and to answer 'any other questions you might have' and wondered if Harry and a colleague would like to join him for lunch at his home the next day. Harry said he would like that very much and was about to ask about the *sicarios* on the beach when he realised that Voldrev had rung off.

At 8 a.m. – although he wasn't sure he had actually slept – he was phoned by reception to say that his lunch host would be sending a boat to pick him up at noon and looked forward to meeting him in person.

'Why me?' asked Carol when he called her to say that he wanted her to accompany him to the island. 'I'm your nerdy forensics officer, not an experienced detective.'

'I know that.'

'Come on, this is a real chance to get under Voldrev's skin. All I can ask him about is isotopes and oxidation states – I'm not so hot on drug busts and throat-cutting. You should take Iris or John, obviously. I'm a total novice when it comes to interrogating bad guys.'

'That's exactly why I want you to come. This is absolutely *not* going to be an interrogation. It's Voldrev's show, on Voldrev's turf. If I ask him the kind of questions I would in a routine questioning, the whole thing will be a waste of time. He'll clam up. He'll clam up anyway – at least as far as his own activities are concerned. It's the asides, the poker tells I'll be looking for.'

'OK. But where do I fit in?'

'You're by far the smartest of us— No, of course you are, don't even bother protesting, it's a waste of time. That's why you're here. Voldrev will be flattered that I brought a brilliant scientist and not a caddy.'

'A caddy?'

'You know, a junior detective. He'll also know who you are and what your specialty is. Which means he knows we're serious and that he has to watch his step when talking about the radioactive rock – if he does, which he might well not. Remember, he's a career KGB boy at heart, who made his bones in a country that could barely feed its people but flexed its muscles on the world stage with nuclear power. I doubt he knows much science, but he'll have grown up hearing about it and how important it was to the glory of the Soviet Union to have lots of scientists on call. See my point?'

She nodded. 'OK then. I'll do my best.'

'Just follow my lead. If I'm right, he's planning on doing two things. He'll want to impress the fuck out of us – I mean, that's his shtick, right? – and charm us. But he'll also want us out of his life and on the next flight back to Heathrow. So he'll distract us with his own theories about what's going on – you know, a false scent or two – and maybe, if he's in the mood, throw in a lightly veiled threat somewhere. Either way, I'd be surprised if we get another shot at profiling him. If nothing else, Robinson will be pleased that we got this far.'

She paused. 'Doesn't this all strike you as a bit odd? I mean, his men appear from out of the blue late at night and save John from God knows who. They take them out there and then, without thinking twice. Corpses dragged down the beach to their boat. And *then* he invites two Met officers with no jurisdiction to speak of to a spot of light lunch at his Caribbean chateau. Does that all seem . . . rational?'

Harry shrugged. 'Well, all villains have a streak of the performer in them. Especially at his level. What's the point of building a palace if you can't flaunt your power to poverty-stricken coppers occasionally, right? Even power over life and death. But also, if the rock really is in play, and plenty of people seem to think it is, then Voldrev will be fishing as much as we will. Is he really a suspect? Are we working with the Yanks or anyone else? Is our little mission just a diversionary tactic before Navy SEALs storm his island? Which, by the way, it could well be. Don't rule it out. The up-tops are not above throwing a few coppers in as the unwitting warm-up act before they launch the big guns. It's been done before, and the cops involved are always the last to find out.'

'Do you actually think that's what we are? Canaries in a coal mine?'

'Possible. But I doubt it, actually. There'll be lots of other investigations by other agencies going on – that's par for the course. But I can tell that Robinson is under real pressure from his real bosses – I mean, the people in Downing Street and the Cabinet Office that call him when the shit hits the fan. They really *do* want results from us. They're worried that the blue chips – you know, Five, Six, whatever – will run around like headless chickens, produce a lot of briefings and COBRA minutes but get precisely nowhere. Not in time, anyway. That's where we come in. We got to the Devereux lair a bit too late – all the throats had been cut already – but at least we got there. Just by standard police work. Do you see what I'm saying?'

'I do,' said Carol. 'Like I said, I'll do my best.'

As he leant back in the sun, the swell below the boat a little choppier than when they had set off, Harry thought about the grimy warehouse off Brick Lane and the bloody crime scene he and Iris had walked in to. So much for a pleasant night out at the Cube, clubbing with a beautiful colleague. From that moment, as he considered the vicious bloodshed that this case had already caused, he knew that his immediate future – and that of his team – was going to be very perilous indeed. His antennae were still sharp in that respect. He recognised the distinctive scent of real trouble when it entered the neighbourhood. And the danger in this case was not just the deadly potential of missing uranium. It was the things that he knew bad men would do to get hold of it.

'Approaching Elena in five minutes, sir and madam,' said the skipper.

'Elena?' asked Harry.

'The island. The name that Mr Voldrev bestowed upon it.'

A small wharf with what looked like a pine jetty was now in view. There was a large boathouse at the beach end of the pier, and plenty of moorings for vessels great and small. Among the lavish green wall of macaw palm trees, Harry and Carol could see a handful of guest cottages, with their own swimming pools and sun decks. A series of tiled pathways led away from the beach into the interior of the island.

The speedboat docked quickly as a team of uniformed staff worked with ropes and attached them to cleats, pilings and posts until the vessel was secure and the short gangway firmly in position. On the jetty, there was a smartly dressed woman who seemed to be in charge. She waved to Harry and Carol and beckoned them to disembark.

'Greetings,' she said. 'Detective Chief Inspector Taylor, Inspector Walker. I am Natalya Semyonova, Mr Voldrev's chief of staff on the island. Welcome to Elena.'

'Thanks very much,' said Harry, shaking her hand. 'It's, it's quite something.'

Natalya laughed. 'Yes, we hope so. Mr Voldrev has worked very hard to make this place special – for our honoured guests, as well as for himself and his staff.'

'How long has he owned the island?' Carol asked.

The question was ignored. 'We go?' said Natalya. 'Mr Voldrev is excited to meet you. He is in the gardens, taking business calls. It is a short walk.'

Harry leant over to Carol. 'I tell you what. We're going to find out fuck all from this girl.'

Carol struggled to suppress her laughter and nodded quickly before Natalya could register their amusement.

The path to the left of the jetty led to the main house, she said, as if she were describing a regular six-bedroom villa or a finely renovated farmhouse. But something told Harry that what awaited them was very much more impressive than that.

What he had assumed was a stockade of tall trees to keep prying eyes at bay turned out to be much more like a jungle. There were fig trees, thick baobabs, cassias and creepers hanging to the forest floor. Overhead, green monkeys leapt from branch to branch, and the air was full of birds – exotic and noisy, most of which Harry did not recognise. A pair of panting German shepherds loped along beside them as they walked: Harry, Carol, Natalya and the two button-men from the boat. Along the way, he spotted at least ten more staff; mostly construction workers or foresters busy in the dark recesses of the woods. But also one or two men in white shirts and shades, patrolling the area with sub-machine guns slung over their shoulders, with pouches of extra ammunition across their chests. If this was indeed an island paradise, it was also a place where the possibility of violence was taken seriously at all times. But then, what else had he expected?

The path curved eastward into what they assumed was even deeper jungle – but turned out to be a large clearing. Or, rather, a clearing that led to a driveway, full of gleaming vehicles: a trio of Range Rovers with blacked-out windows, a blue Bentley Continental GTC and a silver Porsche 911 GT3. Now this *was* impressive, Harry had to admit.

'I see you admiring the cars?' said Natalya. 'These are only those in use today. Mr Voldrev has a hangar on the other side of the island in which he keeps his most treasured vehicles. He is a dedicated collector, did you know?'

'I didn't,' said Harry.

'Oh, yes. Very much so. It is – what is the word? – his *hobby*, if you like.'

'I suppose that is the word, yes. In a manner of speaking. How many motors does he have?'

'Oh, worldwide, many hundreds. Perhaps eighty here on Elena.'

'That is quite a hobby,' said Carol.

'Well,' said Natalya, 'he is the first to admit his love of beautiful things.'

Beyond the driveway was what looked like a neoclassical façade. Four storeys, tall arched windows and a portico topped by a magnificent sculpted pediment. Beyond its columns was not a door but an archway, wide enough to afford them a glimpse of the courtyard that lay within.

'Come, please,' said Natalya. The dogs scampered off in pursuit of some imagined prey but the hoods stayed with the party, a few paces behind but never too far away. They climbed the marble stairs and went through the archway.

After years in the special forces and the police, after seeing, on a routine day, things that civilians were spared their whole lives, Harry Taylor was rarely lost for words. But the spectacle that he now beheld was extraordinary: no other word would do. Somehow, in the middle of a Caribbean jungle, with blistering heat and 80 per cent humidity, Vladimir Voldrev had managed to build a homage in stone to the Palace of Versailles itself. Insane, or heroic? Or both?

'You see the black and white marble tiles?' said Natalya. 'This is inspired by the work of André Le Nôtre, who was architect and gardener to Louis XIV himself. Like much else on Elena. On the terrace, we have a version of the Latona Fountain. There is a hall of mirrors and a hedge labyrinth. The gardens replicate the original design, too – though on a smaller scale, of course. A chapel, too, and several galleries where Mr Voldrev has hung some of the classical paintings he has acquired.'

'He's a collector of art, too?' asked Carol.

'Oh, very much so,' Natalya said. 'But here on the island, he displays only paintings completely appropriate to the style of the chateau. Many of the artworks he owns are on loan to museums and galleries around the world – though he never advertises the fact. He likes to keep his collection private, as most people in his position do.'

How many people, exactly, were in Vladimir Voldrev's 'position'? Harry wondered. A Russian oligarch living on an island like the Sun King. An international drug lord who had evaded capture for decades – a former KGB killer, for that matter – now posing as an *ancien régime* French aesthete, as if that would just wash all the blood off his hands. Fucking cheek.

Natalya, still wearing her suit jacket, and not even perspiring, continued the tour. 'So let us go into the next courtyard, the Cour Royale.' They walked through a second archway and into an even larger quad. It was spectacular, no doubt about it. A miracle of masonry, carpentry and artistic detail. And a testament to what you could buy if you were a billionaire who paid lower taxes than your cleaning staff.

This courtyard was dominated by a bronze equestrian statue – perhaps twenty feet in height. It was, Harry saw, an effigy of Peter the Great, rather than a pre-revolutionary French king or aristocrat: a reminder of the owner's true heritage.

Carol looked up to the attic windows. 'There must be more than a hundred rooms in this place. Are they all used?'

'Not all,' said Natalya. 'But of course you must remember that Mr Voldrev is also a very modern man. So what looks like Versailles on the outside may in fact be very different inside. Like a trompe l'oeil! We have conference rooms for our business associates, a state-of-the-art gym and spa, even an IMAX cinema, would you believe! Mr Voldrev works very hard, as you know, so he loves nothing more than to watch an action movie on the big screen at the end of the day. It is what he calls "an indulgence".'

'Bloody hell,' Harry whispered. 'Is that the only thing he calls an indulgence round here?'

'It *is* amazing,' Carol replied, also keeping her voice down. 'I'll give him that. But it stinks of villainy. I wish she would stop saying "as you know". Because, no, we don't bloody know, do we? I mean, that's probably the point.'

'It certainly is.'

'Now, we are almost there, and I can leave you to enjoy your lunch,' Natalya said.

They crossed the second courtyard and walked out into the full blaze of the sun. As far as the eye could see, there were immaculately tended lawns, hedge walls, statuary and, in the distance, a handful of peacocks strutting across one of the lawns.

On the terrace was a long table, set for their meal. It could easily have seated thirty but there were only three settings. Three golden ice buckets were on a side table, two containing what looked like two bottles of Cristal – what else would Voldrev select? – and a white wine the quality of which, Harry felt fairly sure, they would be told all about.

Natalya extended her hand to say her farewells. 'I will take my leave now. I have matters to attend to for Mr Voldrev elsewhere. As you can imagine, there is always much to do! I hope that the rest of your day on Elena is very pleasant.'

They thanked her with, Harry felt, a politeness that was slightly over the top and very English. The two hoods were now standing by the archway, motionless, looking as though they might turn into stone at any moment.

A waiter approached them with flutes of champagne. Though they were on duty, neither hesitated before accepting. First, it would seem rude not to. And second, they both badly needed a drink. As Carol said to Harry later: 'There's only so much fucking weirdness a Cambridge physicist can cope with in one day.'

For now, they sampled the champagne. 'Christ, that's incredible,' she said.

'Louis Roederer Cristal 2008,' said the waiter, sounding suddenly more like a sommelier. 'Some think it the house's finest vintage yet – very little yeast is used in its production, which means that it has aged especially well.'

'Slips down nicely,' said Harry.

'Indeed it does!' a voice boomed out.

They turned round and found themselves facing Vladimir Voldrev.

Not a snatched long-lens photograph. Not a decades-old Russian stock photo of a soldier who was still really a boy. Not a circled, blurry image distributed by the FBI to friendly partners abroad. The man himself, in the flesh.

He almost detonated with immediate affability. 'DCI Taylor! Inspector Walker! So good of you to come! Welcome to Elena. It is so wonderful that you are here!'

He was tall, commanding, clean-shaven, his dark hair still thick for a man of his age – had he had work done? The perfect white teeth that were now mandatory for men and women much lower down the food chain than him. Decked out head to foot in the Vilebrequin beachwear that Harry remembered John telling him was standard for showy players during playtime in the sun. Old espadrilles, as if he had just stepped off a yacht – which might well be the case. His forearms were exposed and almost every inch of visible skin was covered in tattoos. They could see dark ink climbing up his neck, too. *Yes*, thought Harry, *from Russia with love, all right.*

'Quite the place you have here, Mr Voldrev,' Carol said.

'Oh, please, call me Vova, everyone does.'

'Natalya doesn't,' said Harry.

Voldrev laughed. 'That is true. Miss Semyonova is a punctilious employee, and, I should add, an invaluable one. She runs everything on Elena so that I can relax and enjoy the sunshine. And the peace and quiet.'

'Are you here much of the year?' asked Harry.

'I travel a lot, Harry – may I call you Harry? And Carol? – but this is my home. Business calls me away. A brutal muse. But, these days, with technology, there is very little I cannot do here with my laptop and a glass of good chablis. I much prefer that to flying all over the world, always jet-lagged, always exhausted. I'm not as young as I used to be! Though I have been trying to stay in shape these last couple of years.' He patted his gut.

'I hear you have a fitness centre here,' Carol said.

'A fitness centre! More like a torture chamber. Eddie – one your fellow countrymen, in fact – puts me through my paces every morning at six a.m. sharp. He was a mixed martial arts champion before he retired, you know, and then he became a personal trainer. I discovered him in New York and took him on as a permanent member of staff. He is so tough with me. "Mr Vova, you have the arms of a girl!" "Mr Vova, you don't deserve to be trained by me!" I like him enormously. Ah, thank you, Michel.'

Voldrev took a glass of champagne from the waiter. 'Well, my friends. What shall we drink to?'

'Mysteries?' said Harry.

'Yes! I like this. Very Conan Doyle! To mysteries – and to new friends!'

They toasted one another and sipped the gorgeous vintage.

'Now, shall we sit down? I have asked Chef Hugo to make us something light. Not only for my waistline but because I find a heavy lunch makes for a sleepy afternoon. Don't you agree?'

'Oh,' Harry said. 'Indeed.'

'Good. I believe he has prepared us some of his magnificent gazpacho and then a lobster salad. The lobster caught this morning, of course, and the mangoes from our own trees. And we have a 2014 Montrachet, which is drinking very well.'

'This is all very kind of you,' Carol said.

'Not at all. The pleasure is all mine. I entertain guests all too seldom these days and it is wonderful to have some intelligent company.'

The chilled soup arrived. Voldrev declined bread.

'Well, my friends. Bon appétit!'

The gazpacho was indeed delicious. Substantial, tart and chilled to perfection.

'So,' Voldrev began. 'Before anything else, you must tell me how your colleague is. Detective Inspector Williams. My men were on the main island by coincidence and heard what had happened.'

*So you were already watching us,* thought Harry. *And you want us to know that.*

'They heard that the attack was quite savage. Most regrettable. Though, I gather the assailants were – seen off?' A smile flickered across his features. 'Of course, I called as soon as they informed me. As I said, I try to avoid entanglement with the authorities. There is a lot of corruption in Barbados and I keep a very clean house. I have no time for such . . .

distractions.' He paused. 'Though I understand that Deputy Commissioner Tennyson is an honourable man and very much to be trusted.'

*So you know about that, too.* Voldrev was toying with them already. That much Harry understood. He also grasped that it was important not to rise to the bait – at least, not yet.

'That's good to know,' Harry said. 'The Met has strong connections with the police service here. But my team has only just arrived, so that sort of local knowledge is invaluable.'

'And Mr Williams?'

'Bruises, mostly. No cracked ribs or abdominal damage. He'll be fine. Wounded pride, mostly.' Harry paused. 'Though whoever intervened was pretty ruthless. At least two dead, we believe.'

Voldrev ignored this. 'Yes, well, this is good news. Please send him my best.'

'I certainly shall, thank you. Mr Voldrev, I hope you don't mind me asking—'

'Vova!'

'Vova, apologies . . . but do you, or your employees have any idea who might have attacked DI Williams? I mean, it was – at the very least – intended to be a very serious warning. And maybe much worse, had it not been . . . stopped.'

Voldrev nodded his head in recognition. 'You know, I abhor violence. For ethical reasons, of course, but also as a businessman. It is simply unacceptable that a British police officer cannot take a stroll down a Bajan beach without being attacked. Anyone, for that matter.'

*You're not answering my question, you slippery bastard,* thought Harry.

'As to the identity of the assailants, this is, regrettably, an easy question to answer. The people in question are becoming a menace on the island, and, I know for a fact, a growing headache for the authorities.'

'Who do you mean?' asked Carol.

Voldrev waited until the staff had cleared the soup bowls. 'Does the name Xavier Ramirez mean anything to you?'

*Careful,* thought Harry. 'I've heard of him. Mexican cartel boss, right?'

'Correct. His operations are mostly based in Juarez, and he is one of the two or three most powerful figures in the cartels – now that the centre of the action is Mexico not Colombia. He fancies himself as the new Escobar, but he is no such thing. His coyotes probably make more money people trafficking across the border than they do shifting product into the United States. And his methods are . . . well, barbaric.'

Harry wanted to say: *Unlike pushing people off the roof of the Lubyanka in your KGB days, eh, Voldrev?* But he didn't dare interrupt the flow of the Russian's monologue.

'He kills women. He kills children. He takes his enemies to the desert and skins them alive. There are no rules, no boundaries with his kind. But he has established quite a grip on the south-west American drug market. And, crucially, he is expanding into Europe.'

'Really?' Carol said. 'Recently so, or for a while?'

'Quite recently. That is the point, I think.'

'How do you mean?' said Harry.

'My knowledge is second-hand, remember. But, as you know, I have many contacts still in Russia and so I hear many things about the changing scene there and in mainland Europe. Ramirez is certainly shifting a lot of his narcotics to the UK and the continent now. Or rather he is trying to.'

'Trying?' Harry prompted.

'Yes, Europe is – how to put this? – quite a *mature* market. There is a well-developed network of sellers who work for suppliers all over the world. Many of them have political, judicial, even, I fear, police protection at the very highest level. But they have grown complacent. They have been caught off guard by the sheer ferocity of the Ramirez operation and the man's personal ambition. And they cannot work out how he is getting his product into the European market. It certainly isn't arriving by plane, and there is too much of it to be accounted for by mules. All his chartered vessels, including his personal yacht, are regularly checked from bow to stern with a microscope. The police, customs and intelligence agencies have found nothing. No, he has devised an import procedure that is new. I will give him that much.'

'Have you met him?' Carol asked.

For the first time, there was a frisson of anger in Voldrev's response. '*Met* him? Dr Walker – Carol – I do not have dealings with such men. I am a completely legitimate businessman and investor, and I have never been charged with a crime in any country. Xavier, on the other hand . . . well, I am told that he spent five years in Cefereso 6 for attempted murder – a prison so horrific that it has since been closed, I believe. Were he less powerful, he would be in another penitentiary now, or have been shot like a dog by some right-thinking police officer.' Voldrev collected himself. 'But all this is none of my affair. I simply detest such inhumanity and its consequences.'

Harry decided to dive in. 'Of course. But you must have seen your fair share in the KGB?'

Voldrev's reply was calm, almost genial. 'Well, yes, very much so. Like you, Harry, I served my country in various ways and that was one of them. It was a very different time. Did we make mistakes? I am sure we did. Do I have regrets? Who doesn't? But when the Wall came down and the Soviet

Union collapsed, I realised that I wanted to live the life of a private citizen and to build a business. To create something. I am sure Natalya would tell me that my figures were out of date, if she were here, but did you know that the companies and businesses I own or part-own around the world employ three hundred thousand people? And that I personally have a payroll of several hundred? The image of Russia has been very bad, especially since Ukraine. Well, I am the first to recognise this. But we are not monsters, you know. My charitable foundation – the Elena Trust – made donations of more than fifty million dollars last year. I do not mean to boast – perhaps a little! – but I do want you to see me as I am, not as some hardened recluse in the shadows. Things aren't always what they seem, you know.'

'Of course not,' Harry said.

Waiting staff appeared, as if out of nowhere, and presented the next course with a flourish.

'Ah, the lobster! I hope you will like it. Michel, make sure everyone is topped up with the Montrachet – and anything else they might like.'

'Thank you very much,' Harry continued as the staff bustled around. 'I understand that your knowledge of the Ramirez cartel is limited. But I'd be very interested to know if you have any theories about the attack on John – DI Williams. Why make such an aggressive move? What could it really achieve?'

Voldrev savoured the wine. 'What could it achieve? Well, it is impossible to be sure. These are men of great volatility and that, of course, is very dangerous in the trade that they pursue. That particular business, I need hardly tell you, requires a measure of order and predictability to function. Violence needs to be a last resort, not an opening gambit. The politicians who protect Ramirez – well, he makes it very difficult for them sometimes. His impulsiveness will be his downfall.'

'We assume that his thugs intended to kidnap DI Williams.'

'Yes, that would seem logical.'

'But why? What do we have to offer Ramirez and his crew?'

Voldrev pushed his chair back and stretched his arms. He paused for a moment then returned to his original position, cupping his chin as if in deep thought. 'Well, Harry. Ramirez is a hothead but he is a powerful hothead now. He has connections. He evidently knew of your team's arrival on the island—'

'As did you.'

'True enough. I think you will find that it was, so to speak, an open secret.'

'All right,' said Carol. 'But why shake us down?'

'Please bear in mind that everything I know is second-hand. You must verify all this for yourselves, especially if you are reporting back to your superiors. That is the – what is the expression? – health warning.'

'Understood,' said Harry.

Voldrev sighed, as though it was lowering to have to pass on such details. 'I understand that he believes you are on the trail of some – 'material'. Some material that could be extremely dangerous if it fell into the wrong hands.'

'Go on,' said Harry.

'Well, is it not obvious? He *wants* it. He believes that you and your team can help him find it, but that he would have to apply – what is the word? – *pressure* to get you to reveal that information.'

'Christ. So he was going to sweat John?'

'Yes, you can be sure of it. And not just "sweat" him, either. His *sicarios* specialise, I believe, in slow dismemberment. Many of those they interrogate give up the ghost through sheer blood loss. As I say, we are dealing with a barbarism that is quite shocking.'

Carol looked down and turned pale, as if she was questioning her presence here. Harry could read her thoughts from her expression. Shouldn't she be back in Cambridge talking to her colleagues about quarks and hadrons, worrying about her lecture notes rather than the interrogation methods of Mexican *sicarios*?

Harry persisted, 'What does Xavier think we might know? I mean, what is he trying to get hold of?'

'Really, Harry,' Voldrev said, 'let us not be coy. We'll only get indigestion. We are speaking of the uranium-235 that was discovered in London very recently and that went missing shortly afterwards. It was taken, was it not, by somebody from a dump in the east of the city? With some violence, I gather. Or do you not think the raid was successful? That it is elsewhere?'

'Well, I'm not going to speculate about the nature of the material, Vova, if you don't mind, not having seen it myself.'

'And yet I notice that you have brought an expert nuclear physicist with you to lunch. Not a coincidence, surely?'

'Well, Inspector Walker is helping the team with a number of aspects of our inquiry. She covers the waterfront when it comes to forensic science.'

'Indeed. And she and her father, the legendary Professor Walker, are both renowned in the field of atomic science. Are they not?'

'You're right about my academic specialisation,' said Carol. 'And, of course, my father's. That information is all readily available online. But it's important to understand that I am a police officer now and that my role here is exclusively to follow orders from DCI Taylor.'

'Of course, of course,' said Voldrev. 'Please do not take

offence. I was being arch. Forgive me. It is a habit of Russians to look for irony and wit where perhaps none exists.'

'So to return to the question,' she said. 'What does Ramirez think we know?'

'Well, that I cannot say, not having any contact with him. But my strong hunch would be that he thinks you know – or are close to knowing – who has the uranium. Forgive me: the *material*. That's why he made his move so quickly. And, it turns out, ham-fistedly. He can be the bluntest of instruments, I am afraid.'

Harry locked eyes with Voldrev. 'All right. Well. That makes sense, as far as it goes. So my follow-up question, Vova, is this: Where do *you* think the material in question is?'

There was silence. Carol wondered for a moment if Voldrev was going to draw a knife – or a gun?

Instead, he burst into peals of laughter, real belly laughs, as if Harry had delivered the punchline of the century at a stand-up show. He wiped his eyes with his napkin and allowed his mirth to subside.

'Priceless, Harry! Priceless! Where do *I* think it is? I have not the *slightest* idea. How would I know such a thing? Am I a terrorist? No. Am I an arms dealer? No. Am I engaged in complex scientific research? Regrettably I am nowhere near clever enough for such undertakings. You think too much of me, you really do.'

Harry was not amused. 'I'm not sure about that, Mr Voldrev. You seem pretty plugged in as far as I can see.'

The Russian was still for a moment, his eyes narrowing slightly. Gone, momentarily, was the genial host, replaced by something steelier, braced, as if weighing up options. The mask had slipped a little, that was for sure. The silence felt like it would never be broken.

When Voldrev finally spoke, it was more quietly, with

greater deliberation. 'Well, it is true that I keep my ear to the ground. It pays to be well-informed, believe me. I am subject to much malicious, envious gossip. Even threats to my own life. I have to keep open – what do you English call it? – the "usual channels". In this life the simple matter of earning an honest living can get you killed. I have made a habit of being both cautious and vigilant. Death will take me when it is good and ready. Every Russian knows this about death. But we are in no hurry to accelerate the process . . . to chase death, so to speak.'

'I dare say,' said Harry. 'So, what are the "usual channels" telling you about the material we have been discussing? What is the gossip? What *rumours* reach you here in Xanadu?'

'Really, now, Harry, there is no need for sarcasm. We are all on the same side here, no?'

*Like fuck we are*, thought Harry – but kept his own counsel, hard as it was in the face of such mounting impudence by this jumped-up Russian gangster.

'My apologies. Anything you could let Inspector Walker and me know would be much appreciated,' he responded reluctantly.

Voldrev cleared his throat, as if preparing to make a toast. Instinctively, the staff replenished the Russian's glass – and then his guests'.

'I know you have come a long way hoping for an answer. I'm afraid I don't have anything like that for you. As for rumour, I have indeed heard gossip that the Ramirez operation is preparing to make its biggest shipment yet to mainland Europe. Perhaps you have heard this already? The cargo may already have left, I am not sure. It is said that Ramirez himself regards the shipment as being so crucial that he himself is overseeing it. This is known to the cartel's competitors, and there is a mood of – how can one describe it? There is a mood of extreme tension between the cartel and those they would displace in the European markets. My strong impression is that both sides in that battle are looking for an insuperable advantage over their enemies. Corrupt politicians, guns, bombs . . . all these play their part in the world of the *narcotraficante*, they always have. But possession of the . . . material that you are chasing? Well, that would transform a criminal operation of any sort from a business into a global corporate power. It would compel the other side to back off completely. If the other side were *sure* that it was facing such devastating odds, that is. And we all seem to be a fair distance from *sure*, don't we? Russians love chess, my friends, but I know a poker game when I see one.' Voldrev settled into his chair again. 'I can only say that I am glad I do not have a seat at this particular table.'

'But who does?' Carol asked. 'I mean, who does have a seat? You clearly believe that Ramirez is in hot pursuit. And that makes some sort of sense. His cartel's ambitions won't last long if his enemies get there first. But which of his enemies do you sense he is competing with?'

Voldrev drained his espresso and took a cigar from the cedar box held out by the waiter for him to peruse. Harry declined the offer, watching as the Russian prepared his smoke with monogrammed Davidoff cutters. The cigars were not the same as those he had found in the Devereux lair – Arturo Fuente Opus X – being instead a mixture of the highest quality Padron and San Cristobal. In more relaxed circumstances, he would certainly have indulged himself. But Voldrev had made him sick with rage. He wished he could put the bracelets on this villain there and then, cart him back to the main island for extradition and make the world a safer place. The fact that he had no grounds to do something like that – to do his job – only made him feel more bloody frustrated.

Was Voldrev baiting them by smoking a cigar in the first place? Had he or his representatives left the cigar box amid the carnage as a calling card and a 'fuck you'? And was this minor theatricality the oligarch's way of letting them know, here in his crazy Caribbean palace?

The Russian resumed. 'I do not think the Colombians have sufficient reach any more to take on Ramirez in this way. Once, they covered the planet. But not now. As for the continental market itself? It is, as far as I understand, a patchwork of interests – organisations that sometimes collaborate, sometimes compete. Sooner or later, one of them will make a move for dominance. But of course, the question is, which one?'

Carol did not hesitate. 'And which one will? In your best judgement?'

'Hard to say. Very hard. There are ambitious groups in my homeland who would still like to control the whole European underworld. Especially now they have been, if you like, banished from polite society. There will be more Russian drug crime, not less, mark my words. Albanian organisations, too, though they are not sophisticated in methods or strategy, and would, I think, struggle with the technicalities of which we are speaking. Perhaps they might be capable ten years hence, but not yet.' He paused. 'There is one individual who, I know for sure, resents the brashness of the Ramirez cartel. Who despises Ramirez himself.' He laughed quietly. 'Who despises me, for that matter.'

'You're talking about Julian Smythe, aren't you?'

Voldrev was not a man given to flinching, Harry was certain, but the name caused him visible discomfort. When he spoke, his voice was cold.

'Indeed, Harry. A man of deep vindictiveness. Or, more precisely, given to pursuing vendettas for non-existent reasons. Have you come across him? I mean, in your various operations?'

*You know fucking well that I have,* thought Harry. He wondered how long Voldrev had been following them. How much he actually knew about his encounter with Smythe in Belgravia and what was said in that very different citadel of wealth.

'A little bit. He has crossed our radar once or twice, if that's what you mean. Ours, and the radar of many other law-and-order agencies. Never been able to pin anything on him, though.'

'You will struggle to do so. Smythe's speciality is impunity. Like Moriarty to Sherlock Holmes, he simply slips away. He is more ghost than man.'

'People use the same word about you,' said Harry, remembering what Pépé had said.

'Do they? How extraordinary! No, I am very much flesh and blood like anyone else. Well, people say many things about me and a very small percentage of them are true.' He drew on his cigar and puffed out a smoke ring with an air of satisfaction. 'In any case, we were speaking of Mr Smythe. *Sir* Julian, actually. He is a baronet, though he never uses the title as far as I can tell. He is, as I say, very adept at concealing his operations. He leads a double life, as you know. A respectable art dealer, as far as the *beau monde* of London is concerned. But, really, a man whose life has been mostly dedicated to the distribution and sale of prohibited narcotics. A vicious man, too.'

'He claims that you and he have a disagreement that goes back to Moscow,' said Harry. 'And it is said that there is much personal bad blood between you.'

Again, Voldrev waved this away. 'Fantasy. I am not aware of ever having met Smythe. Certainly not in the motherland – though, of course, I understand that he spent some of his formative years there. He is the kind of man I avoid, on principle. Perhaps that is part of the reason that he is so hostile to me.'

Harry checked his watch, wondering how John was getting on and whether Iris had checked in with Tennyson as he had earlier instructed. 'What form does his hostility to you take?'

'*Lies*. Always lies. Falsehoods, fabrications. He says things about me that are so fantastical – I mean, there is no villainy so deplorable that he is not ready to accuse me of it! It has caused me some inconvenience over the years, I have to say. Visits from law enforcement agencies that have not been, shall we say, as agreeable as this lunch. All for nothing, of course – trumped up nonsense.'

'How often?'

'Not for a few years now, but I always prepare myself for the next bout of mischief. I am no psychologist, Harry, but I do wonder if he somehow chooses to project on to me and my life the criminality of his own. After all, let us not be naïve: people are more willing to think ill of a low-born Russian businessman such as myself than they are of an aristocratic Englishman. In the battle of snobbery, I don't stand a chance!' He reflected for a moment. 'But such games are of no real consequence. For me, that is. For you, I would say that Mr Smythe's *ambitions* are very much to the point.'

'How do you mean?' Carol asked.

'What I mean, Dr Walker, is that – back to chess, here – the logic of the board requires Smythe to get hold of this material, or at least to prevent his rivals from doing so. I have no specific intelligence on his efforts to do so, you understand – I am merely speculating. But it is logical speculation, if you like, based on where all the pawns and the bishops and the knights are positioned. He will be delighted that you have come all this way. It is a classic misdirection, I have to admit.'

'You think he wanted us to come all the way to Barbados just to get us out of the way?' said Harry.

'Without question,' said Voldrev. 'I mean, I am not suggesting that you took instruction from him. That would be ridiculous. But Mr Smythe, I regret to say, will be *thrilled* when he learns – as doubtless he will – that you have been sitting with me, eating lobster on Elena, while he gets on with . . . well, whatever he is doing.'

'He is that fixated with you?' said Carol.

'I believe so. For his own psychotic reasons. And it is a matter of convenience, too. I make a useful enemy in his great game. He accuses me of the very things that he is doing or wants to do. It is as though we are twins. Of a sort.'

'Takes sibling rivalry to a new level, doesn't it?' said Harry.

Voldrev shrugged. 'I do not regard him as a *sibling*. Or feel any other form of affinity to him. His antics are . . . a *serious* waste of my time.'

Harry stood up suddenly, causing Carol to catch his eye, as if confused. 'Speaking of which, Mr Voldrev – Vova – we have already taken up too much of your time. And we are very grateful for your hospitality.'

'You must leave?'

'We are only in Barbados for a short while. And I imagine you have a million things you need to be getting on with. I hope the rest of your day is very pleasant and productive. And thank you again for your advice – and a delicious meal.'

'So soon?' said Voldrev. 'Well, you are a busy man, too. And a busy woman! I shall get Natalya to take you back to the jetty and the launch will return you to your hotel.' He nodded to one of his henchmen who relayed the instructions into a wrist mic. 'And may I say what a pleasure it has been to spend some time with you? People often say that Elena is a paradise island, but what is the point of living in paradise if you do not get to share it with others?'

Like a spirit materialising from the ether, Natalya was suddenly at her boss's side. Voldrev embraced Harry and Carol, who put up little resistance to his raucous farewells and the sheer power of his bear hug.

As Natalya proceeded towards the archway, he held Harry back and whispered something in his ear. Harry nodded.

'Do we buy any of that at all?' Carol asked as they sped across the surf back to the resort.

Harry nodded his head. 'Some of it. Not all, of course. He knows more than he's saying, you can bet on that.'

'Do you think he has the uranium?'

'If he does, it's not on his island. That was part of his message: I'm here, come and do your worst with any warrant you can get. No, it would be a complete waste of time to go back. You could have one hundred officers combing that island, but they won't find any trace of it – if he has it.'

'All those rooms, though? It could be anywhere.'

Harry shook his head. 'That island is a fortress, and I'm sure it has criminal uses. But that's not its main purpose. The whole thing is just one big vulgar declaration to the rest of the world: I'm pharaoh, I'm the Roman emperor. Whatever. It's his fucking chocolate factory to impress us all.'

'So we rule him out?'

'Did I say that? We absolutely don't. He could easily be our man. And if he is, we're going to have to be smarter than we have been so far. Of course he wants us to think it's all Smythe – they fucking hate each other. But the stuff about the Ramirez cartel . . . that's important, whatever happens next. We need to find out everything we can about Xavier and his beef with Smythe – and anyone else. We're only seeing part of the picture. And time is not on our fucking side.'

'What did he say to you?' Carol asked. 'When he pulled you back, as we were leaving?'

'He said, "Do not forget that, in the eyes of history, your country is still a part of Europe."'

'What the hell does that mean?'

'It means that something is about to go down back home.'

# 20

What is true power? As the ship ploughed through the ocean, furiously churning foam and spray in its wake, this was the question that occupied him.

From the prow, he looked eastward, the trade winds gripping his face, towards a horizon of infinite possibility. Now was surely his moment. One for which he had prepared, fought and spilt blood for in so many places and for so many years.

But what was the power he sought? Wealth? Of course, always money. There was no such thing as 'enough', and those who believed such nonsense were usually destroyed by the natural selection of the marketplace. Money's only honest instruction to those who acquired it was 'more'.

Yet he knew that was not the authentic essence of his plan. It had so many levels, each of which would reveal itself only at a moment of his choosing. He would fool them all.

If not money, then what? Status in society? No, that wasn't it. The sudden deference that comes with the first phase of true success: the phoney friends, the women, the cars and the yachts and the helicopters and the invitations to elegant homes . . . All that was welcome enough, a sensual surge for the newly empowered. But the excitement faded fast enough. The platinum playground, you soon learned, was much too full to be considered truly exclusive. And the hedonism, sycophancy and cosmetic grandeur, all that quickly lost its appeal if you were a man of substance. A man who aspired to greatness.

That was the heart of the matter. How to achieve greatness, real greatness.

As he thought about the past few weeks, and the path that had brought him to the middle of the sea on a boat bearing great treasure, he realised suddenly, with total clarity and precision, how such power was secured. And there was only one way, really.

Not money, love, spectacle, prestige. Not cash or bullets or even freedom from the dreary rule of law (an expensive privilege, it had to be said).

No, it was fear. Fear. Only fear would give you true control. Only terror would make other men bow to your will without question. Would make them scuttle out of your way before you even moved. Dread was what he required in others.

And soon they would all dread him. They would fear his will. They would fear the fire that he could conjure, as if from the skies.

# 21

'What do you mean "moved off"?' Harry thundered, his knuckles white as he gripped the edge of the table in Robinson's office. 'We've only been back a day.'

'I mean what I said, Harry,' said his boss.

'You're having a fucking laugh.'

'I wish I were.'

Robinson stood and returned to sit behind his desk. He pulled a bottle of Scotch out of his bottom drawer.

'Refreshment?'

'No thanks.'

'Please yourself. I'm having one.'

'Explain.' Harry breathed out, trying to control his fury. 'Please. Bill.'

The other man knocked back the double he had poured for himself. *What must his liver look like?* Harry wondered.

'Your Barbados trip—'

'Which has generated more leads than all the other agencies have come up with put together! Answer me this: How many one-on-ones with Vladimir Voldrev have the fucking NCA had recently? Tell me that anyone at the DEA or in Washington, Springfield or Langley knew about the Ramirez shipment? Or the potential drug war between Smythe and the cartel?'

'It's all good intel, Harry. Don't get me wrong.'

'Well, thanks a million. I *know* it's fucking good intel.

I nearly lost a man getting it, don't forget. Lying in the sand, listening to an execution party all around him!'

'How is Williams?'

Harry waved away the question. 'Fine. He's got nine lives, that one.' He could see Robinson really wanted to know. 'Look, he had scans at St Thomas's this morning. In addition to the paramedic treatment he received at the hotel, courtesy of Tennyson. All fine. OK?'

'What did you make of Lance?'

'Good man,' said Harry, calming down a little. 'Thanks for connecting us. He helped a lot.'

'Look,' said Robinson. 'Here's what is happening. It's the usual SO22 bollock-crusher. On the one hand, you're the blue-eyed boy upstairs for having brought this much in, and so quickly.'

'But? I'm sensing one of your gold-plated "buts" here, Bill.'

'Yeah, you're not wrong. The problem is that good intelligence creates a feeding frenzy. You're a four-man unit, right?'

'Right.'

'So all the lumbering giants now want a taste of the action. The word from on high is: "Thanks very much, we'll take it from here."'

'Who's "we"?'

'I asked that very question. The answer was not very clear.'

'So they are shutting down a focused op with four officers making serious headway and dispersing all that on the basis of fuck-all logic around the big agencies. Right?'

'That's probably about the length of it, yeah.'

Harry stood up. 'You know, this is where we always go wrong. Coppers, I mean. Or our bosses. Whichever. Both. You get told, and I get told by you: "Go off and cut through all the red tape and do *proper* bloody police work while all the committee meetings trip over themselves." That's what we're here for.'

'Yup.'

'So that's what we do. And then they cut us off at the fucking knees.'

'True. All true.'

Harry pulled out his police ID from his jacket and slammed it on Robinson's desk. 'Well, how true do you think *that* is? I fucking well quit! Yeah, Bill. Adios. Arrivederci. Toodle-fucking-pip. Get somebody else to be your stooge from now on.' He turned and headed for the door.

Robinson stood and, like a giant awakened, roared as if he didn't give a damn who heard him. 'DCI Taylor! Stop right there, and start acting your age, not your shoe size! I won't tell you again!'

The sheer rarity of Bill Robinson raising his voice like a square-bashing sergeant major was enough to make Harry stop in his tracks. He looked around, put his hands in the air.

'What, Bill?' he said. 'You going to shoot me, are you? This is a free country, you know. A man can still quit his job if it becomes a total bloody farce. Sometimes, dignity requires it.'

'Sit down and shut up for a minute, will you?'

For the first time in this very awkward conversation, Harry thought he sensed the beginning of a return to something like business as usual. He complied with Robinson's request. Outside the office, it was as if time were standing still. Officers and support staff gawping, immobilised, utterly transfixed by this clash of the titans. As soon as they clocked Harry's scowl, they quickly returned to whatever it was they had been doing before.

'I'll have that Scotch now, Bill, if the offer still stands.'

'I'll have another myself.' Robinson poured out two healthy measures and handed Harry his glass. 'Cheers.'

'Cheers.' He took a sip. 'So, look, Bill. As a friend. What am I to do now?'

'You mean, personally? Let off some steam however you do that. Take a week's leave, if you're capable. And wait for the next op.'

'Can't do that. Got three officers on the fifth floor who are expecting to be scrambled to their next destination today. Can't just tell them: "Sorry, gang, your services are no longer required on this job. Stand by for the next op." Can I?'

'That's *exactly* what you tell them. You know as well as I do that at least half of being a boss is managing disappointment. They're professionals, aren't they? Davies and Williams are devoted to you. They'll go along with whatever you say. And Dr Walker will return to SCD4 with our gratitude and a glowing letter from you to her commander.'

'Carol. She's *good* that one, Bill. We should try and keep her. I mean, keep her as an SO22 officer full-time. I'll get Iris to teach her how to punch people and shoot villains. She'll pick it up in no time.'

Robinson frowned. But Harry could tell his boss was frowning at something other than what he had just said. After a few seconds, he unlocked the bottom drawer of his desk and pulled out a file – then tossed it across to Harry.

'Take a look at that. Tell me what you think.'

The file, marked *Top Secret – Eyes Only*, was slim, but its contents were extraordinary. Some black-and-white stills, a series of confidential encounter reports and what looked like shipping documentation. A few other items. But that was plenty. Harry took his time, giving it his full and undivided attention.

'This should be in your safe, Bill. You do know that, right?'

'Probably.'

'And this guy.' Harry held up one of the photographs. 'Ramirez?'

'Yes. Facial recognition pretty much matches that image

with the last known snap of Xavier Ramirez, which was snatched in Juarez after a cartel meeting three years ago. The guy who took the Juarez photo is dead now. When he was unmasked as an FBI snitch, Ramirez made him watch as they killed his family. Then they made him dig his own grave and buried him alive. These are vicious bastards, I'm telling you. And not just your common-or-garden vicious bastards.'

'Christ,' said Harry. The more recent picture showed a sleekly groomed man in a sharp business suit, dark sunglasses, surrounded by his security detail on a quayside somewhere. He was engrossed in a phone call but his expression was impassive, his sharp features giving no hint of his inner emotions. There was, Harry thought, a scar below his right eye, though the pixelation of the picture – clearly taken from a fair distance – was not so fine that he could tell for sure. So this was the man who had, according to Voldrev at least, pissed in Julian Smythe's soup.

'Where and when was this taken?' he said.

'Miami, last week. Unusual for Ramirez to cross the border but he does occasionally to see his mother, whom he moved out of Juarez some years ago. Also, he apparently has a mistress in Florida. Not to mention a bunch of lawyers and politicians on the payroll.'

'Bold move, though.'

'It backs up what Voldrev told you about Ramirez taking personal charge of this job. Unusual to the point of foolhardy for a man of his seniority, frankly. It shows strength, or weakness, or maybe both.'

'How do you mean?'

'He wants the right people to know that he's not a prisoner in his Mexican castle – that he can move freely, or almost freely. That's the strong bit. The weak bit is that he obviously doesn't trust his own people enough to make this big move for him. Which means he thinks there are traitors in their ranks.'

'Are there?'

'We don't know.'

'Do you think he might have the uranium?' said Harry.

'Do you?'

'I bloody hope not. He definitely wants it, I think we got that message loud and clear. And all this' – Harry gestured towards the file – 'makes me think he is getting more confident all of a sudden.'

'Or more desperate.'

'Yeah. I keep coming back to what Voldrev said about Julian Smythe. I mean, you can't take anything those two say about each other at face value.'

'True,' said Robinson. 'But you are one of the few people – maybe the only copper – who has spoken to both of them, at least recently. What do you reckon?'

'I think, as much as Voldrev loves spreading poison about Smythe, that he wasn't bullshitting about the tensions between the Ramirez cartel and his old enemy Julian. That tallies with what we know about Smythe. He hates disruption, anything that messes up the smooth surfaces of his operations. He's almost frictionless. I mean, that's why nobody has ever been able to nick him. A lot of what Voldrev said to me and Carol was purest horseshit, and he knew we knew that. But I think he was telling the truth about the beef between Julian and Xavier. I think it's in Voldrev's interests that we focus on that.'

'While Voldrev himself has the rock?'

Harry paused. His head was pounding as he thought of the deadly wheels within wheels. 'Possibly. Or maybe he's close to getting it. Either way, this shipment – and what it means for Smythe – is important.'

'I'll say. Christ. The scale of this . . . It gets worse and worse.'

'Who gave us the photos?' Harry said.

'Oh, a gift from our cousins at Langley. Sent it over to Vauxhall and the NSC – who quietly passed it on to me.'

'Helpful spooks? Wonders never cease.'

'They have their moments. What do you make of the other docs? I mean, apart from the happy snaps.'

'Well, the shipping manifest is for a vessel arriving in Marseilles next week. Nothing unusual at first sight. Cargo is supposedly – what? – food products, some construction materials, an unspecified container.'

'We checked that. It's a removal company, shifting somebody's gear from Florida to Europe. Legit.'

'Do we know who owns the ship? The *Argonauta*?'

'A shell company registered in the Bahamas, which sent up a red flag. It's being checked out. The working assumption is that the ultimate owners are either the Ramirez cartel, or attorneys acting on their behalf. As I say, that's only an assumption at the moment.'

'Anything unusual about the vessel's recent history?'

'Not at all. It's been in dry dock in Tampa for six months undergoing renovation and repairs. Before that, its movements were mostly in and around the Caribbean. Basic commodities, bits and pieces. It hasn't crossed the Atlantic in five years.'

'Well, it's interesting that it is coming over now, I suppose.'

'Not enough to hang our hat on in itself. I think we need to know more about the ship's ownership and a lot more about what's waiting for it in France. We know Ramirez has the skeleton of an operation there, but we'd struggle to roll up his distribution network because we don't know if he has one yet.'

Harry nodded. 'And even before you get to the question of how he sells the gear, I'm puzzled.'

'Go on.'

'Well, look. This is a cargo ship that will be coming from Florida, no recent history of transatlantic journeys. Even the sleepiest frog customs officer is going to give it the once over. Probably not just customs officers, either. If it's carrying a big shipment of coke, then Ramirez is taking a huge risk. I mean, especially now – but even before that. It doesn't make sense. He's gambling on nobody boarding the boat at any stage or taking a peek in the hold. Or getting a warrant to break open some boxes. It only takes one officer with a hard-on to strip a ship to its bare bones.' Harry shook his head. 'I know Xavier is supposed to be impulsive but this . . . this is daylight madness.'

Robinson brooded on this. 'Listen, Harry. How much paperwork have you still got to do on Crick? I mean for the file?'

'You're kidding, right?'

'I'm not.' He lowered his voice. 'What I mean is this. I have to log you off officially from the uranium op. That's out of my hands now – my protests noted and summarily overruled. There is a multinational task force already heading for Marseilles. Some of them got there yesterday. That ship will be stripped down to its last stainless steel bolt. But something tells me that, whatever they find, this isn't the whole of the story.'

'Not even close,' said Harry. 'Even if they find twenty tonnes of the white powdery stuff on board – and I'm still wondering whether they will – Ramirez will have something up his sleeve.'

'So, if I were to write you and the team up as ever-so-bloody-busy for the time being with your reports on your recent holidays and previous op . . . You know, being *very* thorough with the record-keeping? Well, could you be discreet? *Imaginative* with your use of the time? If you know what I'm saying?'

Harry allowed himself a smile. 'Discretion is my middle name, Mr Robinson. And I like to think I'm always imaginative. In my own way.'

'Good. Now I'm off for a slash. Don't touch that file while I'm out the room.' He stood up. 'Oh, by the way. Have you seen my fancy new printer? Just down by the desk here? Turns out you can use it to make copies, too. Very handy.'

Harry absorbed this, then said, 'Hey, Bill. One thing I can't really get my head round.'

'What's that?'

'What constitutes a win in this mess?'

'Simple: Get the rock back, with as few dead bodies possible.'

Robinson left and Harry acted quickly. He returned the file to its drawer, picked up his police ID, which was where he had flung it on his boss's desk, and headed out to tell the team that, as of today, they were going rogue, dark, off books, free to cause mayhem in a manner of their choosing.

# 22

They wore long sleeves and beanies. 'Don't stand out,' the boss had said. 'Hide the tats and keep your lumps covered. Don't want anyone seeing a couple of skinheads with swastikas on their arms. Sweet?'

They did as they were told, as was their only option. He was not a man to question, much less to argue with. The last to do so was his predecessor, a giant of a man acknowledged as the most powerful right-wing paramilitary in England. He had run the show for more than ten years, drawing up kill lists, building up the war chest with increasingly professional heists, targeting politicians, journalists and left-wing campaigners for intimidation, on- and offline.

Only a handful of his closest lieutenants knew his real name. To his many followers, digital supporters and active soldiers, he was only the Patriot. That was his title, his call sign, and his way of ensuring something close to anonymity. Among those in this circle of trust was a man ten years his junior, Jon (no surnames, ever), an ambitious and able commander in the field who, in the space of six months, had firebombed a mosque, forced a synagogue to triple its security and, from a speeding car, shot a British-Asian MP (the politician had survived, but the mission was counted a success in the movement: nobody was safe now from the armed struggle of the New English Front).

The Patriot commended Jon to all and looked upon him

as pupil and eventual successor in the great race war that they had been chosen by the ancient gods to fight. But Jon wasn't interested in waiting. He had come to believe that the Patriot was too cautious, insufficiently attuned to the call of history and the urgency of the Great Task. On the rare occasions that the high command met in person, Jon started to voice his frustrations: initially with respect, and then less so. They had quarrelled, the Patriot and Jon. Factions had begun to form, tempers frayed, arguments turned nasty.

One night, at a Valhalla gathering in a field in Essex, as a hardcore band screamed racist lyrics under the canopy of a circus tent, and those who weren't smashing against one other in the mosh pit, filled up on barbecue food and plastic cups of lager, the Patriot, flush with vodka and speed, had walked up to Jon and whispered something snide into his ear.

There were many accounts of what happened next, as is often the case with a sudden act of violence. What nobody doubted was that Jon had put the Patriot on the ground with astonishing power and speed, pounded him repeatedly, and then proceeded, without warning, to gouge out his eyes – either with a blade or his bare hands. As the Patriot screamed for help, Jon had yelled mocking obscenities into his blood-streaked face. And then, when he was breathless himself, still straddling his enemy's chest, he stopped and looked around. Nobody came to the Patriot's assistance or urged Jon to walk away so they could get what was left of him to hospital. The small crowd that had gathered was united in its terror and paralysis.

Jon nodded, as if confirming to himself what he had already suspected. He pulled a pistol out of his bomber jacket and shot the Patriot twice in the forehead. A few people probably screamed, but it was hard to tell with the noise of the band still drowning everything out.

Thereafter, it was as if the Patriot had scarcely existed. Jon ruled the movement with fury, impatience and violence. He told his growing army of young men that this was Year Zero, that the white man was being steadily and speedily replaced by other races, and that – unless drastic action were taken very soon – the war would be lost and England, real England, would be dead and gone before their children had grown up. Only in bloodshed could they prevail. Only as a true military force, with help from their brother movements overseas and friendly nationalist governments, could they see off this existential threat.

Which was why these two disciples followed his instructions to the letter. He knew about the rock. He wanted the rock. And he believed that he knew how to get it.

They both watched as Harry, Carol, Iris and John left the Yard, and texted command to let them know everything was falling into place.

# 23

'Is this our new office then, guv?' asked Iris. 'I mean, now we're on the run?'

Harry put the drinks down. Pints for him and John, a glass of wine for Carol, and – of course – a G&T for Sergeant Davies. Her second.

'Very funny. Witty as well as glamorous, is that the deal?'

'Absolutely,' she said. 'Don't you know it.'

*Yes,* Harry thought, admiring her slender figure and the elegance of her hands. *I do, actually. Oh Christ: do I fancy one of my own team?* He had no time for this, not right now. But the feeling was there all the same. It had been since the night at the Cube when she had turned up looking like a film star. For a moment, his confusion got the better of him.

'Well, sit down, guv,' said John. 'No point standing there looking like one o'clock half struck. Clue us in on the latest.'

Harry looked around at the other tables in the Lamb pub. Why had he brought them here? There was nothing to celebrate. If he was honest with himself, he just didn't want to be at the Yard. He wanted them to feel like a team, and act as one. But he wasn't sure that was going to be possible in the office. Walls had ears. He trusted Robinson, but not many others. And they had a lot to do.

He filled them in on the Marseilles connection and the plan to intercept and board the *Argonauta* just before it docked. Helicopters, a fleet of police vessels waiting just off the cove, snipers in place on the quayside, even a unit from his own regiment on standby in the port – dressed in civvies, of course – in case the Ramirez cartel travelled with their own private army. There must be hundreds involved in the operation, he said, and from at least four nations. He'd never heard of such a reception committee. Smythe would be delighted.

'Shouldn't we be down there?' said Iris.

Harry shook his head. 'We're barred from the scene. Officially. But – in any case – we wouldn't get within a mile of the boat. I can bullshit my way past most cordons but that quayside is going to be locked down like a military base. Which is basically what it will be for a few hours.'

'What do your instincts tell you?' asked John.

'Robinson confirmed about an hour ago that the ultimate owners of the ship are an Atlanta law firm that definitely has senior cartel figures on its books. Not Ramirez himself but his most important jefe, amongst others. I think it's safe to say that the boat is cartel-owned. Which means that *something* is about to happen.'

'So what do we do?' Carol asked. 'Watch the news and wait to hear how brilliant the DEA is?'

Harry smiled. 'Very funny, Two-Brains.' His phone pinged. 'Hold up, this'll probably be Robinson now.'

He looked at the message. What the hell was this? Made no sense at all. Undisclosed number. He frowned in silent exasperation.

'What is it, guv?' said Carol.

He showed her the text. It was a run of numbers: *53184624439*. What the hell did that mean? Who was fucking with him, and at this particular moment?

'That means fuck all to me,' he said. 'But then I'm more from the running, punching and arresting school of detective work. Does it mean anything to you?'

'Hold on a second.' She pulled out her laptop. 'What's the Wi-Fi in here?'

'Reg!' Harry shouted to the barman. 'Be a doll and give us the Wi-Fi, would you?'

Reg chucked him a card, which Harry handed to Carol. She typed in the password.

'What do you reckon?' he asked.

'Patience, boss,' she said, typing furiously, as focused as she could be in a busy pub.

'Is it cryptographic?' John asked. 'Any patterns observable?'

'Ok, well, first up . . . It's a prime number, which is interesting. Eleven digits. Could be a key. Let me run some cryptography algorithms on it.'

'Christ,' said Iris. 'This is getting a bit *Mission Impossible*, isn't it?'

'"Impossible" is the word,' said Carol. 'No, not coming up with anything yet. Shit, that's annoying. I'm putting it through an AI software now that will scour the whole internet for matches. You know, telephone numbers. Genetic codes. Tax records. Credit cards. Anything.'

'Who sent it to you, Harry?' said Iris. 'I mean, who do you think?'

He shrugged. 'I've no idea. If I had to bet my kidneys, I'd say it was probably Voldrev. He likes to play games, doesn't he? He's his own court jester. And he'll have made it his business to find out that we're off the case, you can bet. So it would be in character for him to throw me a morsel, if only to see if he gets a reaction. He talks about chess, poker – supposedly Smythe's great game, but I think he could be talking about himself.' Harry turned to Carol. 'Anything?'

'Hold on,' said Carol. 'Give me a chance . . . wait.' She frowned and shook her head. 'There's a guy at Cheltenham who owes me a favour. I'll send it to him, see if it makes any sense. Without context, of course.'

'All right, but on the down-low, Carol, OK?'

'Sure,' she said. 'That's sent. But let me try . . .'

A mood of frustration descended on the table, but Carol kept working, grouping and regrouping the digits.

After a while, the team sipping nervously at their drinks, Carol smacked her hand against the table. 'Christ. Of course! Why am I so thick? Yeah, I reckon I know what this is.'

'What?' said Harry.

'This is a geolocation. The number of digits . . . I *knew* it reminded me of something. Coordinates are basic training in geophysics.'

'Go on.'

'OK, been a while since I did this. But . . . you add in degrees, minutes and seconds. Then compass points. Which isn't too hard. And then you come up with . . . this.'

She held up her laptop, on which she had enlarged a line of script: *53°18'46"N    2°44'39"W.*

'Fucking hell, Carol,' John said. 'That's brilliant. Where is—?'

'Is it Marseilles?' Iris interrupted. 'Or nearby?'

'Not even close,' said Carol.

'Where then?' Harry said.

'Here,' said Carol, turning her screen round so the others could see.

'Weston Marsh Lock?' said Iris. 'What . . . and let's see, it's right by the Manchester Ship Canal. Connection to the Weaver river . . . Bit of a bloody wasteland, isn't it?'

John took his own laptop out of his backpack. 'Let's take a look.'

Iris continued, 'Well, this lock is for smaller boats. But the canal . . .'

Harry interrupted, '*That* can take almost any kind of vessel. I've been down there once. Close by, anyway. On a job, years ago. Straight from the Mersey Estuary into the heart of Manchester. About thirty or forty miles. You can get a tanker in there. Bloody hell, that's unexpected.'

'No Russian vessels, though,' said John. 'The canal was barred to all shipping "owned, controlled, chartered or operated by any person connected with Russia" on twenty-eighth of February 2022.'

'Four days after the invasion,' said Harry. 'Yes, makes sense. Rules out Voldrev himself, I suppose. Or at least any vessel associated with him. Which isn't quite the same thing, come to think of it.'

'Is that where the *Argonauta* is really going, then?' said Carol. 'Is this Voldrev's way of tipping us off?'

'Could be, but I'd be surprised,' he said. 'I mean, somebody's clearly tipping us off to something connected with all that. But the *Argonauta* will be under satellite surveillance. If it hangs a left and heads for Manchester, the DEA, the world and its wife will know immediately. There's no real purpose in changing course.' He looked at John's screen and the dismal scene of patchy grass, a canal lock and the expanse of water beyond it under a heavy Northern sky. 'I think the message is: While your mates are in Marseilles, you should be *there*.'

'No offence, Carol,' John piped up, 'but doesn't it seem a bit – well, easy, even for our resident genius? Would Voldrev just send us the coordinates as readily as that? Are we being led into a trap?'

'Maybe,' Harry said. 'Ease of acquisition is always suspect, you're right. Let's do some more digging first, ensure we've not missed something. But I think we have to follow this up. It's a risk, but so is doing nothing. Tell you what,' he said,

'Iris, get on to the port authorities and the harbour master. Get a list of all vessels authorised to travel down the main canal in the next ten days. Then we can cross-reference and see what we come up with.'

'On it,' she replied.

'What do you think it means?' Carol said.

'All I know is that someone wants us there. Whether they're trying to help – well, that remains to be seen, doesn't it?' He stood up.

'Where are you going?' said John.

He smiled. 'To get some backup. Old-school backup.'

# 24

Otis Walker could not settle. Normally, at this time of the evening he would be reading a book, or watching *Newsnight*, or sitting in his old leather armchair, petting Daisy, the gentle Burmese cat that had been so adored by his late wife and outlived her by – what now? – seven years. But he found himself pacing the drawing room, his mind paralysed by some deep, unspecific sense of apprehension.

As Otis had long known, there was a cost that came with the sort of brainpower that had been bestowed upon him. Yes, it had been the engine of his remarkable career and his eminence as a scientist. It had enabled him to publish, to teach, to engage in deep research at the very best facilities, to travel and to see what the world had to offer. But his cerebral firepower was also a curse. He never really stopped thinking. Even his dreams were troubled by the capacity of his mind to see six moves ahead; and often, as he slept, his intellect and his emotions would wrestle in the most unsettling way, filling him with fears for the future and anxiety about past failure.

What was agitating him so much? He knew full well. It was the new life that his daughter had embraced and the world into which she had been catapulted by her secondment to SO22. In her forensic role, she had, at least, still primarily been a scientist; working in the labs, assessing evidence and offering opinions to her senior police colleagues about the meaning of what they had found – or feared that they might find. She was their guide to the rarefied world of physics, organic chemistry, quantum mechanics, biological engineering, and the terrible forces they might unleash.

But her work now was different. Suddenly, she was in a unit of frontline specialists, specifically tasked with the hardest and deadliest missions; called upon when routine police work was not enough and a more aggressive approach was needed. Not only did SO22 face gunfire, they ran towards it.

No, he must stop this destructive thought spiral. It would do nobody any good. Not him, not Carol. He knew that she had detected the malaise in his voice whenever they had spoken on the phone in recent weeks about her ambition to find fresh challenges in her work. That she was concerned that he was concerned: especially since her mother Betsy's death, she had been a protective child, always solicitous about his wellbeing and peace of mind. It embarrassed him that his adult daughter, busy with such important work, should be devoting any bandwidth to his irrational worries.

But were they irrational?

Enough. He would call it a night and go to bed. He ran the cold tap in the kitchen, filled a glass with water and added some ice. Put an offprint article from the *Journal of Synchrotron Radiation* that a colleague in Mumbai wanted him to read back in his briefcase. Then he turned off the lights downstairs and headed up. Yes, he would try one of those sleep apps that Carol kept recommending to him and seek some respite from his overactive mind. In T-shirt and sweatpants, he checked himself out in the mirror. Yes, he was still in reasonable shape. No significant health worries and still running two miles every morning at 5 a.m. *There are a few laps left in these bones*, he thought to himself.

The app was a little saccharine for his taste – '*Find the*

*inner space at the centre of the body that reminds you of sunshine and a happy beach*' – but the sound in his earbuds of the voice and birdsong and of waves lapping against a shore was undoubtedly soothing. He drifted off on a tide of reassurance and New Age banality, pleasantly and with much less effort than he had feared.

It was 3 a.m. The first thing he noticed when he was startled by his phone ringing was the time on his digital alarm clock. Red digits warning him that it was the very time of night when, supposedly, people are mostly likely to die. Who could be calling him at this hour?

Still half-asleep, Otis accepted the call – and was jolted into full consciousness by what he heard.

'Walker. Say nothing.' The voice was disguised, unnaturally low and mechanical. 'We have your girl. And we know you know where the ore is. If you hand it over, she lives. If you don't, she dies. Stand by for further instructions.'

Otis started to speak, but the call had ended. He called Carol's number. Straight to answerphone. Again. Same result. He tried five more times – the deepest panic now rising within him.

Could this possibly be so? Was this a waking nightmare? Did anyone *seriously* believe that he himself had access to a cache of uranium – of whose possible existence he only knew because he had signed the Official Secrets Act years ago and had often been entrusted with such information by men like Harry Taylor – and by men much more senior? Did the cyborg-voiced individual at the other end of the line really think that he would be able to locate it? It was madness.

He tried to clear his head. *No, whatever else it is, it isn't madness.* These people – was it people? Or just a lone wolf? – understood enough about parental love to know that he would do anything, *anything*, to ensure his daughter's safety. That he had connections all the way up to Downing Street, and across the ocean to the American NSA, and that he would lean on anyone he could, use any ploy, to get her back. That the one thing Otis Walker treasured more than his professional integrity was Carol. Yes, they had spotted his vulnerability all right, and they were exploiting it well.

She had left him emergency numbers before she headed off to Barbados, knowing that he would not need them but that it would make him less fretful if he had them. *Well, you were wrong, darling*, he thought. *I* do *need them now.*

An hour later, the two men were sitting in Otis's kitchen, drinking coffee. Harry had stationed an additional trio of plain-clothes officers outside the house and a squad car across the road to maintain surveillance on the house and its vicinity. This was a next-level attack on SO22 and he was taking no chances. John was on his way.

'Look,' he said. 'I'm very sorry, Otis. I really am. I know how you must feel – well, I think I do. Don't have kids myself but I know enough from those that do to understand how terrible this must be.'

'I feel responsible,' said Otis. 'I should never have let her leave university life.'

Harry shook his head. 'It absolutely isn't your fault. First of all, Carol chooses her own path. I've learned that about her already and I admire that quality. Second: if anyone is to blame for involving her in all this, it's me. And I'm going to get her back for you. Personally.'

'Who do you think it is?'

'I don't know. There are so many groups and lone operators who are chasing this bloody rock. And they all think *we* know more than we actually do. So, they've taken Carol as if we had the stuff stashed in a deep bunker underneath the Yard. Either that, or they're completely stupid. Which I doubt. Or – third possibility – they're just covering all the bases to find it. This stopped being a case of lost property a long time ago. It's a *race*. And there seem to be a lot of bloody competitors for the prize.'

Otis shook his head. 'So we know *nothing?*'

'Not yet. But we will soon. He told you that explicitly. Whoever these muppets are, they'll reveal themselves quickly. We'll get your girl back.'

But how? How, Harry Taylor wondered, would he ensure the safety of Carol Walker? Everything was connected, he was sure of that. But he couldn't see the whole board yet, couldn't tell how all the elements of the game were connected, or who was moving where, or why.

What he did know was that he was going to fix this himself. On the way to Otis's house in Islington, he had woken up Robinson to brief him. His boss had firmly instructed him to involve MO7, the kidnap squad, at once.

'Not a chance,' said Harry. 'I reckon we have twelve hours at most to save Carol. Absolute tops. This is a direct attack on SO22, and SO22 has to fix it. Our way. If we bring in other units and flood the zone with officers, she's dead. She might be dead already, is the honest truth. We don't have time, Bill. And, at this point, we don't know who to trust.'

Robinson had protested, but Harry could tell that he was just doing so for the sake of good form. Of all the officers he had ever known, Bill Robinson would understand that this was now, in every sense, a family affair. He also knew that he had a strictly limited window of time in which to get Carol back – after which even Robinson would be professionally obliged to call in other sections of the Met and to notify Five.

The doorbell rang. It was John, visibly frantic. A good man, John. He had only known Carol a few days, but a comrade officer was a comrade officer. Like Harry, he would not stand for this and would do just about anything to ensure her safety.

He expressed his sympathy to Otis and declined the offer of a coffee.

'What's next?' he said. 'I saw you've got some guys outside.'

'Yeah,' said Harry. 'I don't want any foul-ups. We're going to keep Professor Walker safe and we're going to get Carol back. And that's all there is to it.'

'Excuse me,' said Otis. 'I need to splash some water on my face.' He headed upstairs to the bathroom.

John lowered his voice. 'This is really fucked-up, boss. When was a serving police officer ever abducted?'

Harry leant on the kitchen counter. 'In this country? Never, to my knowledge. There have been cops in hostage situations. There was that French guy who died in 2018, remember him?'

John did indeed. 'Do you think this is linked to the Manchester tip-off?' he said.

'I really don't know yet. I mean, yes, in the sense that it's all linked, everything joins up somehow. But I keep thinking about the people in play: Ramirez, Smythe, Voldrev. Are they capable of lifting a British police officer and holding her to ransom? Yes, they are. But would they? I'm not so sure. This feels more like the kind of thing a jihadi group might do. And we know they have been looking for nuclear material for decades. It's possible. But this is only me speculating.'

'Do we know when Carol was last seen?'

'Yes,' Harry said. 'A neighbour met her on the way into her flat in Greenwich earlier tonight – around ten, but he couldn't be sure. That was the last time she logged into the database too – ten fifteen. After that . . . nothing.'

'Any sign of breaking and entering at her flat?'

'No. Which means she must have been tricked into leaving

home later on. Or gone out to get a pint of milk from the corner shop. God knows. But there's no CCTV on her street, and her car is still parked outside. No incoming calls or relevant emails either.'

'Doesn't make sense. She's pretty sharp, Carol. Well, obviously.'

'If I had to guess, I think this crew are playing the Walker family in a very horrible way. I wouldn't be surprised at all if the person or persons who took her claimed to her that they had her dad too. Mind games. You can imagine. A voice at the door, a warning. She'd have gone with them if she'd thought Otis was in danger.'

'And now she's the one in danger,' said John.

'Yeah. We can't be having this. This goes beyond normal villainy. We *can't* set a precedent where it's OK to kidnap coppers. So, listen, John. We have to wire up Otis's phone and computers immediately for trace. You can do all that, right? Good. And we need to take decisive action, very fast. Gloves off. Whatever else happens in this case, I am *not* losing an officer.'

'Absolutely,' said John, his fist in his palm. 'Abso-fucking-lutely.'

Back inside, they met Otis in the hallway. As the morning light began to fill the room, Harry could see the worry etched in his face. He looked suddenly older, frailer.

'All right,' said John. 'I need to do a few bits and pieces with your phone and computers, Otis, so we can trace any communications. They'll know we're trying and will probably ring off before we can get a lead. But it's worth having a go.'

Otis appeared to be only half listening. 'Sorry? Oh. Yes. Yes. Here's my phone. And I only have one computer at home. It's in the study. Password is "Heisenberg1901".' Then, quietly: 'It was the year of his birth, you see.'

'Sure thing,' said John. 'Thanks, Professor. Won't take a moment.' He opened the army medic bag he always carried on a job, which was full of the equipment he would need.

Harry drew out his own phone to check in with Robinson when Otis's phone rang.

John reached for the handset but Harry took it from him.

'Hello. This is Detective Chief Inspector Harry Taylor. I'm answering Professor Otis Walker's phone.' He put it on speaker.

It was the cyber-voice that Otis had described. 'In the name of the Fourteen Words: hand over what we want, or she dies.'

'I want proof of life. Put Inspector Carol Walker on the line. Now.'

'What you want is irrelevant! Today, one p.m. sharp. Roscommon Way. Canvey Island. You'll see us. Just you, Taylor. Nobody else. Not another single soul. Park your vehicle on the road after the roundabout. If you bring anyone else, she dies. If you play any tricks, she dies. You have one chance to keep your officer alive, Taylor. Don't blow it.'

The call ended.

Otis could barely speak. 'The . . . the Fourteen Words . . . What is that?'

'It means we're not dealing with jihadis. Or Mexican *sicarios.*'

'What, then?'

John read out from his phone. 'The Fourteen Words are: "We must secure the existence of our people and a future for white children." Bastards.'

Harry nodded. 'It means that we have neo-Nazis in play now. Far-right militias.' He thought for a moment. 'Well, we knew their ambitions were growing, especially after the January 6 palaver in America. They want some muscle, too. This is them trying to get it.'

'But *nukes*, boss?' said John.

'Remember, Carol's main point from the beginning has always been that the technology required to rig up a device is not *that* complex. Do I believe that a bunch of skinheads know how to handle uranium-235? I bloody well don't. But might they be in partnership with people of like mind who *do*? Ten years ago, I'd never have credited it. I'd have laughed it out of court. Now, I can just about imagine it. They're all linked up, these groups.'

'DCI Taylor,' Otis said. 'Harry. What will you do?'

'Simple. I'm going to Canvey Island, and I'm going to bring Carol back to you this afternoon. That's what's going to happen.'

'How much backup do you want?' said John. 'Do you want me to drive you. I can—'

'No backup. And you stay here with Professor Walker and handle any further calls. No, no arguments, John. This isn't a day to take risks. You heard what they said. If they see one other copper, let alone a SWAT team and a couple of helos, Carol doesn't stand a chance. Nope. This is just for me.' He headed for the door. 'Try not to worry, Otis, as much as that's possible. And stay in touch, both of you.'

Then he left.

## 25

*Oh Christ, Dad. I'm sorry.* Carol could hardly move, and it was hard to breathe under the hood. She felt fear in a way that she had never experienced before: nothing close. This was what it felt like when death was in the next room. When you could feel death's cold breath on your shoulder.

*I'm sorry, Dad.* That was what Carol Walker wanted to say.

Where was she? Hard to tell. She had been hooded, cuffed and thrown into the back of a van by men in masks before she could really register what was happening. After shouting at the top of her lungs that she was a serving police officer, and they would do well to let her go if they wanted to avoid years in prison, she realised that she was wasting precious energy. Nobody spoke to her. All she could hear was the engine and the sound of passing vehicles.

Her mind wandered backwards in time. To a particular conversation.

How could she forget that morning? Their surroundings could not have been more perfect: close to the cathedral, al fresco breakfast at the hotel, sunshine soothed by a pleasant breeze. Still, she had been nervous.

Milan was one of her father's favourite cities, and so he was delighted when she told him that their first conference as fellow attendees would be in the Lombardy capital. It was one of the egghead jamborees that he claimed not to like – 'Such an interruption to my work!' – but all too clearly relished. He loved seeing his colleagues from around the world, he loved the gossip and chatter of lab-based academia, he loved spotting the stars of the future at the plenaries and break-out sessions. One of those stars, he hadn't been shy to point out, was his daughter.

Otis, of course, was one of the keynote speakers, delivering a paper entitled: 'Practical Extraction of Plutonium-239: Methodologies, Risks, Opportunities.' Never one for a snappy title, her dad. Carol, meanwhile, was merely a regular delegate, a postdoctoral fellow in experimental physics at Trinity College, Cambridge, picked out because of her exceptional promise and the growing assumption that she was not only a chip off the old block but already showing signs of being a pretty impressive block in her own right.

Her father's lecture was set for the following morning in the main auditorium and, she knew, had been finished almost a month before: emailed confidentially to a few very senior and trusted friends for peer review. So eminent was Otis Walker in his field, so eagerly were his researches and teachings awaited that everything he said had to be perfect first time around. No state-of-play disclosures of half-finished work. All his significant lectures found their way on to YouTube, sometimes within minutes of his leaving the lectern. The geekier corners of social media would be buzzing with reports and reaction even as he was speaking. The pressure was immense. But he seemed to thrive in the spotlight. Though he had chosen a notionally solitary path in life – a life in laboratories, libraries, facing the blankness of the white-board – he did love to ham it up.

This was no surprise to his daughter, who knew his playful, mischievous side, and loved him for it. But it still shocked some of those who had never seen him on stage before: when he performed, he performed. 'The search for the truth,' he liked to say, 'is a drama. You have to keep people's attention if you want them to follow you down the road – even if it is a very technical road.'

And now, as they sipped their espressos, she could see how contented he was. Still a strikingly handsome man in his early sixties: tall, strong-featured, greying at the temples but still visibly athletic. A smile that could light up a room when he walked in, and a presence that gave him a natural command. And here they were, at last: the two of them, venerated grandee of his discipline, and his brilliant daughter, already climbing the greasy pole of academia, making a name for herself. Scientists are meant to be ruthlessly objective, and her father could, it was true, disappear for hours into zones of coldness and deep thought as he tried to excavate the deepest secrets of the physical universe. And – from time to time – brooded upon the practical, even deadly uses to which those secrets might be put. But Carol knew how emotional a man he was, too. How loving he was, how proud of her achievements and her steady passage out of his shadow and into a career of independent excellence. 'You'll be better than me, Caro,' he would say. 'Wait and see! I'm just the Nokia Walker – you're the iPhone!'

And, yes, she could see why he might think that. She had left school at fifteen with four A* A-levels, gone straight to Cambridge to read natural sciences and graduated with first-class honours all the way through, completing her doctorate in only two years, landing a postdoctoral fellowship at Trinity; prizes, citations, her name on the lips of talent-spotters at universities around the world looking for the young scientists who would advance the frontiers of knowledge in the coming decades.

Everyone assumed that he had driven her relentlessly towards her achievements, like a ferocious sports father yelling from the stands. But the truth was that Otis Walker really *was* smart. He had spotted his only child's ferocious ambition early on – and left her to it. No plan, no playbook, no pressure. When she sought his advice, which she often did, he was happy to oblige. But she was left to make her own decisions. That, she had reflected, was a measure of her father's wisdom.

Of course she knew he wanted her to follow in his footsteps, to take the family firm forwards. He wanted her at his side, too, as he grew older, to relieve the solitude of his vocation and keep him up to date with their fast-moving field. But – in his hyperintelligent way – he had understood that the worst possible parental strategy when raising a prodigy was to tell her what to do. They had ended up, exactly as he had hoped, in this very place: colleagues, albeit at different levels in the hierarchy, enjoying each other's fellowship and conversation at a distinguished conference in a beautiful Italian city.

So how could she break the news without hurting him? Carol had considered waiting until after his lecture. But that, she decided, would be cruel. It would ruin the whole day for him: ruin the sense of adrenaline-soaked achievement he always felt when he had delivered an important lecture. There would, she was sure, be a buzz around the conference centre after he had spoken, and much animated discussion about the implications of what he had said. In the evening, there would be a small dinner in his honour, hosted by friends and collaborators, and the talk would carry on long into the night: plenty of intellectual jousting and jokes and pitchers of bonarda, boisterous and collegiate, exactly the sort of social occasion he most enjoyed. No: she didn't want to ruin all that. She needed to get the bad news over with now.

'Dad,' she said.

He looked up distractedly from his *Financial Times* and over his spectacles before turning back to an article on page two. 'Yes?'

'I need to discuss something with you.'

'Sure.' Still focusing on the page.

'It's important.'

'OK.' Otis theatrically folded up his paper and smiled. 'You have my full attention, love.'

'Good.' She drained her cup, ordered two more for them from the waiter. 'This is difficult—'

'Oh, God,' said Otis. 'It's not you and Richard again, is it? Because—'

'No, no. I haven't spoken to Richard in months. He's at Columbia now – engaged, I think.'

'Good. Somebody else's problem now. That boy was *not* good enough for you.'

'Dad, can we not audit my romantic history again? Please?'

'Of course. I'll shut up.'

'OK. Well. Look. You know we were discussing what I might do after my two years at Trinity ends. Whether to apply for a longer-term gig in Cambridge, or go for MIT?'

'Yes, of course. You were inclining towards MIT when we last spoke about it. Having second thoughts?'

She drew breath, hunched a little. 'Well, not so much second thoughts as – ah, Christ, this isn't easy – more like *third* thoughts.'

Otis was now scrutinising her with a mixture of concern and mild irritation. She knew that look very well. 'Well now, you're just talking in riddles, child. Which is, frankly, not your style. Nor, more importantly, is it mine.'

She laughed. 'No. That's certainly true. Fair point. So let me come to the point. You see, I'm thinking of leaving academia.'

Her father frowned. 'What, on a secondment? Did you get offered big money to do research for a couple of years? Private sector? A cash dash?'

'No. Quite the opposite, really.'

'Well, what then? You're starting to worry me, Carol.' He only used her full first name when he was genuinely anxious.

'I've had an offer from SCD4. Do you know who they are?'

'Spies?'

Again, he could always make her laugh. 'No! It's a specialist forensics section. At the Met.'

Very rarely was Professor Otis Walker lost for words. But this was one of those moments. He pursed his lips as if to whistle and then opened his mouth as if to speak. But no words came out. Until, after what seemed a long time, they did.

'Wow.' Pause. 'The *police*.'

What, she wondered, did that word really mean to her father? His parents were part of the Windrush generation, immigrating from St Lucia in 1958 when little Otis was only five. They hoped for a better future for their son and worked crazy hours to see that he got one. Elsa had managed to hold down three jobs, while her husband, Trevor, drove a cab ten or twelve hours a day, six days a week. Otis went to church school and then received full scholarships to a prep school and City of London. Academically, he had flown – 'like a bird' her nanna used to say. Within weeks of arriving at university – Imperial College, London – he had known he would never return to civilian life. His parents, through their determination and sweat, had made it possible for him to reach for the stars in the world of pure intellect.

Still, it wasn't all easy, not by a long chalk. There was plenty of racism where they lived in Shepherds Bush, some of it explicit, much of it unspoken, but still palpable. Elsa knew that there were some homes where her cleaning services were not welcome. Trevor could tell that his skin colour made some passengers ill at ease, and that his attempts to strike up cheerful conversation could make a few even more twitchy. Otis sensed some of this at school, often the only Afro-Caribbean boy in a class of affluent white kids. He was rarely bullied – his build saw to that – but he often experienced what he later discovered was the feeling of being 'othered': an 'out', not an 'in'.

Then, from adolescence, as a tall young Black man on the streets of London, he experienced this in a rather sharper form: being stopped by the police for no reason. Called racist names. Searched only minutes after he had left the library, pinned to a wall with a beat copper yelling in his ear, asking where he was hiding 'the ganja'. What ganja? He was in his O level year, studying hard. And this was what they saw? A drug dealer? More than once, he had been picked up, taken to the local nick and questioned about random car thefts and burglaries. Of course, he knew nothing. Why did they bother? Force of habit, or just bigotry? Or a bit of both?

Everywhere, he read that London in the sixties was a swinging city, the centre of 'new freedoms' and 'cultural revolution'. But not for everyone, it seemed. The bands on *Top of the Pops* and *Ready Steady Go!* were mostly white. When the Beatles hailed Jimi Hendrix as a genius, they didn't mention that he was simply reclaiming the music that had been pioneered by Black musicians in the Mississippi Delta and then adapted by Elvis and white groups from Britain as chart fodder. Alongside his school books, Otis hoovered up the writings of Malcolm X, Martin Luther King Jr, Bayard Rustin, and other civil-rights authors.

Much later, he made sure that his daughter knew those

writers, too. He wasn't much given to political declarations, or sociology, but she knew that, for all his success and the public prominence he had achieved, there had been adversity along the way. The words 'systemic racism' would never pass Otis Walker's lips. He hated what he regarded as jargon. But – even if he didn't speak of it – he knew all about it. So what must he think of his daughter signing up to the police service?

'Say something, Dad,' Carol said. 'Can't bear you being silent like this.'

He looked down at his coffee and sighed. 'I'm surprised. That's all.'

'Look,' she said. 'I get it. Me being a copper. It must seem – odd. Like, oh, I don't know—'

'You think I see it as treachery?'

'Well. Perhaps. Maybe. A bit.'

He smiled faintly and sat back. 'Come on. Give me some credit. You know about what it was like when I grew up. How it still is, a lot of the time. But you also know that I've probably helped UK law enforcement agencies more than any British physicist now living. Right?'

'Yes. Yes, I guess.'

'I mean, who do you think they came to when they were convinced that Saddam had nukes? Hmm? When they were trying to make two and two make four and kept coming up with five?'

'You. Yes, you, of course.'

'Right. I told them that they were wrong, that Iraq really didn't have yellowcake or any other enriched material. It was a wild goose chase. I *told* them.' He paused. 'Much good it did.'

'Hardly your fault.'

'Well, that's for others to judge. Point is, I understood long ago that I live a double life. On the one hand, as a Black man, I have had experiences that make me wary of authority. That bridles when I see a police uniform. That's part of me. I still embrace it. But – on the other – I've developed an expertise and a reputation which makes me occasionally useful to society. They *need* me.'

'They do, Dad. And you *have* been useful to society. Lots.'

'And – now you mention it – I have taken calls from your SCD4 myself, or whatever they've called that unit over the years. From time to time. When they think about certain numbers. Like, for instance, eleven.'

'Why eleven?'

'That's the number of US nuclear devices that are believed to have gone missing. My favourite was the bomber in 1958 that was damaged and was ordered to drop its payload into the Atlantic. It's never been recovered! Imagine! Just sitting at the bottom of the ocean, somewhere off Savannah, Georgia.'

'Point taken. I didn't know you'd dealt directly with the Yard.'

'For sure. Who else? Well, of course.' He chuckled. 'I've answered my own question, haven't I?'

She blushed. 'So if it's not the police in principle . . . I mean, if that's not what bugs you, why are you disheartened? I can tell you are, don't deny it.'

'Well, it's a surprise. Grant me that.'

'Yes. To me, as well. I didn't know that the idea would appeal to me until they approached me. And then, as soon as they described the work, it really did.'

'Don't think I don't get that,' he said. 'The life of the mind is costly. And you're a young person, full of life – a bit of *vita activa* appeals to you, of course. Breaking down a few doors, stopping the bad guys.'

'The *worst* guys. The jihadis, the far right, drug barons,

nationalist movements, God knows who else. Cults every-where. It's a digital world now, Dad. They hide in the shadows. They're not armies you can see – they're networks, all around us.'

'And you want to help stop them?'

'Yes. Well – if I can. I mean, it's a change of pace from long hours at the Cavendish, working on a quantum computer.'

'It certainly is. But I don't think you'll find it that hard to adjust.'

It was Carol's turn to frown now. 'So, if that's the case . . . I'm not sure I understand—'

'Why I'm not turning cartwheels? Listen. When have I ever stood in your way, or questioned your sense of your own destiny?'

She put her hand on his. 'Never, Dad. Not once. And don't think I'm not grateful. Because I am.'

'No, I don't mind you changing lanes. It often happens, especially now as people are living longer lives. I think my kind of career – signed up at twenty-one, the same thing until retirement – will be a thing of the past soon enough.'

'So . . .'

'So this new life you're thinking of. It's not that I think you'll be *wasting* an academic career. It's that you'll never look back.'

'What do you mean? If it doesn't work out, I'm not so proud that I won't come back with my tail between my legs and try to wheedle my way back into some campus or other. I accept the risk of failure. This would be a real step into the unknown.'

'Yes, but everything is, in the end. When I got my first chair, nobody seemed surprised – except me! *Professor* Walker. That *meant* something. Still does. I had a responsibility. I didn't know if I was ready or up to it . . . We all have these doubts, Caro. It's when they stop that you have to start worrying.'

'I agree, Dad. But I still can't work out what's really worrying you.'

He shifted his chair round the table so he could be closer to her and speak to her more seriously. 'Listen, Caro. If you take this job, you'll do what you always do. You'll give it your all. And that means, as sure as night follows day, you'll end up in *danger*.'

'Oh, Dad, really?. . . The offer is a crash course in police training and then a senior forensic role at the Yard. NBC war-gaming. Ops planning. Systems analysis. Not field work at all. I'd be swapping the lab for an office and – well, another kind of lab. And no high table or common room. Just a ropey canteen.'

'Don't kid yourself, Carol. You'll start that way, sure. But you'll *never* settle for less than the maximum on offer. It's in your nature. You can't fight it.'

'Well,' she said, with a shrug, 'even if that's true, and I'm not sure it is, the maximum on offer is inter-agency radiological work. I mean, it's hardly *Grand Theft Auto*, is it? I won't be going into nests of criminals, all guns blazing. Let's get real. Plus, the money is shit.'

He waved this away. 'Not at first. But the day will come – it really will – when the bad men *do* get hold of something that could harm a lot of people and you will find a way of being on the front line. I know you. You just will.'

She looked up in disbelief. 'Oh, *come on*, Dad. Do you really think I have it in me to do something so rash? I'm a *scientist*. I don't want to be in the line of fire or be a hero. I don't have it in me.'

'You're wrong.'

'No, *you're* wrong.'

'I really hope I am.' Otis Walker looked up at the Milanese skyline with rueful clarity. 'But I know I'm not.'

Now, four and a half years later, she was struggling for air in a stinking hood, wondering whether she would see another morning, whether this would be the night that she died. All the terrors coursing through her, all at once.

*I'm sorry, Dad. You were right.*

# 26

A few hours' kip and then off to the meet. But it never worked like that, did it? Harry lay awake, totally awake, wondering irritably why he had bothered to go home at all. Well, a shower had done him no harm. And some fresh clothes. But shut-eye was out of the question. His head and heart were pounding, as they always did before an op. This was like Helmand, only, this time, he was barely leaving London to confront the monsters.

They were everywhere, weren't they? That was a safe conclusion, after all these years. The world needed men like Harry to stay alive long enough to stop the kind of men who crossed the line like this; who thought, in ever greater numbers, that this was the way to get what they wanted.

Well, *fuck that*. Fuck them all. Fuck Voldrev, Smythe, Ramirez, and now this demented Hitler tribute act who seemed to think they could mess with his team and get away with it. Deep inside, he felt what one of his best commanding officers in the regiment had called the 'gear-change': the moment when an op entered your bones, your blood, your viscera. Much more than taking it personally, it became your whole reason for existing.

Harry felt better once he was back in the car, on his way, checking the clock more often than he needed to, keeping a lid on his anger as best he could and preparing himself for what he knew would be a hugely dangerous encounter. People like Voldrev, they were more lethal in theory, but they also played by a set of rules that you just got used to over the years. He knew that he and Carol had never been in serious peril when they were on the island. Any more than Smythe was ever going to pop a cap in his head when he had visited him in Eaton Square. It didn't work like that with such men. They had a certain way of doing things which didn't make them predictable, exactly. It just meant that they took pride in scalping their enemies with a bit of subtlety and (almost always) a bit of distance. Face to face was often the safest place to be with the worst villains.

But who knew what to expect from a bunch of skinheads with delusions of grandeur, who seemed to think that they were going to get their hands on a tidy cache of enriched uranium? Because, Harry already knew, they *did* think that. This was a big play by previously small-time players. And that made it a crapshoot – and all the more dangerous. Voldrev, Smythe, Ramirez, they had nothing to prove to a DCI from the Yard. Their ambitions spread across continents, through time zones. Harry was just the next guy in the way.

But with these little Adolfs? Well, the whole *point* for them was to prove themselves. The whole wretched business was a show of virility – to make the world believe that they were a force to be reckoned with and a force to be feared. If that meant killing him and Carol, they wouldn't hesitate. That, he knew with certainty, was what he was dealing with today.

He stopped off at a Co-op and bought himself a sandwich, an apple, some biscuits and a big bottle of water. In the intensity of recent days, he had noticed that he was forgetting meals, which, when added to the inevitable sleep deprivation and oversupply of adrenaline, increased the risk of poor decision-making. And he couldn't afford a single bad decision. Not now. Not today.

He'd been in hostage situations before; in the regiment rather than during his years as a cop. A good third of the covert operations that had occupied his unit had involved springing the victims of abduction from some God-forsaken cellar, or jungle stockade, or (on one occasion) a fortress in an icefield. The job was the job, but it was always that much harder when the hostage was a comrade-in-arms; which was more often the case than the public knew. He had been involved in half a dozen rescue missions to free UK military personnel – including men from the SAS itself. Mostly, he and his team had succeeded. But not always. He could still hear the screams of a captured combat signaller in a Bolivian swampland as his drug-lord captors cut him to pieces, the exfiltration team having arrived two minutes too late. Two minutes was an age in these situations. Two minutes was the difference between life and death. He was not going to make any mistakes on this mission.

He opened the glove compartment and pulled out his service pistol. How long was it since he had fired the SIG Sauer P226 in the field rather than on a range? Many years. More than he cared to think about, really. How many men had he killed with this particular weapon? Twelve that he knew of for certain, all at close quarters. Probably more. It was not something he chose to dwell upon.

Would he need it today? Yes. He would need it in case the brutes that had taken Carol were not serious about releasing her. But then . . . No. Obviously they would frisk him when he arrived. He could not be carrying a weapon, could he? Damn. Fuck it all. He replaced the pistol and closed the compartment.

He sped through Poplar, following the signs to Barking and Dagenham. Classic British nationalist terrain, naturally. This outfit was not straying far from its roots, clearly. A quick database check by John listed a dozen or so far-right groups believed by MI5 and the Met's Counter Terrorist Command to be 'actively engaged' in training, arming and preparing recruits to commit acts of violence. All interconnected, some having recently risen from the dead – the Blood and Soil Army, for instance, thought to be long disbanded had reappeared on the spooks' radar in the past year. The New English Front, of course. The British Aryan Brotherhood, still beating up innocent people and spreading hate. A crew that called themselves Thor's Hammer . . . Christ, how could people be so embarrassingly stupid, as well as so vile?

But that, he knew, was all part of the neo-Nazi mindfuck. These bastards *wanted* to be underestimated by people like Harry, dismissed as thugs and blundering pissheads. Plenty of them still were. But this wasn't the 1980s. The new breed of paramilitary nationalist was different: in touch with similar movements all over the world, emboldened by white nativist success in mainstream politics, more focused and more disciplined. They truly believed that their race was at risk of 'replacement' and that a great ethnic war was at hand. The fact that they were deranged only made them more dangerous. Most of them didn't care whether they ended up in prison (though they minded about the race of their cellmates) or even if they were sent to Valhalla after a glorious death in battle. They believed in their insane cause. And their numbers were increasing, at an alarming rate.

And a meet in Canvey Island? Yes, that made a sort of sense. He had been to the beaches as a kid and remembered it as a place of fun and sunshine. But there were also plenty of derelict vacant lots and wildland, where a criminal organisation could carry out its ugly business – if it acted fast – without being detected. Roscommon Way, lined with trees, would not be deserted. But, with its great expanses of parkland, dunes, building sites and industrial units (many of them empty), it would serve its purpose for the kidnappers. They had him by the short and curlies, and they knew it. A motorcade of police cars, even a single support vehicle or an ambulance hovering nearby would seal Carol's fate. And he couldn't afford to take that risk.

In Orsett, he hit traffic on the A13. Roadworks. A slow contraflow, and no means of getting through, even with his police siren and lights. Shit. It was already noon. This was the last thing he needed. He could see a fire station ahead and the dismal crawl of the vehicles that stood between him and his rendezvous with the local branch of the Nazi Party. Finally, after a wasted twenty minutes, he was off again, passing by Basildon Cemetery and towards the Sadlers Farm roundabout, where he turned right down Canvey Way.

He reached Roscommon Way and took the long dual carriageway towards the Waterside Farm roundabout. The traffic was light as it often was out of rush hour – which was why, he remembered hearing, some local kids had started using it for mad *Fast and Furious*-style races in the dead of night at 130 mph.

But not today.

Had he not been keeping a look-out, he wouldn't have spotted the black Mercedes Sprinter van parked about twenty yards off the road, behind a small copse. Yes. This was definitely it.

He slowed a little and saw that the driver, obscured behind

tinted windows, was flashing his headlights. Which meant: 'Slow the fuck down and don't make a big deal of it.' Which is exactly what Harry did.

He parked off the dual carriageway and, opening his boot, quickly set up a police road sign. In other circumstances, this would have been madness – but, within the time frame he was looking at, it was the smart move. It meant that no civilians would interrupt what he was doing. And it was placed at a particular distance from his motor that would signal to his fellow officers that he was only dealing with a spot of car trouble and that they didn't need to get involved. If he was lucky, nobody would interfere.

Zipping up his leather jacket, he walked slowly in front of the car with his hands clearly up – but not showily so. Again, anything not to attract attention. He knew the driver of the Merc would see. He kept his pace careful and even. They would be able to see that he was alone and that he fully expected to be patted down before the parley.

He got within thirty or so yards of the van and stopped. Any closer might be seen as taking liberties. Hands still up, waiting patiently. For a while, nothing happened. More fucking mind games, was it?

Finally, the passenger door opened and a burly man jumped out. He was wearing black jeans, a black bomber jacket, a flat cap and a grey scarf worn like a Covid face mask so that only his eyes and the top of his nose were visible.

He looked Harry up and down with evident contempt. Sizing him up. Getting his measure. His stare was steady, unruffled. His manner unhurried. He might be a neo-Nazi idiot but he was also, Harry thought, no stranger to moments of tension, violence and confrontation.

'You Taylor, then?' he said finally, his voice deep and confident, cutting through the gusts of wind on the common.

'You know I am.'

'Don't be fresh, DCI. You're in no position to mug anyone off today. Let's not start with any nonsense, eh?'

'Fair enough,' said Harry.

'So shut your noise and listen. Otherwise, your girl is going to have a very nasty, very final day.'

'I'm listening. What do I call you, by the way?'

'You don't call me anything, son. You just answer questions.'

'All right, then. Fire away.'

The other man looked away for a minute. He lifted his left hand slowly. The driver's door opened and a second thug jumped onto the grass – dressed more or less identically to his boss, but with a plain navy blue baseball cap.

'My associate here is going to pat you down first and check your motor to make sure you're not playing silly cunts. Because, in my experience, you race-traitor coppers are always playing silly cunts somehow or other. Always finding new ways to let your own people down.'

Harry shrugged as the second man lumbered over to him. He raised his arms higher so that he could be patted down. The driver checked his shoes, opened his jacket to see if he was wearing body armour, or a comms system – he wasn't – and then spun him round roughly to take a look at his back pockets and belt.

The driver turned round and shook his head.

'Now do the motor. *Thoroughly*,' said his boss.

Harry wasn't going to take the risk of turning round but he could hear the doors and boot of his car being opened and then silence as the man gave it the once over. It took him a surprisingly long while to find the pistol which was, after all, only in the bloody glove compartment. As soon he did, he marched furiously back past Harry across the grass to his boss, who looked at the weapon with disgust.

He cradled the gun and examined it, as if baffled. At last, he broke the silence.

'Nice piece,' he said. 'Army service issue, right? I heard you had served. Odd that you should be betraying your country now. But then so many do.' He shook his head. 'Trouble is, this gun – this *thing* – is exactly what I meant by "silly cunts". This is what I hoped you'd be smart enough *not* to do. Coming armed. Makes things a lot more difficult.'

Harry interjected. 'I'm a senior SO22 officer. I always carry a weapon. The point is, I left it in the car. I walked out with my hands up. Your . . . associate frisked me like I was Osama bin Laden's auntie at Heathrow. That's the opposite of "silly cunts", if you don't mind me saying so.'

The man in the flat cap paused again. 'Still stupid of you. Doesn't encourage me to trust you. Give me one good reason why I shouldn't put one in your head right now and then feed you and your *foreign* colleague to the pigs on a farm I know a few miles from here?'

'Because, Mr Herr Sunshine,' Harry replied, 'you want something from me, and you aren't going to get it from two corpses, are you?'

Almost imperceptibly, the boss smarted at this arrogance. 'Well, now. I'm going to attribute that stupid fucking cheek to the chilly weather and middle-aged nerves. But you ought to know by now that I don't appreciate being talked to like that.'

'But I'm right, aren't I? You want something from me. And I want my fellow officer back safe and sound. I was hardly going to dive in blasting bullets. Was I? Behave, for Christ's sake.'

The boss waved his lieutenant back to the van and pulled a pack of cigarettes from his jacket. In the wind, it took him a while to get his lighter to work, but when it did, he pulled down his scarf and drew long and deep on his smoke.

'All right, then. I see you put a sign up to keep people away. That was almost intelligent. So – I'm assuming you have an idea what we're here to discuss.'

'I have half a hunch, yes,' said Harry.

'Good. Good. Because that means that you and your colleague – or whatever you call her – have at least a five per cent chance of making it to the end of the day without being zipped up in body bags. Or buried alive.'

'All right,' said Harry. 'So why don't you tell me how I can get into the lucky percentage zone?'

The boss shook his head. 'You see, again. That tone of voice is not what I want to hear. You know precisely what I want. And while I didn't exactly expect you to bring it in the car, I do regard it as your job to explain how, exactly, you're going to get it to me.'

'Get it to you?' said Harry.

'Well, yeah. Because if you don't, you, your girl, her fucking father and, to be perfectly honest, anyone you ever called family are going to be found in about two hundred different locations.'

'Oh,' said Harry. 'I thought you said we were tonight's piggy supper. I'm confused now.'

'Don't be, Taylor. I can be very innovative when it comes to expressing my anger. *Fickle*, even. Trust me, I didn't get to this position without a fair amount of – what's the word? – *demonstrative* behaviour.'

'I don't doubt it,' said Harry. 'I've known your sort all my life. Pisspot bigots giving it large with broken bottles and thinking you're Adolf Hitler. Kicking in any head you can find. Lighting fires so that people die for *nothing*.'

The boss took a step forwards. 'Not for nothing! Not for nothing *at all*! Your disgusting generation of cowards has turned this country into a cultural sewer. And you've made coolies of decent white people, third-class citizens in their own homeland. Proud of yourself? If you had any honour, you'd all fucking top yourselves.'

Harry snorted. 'Well, that figures. I know your lot like a bit of the old self-destruction down in the bunker when things get hairy. Don't you? It's your style. Before the Russians get to Berlin, I mean.'

'No Russians coming today, Harry boy. So best mind your manners. For what I promise will be the *last* time.'

'OK, sunshine. I just want to know exactly what you want for the safe return of Dr Walker. Let's get down to practical action, shall we?'

The boss lit another cigarette. 'All right. All right then. First of all, this is a game of two halves, Taylor. We talk today about ways and means. That's the first bit. Then you shut your fucking trap and do whatever is necessary to keep the dogs at bay while you work out how to get the rock to me. I don't care how you do it. But you need to work fast. And if you work fast and get it done – well, that's the second bit, isn't it?'

'You're assuming I have it. Half the world has been looking for that uranium since it was half-inched in Stepney. As I'm sure you know. Quite the rush to get it, there's been. And the bodies have been piling up ever since. What makes you think that us feeble race traitors at the Yard would have struck the jackpot?'

'Because we've been watching you, Taylor. We have a lot of assets around town these days, patriotic foot soldiers keeping us clued in. All walks of life. You've been at the centre of the whole story, haven't you? Out the country, bouncing around like nobody's business. Everyone's after you. You bloody well *know* where it is, Taylor. Why else would I be wasting my time with a middle-ranking has-been like you otherwise? I'm not some skinhead in braces from the eighties, boy. Things have moved on.'

'If you say so,' said Harry. 'So let's go one step further and say you're right. For the sake of argument, you understand.'

'I know I'm fucking right. That's the premise. Not a discussion point.'

'OK. So, how am I supposed to remove a tidy quantity of weapons-grade gear from – let's just say – a military-level, top-secret storage facility, swarming with top brass, spooks and God knows who else, and get it into your hot little hands? As you keep saying: I'm just a copper. We're not really trained to do nuclear heists, if you know what I mean.'

The boss waved his hand, as if in boredom. 'Details, details. If I know one thing about you, Taylor, it's that you're not regular law. You have fingers in a lot of pies and you do a lot of stuff off the books. So you'll find a way. This is what you do. This is the *point* of you, why you weren't drummed out of the force years ago for being a general pain in the arse.'

*God, he's beginning to sound a bit like a Cockney SS officer,* Harry thought. *Better wind this up soon. He's losing his patience. And that can't happen.*

'OK, OK. So you understand SO22. All right. I don't know how yet, but I'll find a way.'

'At *last*. We begin to make a tiny bit of progress.'

'It won't be easy. But, look, I'll sort it.'

The boss looked away towards some demented horizon. 'Yeah. Best you do, Taylor. I want that rock and I'm prepared to do some pretty fucking horrible things to get it.'

'Yeah, I think I got the message.'

'Good. Well, then. Why are you still here? Fuck the fuck off and get on with what you have to do.'

*Here we go,* thought Harry. *Deep breath.*

'Because I need proof of life.'

The boss burst out laughing. It was as though Harry had started juggling or pirouetting. 'You must be insane! You think I'm here to *negotiate*? Christ, you coppers never fucking learn, do you? You always think you're in the driving seat or that you can pull one over on us. Well, like I said, it's *our time* now. You're here to take your orders, you fucking *melt*. And that's it. Now run along before I get my tools out and go to work on your girl.'

Harry stood his ground. 'But how do I know you've even got her? That she's alive and unharmed?'

'*Really?* You're ready to take that chance?'

'All I know for certain is that Dr Walker has gone missing. And that you called her father. And ended up speaking to me. You're assuming that nobody else has been in touch. Which, if you'll permit me to speak freely, is a bit of an assumption.'

'How's that, then?'

'Well – as you pointed out, a lot of people are very interested in my team right now. And so it's safe to assume by now that a lot of people know that Dr Walker has gone missing. What makes you so sure you're the only interested party that claims to have her? I could just be doing the rounds today, couldn't I? Stop off to talk to the Mafia in Soho, Russians in Mayfair, Mexicans in – where do Mexicans live in London? Dunno. Then, of course, you scruffy lot here in the middle of fucking Canvey Island. She could be anywhere, really.'

'You're a shit poker player, Taylor. Even if I believed you – which, as it happens, I fucking don't – you're not going to risk me getting my boys to cut her ear off and bring it out the van so you can see. Are you?'

'See, I was hoping you could just let me see that you have

her. I mean, it's a bit early in our business relationship for slicing and dicing, isn't it? And, anyway, one ear looks much the same as the other. Doesn't it?'

His adversary stared at him with cold fury.

'I'm not asking much,' said Harry. 'I won't move. *Obviously.* You get your associate in there – or whoever – to bring Dr Walker out. So I can see her for *two seconds*. And then I can start working out how to get you what you want.'

'Why should I trust you, Taylor?'

'I'm not expecting you to trust me. You have the cards, or so you say. If you have Dr Walker, I'm obviously going to do all I can to get you to free her. Look up. No helos. No backup team. No comms. It's just me. Like you asked. All I'm saying is, show me that you've actually got her, and I'll be in my car and on the road in ten seconds flat.'

The boss's eyes narrowed. Harry could see that, with every fibre of his being, he wanted to slash him from ear to ear and bury him in a shallow grave. But that this primitive instinct was quarrelling with the beginnings of a strategic mind, and that, having put everything on the line in the name of taking his movement of thugs into the big league, he needed to make something like a calm, rational decision.

After what felt like an eternity, the boss raised a finger. '*One second.* I'll get her out for *one second*. If you move, she's dead. If you don't go straight to your car once you've clocked her, she's dead. If you put any form of trace on us, she's dead. And then you get me my rock. OK?'

'OK,' said Harry.

The boss raised his hand again and the driver leapt out, running over to take instructions. He nodded as he was told what to do and headed for the back of the van. He opened the door and seemed to be talking to someone. Harry could see him gesticulating and arguing. The driver was much less of an operator than his boss.

And then, from the back of the van, a third man emerged, with his arm round Carol's neck. The two of them shuffled just into view. To his disgust, Harry could see that Carol had been blindfolded and gagged, and that her wrists were bound tight by duct tape. She was not resisting, which was smart.

'Right,' said the boss. 'Your second is up. Back she—'

Before he could finish his sentence, the top of his head came off, flat cap and all, and blood and brain tissue sprayed across the green behind him. He fell to his knees, quite dead.

That was shot one.

Shot two: the driver slumped to the grass, with a new scarlet hole perfectly centred in his forehead. He exhaled once and was still.

Shot three: Carol's captor didn't even finish his cry – 'Fucking he—' – as the third bullet entered his left ear, passed through his skull, temporal lobe and out the other side, killing him instantly.

Carol, feeling herself suddenly free from his grip, yelled out, her words muffled by the gag. Harry rushed over to prop her up, and let her know everything was OK now.

He removed her gag first and she took deep, gasping breaths.

'Carol, it's me, Harry. Harry! They're all dead. You're safe. You're safe.'

He removed her blindfold, and she screwed up her eyes, the sudden blast of light painful after hours of enforced darkness.

She leant into him. 'Harry! What the actual *fuck*? Who were they?'

'Just a bunch of two-bob cunts who fancied having a go at making history. Sorry you had to be involved. Christ, you all right?'

She was leaning over, winded and holding her knees as if she might throw up. 'Yeah. Yeah, thanks. I'm just . . . taking in the fact that I was kidnapped on the pavement by the – what were they? The fucking Fourth Reich or something?'

'Not even,' said Harry. He checked the road: mercifully free of traffic. 'Just another gang of skinheads who think that reading *Mein Kampf* makes you some sort of hero. Assuming they could read. Total scumbags.'

'Jesus Christ. How many people are after this bloody rock? It's mounting up.'

'I'll say. Be the Hare Krishna next.'

She managed a laugh. 'Yeah. Probably.' Then, 'By the way, Harry . . . Who took them out? I can't see any backup.'

'Oh, that'd be our very own colleague DS Iris Davies who is two kilometres away in her very own sniper's nest. She said she could make the shot at that distance, and it turns out she was right. I'd say we owe her a drink, wouldn't you?'

'A big drink,' said Carol. 'Here, Harry. Have you got some cutters to get me out of this bloody tape? And some water, or something. I'm parched.'

'Yeah,' he said. 'Come to the car, where it's warm. I'll call this in and we can get you checked out.'

'Oh, just bruises I reckon—'

'Yeah, but just in case.'

'I know. Thanks, Harry.'

Harry waved with both hands knowing that Iris would see him. Which, from the roof of the apartment block two kilo-metres away, she did, and smiled to herself on – though she said so herself – a job well done, and three less Nazis for the world to worry about.

She started to pack up her kit as she waited for Harry to call.

# 27

'Christ, it's cold,' said Iris. She shivered in her US Army surplus combat fatigues, camouflage webbing and shooter gloves. The nest they had built was, she said, much too exposed. But it would have to do.

'Stop complaining,' said Harry, looking through binoculars. 'Unit Two have it much harder down by the canal.'

About a hundred and fifty metres ahead, John had taken up position behind a shed that was close to the water. With him were two of Harry's mates: Gerry and Spike, or so they called themselves. Broad-shouldered, bearded men, who had been waiting at a motorway service station not far out of London and seemed to have brought along their own private armoury in the boot of their BMW. John and Iris had been uncertain about teaming up with a couple of civilians but were sharply overruled by their boss.

'They're not fucking *civilians*,' Harry had said. 'They've seen more action in defence of the realm than either of you ever will. They work in the private sector now. I'll mark them down as "expert observers", OK?'

'Oh, yeah, Robinson'll buy that,' John replied. They sped up the M40 in the unmarked Range Rover that Harry had taken from the pool for the week, his Jag not being quite the vehicle for this expedition.

'Of *course* I'm not going to mark them down. Obviously, they were never here. Jesus, do I have to spell it out? Yes, apparently, I do. Listen. Robinson wants us wherever the trail takes us. He's not certain about Marseilles either and he definitely wants a Plan B. And that's us. He just doesn't want to know the details. It's called "plausible deniability", John. It stinks, but it also makes the world go round.'

'Are they good, though? This "Gerry" and "Spike"?'

'Bloody hell, you really are looking for teeth in a basket this morning, aren't you? Those two are better than you could be in ten lifetimes and the best couple of—'

'All right, boss, all right. I get the picture. "Who Dares Wins" and all that.'

'Yeah, well,' said Harry, concentrating on the road and speeding up to ninety. 'You never know. We might need a bit of extra today, if you know what I mean. It's got that feeling about it.'

There was nothing 'extra' about this windswept location, Iris thought. Though they had settled on a small hillock not far from the lock itself, which gave them a clearer line of sight, most of the terrain around was flat and desolate – interrupted only by nondescript brick warehouses and a giant Victorian gas holder.

'I tell you,' Iris said. 'Carol will be so pissed off she got left out of this school outing.'

'Yeah, well, she's officially on compulsory leave. Recovering and that. Which is fair enough when you think what she went through. Truth is, Robinson wants her close by, in case of developments with the rock. She can't afford to be out of London right now – I mean, they might need her scientific talents at short notice.'

'Lucky her.'

'Actually, I think she was a bit annoyed to tell you the truth. She's getting a taste for proper police work.'

The Range Rover was parked about five hundred metres

away in an area that had been concreted over for no clear reason. All the bleakness, the greyness, somehow this felt like the end of the line, the end of the world, even. To Iris's left, there was a patch of ground hemmed off by old chicken wire and a fading *KEEP OUT* sign, clearly related to the former use of the factory compound further down the path. Now, the broken windows and unhinged doors of its buildings looked like a snaggle-toothed sneer. Nothing to see but the ruins of the industrial age beneath a gloomy sky that promised rain at any moment. It was already spitting.

Under the makeshift shelter of her backpack, Iris looked at the plastic-covered screen of her iPad. They now had a complete roster of the vessels expected down the canal that day – and only two looked even remotely interesting. One, due around 6 p.m., was a German-registered cargo boat, the *Sieglinde*, whose true ownership had proved impossible to verify, and was therefore, in the circumstances, suspicious. Earlier in the day – in less than twenty minutes, in fact – they expected to see a smaller freighter, the *Gabriella*, registered in Vancouver, with owners traced via the Caymans to a shell company notionally based in New York. There, the trail went cold. Alarmingly so.

She and Harry formed Unit One. Broad surveillance was the key, he said. What were they looking for? They absolutely didn't know. But they needed to be ready for anything. John, Gerry and Spike were closer to the canal, and ready to take whatever action, if any, was necessary. John was stationed behind his prized Oberwerk binoculars, which he had managed not to return when he left the NCA, and had seen him through many an op over the years. Gerry and Spike carried M4A1 carbines which, they revealed proudly, had been presented to them as a thank-you gift by Team 7 of the US Navy SEALs after a successful joint exercise in Paraguay back in the day. John hadn't wanted to hear any of the details.

He'd wondered out loud just before the teams split if it was even legal for these men to be carrying those weapons. What were they *doing* here? he'd asked Iris. She's said it wasn't their place to question Harry's thinking. Just trust him.

Iris had rigged up a secure digital comms system so they could stay in touch with minimal risk of a breach. 'Unit Two, come in,' she said. 'What's your status?'

'Unit One,' John replied. 'Nothing unusual. It's going to piss it down soon, isn't it?'

'Unit Two – yes, definitely, especially on you three twats.'

'Unit One – fuck off, Iris. It's bloody freezing down here. Nothing to see since that Swedish trawler about half an hour ago. Light traffic today, the harbour master said. He wasn't kidding.'

Harry stood up and walked to the crest of the hill. There was indeed nothing to see, except a grey expanse of water with a few rowing boats moored close to the lock, rocking in the wind. The silence was broken only by the occasional squawk of gulls or the distant sound of a plane. Odd to be so alone, he thought. Not even the comfort of a circling police helo in the sky.

He called out to Iris. 'No sign of anything?'

'Nothing. Not even on the towpath.' She looked through her scope and assessed the chances of making a kill-shot to a target on the other side of the canal. Decent, even with the wind. A moving vessel was another matter, but even then, she was confident she could get the job done if she needed to. But what *was* the job? She had stopped asking Harry that question because he clearly had no better idea than she did. And the tension was high enough already without drawing attention to the scale and number of unknowns in their situation – not to mention the lack of backup, legal cover, stuff like that. *Focus,* she said to herself. *Breathe.*

Her earpiece crackled. 'Unit One,' said John. 'Are you seeing this?'

She looked as far as she could westward and spotted it. The shape of a vessel, blue and red, its twin cranes resembling metallic arms reaching to the heavens. It lumbered towards them, its deck loaded down with containers.

'Unit Two,' she said. 'I see it. Is it our girl?'

'Unit One. Hang on. Can't see insignia. Wait a minute – yes, Canadian. That tallies with Vancouver. Should be the *Gabriella*.' He looked down at his tablet. 'And . . . yes, it looks like the image we sourced. Plus a few more years of wear and tear.'

Harry spoke into his mic. 'Unit One. Gerry, Spike, take up forward position but maintain cover. Brace for hostiles. This looks like an ordinary cargo ship but it could be anything.'

'Unit Two,' said John. 'Roger that this end. There's a smaller vessel heading towards us from the Manchester end. Just a feeder ship. I think it's on the list but it may cross over when the *Gabriella* is in our sights.'

'Unit Two,' said Harry. 'Understood. Assume neutrality unless we have reason to think otherwise.'

He turned to Iris. 'The last thing we need is a bloody audience for whatever this is.'

'Yeah. Let's hope that feeder gets past us sharpish.'

'Hold up,' he looked through his binoculars. 'The *Gabriella* is . . . Is it my imagination or is it slowing down?'

She checked her scope. 'No. It's not your imagination. Definite decrease in speed. Visible to the naked eye. Is she planning to *dock*? Where would a ship that size moor itself round here?'

'It makes no sense,' said Harry. 'Unit One. Stay sharp.'

'Unit Two,' said John. 'Roger that. Something's definitely up.'

In the distance, Gerry and Spike were raising their carbines, fully prepared for battle. Iris watched Harry as his whole body tensed, ready for action. He was leading them into a battle that might not even exist; or might be a true nightmare. For the first time in all his years danger, the uncertainty would be killing him.

'Unit One. This feeder vessel. Weird . . . it's slowing down, too.'

'All right, Unit Two,' said Harry. 'Stand by.'

Iris curled her finger round the trigger of her rifle, preparing to respond to whatever happened next.

The *Gabriella* was closing in. An ugly ship, by any standards; a floating steel box, really, an eyesore carrying hundreds of tonnes of cargo around the planet, day after day, week after week. Food, fuel, vehicles, timber, trafficked human beings: it might be carrying *anything*.

Harry's iPhone buzzed. It was a text from Robinson.

URGENT: Mrslls op is a dud. *Argonauta* still being strppd by DEA. But nthng there. Fiasco. More ASAP. BR.

'Shit,' Harry said. He told Iris, and she only nodded grave assent. If Marseilles was a bum steer, what was this? Another sleight of hand? Just another show to keep more coppers away from the real action?

'Unit Two,' Harry said. 'Be advised. Our intel is that the Marseilles op is a dead end. Nothing there. So prepare for anything here.'

'Unit One,' replied John. 'Roger that. Hold on, can you see this?'

Harry looked into his binoculars. 'Unit Two. What am I looking for?'

'Unit One. Starboard side of *Gabriella* . . . just by the surface of the water. Movement.'

Harry looked harder. Christ, John was right. A froth of foam was building up at the plimsoll line of the hull. And . . .

'Jesus,' said Iris. 'That is *not* possible.'

But it was possible. What looked like a steel panel in the hull was opening up to reveal bright lights and something barely breaking the surface of the water. As the hatch opened fully, the foam grew in scale and something like a great iron fish could just be seen below the churn.

'Unit One,' said John. 'I can't believe what I'm seeing. Unless I'm very much mistaken, that is a fucking *submarine*.'

'On deck, Harry,' said Iris. 'Two men. Looking down. Can you see?'

He adjusted his binoculars. 'Yes, copy that. One is about six foot, the other slightly shorter. They are very interested in what we're interested in. Hard to see their faces under those parkas and with the goggles. But is the one on the left . . . *Ramirez*?'

'Unit One,' said John. 'I can't make a positive ID. Could be. Yes, *looks* like him, for sure. Hard to imagine he'd be here, but it does . . .'

Iris interrupted. 'I have a clear shot on both. Waiting for your green.'

'Stand by,' said Harry. 'I don't want to kill a couple of fucking innocent Canadian seamen by accident. Unit Two, what's the status of the sub?'

'Unit One. To judge by the surface trail, it's now clear of the ship. And – yes – the hatch is closing.'

'Unit Two. Copy that. Oh, hold on. Looks like we've got bloody company.'

The feeder vessel was now barely fifty metres from where John, Gerry and Spike were stationed. And it, too, was slowing down.

'What the hell?' said Harry.

'Unit One. The second vessel is almost at a standstill. We still have a clear sight of the *Gabriella*. Awaiting instructions.'

*What are you doing, Ramirez, you cunning bastard?* Then, with grim clarity, it dawned on Harry.

'Unit Two. It's a *handover*. The shipment was never on the *Argonauta*. That was all a feint. The *sub* is making a delivery to the feeder. I can't see anyone on the deck of the smaller ship. Can you?'

'Unit One,' said John. 'That's a negative. There's a hell of a noise coming from the hull of the feeder, though. Must be getting ready on its starboard side to receive . . . whatever.'

'Unit Two. OK, copy that. I'm going to get Robinson to call in air cover and full backup. We must now assume that there is a bloody great cache of class A narcotics on that sub – which will soon be on that feeder. What's it called?'

'Let me – the *Avalon*. I can just see it in white lettering on the hull. And yes, it's on the list.'

'Unit Two, don't worry about its owners right now. I need real-time intel on absolutely every cough and spit of what you see. Stand by, am about to call Bill.' He pulled out his phone. 'I hope to Christ he despatches what we need, and, you know, by yesterday.'

'Guv,' said Iris. 'Three o'clock and closing in. You'll need your bins to see it.'

He took a look. Now, what the *hell* was this?

'Unit Two. John – you seeing this?'

'Unit One,' John said. 'Affirmative. Very much so. Moving fast. Gerry has it in sight. Spike covering the two herberts on the *Gabriella*. What is it? Can't be. Makes no sense. A *bike*?'

On the towpath, heading towards the larger vessel at a speed of no less than sixty miles per hour, was a quad bike, the rider clad head to foot in black.

'Iris,' said Harry. 'Shift target to bike rider immediately. What the fuck are *you* up to, sunshine? Jesus, it's all go today.'

'On it,' she said. 'I can take him on your command.'

'Not yet,' Harry said. 'Might just be a kid.'

'Doesn't look like just a kid, guv,' she said.

And then, as if the rider could hear them, the quad bike slowed down dramatically. It drew to a halt by the prow of the *Gabriella*, its rider still just visible from the other side of the canal.

What is *this*? Harry thought. Was the bike delivering something else, as the sub docked with the *Avalon*?

They weren't the only people who had seen the quad bike and his driver. The two figures on deck were pointing at the towpath and seemed to be shouting something. They were joined by – how many? – at least five more of the crew.

'Activity on board the *Gabriella*!' said Harry. 'They won't like this one bit, whatever it is.'

'Unit Two,' said John. 'The rider is pulling something off the side of the bike . . . like a pipe of some sort. What the fuck would he want with a length of piping?'

Gerry intervened for the first time: 'Unit One. Harry, that ain't no pipe. That is NLAW kit. Over.'

John said, 'What the—?'

'NLAW, man!" yelled Gerry, "Shoulder-mounted missile launcher! Next-Generation Light Anti-tank Weapon! Fuck, we've been dishing those out to Ukrainians like sweets. That is *not* standard kit to see in the north of bloody England! Charlie Mike?'

'Unit Two. Charlie Mike,' Harry said. 'Await—'

'I have him,' said Iris. 'Waiting on your green.'

But it was too late for a green because with a dull thud the weapon had been fired and its payload landed on the deck of the *Gabriella*.

Meanwhile, Ramirez – if it was Ramirez – had something on his shoulder. *Christ,* thought Harry, *Is that a bazooka?* The distant figure took aim and fired.

A mighty fireball burst the side of a warehouse on the other side of the canal with an explosion that would be heard for miles. Smoke, ashes and debris filled the air.

But Ramirez had missed.

Unfazed, the rider returned his own launcher to its mountings on the side of the bike and scorched off down the towpath.

Where was the second explosion? Harry wondered. Had the shell failed to detonate? Or what?

Then, in an instant, as if all his synapses were firing at once, as if the puzzle had never really been a puzzle at all, he glimpsed the faces of his team, of Voldrev, of Robinson, of Smythe, of Adey, of Pépé, of the men with slashed throats in the Devereux . . . and, as if time had stopped, it all fell into place.

'Unit Two!' Harry shouted. 'We are Oscar Mike! Immediate termination of op! Get the fuck out of there!'

He practically lifted Iris off the ground. 'Now! We are leaving now! No questions!'

She grabbed her rifle and backpack and started running. Harry counted to himself as he increased his pace: one, two, three, four, five . . . How long would they have to wait?

From pure instinct, he took hold of Iris's shoulder and pulled her to the best cover he could see: a reinforced concrete wall supporting a two-storey brick workshop.

'John!' he shouted. 'Are you out?'

'Unit One. Affirmative. We are right behind you and—'

Suddenly, the grey landscape ahead wasn't grey at all. It was bathed in dazzling white, as if a thousand floodlights had suddenly been turned on behind them. It filled every space, every fold, every nook and cranny of what they had seen a moment before.

'Get down!' he yelled at Iris. She crouched with her arms over her head. Harry hit the deck.

The blast wave, when it came, was inexpressibly different to anything he had ever experienced. As he and Iris huddled behind the wall, they could feel the building's very structure shudder, hear its windows shatter into tiny particles, sense the force hurtling through their own bodies and their breath being driven from their lungs by the sheer ferocity of the explosion. In nearby cabins and huts, joists splintered audibly, plaster was vaporised into dust and doors flew off their hinges. He felt as though they might be swept from the ground at any moment by the monstrous tornado, plucked and then dropped like ants in a fire.

Then there was only the falling debris, the wind howling like a ghoul and a sky dark with terrible news.

# 28

On the huge flat screen embedded in the wall of his bedroom, the images flickered like a dream being reflected back at him. On almost every channel, too. As if the world had indeed been turned upside down, according to his directions.

This was the order hidden in the midst of the chaos. It was all going to plan, and that was a source of immense pleasure to his rigorous mind. The symmetry of the scene delighted him. All the long and meticulous preparation – years, in truth – now so perfectly rewarded by the rolling news coverage and the panicked voiceover of anchors and supposed experts who had no real idea what was going on. Their commentary was just meaningless babble in a grand drama that was approaching its final act.

This was history, and he had made it.

A surge of pain interrupted his reflection and, feeling suddenly nauseous and trembling, he reached over to the side table, grabbed a bottle of pills and some water and swallowed three – more than he was supposed to, less than he would have liked.

Yes. This was the endgame, all right.

# 29

The circular pews were filling up fast, and the verger wondered if the plastic chairs that he had set up that morning at the back of the church might indeed be needed. Might he need to fetch more? St Stephen Walbrook in the City of London can accommodate a congregation of around three hundred and fifty, and it looked as though that number would be reached quite easily.

Around Henry Moore's famous circular altar, the mourners who were already seated whispered to one another, examined the order of service or looked up at Wren's dome. The organist played a Bach voluntary as the church filled up. One of the last to take their place was Sir Muhammad Baqri, the Met Commissioner, who was due to read a passage from Corinthians.

Harry sat a few places to his left, uncomfortable in his suit and still – why deny it? – dazed and unsettled by the events of the past few days. Rarely had he felt so passive, so totally at the mercy of others. And though he understood that they were all just doing their jobs – as he had been – he hated every second of it.

While the endless tests were carried out and each result was awaited with apprehension, he boiled with anger at his confinement: first at Manchester Royal Infirmary, where a floor had been cleared to deal with the attack; and then at a more discreet facility near London where his health was monitored by doctors and nurses seconded to the Ministry of Defence.

Even as he was first wheeled into the hospital, slipping in and out of consciousness, it was clear to Harry that he was as much a specimen as a patient. All his medical carers wore full hazmat suits, as if he himself might be pulsing with radioactivity. They subjected him to every conceivable assessment, taking bloods and urine samples each day, monitoring a Geiger counter around the clock. His room was vacuum sealed and his conversation with the staff limited and muffled – his deafness from the explosion clearing only slowly. He felt like a bedbound stick of polonium rather than a person, and, as exhausted as he was, longed to yell at somebody that he was a serving police officer with a job to do and wanted to speak to whoever was in charge.

But he was experienced enough to know that a tantrum would do him no good. He could also tell that the doctors, nurses and occasional military personnel that visited him were frightened and uncertain themselves. They weren't going to let him out, or even brief him in anything other than the most minimal way, because they were acting under strict instructions from the very highest authorities.

Everything had changed. That much, if little else, was certain.

On the fourth day, as he awoke from another fitful sleep, one of the doctors presented him, without commentary, with an iPad. It was a secure video call with Robinson.

'Harry?' said his badly lit boss on the screen.

'Most of me, anyway,' he replied.

'Thank Christ. Great to see you. Hear you. How are you feeling?'

'Like a bloody atom bomb kicked me in the arse, to be honest. Apart from that, fine.'

'They tell me you're fine. Amazingly so, actually. All things considered.'

'Well, I'm glad they're amazed. I could think of some other adjectives.'

'Bumps, bruises, a spot of concussion. But here's the thing, the radioactive impact was almost negligible. It was incredibly localised. That bit of the canal will be unusable for decades, of course, maybe longer. But where you and Iris were was more or less OK.'

'I don't get it,' said Harry. 'Shouldn't my bloody face be melting by now? I mean, I've not even lost any hair. Doesn't make sense.'

'Going to patch in Carol,' Robinson said. 'She's at Imperial today briefing their new task force. But I set her up in a secure office here so she could speak to you.'

Beside Robinson's face appeared Carol's.

'How's my favourite kidnap victim?' said Harry.

'Better than you, I'm guessing.'

'Nah, I'm Captain Scarlet, me. Fucking indestructible.'

'Well, you're not. But, as I expect the Super has told you, your health stats are basically fine. Big relief. Iris, too. Nothing serious and certainly nothing long-term. They'll keep you both on potassium iodide as a precaution, but you'll be back on the beat pretty soon.'

'Well, I don't mean to sound ungrateful, but isn't that impossible?'

'As it turns out, no. I mean, you're lucky, no question. But your hunch turned out to have been spot on, Harry: whoever got hold of the rock wanted to use it for very limited purposes indeed. Or rather, to show that they had access to nuclear weapons without flattening a city. Which is to say, they *could* flatten a city—'

'But they aren't going to right now. I mean, what they did,

as far as I can see, was wipe out Ramirez and stop his expansion into Europe in a pretty bloody unambiguous fashion. Nobody will be trying that move for a while, will they?'

'Exactly,' said Carol. 'It's a completely new way of using these weapons. Small sting, relatively speaking. But it disrupts *everything*. It changes the game. Maybe forever.'

Harry tried to wrap his head around it all. 'So what next?'

'I'm dropping off now,' said Carol. 'Feel better, Harry.'

Robinson proceeded to fill him in on what had happened in the past few days. The whole world was still adjusting to the first use of a nuclear device in anger in almost eight decades, and to everything that meant and might mean for the future.

It was the first aggressive use of nuclear weapons on western soil. An apparent attack on a NATO member. Mass panic in the north of England – the motorways jammed, trains packed with families fleeing the scene. The airwaves fizzing with talk of a new kind of terrorism or a direct attack upon the UK by a hostile state – take your pick: Russia, China, Iran, North Korea. Daily meetings of the Civil Contingencies COBRA Committee, chaired by the Prime Minister, who was (according to Robinson's sources) sufficiently rattled that he might declare a national emergency at any moment. Even martial law, evacuation of the big cities, if the attacks continued. 'Proportionate reprisals' under active consideration, the nature of which was far from clear.

'Christ almighty,' said Harry. 'I get it, Bill – I mean, of course, all of it . . . but hearing you say it . . .'

'I know. It's a lot to take in. But you're right: the minute the word "nuclear" is involved, everything changes.'

Harry tried to sit up properly in his bed. 'And we've still only accounted for a tiny quantity of the rock.'

'Exactly. I mean, thank God it was a small device. Relatively speaking, anyway. I bet it didn't seem small out there and— Christ, I'm sorry, Harry. Fact is, though, there's still a lot of uranium in play and that's making everyone above me on the food chain very nervous indeed. Not to mention seven billion other people.'

'Yeah,' said Harry. 'I'm not wild about it myself. But the key is, do the politicos and the spooks get that this isn't a great declaration of international war, or a new global jihad? Those Nazi pinheads that took Carol – no way they could have pulled off something like this. This was proper tradecraft. I mean, do the up-tops get that this was all about organised crime and what it can now do?'

Robinson looked suddenly weary. 'That's what I've been trying to explain from the moment I heard what had happened. I was still in Marseilles. We'd been well and truly suckered, and that never happens without a greater purpose in mind. So when I got the read-out of your comms . . . I could see immediately what was going down. And I had a gut feeling that we had stumbled into an incredible escalation in the global drug trade. Voldrev, Smythe, Ramirez – it all connects. It's a battle for total control. All or nothing.'

'Yeah. Not the warm-up to an invasion by Russia. Or a slap in the face by the Iranians, or whatever.'

'Exactly. But the chiefs of staff and the spooks aren't having it. They see a mushroom cloud, they see a geopolitical threat. They think: new Cold War, or the Islamist bomb. Meanwhile, the real bad guys could be planning just about anything.'

'Have you been able to knock some sense into them? I mean, they have to see that this was the international narcotics trade shifting up about ten gears in a single day,' said Harry. 'Every drug agency in the world should be all over this.'

'I got to speak to Fincham – National Security Adviser, close to the PM. I've met him briefly a couple of times and

Otis helped smooth the path to a call. Strictly off the books, as he isn't supposed to speak to someone as junior as me.'

'Did he get it?'

Robinson paused. 'He was . . . sympathetic, I suppose. In that Eton toff sort of way. I walked him through the SO22 op and everything you've uncovered so far, and he definitely saw how we'd reached the conclusion we've reached.'

'But?'

'But that's not how the national security apparatus sees things. They're wired to think in terms of nation states, global terror groups, rogue regimes. They're feeding the media panic and responding to it as well. Drug cartels don't really fit into all this, unless the cartels are acting in partnership with any of the above. And remember, there was no evidence left. If the *Gabriella*'s sub was carrying a shit tonne of drugs, and Christ knows what else – well, that's all gone. They don't buy the idea that any of the vessels were owned by proxies of Ramirez. Or they're not interested. We're "reaching", apparently. They just don't believe this has anything to do with *narcotráfico*.'

'Well, what about the quad biker? Did he attack the *Gabriella* just for fun?'

Robinson shrugged. 'As far as they're concerned, this was just a warning. An attack that would level a small part of a major British city without causing huge casualties – ten so far. But it would signal to the world that there was a new nuclear player on the block. And not necessarily a state actor.'

'So, they're fighting the last war? As usual?'

'Yes. Seems so. There's a school of thought at Vauxhall that this is rogue Russian. A breakaway group seeking actively to destabilise and break up NATO with a view to occupation of the Baltics and then Eastern Europe. Or a "Did you miss us?" message from an Iranian-sponsored cell, with major tech support, just to remind us that they're still there and thinking big. Really, when it comes to theories, you can take your pick.' Robinson paused. 'It's a godawful mess, is what it is. People scared out of their wits. Bulk buying. Panic everywhere.'

'So how did you leave it?'

'Fincham said that Voldrev wasn't on anyone's radar right now – and I can't locate *him,* either. Nor can Tennyson, though he's got two armed units scouring the island for intel. MI5 interviewed Smythe, who it turns out was in London on the day of the attack, and apparently thought the whole idea of questioning him was ridiculous in the circumstances, and told them so. They don't have anything on him. And nor do we, Harry.'

'No, but we need to squeeze him, don't we? Him *and* Voldrev? I mean, this is a clear and present danger now, isn't it?'

'I agree. But the top brass don't. They don't want SO22 involved in any way. They don't want us "complicating the picture" – as Fincham put it. Worried the press will get hold of your investigation and that the whole thing will spin even further out of control.'

'Well, it's pretty fucking far out of control already, I'd say. Wouldn't you, Bill?'

Robinson sighed. 'Of course. They're already talking about emergency powers even martial law if the panic gets worse. Listen, I'm on your side. But you're going to have to tread with extreme care, Harry. Even more than before, I'm afraid. You and Iris are not just being held in hospital for your health, as you'd probably worked out.'

'Yeah, I'd kind of got that. Listen, Bill – just get me out.'

Which Robinson, pulling every string he could, had managed to do – but not before they had been transferred to the second facility for a few days where the tests and the monitoring continued. By now, he and Iris knew full well that they didn't have radiation sickness. But their custodians had evidently been instructed to keep them out of circulation for as long as possible.

Now Harry was out, and sitting in a church with friends, colleagues, and people he had never met before. Iris, who had not been allowed to see him since the explosion, laid her head on his shoulder. She was still in a partial state of shock, he thought, trying to process an experience that was almost impossible to understand. She would get over it; her innate toughness and sense of duty would ensure that. But – for now – he had urged her to take her time.

Finding her had been his first instinct when he managed to scramble up after the unbelievable blast – and saw that she was no longer at his side.

How long had he been out? Seconds? Minutes? The air was thick with dust and a thin rain of tiny shards from the buildings. He could barely see as he swayed in the ferocious gale that had transformed the scene into a prairie of destruction. He yelled her name, though he could not hear himself. Still, he kept shouting in case she had not been totally deafened.

They had been together behind the wall – that much he remembered – and that was still standing. Had they been hurled forwards by the explosion, rolled along the ground like tumbleweed? Must have been. But that didn't mean that Iris had ended up where he had.

Stumbling around, Harry looked back and could see nothing but a dark cloud and a surreal landscape of wreckage from the ships – a mast, a ruined container, part of a hull – hurled on to land by the force of the blast. It was impossible to see whether the canal had been suddenly, biblically dried up.

Finally, and (truth be told) by accident, he had located her, still unconscious and lying face down on the track. He shook her awake, or at least semi-awake, and put her arm round his shoulder and his own round her waist. No time to think this one through. All that mattered was to get as far away as possible, as quickly as possible.

He felt a twinge in his bad knee – and feared for a moment that his leg would give way. But it didn't, thank fuck. He lumbered on, through the impenetrable fog of grit and debris that looked, for the moment, as if it had no end.

Swallowed by the haze, he lost track of time and distance. All he had was a sense of purpose – not to let this lovely woman die and, if possible, not to die himself. By the time he saw the lights of emergency-service vehicles, he had no idea if he had covered a few hundred metres, or a couple of miles, or been walking round in circles. He handed Iris over to medics in protective suits. He noticed that they were struggling to concentrate on the job in hand and not to stare into the eye of the abyss ahead of them. Then, his breathing laboured and his temples pounding, he had fainted again.

The organist began to play once more, this time Elgar's 'Nimrod'. A stately procession entered the church, the Bishop of London at the front, the vicar of St Stephen herself attended by other clerics and City of London dignitaries that Harry could not identify. Behind them, in dress uniform, six police officers carried the casket, their faces a mask of focused responsibility; each of them having been closely connected with the deceased over the years, their sense of grief kept under control for now as they concentrated on the job in hand.

It enraged Harry and broke his heart that he was not among their number. Officially – and this came from the top of the Met – he was barred from doing so on the spurious grounds that he was still supposed to be convalescing and was not cleared for any sort of duty; including, he was informed, helping to bear an empty coffin. He was permitted to attend the funeral – but in civilian clothing.

Which told him all he needed to know. There were to be no press pictures or footage of DCI Harry Taylor in a formal role at the funeral of DI John Williams. No SO22 involvement at all. Nothing that might connect his team with the ceremony – even though his team had been John's team. Even though he had been John's mate and his mentor. Even though he had been there – *right there* – when John had evaporated from the face of the Earth in the first nuclear attack to be launched upon the country that he had served for many years.

He looked across the altar at little Livvy and Justin, who had lost a father; no sign of John's ex, but the children were being comforted by an older woman whom he assumed was their maternal grandmother. How unbearable that they had been denied more years with their loving father by such a vicious twist of fate, and one that would have been simply incomprehensible to their young minds.

He looked at the order of service: the hymns John had chosen when writing his will – 'Jerusalem', 'I vow to thee my country' – and then, to be played through speakers after the coffin had left the church, 'The Return of the Los Palmas 7', a classic instrumental number by Madness that he had always recommended to mates to raise their spirits. A few readings, and a eulogy, which Harry knew would be safe in Bill Robinson's hands but – by rights – he himself should be delivering. It made him feel sick that, at this of all moments, the memory of John should be tarnished by office politics and the fears of Whitehall placemen who weren't fit to speak his name.

The choice of venue was explained in italics as a note at

the end of the order of service. *John chose St Stephen Walbrook,*
*the birthplace of the Samaritans, because of his close association*
*with that charity.* And then details about how those in the
congregation could make donations.

Harry felt himself welling up. He had never known that
his friend had shouldered that additional responsibility in life,
helping those who believed themselves at the end of the line.
But it made all the sense in the world. John Williams, as a
police officer and human being, had been carved out of the
timber of the suffering to which his brutal stepfather Declan
had subjected him. And that suffering, Harry had learned in
their long conversations, had pushed him to the very edge
when he was young.

How had young John pulled himself back? Now the picture
was clearer, in a way that made his loss all the more tragic.

Harry had told John that he wouldn't lose an officer during
this operation. And now it was John himself that he had lost.
A good man, reduced to a mist of particles on the quayside
in Manchester by the greed and insatiable hunger for power
of bad men. Lifted clear out of history for – what? Nothing
important or meaningful. Just another moment of destructive
mayhem, and a kick in the teeth for the people who loved
him.

And for that crime against common bloody decency, Harry
Taylor was going to make sure there was a reckoning.

As for Gerry and Spike, who had perished at precisely the
same moment as John, Harry knew well enough not to ask
about their funeral arrangements.

# 30

From the road, the house looked like an ordinary semi-detached in an Ealing cul-de-sac. A family home, probably. Freshly painted, the front garden neat and well-tended. A mountain bike padlocked to a ground anchor. Three storeys, and all the blinds closed. As inconspicuous as Harry had hoped.

'This'll do just fine,' he said.

'How did you get hold of this, then?' Iris asked. 'I thought you were on a short leash?'

'Well,' he said. 'That's what it says in the file, yes. I'm signing in with Robinson daily, in person, until I'm officially discharged from "medical observation". You too, my dear. But all that paperwork has already been done. In advance.'

'Christ,' said Carol. 'He's taking a bit of a career risk, isn't he? I mean, word is out that you two were there. In Manchester. Deniable, sure. But the press are bound to be looking for you. Bill can't let you go roaming. Can he?'

'Yeah, well,' said Harry, leading them up the stairs to the porch. 'You're right. But he also can't afford not to. He knows full well that we need to keep chasing this, because we're the only ones who have been working on this case since the beginning. He could reach out to Europol or the DEA, and maybe there would be people who would give him a hearing. But there are also people who would shut him down.'

'The bigger this gets,' said Iris, 'the more stupid the response.'

'Welcome to elite law enforcement,' said Harry, tapping in the code on the door keypad. 'By the way, this code changes every twelve hours, so don't get locked out.'

Inside, the house seemed, at first glance, to be the well-appointed home of – what? A mid-ranking financier? A lawyer? Someone doing quite well in advertising? The hallway runner was tastefully old-fashioned in design, and the walls of the corridor were lined with Hogarth prints on one side and high-end framed movie posters on the other. A couple of items of post were placed on a console table, lit by a green library lamp.

But, as if running out of breath, the house quickly revealed its true identity. The downstairs living spaces were beautifully furnished and there were expensive sound systems and televisions in both. On one of the coffee tables stood a vase of fresh-cut lilies. There were unlit church candles on the mantlepieces. But there was no true evidence of habitation, of the life of an individual or a family. This was certainly a house with a purpose – but that purpose was not day-to-day living.

They emptied the Range Rover of the kit they had hastily assembled. Weaponry, surveillance gear, body armour, three suitcases of comms gear to keep them in touch with everyone and everything. This was their mission to complete, as a unit.

For the first two hours, they checked and rechecked everything. The larger sitting room was quickly turned into a makeshift ops centre, with a series of monitors spread out on trestle tables carried up from the basement. Iris found a small study to convert into an armoury where she laid out three sniper rifles and the team's handguns. Hand grenades, flare kits, tear gas and more. Harry said he didn't want to know where she'd got it all. Just to make sure she had the receipts and to triple-check that nothing would jam in the field. They were in a zone where there was no scope at all for mistakes.

When everything was in place, they gathered in the kitchen.

'So, Airbnb, is it, Harry?' asked Carol.

'No chance. For a start, I'm not putting my hand in my bloody pocket to pay for our temporary digs, and nor will the Yard. You can be sure of that. No, this happens to be a safe house belonging to His Majesty's Security Service. God knows what they use it for. I doubt it's for *treffs* with agents. Much too obvious. Who knows?'

'Well, how did we get it?' said Iris.

'Remember that big oaf Neary – Gordon Neary – we met on the very first day in Stepney?'

She nodded.

'Well, it turns out that he's not a total oaf after all. I called him a couple of days ago – a fishing expedition, really. And it turns out, fair play to the poor sod, that he's banging his head against a wall, too. Seems nobody in Thames House will give airtime to any theory that doesn't involve the mullahs, Russia, China . . .You both know the list by now. Straightforward villainy plus nukes just doesn't stack up for them. And though Neary isn't getting anywhere in nailing it all down, he's intelligent enough to know that this is something new – and not just in the obvious sense.'

'Can he help us?' asked Carol, sitting at the table.

Harry started to open the cupboards, looking for tea. 'Neary? Well, not much right now – I mean in terms of usable intel. But he might prove helpful when whatever happens next – happens. And he did fix me a covert loan of this place. Mainly because he's pissed off at his bosses, I reckon.' Ah, there you are, you fucker. Brew, anyone?' He grabbed the box of tea bags. 'Brew?'

'Yes, please,' said Carol. 'Just milk.'

'Yeah, same please,' said Iris.

'Incidentally, you'll have deduced already that every room in this place is bugged,' said Harry. 'Including the khazies. So you can assume that everything we say is being listened to – probably by a real person. I like to think we've graduated from AI surveillance software looking for keywords, don't you? Bit of a bloody insult if it's just Siri or ChatGPT listening in, really.'

'Doesn't that bother you?' said Iris.

'Not a question of whether it bothers me.' Harry placed the mugs on the table. 'We've probably been under hostile surveillance of one kind or another for the whole of this op, and no doubt by our own side too. They know SO22 is a loose cannon, and the question is always how far it's in their own interests to let the loose cannon stay out of its box and do its work. Course they'd never admit to it.'

Carol looked out of the bay window to a long, well-kempt lawn at the end of which was a small rose garden. All in order, nothing to attract attention. Classic safe house. 'Are you saying we're just guinea pigs?' she asked. 'Or what?'

'What I'm saying is that every time they tell Robinson very sternly to keep us grounded – me, especially – and in his sights, there's part of them that's really signalling to him: Do what you have to do, Bill. Just get this fucking mess sorted.'

'Total bloody hypocrisy,' said Iris.

'Like I said, welcome to elite law enforcement.'

Harry sat down. He raised his mug. 'Here's to John.'

They toasted their fallen comrade and fell silent for a while. They knew that their true grief would have to be postponed for now, while they took care of business.

'So,' said Iris. 'What now?' He noted the edge of steel returning to her voice.

'Well, I think we can be reasonably sure now that Ramirez

got caught in a battle between two giants. He was moving in on Smythe's ops in Europe. Maybe it was his firm, or a subsidiary that the Crick syndicate were dealing with when they tried to buy that gear in that Kent country park. Christ, all that seems a lifetime ago. We'll never know, probably. And Smythe took him out in the most spectacular way he could.' He sipped his tea. 'Which is still a puzzle to me.'

'How do you mean?' said Iris.

'Look. You're Smythe. You have a public life as a big-time art dealer to the super-rich, philanthropist, bit of a dandy. Everyone with a badge knows you have a drug network going, but they can't land a punch on you, and a lot of them have given up trying. Which means two things.'

'Which are?' said Carol.

'He's got protection at the very highest levels. Certainly in the US where the charges against him just melt away. Maybe here too, who knows? And on the European mainland – well, you wouldn't bet against it, would you? I mean, not a *single* successful bust, in any jurisdiction, in all these years? Tell me that's a coincidence.'

'All right,' said Iris. 'What's the other thing?'

'Political protection only lasts as long as you observe a certain level of discretion. Look at the mob in the US. Whenever they lose sight of that – when they go too far and the public gets properly scared of their bloodshed – suddenly there are indictments, convictions, whole criminal enterprises torn to pieces. Corruption depends upon smooth surfaces.' He smiled coldly. 'And a fucking atom bomb really does not count as a smooth surface. The whole country is suddenly teetering on the edge of anarchy.'

'But it does end Ramirez and his cartel, doesn't it?' said Carol. 'I mean, as brute force goes . . .'

'Yeah, but there are a hundred ways of doing that. All of

them drawing less attention than *this*. I mean, Smythe could easily afford a mercenary unit to make an airstrike on the Ramirez HQ in Juarez – assuming he had intel to tell him when Ramirez was there. I mean, he obviously knew that he was going to be on the *Gabriella*, right? Which means he has informants in the Mexican cartel, and good ones. Why not use them to find out where Xavier is and when he's vulnerable, and just take him out like a regular gangster? "Xavier Ramirez, notorious Mexican narco boss, assassinated". That might not even be front-page news in some parts of the world. But "Manchester is new Nagasaki – World War Three Imminent" – well, that tends to capture the public imagination. If you know what I mean.'

'Are you saying that this is somebody trying to *discredit* Smythe?' Carol said. 'That it was Voldrev all along? I mean, just for example.'

'Yeah, that occurred to me. I haven't ruled it out at all, either. Voldrev wanting everyone to think that his arch-enemy Julian has finally lost his bloody marbles and is using fun-sized atom bombs to take out his rivals. So – let's say – Voldrev sends us the coordinates to the Manchester submarine hand-over, having worked out that Marseilles was all make-believe and got a tip-off about the real location of the drug transfer. It's like Vladimir wanted us to *see* Smythe take out Ramirez with the bomb – or, just as possible, to do it himself, but make us think it was Julian. Remember the crazy mind games between these two – I told you about their stand-off outside the embassy when Smythe was a kid. Voldrev has been rubbing him the wrong way for *decades*. This would just be the logical extension of a stand-off that began in Moscow in the eighties. Quite a bloody big one, admittedly.'

Dusk was falling and a smattering of grey clouds loomed in the West London skyline.

'Anyway,' he said, 'whoever did this has a taste for spectacle as well as power. They wanted the world to see – but see *what*? That's what's twisting my melon. It really bloody is.'

At precisely the same moment, all three of their phones began to buzz and cheep like crickets taking a conductor's cue.

'What the fuck's this?' he said. 'WhatsApp from Robinson: "Turn on TV, then call ASAP." Jesus. What now?'

# 31

It was as though the sun had burned itself out. The image on the screen of the Caribbean skyline was terrifying in its brooding intensity: dark, low clouds shifting fast over a land mass made of fire. At a distance, a makeshift floating cordon of buoys and a flotilla of emergency-service launches were tossed dangerously by the choppy ocean. Helicopters circled as close as they could, and two Super Hornets – American? – flew over the cove, as if there was anyone or anything left to fight. A few dinghies with survivors still bobbed in the water, awaiting rescue.

Behind them, Carol was not watching the television. Her attention was fully absorbed by the range of screens on the trestles, patched securely into data feeds from around the world and a scanner system that John had designed to monitor satellite information and red flags posted by police and intelligence agencies everywhere. That particular screen was a blizzard of red dots as specialist cops and spooks all over the planet chased leads, squeezed informants and updated friendly agencies. Only half an hour had passed since the blast, and the entire network was fizzing with chatter and speculation.

'POTUS is going to address the nation at six p.m. eastern time,' she said. 'Jesus. What does a president say at a moment like this?'

'Can't imagine he's got much to say,' muttered Harry. 'His

little speech after Manchester was pretty pathetic. The "wings of angels heard in English homes" – for Christ's sake.'

'Yeah, but this one is right in his own backyard,' said Iris. 'The Yanks will be thinking: ISIS or al Qaeda? They'll take it as an attack on the homeland. Cuban Crisis meets 9/11.'

Harry nodded. 'But they'll be wrong, won't they? I mean, why would jihadis vaporise Voldrev's island? It just doesn't stack up. The island of Elena and a Manchester quayside – what's the connection? Smythe taking out another enemy? Yes, very possible. Voldrev throwing a curve ball by destroying his own base and then – who knows? – disappearing, happy for Smythe to take the rap for it all and maybe end up behind bars?' He frowned. 'Or something else entirely. Something I'm missing. Wheels within wheels.'

The BBC reporter in Downing Street informed them that the Prime Minister would be making a brief statement in a few minutes. Behind her, a lectern was being set up.

'Well, that'll clear everything up,' said Iris.

'They must be like headless fucking chickens in there,' said Harry. 'Robinson said he couldn't even get hold of Fincham and that they were all in a COBRA meeting. God knows what they're talking about. Media management and civil disorder, I'll bet. Food riots. Troops on the streets. Ugly stuff.'

'Lot of Brits in Barbados,' said Carol. 'More than twenty thousand, I think. They'll have to offer them all evacuation, I guess. Though they'll also feel obliged to say that there's no need to leave the island.'

Harry's phone rang. It was Tennyson.

'Christ, Lance,' he said. 'How are you doing?' He could hear shouting and engines and confusion in the background.

'I'm OK, Harry. Well – I suppose. Just about. Still . . . processing it. Listen. I haven't got long. A quarter of a million people are trying to get out of Barbados and we've got to stop the panic somehow. I'm at the airport now setting up a perimeter. Military, medics, and everything else.'

'What are the radioactivity levels like?'

'Low. Like Manchester. This was a surgical attack on one small island. That whole area will have to be zoned off for a very long time – but the levels on the main island are not dangerous.'

'But I'm guessing nobody believes that. Right?'

'Exactly. They just see another nuke going off, and this time the cloud is visible from their homes. And they want to flee. Hard to blame them. All this – it hasn't happened since 1945, Harry. It was never meant to happen again. And now, somehow, it *is* happening again.'

'I'm sorry. This wasn't meant to be your fight, Lance.'

'It is now, Harry. It is now. Listen. One of my men questioned a fisherman who saw Voldrev's plane taking off from Elena about half an hour before the blast. I checked the manifest online and I'm texting you the details we have so you can trace him. Looks like he's heading to Moscow.'

'Moscow? Yeah, that would figure. He can probably afford to pay off the regime for any past sins and retire there. Because, one way or another, it isn't safe for him in the West any more. Everything is different now.'

'For sure. He must have been tipped off that an attack was coming – and, after Manchester . . .'

'Yeah, exactly.'

'Listen, Harry, I have to go. Text should be with you now. Stay in touch, my friend. Godspeed.'

'You too,' said Harry. But Tennyson had already hung up.

He gave Carol the details of Voldrev's flight and watched as, a few keystrokes later, the left-hand screen was filled with a state-of-the-art air-traffic-control image of the western

Atlantic. She zoomed in on a dot somewhere in the Guiana Shield.

'Crafty bugger,' she said. 'He's hugging the coast, flying pretty low.'

'He must know he's being tracked.'

'Yeah. He was unlucky to be spotted making his escape.'

'He was,' said Harry. 'Back to Mother Russia, eh? What a creep.'

'Can we intercept him? Once he's over European airspace?'

'Robinson is looking into it. Sure, Voldrev's on a few wanted lists. But he's officially the victim here, remember? I mean, it's his private island that just ceased to exist. Hard to justify sending a couple of Tornados up to bring him down. Though, personally, I'd do it anyway, and let the lawyers haggle over the details later. We badly need Voldrev in custody. Whatever is going on, you can bet he knows more than we do. And what's he going to do to Julian now? How can he do that from a dacha by the Black Sea?'

'You don't believe he's heading home for good?' said Carol.

'All I know is that we're caught between two huge and dangerous egos, one of whom is using the deadliest weapons ever invented in a great game that's been going on for decades. Games like that are more dangerous than business. They make people do mad things, just to win. And be *seen* to win. I'm just trying to work out what the next mad thing is going to be.'

On television, a drone camera zoomed in on a huge chunk of masonry nestling on top of a coral reef, hundreds of yards from the jagged remains of the shore. The blast had been greater than Manchester, sufficiently powerful to send great fragments of stone and timber spiralling into the air, before sinking into the sea. The wreckage of Voldrev's great monument to his own vanity.

Robinson called to say that Vauxhall had also detected the flight and that efforts were being made on both sides of the Atlantic to contact the pilot. But he also told Harry that his request for an RAF or NATO interception had been categorically rejected. The word from Downing Street was: 'Don't rattle the Russian cage at a time like this.' *What is the right time for rattling?* Harry wondered. *If not now, when?*

The unofficial death toll from the Elena blast was already much higher than Manchester: at least 120 assumed to be lost on the island itself, probably more (Voldrev's official payroll list lodged with the Bajan authorities was sketchy, to say the least). A handful of fishing skips had been caught by the detonation, as well as a chartered pleasure boat. This time, Harry wasn't sure just how high the final count might sit.

He texted Robinson:

**What about Smythe?**

The reply was almost immediate:

**Not in Blgrvia or Sussx estate. Wll kp u posted.**

So Julian was keeping his head down. Possibly out of the country. But not, he imagined, high on any priority list as intelligence agencies and elite police units went on wild goose chases all over the world in search of someone – anyone – who looked like a potential suspect.

Harry imagined all the futile meetings going on at that very moment: in Langley, Washington, Vauxhall, Paris, Berlin, Rome, Islamabad, Seoul, at the NATO HQ in Brussels, the UN in New York, and in secret encampments near the Iranian border with Iraq. Enhanced interrogations at CIA black sites. Station chiefs reassuring their bosses they were following every lead. Senior coppers in situation rooms promising the politicians that the crisis, whatever it was, would be resolved in twenty-four hours. Looking at the big picture but forgetting the *smallness*, the sheer pettiness of the hatred between two men and the horrors it could unleash. At least when nations went to war, there was some sort of playbook. But two individuals, hell-bent on destroying each other at any cost? Well, he thought, in that case, it turns out that *anything* can happen.

'Voldrev's heading north,' said Carol. 'The flight is still officially Moscow-bound, just like Tennyson said. No legal infringements or improprieties.'

'I know,' said Harry. 'I don't see how we're going to get our hands on him unless – well, unless he does something stupid, or something changes. Which, let's face it, is more likely than not.'

'Yeah, so we also need to get to Smythe,' said Iris. 'Somehow.'

'He's gone to ground,' said Harry. 'We may have to go looking for him and dig him up, the smug bastard.'

'Absolutely,' she said. 'But where?'

'He'll turn up,' said Harry. 'Remember, he admitted to me that his weakness is a love of drama. All those fucking playbills. And I don't think he was just passing the time of day. So, if he is the producer of whatever this is – this global horror show – he'll want some sort of curtain call, won't he?'

'Assuming it is him,' said Carol.

They were distracted momentarily by images on CNN – fresh drone footage of the blast zone. The acres of lush forest through which Harry and Carol had walked were now obliterated, reduced to smouldering ash and grey twisted roots. What looked like the scorched metal of vehicle parts lay scattered across this newly desolate plain. The chateau itself had been hammered into a flattened ruin, a two-dimensional version of its former self. The Caribbean court of a Russian mobster, his gold-plated homage to Versailles, was now an apocalyptic hellscape.

'Jesus,' said Harry. 'It really *was* bigger than the first device.

There's just – nothing left. Will the third be even—? I mean, where is this heading?'

'Wait a minute,' said Carol. 'Voldrev's plane has disappeared.'

'How do you mean?' said Harry.

'Just that. One moment it was on the scanner – then, gone.'

'When?'

'Now. Literally seconds ago.'

He looked over her shoulder. 'How's that possible? Crashed?'

'No, probably flying very low. Dangerously low. He knows we're tracking him and he's trying to throw us off the scent.' She paused. 'I guess he's hoping we'll lose interest.'

'No fucking chance.'

'He'll pop up again. He has to. Don't worry, Harry, I'm on it.'

'I know.'

For the first time in years, Harry felt the craving for a cigarette. Thank fuck he didn't have any. The waiting was agony, even though his whole career had been built on the cultivation of patience. You waited until the other guy made an error, and then you pounced. That was the job. In camo gear in the jungle, or on an East End stake-out, timing was all. He had to keep his nerve, especially in front of the others.

But this was different. He had to accept that. Nuclear weapons deployed in democratic countries, outside official wartime. Almost certainly by non-state actors. The sum of the world's fears. And he was at the sharp end, bearing an absolute responsibility to bring whatever this was to an end. To find whoever was doing this and take them down – no matter what. He had lost a close mate already and had much too little to show for it. As frustrated as he was, he knew the moment of resolution was drawing close and that he had better be equal to it.

He went outside into the back garden and sat on the bench. Sent texts to Robinson, Tennyson and Neary. Then he drifted off, half dreaming of bone-shaking explosions, John's funeral, his old barracks in Hereford, the face of Voldrev, a plume of cigar smoke morphing into a mushroom cloud. It was not sleep, really. More like a fever dream of unresolved business.

'Harry.' Iris put her hand on his shoulder.

'Christ,' he said. 'I was dozing. What time is it?'

'Gone nine. I ordered in some Indian. Come on, let's eat.'

They ate in near silence around the kitchen table, taking turns to monitor the air traffic screen. At 9.36 p.m., Voldrev's flight reappeared.

'Cheeky bastard,' said Harry. 'Was he flying low all that time?'

'Not necessarily,' said Carol. 'The detection's not foolproof and he might even have rudimentary stealth tech on his jet. He can afford it.'

'What, actually invisible to radar? On a private plane?'

'Not as sophisticated a shield as a fighter has. Just a bit harder to pick up. The oligarchs love it, as you can imagine.'

'I'll bet. Where's he heading?'

'Still on course for the motherland. Heading home.'

'What are you up to, Vova?' said Harry.

'I know what you're thinking,' Carol said. 'The guy we met on Elena . . . I don't see him just doing a fade and leaving the stage like this. He was like a big sack of twitching adrenaline, that one. With tattoos.'

'I agree. Let's see if we're right.'

Just before midnight, Voldrev's jet disappeared from the monitor. But this time he wasn't gone for long: only thirty minutes.

'Bloody hell,' said Carol. 'Bloody hell. Harry! Look. He's turned west and – heading for UK airspace. His course . . . towards Sussex. Must be Gatwick. They support private jets, don't they? Bit obvious though, isn't it?'

'He's not going to Gatwick,' said Harry.

'He's not?' said Iris.

'No. Sussex, you say. Voldrev's not going to Gatwick. He's going to see his old friend Smythe.'

# 32

The drive from Ealing to Raxall Manor took less than an hour and a half – though it felt longer. They were stopped once, at an unexpected military checkpoint about a mile before they hit the M25. Harry showed the squaddie his SO22 pass, and they were waved through.

'Army out on the streets already?' said Carol.

Harry snorted. 'Of course. They're setting up vehicle checks all over the main cities – and there's no way the cops can cover that and everything else. Agreed at COBRA about five hours ago. Next step will be schools closing. You watch. Lockdown by stages. Didn't think it was starting till tomorrow, but there you go. Anyway, it's supposed to make people feel safer, seeing the boys in green on the streets. That's the theory, anyway. Not sure that's what it actually does. It's all for show. They haven't got a clue how to deal with this one.'

'Whoever is behind all this must be thrilled,' Iris said.

'Exactly what I was thinking. They've got the whole world's attention. Except nobody knows who they *are*. Quite the thrill, I imagine. Sick bastards.'

The traffic on the motorway was light, mostly lorries and sparsely occupied coaches. The instinct to huddle at home was kicking in. It was like the early Covid lockdown all over again, but much worse this time. Ahead of them, the majesty of the South Downs was mostly shrouded in night. They were led down the spectral road by shimmering cat's eyes.

Iris instinctively checked and rechecked the sub-machine gun and sidearm she had selected – along with the full sniper kit packed in its foam in a metal box in the boot.

'Jesus, will you stop doing that,' said Harry. 'I don't actually fancy a high-velocity round in the back of my neck if we hit a pothole.'

'Sorry,' she said. 'Force of habit.'

'Yeah, well. Keep it under control. I'd like to be back in London for early lunch at the latest. And not in a body bag, preferably.'

'Made reservations, have you?' said Carol.

'Oh, yeah, sure. River Café at noon. We'll have built up a proper appetite by then, I imagine.'

'Do you reckon we'll get to Smythe before Voldrev does?' Iris asked.

'No idea. That's why I'm flooring it. And I've told Robinson we're on manoeuvres and to prepare backup. Broad-brush picture only. I don't want him flooding the area with flashing lights – not yet, anyway.'

'Why? Don't want to frighten the horses?'

'Yeah, but also because I doubt it would do any good. We have to understand what the fuck is going on before we start getting heavy and taking people in. What's the charge? Being in possession of a private jet after the hours of darkness? Owning a swanky manor house?'

'But Voldrev isn't going to just roll up at Smythe's place on his own with a pea-shooter, is he? I mean, this is an execution. Must be.'

'*Could* be. Robinson says that there was no sign of Smythe on the estate today. A few staff, that's it. He's vanished. Nobody knows where he is. Not that they're looking as hard as they might.'

'What's his place like?' Carol said.

'Raxall Manor? Seriously grand. Came into the Smythe family by marriage in the nineteenth century, apparently. Parts of it go back to Tudor times, and a good fifteen thousand acres of land, too, according to the original brief Robinson sent me. Rivals Cowdray House and Goodwood as the jewel of Sussex, if that's your kind of thing. But – surprise, surprise – no public access. No public money. Julian pays for it all himself.'

'Private security?' said Iris.

'Must be. What surveillance we have – and it's much too patchy for my liking – suggests a couple of guys at most. High fences, CCTV everywhere. Fairly standard. Not a fortress, if that's what you're asking.'

'He'll need a fortress if Voldrev is taking this badly,' said Carol. 'Which he will be. Remember what he was like, Harry? Like a big Russian IED ready to go off. And that was when he was at home, in a good mood, full of champagne and God knows what else.'

'Yeah, he's a jumpy one, old Vova. If he's planning what he seems to be planning, he'll be taking more than harsh language with him.'

'More like a couple of MiGs,' said Iris.

Harry laughed. They were not far away now, and he knew that, one way or another, something was about to be settled. In the coming hours, there would be a moment of resolution. But of what kind, he couldn't be sure. And that made him feel more conscious than ever of his duty to get his people in and out safely. He and Iris had been spared John's fate by an accident of distance – just a few hundred yards and a reinforced concrete wall separated them from instant evaporation. And before, Carol had only escaped a grisly end because of Iris's marksmanship. The image of the slain Devereux mob was still fresh in his mind. And what if they had visited Elena the day it ceased to exist? Death had been stalking them for weeks.

He saw the exit ahead and shifted lanes. Raxall was only twenty minutes away now, though the roads would quickly get twisty and potentially confusing – especially in the dead of night. He relied on the satnav and the knowledge that the manor house itself was built on a slope of a valley and would be visible from a few miles. Assuming somebody was home and the lights were on.

His phone rang. It was Gordon Neary.

'You're up late, sweetheart,' Harry said.

'And you're not tucked up in bed at your safe house, are you?'

'Oh, you know. Couldn't sleep. Out for a spin to clear the head.'

'Yeah, I'll bet. Listen, Harry—'

'Yeah, yeah, I know. Tread lightly.'

'Well, yes. That, obviously. But there's something else. I expect Bill will see it, too, but – well, I thought I should let you know, even though I bloody well shouldn't be telling you. Ach, you know what I mean.'

'Spit it out, Gordo. For fuck's sake.'

Neary paused. 'GCHQ intercepted this about half an hour ago. Coded, but only in a rudimentary way. Direct message to the Lubyanka first desk – attention of FSB chief, General Aleksandr Vasiliev. Reads: "Greetings Sasha! Tonight, all will be revealed and all accounts settled. Felicitations. Voldrev".'

# 33

From their temporary woodland base, Raxall Manor looked like a portal into the past: a huge slumbering beast made of brick, timber and stone, its outline just visible through the cedars, beech and oak that lined its long driveway and encircled the building. There were lanterns every fifty yards or so to guide the visitor towards the house. A few windows – not many – were lit up. Somebody was in.

Harry watched Iris scan the scene through her night binoculars, using a mossy log as cover. They had parked off-road, as discreetly as possible. If Smythe had sensors or cameras in the forest, he would know already that they were near. He probably did anyway. But Harry wanted a moment to take the measure of the location and to steel themselves for what might lie ahead. He also wanted to see if Voldrev had already moved in.

'I still don't understand,' Carol whispered. 'The FSB? Now?'

'Neither do I,' Harry said. 'But remember that all this started in Moscow in the eighties. Voldrev was in the KGB, Julian was with his parents. Vasiliev was in military intelligence then, though junior. He didn't move into the FSB until the nineties. But Voldrev must have known him. Worked with him maybe.'

'Was that a friendly message, then?'

'I doubt it. It was meant to be picked up by foreign agencies.

They barely bothered to encrypt it. No, Vova – or someone posing as Vova – is sending a signal to his former masters that they should keep the telly turned on tonight. Or that Red Square is about to be obliterated. It's turning into that kind of week, isn't it?'

'What did Bill say?' asked Iris, without shifting her eyes from the night sights.

'The PM is out of bed and in his dressing gown, apparently. Spoke to the US President. Embassy staff in Moscow being quietly moved out of the city, though I doubt that'll be easy once this leaks, which it will. Robinson doesn't know whether the Russians know that Voldrev's plane just landed in the UK. But – again – they'll find out soon enough. And when they do . . .'

'This place will be crawling with FSB hoods.'

'Maybe,' said Harry. 'It depends upon what they think Voldrev is here for. And their operational capacity here has been weak since Ukraine and all the expulsions. They'd probably need to deploy locally sourced mercenaries.'

'Jesus,' said Iris. 'Wagner affiliates trampling through the woods. That's all we need.' She paused. 'Hello . . . Vehicle pulling up at the front porch. What is it? Looks like an estate motor. Nothing big. It's dumping . . . can't see. Could just be a delivery of food or fuel. Impossible to tell at this distance. And . . . yes, driven away now. Whatever it was, doesn't look like anyone went in.'

Harry looked through his own binoculars. She was right: nothing much to see. But there was no sense staying here any longer. Time to get on with it.

'All right, let's move out. Iris: shotgun, eyes firmly ahead. Carol: keep that scanner on your tablet. I want intercepts on any CCTV you can get.'

'Roger that,' she said.

'Rules of engagement?' Iris asked.

'Hostiles: shoot to kill. Otherwise, stay frosty. I want to try jaw-jaw if I can. Depending upon who's inside. Though it may be too late for that.'

'And if Voldrev and his team are ahead of us?'

'Play it by ear. But if he's come heavy, we pull back, fast, and let Robinson send in proper armed response or special forces, depending upon scale.'

'Are you really going to pull back?' asked Iris. 'After all these two bastards have put us through?'

Harry thought briefly. 'No,' he said.

Back in the car, he turned the engine over until its purr was barely audible.

'Those gates are reinforced steel. I can't break through them. Not with a civilian vehicle. So let's see if we're expected.'

'Rather than advance by foot?' said Iris.

'I don't want to ditch the motor,' he said. 'And I have a funny feeling that whoever's at home might just let us in. Both of those bastards love a bloody audience.'

'Yeah,' said Iris. 'They also love weapons-grade uranium, though.'

'True enough. In which case, God help the lot of us.'

He reversed out of their hiding place and then turned the Range Rover to face the road, and the gates.

'Here we go, then.'

Iris nursed her weapon like a beloved child.

They crossed over, so that the grille of the car was almost touching the metal of the gate.

'There's a buzzer on the right side,' said Iris. 'If you want to be really polite.'

'Aren't I always?' Harry said. He picked up his SIG Sauer from the dashboard and prepared to get out. Even as he did, the gates opened silently.

'I guess we *are* expected,' said Carol.

And then, without warning, they were bathed in light. They braced, by reflex now, for a blast, for an explosion that would leave nothing of them but dust and a few metal fragments of the vehicle.

This time, the blast did not come.

'Jesus fuck!' said Harry. 'I'm seriously losing my patience here.'

'Floodlights,' said Carol. 'Just floodlights on the driveway! Fuck!'

'Yes,' said Iris. 'But switched on by somebody who knew exactly what effect it would have. Bloody comedian.'

'Right,' said Harry. 'Time to have a few choice words with this joker. Maybe Voldrev is already here and laughing his arse off in the control room. We'll see.'

He revved the engine and took the driveway at speed. If there were snipers in place, they would have to take potshots at a fast-moving vehicle driven by a seasoned officer experienced in advanced evasive driving. He was not going to make this easy on – whoever.

'Hold on,' he said. 'Nearly there.'

The Range Rover screeched to a halt outside the manor porch. On either side were flaming gas torches, seven feet tall at least. Above the portico was a heraldic crest, but he could not make out any details. A stairway landing light – a chandelier in fact – could be seen a few feet above, inside frosted glass.

'Headsets all working?' he said.

'Check,' said Carol.

'Check,' said Iris.

'Right. If we get separated, hang fast. I'll get to you. After twenty, regroup in the Rover or on foot at our original base camp. And listen. Just don't take any stupid risks. Let me handle that department.'

As if either of them was going to leave him in the lurch, Harry thought.

They gathered by the doorway. Iris signalled above and to the left, where a camera swivelled to zoom in on them. Somebody was watching their every move. *Well*, thought Harry, *let's not disappoint them, eh?*

He reached for the doorknob and was not greatly surprised to find that it turned. He pushed the door open with his boot and held up a flashlight, motioning the other two to give him cover from behind.

The hallway was magnificent. The pool of torchlight covered what looked like original stone from the earliest history of the house, covered with huge rugs. To either side were broad staircases leading up to a corridor and a long balustrade. Directly above them was a smaller stairwell that seemed to begin on a separate balcony. The walls were covered with oil paintings: horses, ancestors, nobility, images of the hunt and of banquets. It was hard to make out the detail. On the left, a tapestry stretched from floor to ceiling: its design apparently a medley of coats of arms. The vast space had the aura of ancient authority and generations of power stacked on top of one another. In other circumstances, he would have been mildly interested. But, for now, his focus was on the op. Darting like a spirit across the stairs, he saw the red dot of Iris's laser sights.

Aside from their torches and the minimal light from the stairway above, there were no signs of life. He signalled forwards movement, and they advanced in a three-person wedge formation. The next door was smaller and, when he kicked the ancient draught excluder out of the way, revealed a source of light behind it.

He pointed his team to stand back as he opened the door. Moving through into a well-lit, long, warm corridor, at the end of which was what looked like a library or a study. He could see a desk and shelves of leather-bound books. He could also see a familiar figure standing up.

'Ah, Harry! Welcome to Raxall – do please come in,' said Julian Smythe.

# 34

'Now,' Julian Smythe said. 'Unless I'm mistaken, you must be Sergeant Iris Davies? One of the best snipers in the country, at least by reputation. And Inspector Walker – Dr Walker, of course. Quite the polymath, I gather. SCD4 Forensics until only a few weeks ago, and, goodness, now look at you! On a combat recce – without a warrant, I'll bet – but with a Glock in your hands and a mean look in your eyes. My, my, Dr Walker. You really have left the labs of Cambridge far behind, haven't you?'

'Why don't you shut the fuck up?' she said.

Smythe laughed. In spite of the late hour, he was wearing a perfectly cut tweed jacket, shirt, tie and cords. He looked, Harry thought, as if he was about to have a kitchen supper with an old school friend, visiting from Singapore or wherever else his Etonian contemporaries lived these days.

'Perhaps I should,' he said. 'But my spider senses tells me that DCI Taylor has a few questions he would like me to answer.'

'Just a few,' said Harry. 'Cuff him, Iris.'

'Hold on!' said Smythe. 'Before you do anything like that, consider your options. MI5 has already rattled my chain, to no effect. I retain a world-class London lawyer full-time, twenty-four seven. I am his sole client and he has put three children through the nation's most expensive schools and bought a chalet in Gstaad on the proceeds. If I call him, he will call the police – the *local* police, that is – and report a break-in. He'll also make representations to very senior public figures who can vouch for me. Local constables will come here and, one way or another, your respective careers will be over.'

'How will you call him if you're in fucking bracelets?' said Iris.

'Because, my dear Sergeant Davies, the phone system in this house is voice-activated and responds only to my sweet tones. Tech of a quality you can't get on the general market yet, but ever so useful. As ancient as the house looks, Raxall is one big app, really. I can order in Deliveroo while I'm in the bath, should I be so vulgar to want such a thing. Rather reassuring, really.'

'If you call me "dear" again,' Iris said, 'I'll shoot off your kneecaps with a five second intermission between left and right, just so you can work out which hurts more.'

Smythe put his hands up theatrically. 'Dear, oh dear. That sounds very painful. Well, I certainly shan't make that mistake again.'

'Sit down, Smythe,' said Harry. 'Just sit down and shut up for once. The endless bunny is giving me brain ache.'

'Well, Detective Chief Inspector, now you put it like that.' He sat down at the desk. 'Do you mind if I finish my drink? I was rather enjoying this generous slug of Glenmorangie Signet.'

Harry ignored the question. 'Where's Voldrev?'

'Where indeed?' said Smythe. 'I imagine you followed his flight here and thought you might find us wrestling by the fireplace like Oliver Reed and Alan Bates. No such luck, I'm afraid.'

'So he did fly here?'

'Yes. To Shoreham. The manifest said Moscow, as you know, but, very naughtily, he hung a left and headed towards his old pal Julian's gaff.'

'So where is he? And why are you still here? You must know he's coming to kill you. Voldrev won't put up with you destroying Elena. And on global television.'

'Ah, yes. Elena. We'll get to all that,' said Smythe.

'And I'm assuming that it was Vova that tipped us off to your little bait-and-switch with Marseilles and Manchester. You can't be too happy about that?'

'Yes, he did, in a manner of speaking. I'll answer your questions, Harry – well, those of them I want to, at least – but it's important to do things in the right order, don't you agree?'

'I find the most important thing is to get things done, Smythe. The correct order bothers me less. Especially on a night like this.'

'My, my, you have brought a temper with you tonight, Harry. I saw you as the ice-cold copper. *Unflappable*. Clearly an error on my part.'

Harry felt his grip tighten on his pistol. 'Do you see my hands shaking? I'm quite in control, Smythe. So are my two colleagues. We want a lot of answers, and sharpish. We want to know, for a start, why one of our good friends died in Manchester because of all . . . this. Because of your mad fucking feud.'

'Ah, yes, DI Williams,' said Smythe, shaking his head. 'Very regrettable. I heard about that.'

'Tell us some more things you've heard, you ponce,' said Iris.

'Really, really,' he said. '*Manners*, Sergeant Davies. We'll get nowhere without a bit of decorum on both sides.'

'I'm afraid we're all out of decorum, Smythe,' said Harry. 'Supplies have run out. So just stop your big act and start talking.'

Smythe sighed and sipped at his drink. 'I have two favours to ask.'

'*Favours?*' said Carol. 'You think you're in a position to ask favours.'

'Actually, I do rather. Yes. I think as upper hands go, mine is pretty decent, actually.'

'And how's that?' said Harry.

'Well, the first favour will answer that question and it's terribly easy. Please take a look out of that window, if you would.' He pointed to his left, then spoke to the voice control system. 'Mikhail: spotlights, quadrant eight, mid-level.'

To their right, an area of rough grassland lit up.

'Do look, please. You'll see what I'm talking about immediately.'

'Don't take your eyes off him, Iris,' said Harry. 'Carol?'

They went to the window. On a small plinth, about fifty metres away, was what looked like a launcher on a tripod.

Carol looked through her binoculars.

'Jesus,' she said. 'Is that what I think it is? That's not possible.'

'Indeed it is, Dr Walker. I knew you, of all people, would appreciate it. Quite a rarity.'

'The M29 Davy Crockett weapons system,' she said. 'Those beasts were manufactured – what, in the late fifties? Only about two thousand were ever made, I think. Almost all were deactivated and destroyed in or soon after 1968. What the *fuck* are you doing with it?'

'Full marks!' said Smythe. '*Almost* all is exactly right. I acquired this fine specimen under the most unusual circumstances. In Istanbul, as it happens, from a supplier with no sense of history, who thought it was a regular missile launcher. Well, it was quite a bargain. I was very excited, as you can imagine, and had to maintain my very best poker face as I took him to the cleaners. I've kept it here ever since, restoring some of its parts, modernising it here and there. Ensured it was ready for the day I needed it.'

'And tonight you need it?' said Carol.

'Why yes!' said Smythe. 'Isn't that why we're all here?'

Harry turned round and pointed his pistol squarely at Smythe's head.

'What sort of weapon is it? Be quick, I'm in a bit of a hurry.'

'Do lower the gun, Harry. It doesn't help matters, you know. Why don't you ask Dr Walker?'

'What is it, Carol?'

'The Davy Crockett,' she said, 'one of the original battle-field nuclear weapons, delivers a small fission warhead. Casualty radius of five hundred to a thousand feet. Never that accurate, and famous for leaving depleted uranium in its wake. A relic from an age when armies expected to wage war face to face with limited tactical damage. Christ. *Madness*. Fucking *madness*.'

'I agree,' said Smythe. 'Madness it most certainly is. But that's why the world needs to see it. To be reminded.'

'See what?' said Harry.

'The error of its ways.'

'You think tactical nuclear explosions are a *lesson*?' said Iris. 'You really are a sick fuck, aren't you?'

For the first time, Smythe let the mask slip and his anger show. 'I most certainly do! Look at the world today. We're frying ourselves towards slow extinction – when we're not dreaming up bioweapons, or letting half of humanity starve or die of disease, while the rest of us waste our time and money on things we don't need.'

'Oh. Sorry,' said Harry. 'I thought you were just a fucking duplicitous drug dealer who's never been caught and was wiping out the competition one by one? I didn't realise you were modelling yourself upon Mother fucking Teresa. I thought you were just a posh twat of a villain.'

'Well, so I may be – by your lights anyway, Harry. I don't expect a man like you to understand the greatness of what I'm doing.'

'*Greatness?*' said Carol. 'All I can see is a man with too much money killing anyone in his way and scaring the rest of the world to death with nukes for his party games. Not much greatness in that.'

'Oh, but there *is*. These days, if you want to get people's attention, you have to drop a breeze block in their laps. You have to act with panache and theatricality. I *told* you in Belgravia that I had a gift for the dramatic, Harry. Evidently, you weren't listening.'

'I was listening all right. I just didn't make the connection at the time between bloody Sondheim posters and atom bombs. Stupid of me, really. I must be losing my touch.'

Smythe laughed. 'Well, you weren't to know, I suppose.'

'Is Voldrev dead?'

'We're *all* dead, Harry. Sooner or later. It's just a matter of timing.'

'You know what I bloody mean. When is Voldrev coming? Is he already here somewhere? Or has he already been and gone?'

'In a manner of speaking.'

Harry lowered his weapon slightly. 'Look,' he said. 'Enough with the riddles. Just tell us what has happened and what is going to happen.'

'Dr Walker? Would you be kind enough to take a look at the range of medications on that small table by the book ladder behind you? No, just there. That's it.'

'Careful, Carol,' said Harry. 'Take it slow and easy.'

Carol looked where Smythe was pointing and approached

the smorgasbord of pill bottles. She whistled. 'This is – quite a collection, Smythe. An unlawful quantity of morphine, for a start. Midazolam for breathing and anxiety. What's this? Phenobarbital for agitation. Levomepromazine – for nausea, correct?'

'Absolutely correct,' said Smythe. 'And – though I know you're not a medical doctor – what would be your diagnosis? On the basis of the patient's medications, I mean?'

'For whoever's taking this lot? I would imagine . . . they were in close touch with an oncologist, and probably have been for a while.'

'Correct once again. Although it's palliative care now, rather than aggressive oncology. Stage four pancreatic cancer, now, regrettably, spread to my lungs and at least one of my lymph nodes. I have a couple of months left, possibly just weeks. Maybe another month if I fly to Houston and try an experimental immunotherapy. But why bother? Why lie all alone in an expensive private room in a Texan tower block playing hide and seek for a bit with the Grim Reaper? I would much rather die at home.'

His words hung in the air as they absorbed their meaning.

'Well, that's dampened the mood, hasn't it? Sorry, but you did ask.' Smythe grinned.

Harry was the first to speak. 'All right. But why waste your remaining time with all this playground crap with Voldrev? I mean, don't you have any family at all you'd rather be spending time with?'

'I'll answer those questions in a moment. But before that – my second favour.'

'You're not in a position to ask any favours, Smythe.'

'At the risk of repeating myself, which I dislike *intensely*, I rather think I am. Have you forgotten what's outside? Primed and ready to fire? Are you happy to go for the hat-trick,

Harry? Manchester, Barbados . . . and Sussex. Two out of
three in the UK. Well, that *would* look bad for the Yard, now
wouldn't it?'

'All right. What's the bloody favour?'

'On the same table as the pills, there are two hefty envelopes. They are marked A and B. When our business is
concluded here – assuming you are still alive – two people
will arrive in quick succession at the location written on the
note attached to each envelope. I want you to give envelope
A to the first, and envelope B to the second. Again, you'll
see the point soon enough.'

'What is inside?'

'A legacy of sorts. Something to build on. And – just so
you know – if you try to open them yourself, a device in the
centre of London will automatically be triggered. The envelopes are biometrically coded to be opened only by their
intended recipients. I'd hate your curiosity to lead to a
catastrophe in the nation's capital. Wouldn't you?'

Iris intervened, 'This is bollocks, Harry. More distraction.'

'I assure you, it is quite the opposite,' Smythe said. 'What
do you think, DCI Taylor?'

'I'm inclined to agree with Sergeant Davies. We're all tired
of your parlour games, Smythe. But – seeing as you appear
to have a vintage atomic weapon in your back garden – I
have to admit I'm in no position to argue much. So, all right.
Let's play along. We'll hand over the envelopes. If, as you
say, we all get that far.'

'Good. Good. Thank you. Now, as to Voldrev, what if I
were to say he was already here?'

'I would assume he was lying dead in your basement. Or
– at the very least – captive in a very secure location. If he
made it here, and you're still alive, then I'm guessing he's
not in particularly good shape right now.'

'Well, funnily enough, that's true. But not in the way you mean. He's *not* in a good way, old Vova. But then – who is these days? We live in sickly times.'

'Did he come here to kill you?'

'No. Though he might yet kill me, it's true.'

'Christ, Smythe. Just stop the cryptic-crossword crap for a moment, will you? Is he or isn't he here?'

'Both,' said Smythe.

'You know, even if you do have a bloody atom bomb, I'm increasingly tempted to let Sergeant Davies fire one off in your leg. Now, for the last time: what do you mean?'

Smythe reached up to his head.

'Easy there!' said Iris. 'No sudden movements, mate.'

'This won't harm you at all. Look, my hands are empty.'

'OK. There's a red dot on your left leg. Any nonsense and I blow a hole in it. Understood?'

'Perfectly clearly. Now, where was I? Oh yes.'

He removed his glasses, making himself suddenly look older and more vulnerable, and began massaging his face busily, as if warming his skin, following a line that stretched from his epiglottis, along his jawbone, up past his eyes and onto his scalp. It was as though he was loosening something, grotesquely so. As though the face of Julian Smythe was giving way under carefully applied pressure. As though he was falling to pieces before their very eyes, accelerating the work of the cancer with his own fingers and thumbs.

'What the *fuck* is this?' said Carol. 'Is he trying to harm himself? Psychotic episode?'

'Not at all,' said Smythe, through lips that seemed now to shudder and shift, making his speech slightly slurred. He worried away with his fingers at the back of his head, exerting himself now. He was clearly in pain but determined to get the job done – whatever it was.

Then, in two sharp motions, he pulled off the skin that stretched from his throat to his bald patch, and further back. Off, with a sickening snap, came the face of Julian Smythe. And – as in some ghoulish fairground attraction – out came his dental veneers, too, clattering on to the desk. Disgustingly, fragments of skin remained, and he peeled them off in a more leisurely way, patting himself down with a spotted handkerchief.

'Well,' he said. 'Even after all this time, this is *not* getting any easier. You'd think it might. But no.'

'Christ,' Harry said, repulsed. 'What are you, Smythe? What *is* this?'

'I told you in Barbados, things aren't always what they seem. Didn't you listen?'

'What the fuck? You were never in Barbados . . . You . . . That was *Voldrev* who said that to me.'

'Exactly,' said Vladimir Voldrev, smiling back at him, gold tooth gleaming.

# 35

'Tattoos,' said Carol, finally breaking the silence.

'What?' said Harry, still staring at what was, moments before, Julian Smythe, but was now a Russian oligarch, incongruously dressed as a tweedy English gentleman.

'On the island – on Elena – you had tattoos,' said Carol. 'Russian mafia prison tattoos.'

'Well remembered!' he said. 'Yes, I did indeed. My skin gear – I suppose your forensic teams would call it "prosthetics", but it's really state-of-the-art "identity emulsion" as my lab people say . . . Undetectable by any existing airport scanner or biometric technology. I wish it were open to me to claim the intellectual copyright, as it's quite an innovation. I will admit that it is a bit of an effort to apply and to remove. Especially in a jet while crossing the Atlantic, which is when I usually have to do it. Turbulence can be very irritating in that respect. But you can't have everything, can you? God knows, I've tried.'

He grinned, watching the three police officers absorbing the full import of what was happening. 'Now, in contrast, the *tattoos* . . . well, they are no trouble at all. Not amateur-hour transfers – they are much too easily detected and could cost you your life with the *Bratva*. No, we use an ingenious ink that is applied and removed only with special solutions. And the images were carefully curated to match Vova's back story in the late eighties as a bit of a jailbird – a thief, but connected. The stars of a boss after a while. They have served me very well indeed.'

'But who is "me"?' said Iris. She paused. 'This is very fucked up, you know.' The red dot from her sights was now fixed on his chest.

'Took the words out of my mouth,' said Harry.

The man laughed. 'Well, that is, of course, the question, Sergeant Davies! Vova or Julian? Voldrev or Smythe? Which am I? Either? Both? Neither?' He walked over to the mantlepiece behind his desk. 'Relax, I'm just contemplating this not very good oil painting of my great-great-grandfather, Sir Edward Smythe, the tenth baronet. He was an undistinguished fellow, but he did look after Raxall well, by all accounts, and for that we should be thankful.'

He turned around and sighed. 'I suppose the drearily *literal* answer is that Julian came first. But he was never content being just himself and spending time in Cold War Moscow, and – well, there of all places, it was easy to see that duplicity was the principal element of success. I watched men become obscenely rich and destroy one another by pretending to be things that they weren't. My father was also a professional liar – a diplomat, officially, but his job was to persuade the Russian authorities of HMG's best intentions when the reality was usually quite the contrary. It seemed to me that it was a small step not just to pretend, but to lead two lives. Why build one fortune when you could have two? Why have only *one* global business empire? Why not be twice as feared, twice as powerful, twice as active in the separate networks that I built so carefully?'

Harry said, 'But the key wasn't that at all, was it?'

'Interesting. What do you think "the key" was, Harry? Have you solved the mystery that has been keeping you awake all these weeks? That's been making your old leg injury play up,

I'll bet? The sense that the truth was staring you in the face, but you couldn't quite pin it down?'

'The real point was the *feud*, wasn't it? If every copper and spook on the planet thought that Voldrev and Smythe hated each other, archenemies determined to ruin one another, they would waste time and energy chasing a non-existent rivalry. Cancel each other out, almost. And the chances of anyone working out that you were one and the same person became pretty bloody negligible. Correct?'

The strange hybrid man standing before them smiled once more. 'That's precisely it, Harry. Congratulations on solving the puzzle. Bravo. Many have tried and failed, I'll have you know.'

'Did Vladimir Voldrev ever exist?' said Carol.

'Of course. He's me.'

'You know what I mean.'

'Well, yes. There was a very junior KGB officer of that name who went missing in the field. Afghanistan. No family. It cost me less than ten thousand dollars to buy his papers and use them as I saw fit. And – in case you were wondering – the hood that I had my little spat with outside the embassy in Moscow? His name was Vasily Alekhin. A very undistinguished officer who was killed two years later by Azerbaijani currency smugglers. Anyway, it suited my story very well to claim that he had been Voldrev. But he was nobody. Just another prop in the whole thing.'

'What about this great tragedy of Voldrev's?' said Harry. 'That there was a woman, the love of his life, and that Smythe was somehow responsible for her death.'

He became quiet. 'All true, in a way. There was a woman. The original Elena, in fact. Beautiful beyond one's dreams. She was Russian, knew me and loved me as Voldrev. And then she was killed in an attack that was directed at me – at

Vladimir, that is. So I blamed myself, of course, and correctly so. I hated myself. And, for public consumption, I projected all that hate on to Julian Smythe. Which is also me.'

'You were that calculating?' said Iris. 'Christ.'

'Not calculating. It had become natural by then to consider myself two people. It was true, in most senses.'

'And Ramirez?' said Harry. 'Why level part of Manchester – and kill one of my men – to stop a Mexican cartel from moving in on your turf? Especially as you're dying?'

The man sat down, visibly weary and a little short of breath now. 'Precisely *because* I'm dying. It's what unites the two men I have been all these years . . . a sense of order. I couldn't have scum like Xavier moving in on the European market. The man is a maniac.'

'Sorry,' said Carol. 'Did you just say "maniac"? The man who has been pretending to be an English toff and a Russian mobster simultaneously for years and plays with atom bombs for kicks is calling someone else . . . a *maniac*?'

He frowned. 'It may seem madness to you, Dr Walker, but the way I have lived has been far from arbitrary. Have I made more money than a man – two men – could spend in a life-time from the sale of narcotics and other prohibited commodities? I have, indeed. But I have done so in an orderly way, a way that minimises bloodshed – doesn't end it, but keeps it at the lower end of the spectrum. If Ramirez had moved into Europe unimpeded, the whole market would have become a war zone. All my careful calibrations would have been upset. Trust me.'

'So,' said Harry. 'In the name of *peace*, you took it upon yourself to become the world's first nuclear crime boss. Correct? A one-man nation state? Or two-man, strictly speaking.'

He stretched out his arms. 'Why not? I wanted to do some

fairly . . . *notable* things, shall we say, before I shuffled off this mortal coil. For a start, I was attracted by the idea of reminding the world – again, in a controlled fashion – of the power that its rulers still have at their fingertips.'

'*Attracted* to the idea?' said Harry. 'This isn't a bloody game, Smythe. Or Voldrev. Or whoever you are, right now. You killed people with those explosions and you terrified millions more. Billions, in fact. All over the world. Right now, this minute.'

'Well, as for the killing, I am obviously sorry about DI Williams. Let me repeat: my apologies and condolences.'

'You should be sorry,' said Harry. 'I've half a mind to blow your head off right now. "Identity emulsion" and all.'

'Not much point in killing a dying man, Harry. But – for the record – I apologise once more. It was not personal. And as for terrifying billions . . . well, *excellent*. The world really does need shaking out of its complacency, you know. The ease with which I was able to acquire that uranium was absurd, comparatively speaking. Let this be a lesson to everyone, awakening them from their sleep.'

'Where did it come from? I mean, originally.'

'Well, where indeed? My networks only learned of its existence when it turned up in Stepney. There had been an auction elsewhere in London of a package that originally came from Pakistan. It was an amateur affair, though, and the original buyers – perhaps your friends, the Crick family, maybe someone else – were intercepted by another party. Conceivably, those absurd Nazis that behaved so unconscionably towards Dr Walker. In the end, it doesn't matter. The point is, it was all so *amateur*. That alone was an affront to me, and, clearly, to Senor Ramirez. I was determined to get hold of it and did so – removing it from the custody of those awful Devereux thugs. As if they would have known what to do with it. I believe you encountered a member of my team at their base camp. An ex-member, to be precise.'

'Yes, and I saw what you did to them,' said Harry. 'Very *orderly*, I suppose.'

'I really doubt that you mourn the Devereux gang any more than I do, Harry.'

'But you still haven't answered my question. How did it end up on a Stepney dump?'

'How does anything end up in a place like that? If I had to guess, I'd say the rumours are true and it began its life on the subcontinent, where the trade in such material is occasionally lively. There are insecure facilities all over the world, you know. And it isn't only from the former Soviet bloc that material goes missing, almost routinely. It was brought to the UK and ended up in the hands of bunglers who left it on the dump in a hurry, planning to come back and get it when they could. *That*, Harry, is the most terrifying thing about the whole story, really.'

'You make it sound like Keystone cops.'

'Well, isn't it? Isn't that the *real* scandal? I'm sure I don't have to tell you that it's a matter of public record that there have been *hundreds* of cases of nuclear smuggling and contraband since the end of the Cold War. But there's a difference, isn't there, between public *record* and public *consciousness*? People don't really *want* to dwell upon that sort of thing. The miracle is that it doesn't happen all the time. But this time it *did* happen. And so I stepped in, expeditiously.'

'But to do what?' said Iris. 'To cause mayhem and destruction? To kill people?'

'Just so you know: I evacuated all my people from Elena. Most of them have been relocated to Miami, other islands in the Caribbean, elsewhere. And a handful returned to Europe where they will be able to resume their careers – in the legitimate world, or outside it, it is not for me to dictate their choices.'

'But why destroy the island at all?' said Harry. 'Your mad little replica of Versailles that you – or Voldrev, or whoever – were so bloody proud of? Makes no sense.'

'To me, it does. You're right, in a way. The chateau on Elena *was* a little mad. It was an exercise in performance art, really – a great Victorian folly more than an *ancien régime* palace. I wanted to imagine what a man like Voldrev would build if he had the means, how far he would go. And then turn that dream into reality. The island had its business uses, of course. There were subterranean levels that nobody outside my organisation ever saw that became quite important to my movement of product around the world. But that was secondary to its sheer, preposterous magnificence! I wanted to see how far I could push this great pretence – and it turned out that the answer was: a very long way indeed.'

'And you wanted us to follow you there? I mean, the Barbados cigars at the Devereux lair – that was no accident, was it? You knew we'd make that connection.'

'Of course,' he said. 'Or at least I hoped you would. It was a little touch I insisted upon – details matter so much, I think.'

'You *hoped*?' said Harry.

'Good God, yes. I knew there was a terminus to all this. A medical terminus, if nothing else. I wanted to see if someone on the other side of this great dance we call law and order had the wit to follow me to the end. And, my compliments, Harry – you did have the wit.'

Harry, uninterested in this accolade, continued, 'And the message to the Lubyanka?'

'Oh, pure *pantomime*, I'm ashamed to admit – just like sending all your colleagues scurrying off to Marseilles so I could deal with that fool Ramirez in Manchester. I knew that

General Vasiliev was getting very nervous indeed about Voldrev and thought that little message would put the wind up him. Which, I gather, it well and truly did. It's childish of me, I know, but he's a very unpleasant man. His speciality in the field was shooting Chechen children in front of their parents. He deserved to sweat. A lot worse than that, really.'

'And you knew we would intercept it?' said Harry.

'Naturally. I intended it to be intercepted. But I knew you would look at the flight path and think that Vova was finally heading to Sussex to settle accounts with Julian.' He removed a stray Smythe whisker from his face, peered at it, and discarded it swiftly. 'Which in a sense he was. We're both here now. Aren't we?'

'And you're both going to spend what little remains of your lives on remand,' said Iris. 'Waiting for a trial that you won't live to see.'

'Ah well, Sergeant Davies. That's where I beg to differ. Don't forget what's sitting outside, primed and ready to destroy this ancient house and its immediate precincts.'

'And you're really willing to pull the trigger on that revolting machine?' said Carol.

'Oh, I set that in motion about half an hour before you arrived. It will fire its payload in – well, a little more than ten minutes and that will be that. Tick-tock, tick-tock.'

'Christ's sake,' said Iris. 'You really are insane.'

Harry took a step forwards. 'Not insane, Iris. Just a champion liar. He's bluffing.'

'Bluffing? I'd have thought that after two nuclear explosions, that's the *last* thing you'd accuse me of.'

'You said that two people will arrive soon,' said Harry, 'and we are to give them your mysterious, high-tech envelopes. How can we do that if we're dead and they get here to find a radioactive wasteland?'

'Oh, that rendezvous will take place well clear of the blast zone. On my land, but further down the road. Just by the old monastery grounds. A Benedictine house it was – the ruins are rather beautiful. That's where the transfer will take place.'

'Just deactivate it,' Carol said. 'Do the decent thing, for once.'

'Can't do it.'

'Can't, or won't?'

'The detonation process is irreversible, I'm afraid. Well, unless I punch in a unique-use, real-time code linked to my vital life signs on the control pad itself. Which I'm not going to.'

'But why not?' said Harry. 'What possible purpose is there to destroying this house?'

'Clarity. I want no trace of my life – my lives – to stand when I'm gone. I want the opposite of a monument, if you like. The only legacy I – we – have is in those envelopes. They are all that matters to me now.'

'But you don't have to,' said Carol. 'You can—'

Even in the cavernous library, the report of the gun was deafening. It had the volume of something definitive, a punctuation mark at the end of a long, bitter and often deranged story.

Sir Edward Smythe, the tenth baronet, had not flinched as the brains of his great-great-grandson covered his own face and desecrated his grand portrait. On the desk slumped the body of Julian Smythe and Vladimir Voldrev, a pistol still smoking in one hand, blood oozing from their mouth and what remained of the back of their head.

# 36

With absolute confidence, Harry knew that he had only two tasks left: not to give another moment's thought to the corpse but to get Iris and Carol out of Raxall as soon as humanly possible; and then to make the rendezvous with the mystery recipients.

'Pull out! Right now! Into the Rover. No questions, no looking back, no verbals. Straight to the vehicle!'

He led the exit, swinging the beam of his flashlight around the hallway as they retreated – just in case there was yet another surprise waiting for them in the house.

'Move it!' he yelled. 'He said ten minutes! This place could blow at any moment!'

'Harry!'

He turned round and saw Iris a few steps behind.

'Where's Carol?' she said.

His mind whirred. 'Oh Christ.' He felt the knot in his stomach tighten. 'I know where she is. She didn't follow us, she's . . . Get to the motor – give me ninety seconds. If I'm not out, drive like fuck out of here.'

'But—'

'Just go, Iris!'

He saw the look of dismay on her face. And also her recognition that he meant it. She ran for the door.

Harry sprinted back through the hall, looking for a way out, any way out, to the eastern side of the manor house. He looked behind a heavy velvet curtain, hoping to find the door that Carol must have used to slip out. Just panelling. He checked his watch. Eighty seconds left.

Then, just beside the door to the study, he spotted another hanging tapestry and behind it – yes! – a low hatchway, with an old key in the lock. It was already open. Ducking down, he ran outside, down the stone stairs.

Seventy seconds.

There, on the spotlit lawn, was the insane spectacle of the primed Davy Crockett launcher: a device that was practically an antique, ready to launch an atomic weapon at any moment. At its side knelt Carol, studying what looked like a small box.

'Carol!' She ignored him. 'Carol! Get out *now*! That's an order!'

Still she did not turn round. Well, she might be willing to risk her life to thwart the final plan of a madman. But not on Harry's watch.

He rushed to her side. The box was a small keypad, obviously added to the old rocket launcher by Smythe or one of his team to enable deactivation or remote launch. Carol was deep in thought. Trying to work out the code, the digits that would prevent yet another moment of devastation.

Sixty seconds.

He took a breath. 'Carol. Listen. I know what you're trying to do. Don't. It's not worth it. And he said the code was—'

'There *must* be an emergency cut-out,' she said. 'There always is.'

'Maybe. Maybe not. You heard what he said about the envelopes. It could just as easily be wired to go up immediately if someone enters the wrong code, or even nudges it too hard.'

She was looking under the old tripod, desperately searching for a switch or other mechanism.

'Come on, Carol. Don't get dragged deeper into his games. Don't hand that lunatic another death. Two more, if you count me. Think of your dad. Think of John. Think of Iris taking out those Nazis for you. Don't waste your future on trying to make sense of craziness! Come on – think of *Otis*.'

She looked up at him. Her eyes were welling with tears. Of frustration and exhaustion as much as fear, he thought. He understood exactly how she felt, because he felt it too.

'Let's go join Iris. We still have time.'

Forty seconds.

She stood up and hesitated for a moment as Harry watched her affronted intellect made a final bid to make her stay and solve the puzzle. But some puzzles are not meant to be solved. They are just traps, set by demons.

They ran together across the lawn, and back into the darker corridors of the house. This time, he made sure she was ahead of him.

Into the hall. Thirty seconds. Christ, he hoped Iris had the motor revving.

They reached the porch and, again, he waited for her to run ahead of him.

Fifteen seconds.

Then they were clear of the house, running for their lives through the drive, towards the Range Rover.

'Where are you?' said Iris in his earpiece.

'Right behind you! You should be seeing Carol!'

'I see her!'

'All right. Get ready to put your foot down!'

He saw Carol clamber into the car and, with a last burst of energy, he made it to the front passenger door and climbed in beside Iris.

He checked his watch. Five seconds. *Christ.* Would Iris have left them behind if they had been six seconds slower?

He hoped so. But he was bloody glad it hadn't come to that.

# 37

'I said put your foot down!'

'Jesus, Harry!' said Iris. 'Give me a chance!' The car scorched through the open gates.

'No chance if we don't put at least half a mile between us and the manor house!'

He could feel his heart racing.

'All right,' he said to Carol. 'Send out an immediate all-stations alert – avoid airspace above and around Raxall at all costs. No exceptions. And patch in Robinson and Neary. And Tennyson – he needs to know. We'll need full clear-up detail and emergency services soonest.'

Looking at one of the envelopes, he tapped the necessary figures into the satnav.

'Where are we headed?' said Iris.

'To the rendezvous.'

'You're kidding.'

'I'm bloody not. Remember what he said about the bio-metric codes on the envelopes? And a *fourth* device in London?'

'You believed him?'

'I'm taking no chances tonight, believe me.'

'ETA for the rendezvous?' she said.

'Three or four minutes on these roads. They're public but they cut through the Raxall estate. This place we're heading to is on the very edge.'

Carol made the calls and then fell silent.

The Rover skidded perilously at more than sixty miles per hour round a sharp bend, the wheels screeching and almost losing their grip.

Finally, Carol burst. 'I'm sorry, Harry. I had to try. It was stupid. But I couldn't let that *bastard*—'

'Forget it,' said Harry. 'You did what you always do. You used your brain.'

'It's just, he said there was a deactivation code. I should have—'

'Just more games, Carol. Aimed especially at your scientist's rational mind. To make you think you could persuade him to deactivate it or disarm it yourself. I wonder if there even *was* a code. That was always going to be his exit, end of. I'm not surprised he had a gun in that big desk. But I wasn't expecting him to turn it on himself.'

'Me neither,' said Iris. 'Jesus.'

'What you did was bloody brave,' he said to Carol. 'But it's more important that you stay alive. OK?'

She nodded.

They careered through half a mile of thicker woodland, bisected by the road, past a deer that watched them flash past, and then they headed out towards the clearer space where the old monastery ruins stood.

The two limousines shimmered from a distance. Mercedes Duffy E-Class, unless Harry was very much mistaken. Identical vehicles, jet black, but – oddly – parked facing one another, which suggested that the two occupants, A and B, whoever they were, had arrived separately.

'All right, here they are. I'm going to suggest to them both that we move a bit further down the road, and sharpish. I don't fancy handling these negotiations with my arse in flames.'

'You sure about this, Harry?' said Iris.

'As sure as I am about anything today. But give me some cover, all right? In case things get frisky. And Carol, take the wheel. If I meet a sticky end, just get the fuck out of here, both of you. OK?'

Neither of them said anything. He got out of the Rover. As Carol took Iris's place in the driver's seat, and Iris opened one of the back doors, assuming full sniper position behind it with night vision assisting her view of the meeting spot.

Harry kept his hands in the air, assuming that A and B, and their respective chauffeurs would probably be armed. The question was, who still mattered to Voldrev and Smythe so much that accounts had to be settled even after their deaths? Was he about to find himself face to face with the real pullers of the strings, or with warlords or crime bosses or someone unimaginably more powerful who still needed to be paid off or otherwise rewarded? Was this the final chapter in the saga of these maddened conjoined twins, and their entangled lives – two lives lived by one man?

He approached the left-hand limo cautiously and rapped his knuckles as politely as possible on the back window. It lowered soundlessly.

In the back of the car was not a hefty Russian oligarch or a gaunt man of power but a beautiful young woman. He could see her blonde tresses, an elegant diamond necklace and her slender fingers toying with the buttons of a cashmere coat. She was visibly apprehensive.

He was about to speak, but she interrupted. 'I am instructed to introduce myself as A. You are DCI Harry Taylor, I believe.'

'That's correct. Instructed by whom, may I ask?'

'As yes, this is permitted, too. My father, Vladimir Voldrev. I am Emilia, his daughter. I do not use his last name in my day-to-day life, for reasons he said you would understand.'

'Yes, yes. I do. Listen, I have an envelope for you. But we are in a certain amount of danger here. May I suggest you ask your driver to follow us – my colleagues and myself – a few hundred yards down the road to a more secure location?'

She considered this. 'Very well.' She nodded to the driver who indicated he understood in the rear-view mirror.

'Excuse me while I quickly make the same suggestion to the other car.'

He hurried over to the second Mercedes and repeated his polite request for access. Again, the window was lowered. But this time the occupant in the back of the limo was a young man – perhaps a year older than the woman? He was more confident. 'Good evening. DCI Taylor? Excellent. I am B if that is who you are looking for. My name is Max.'

'And you are the son of Vladimir Voldrev, correct?' said Harry.

'No, never heard that name, I'm afraid. I'm Max Sherwood. My father Julian Smythe owns this estate. If you're confused – I use my late mother's surname for security reasons. At my father's insistence, in case you were wondering.'

'Yes, I understand,' said Harry – at least he was getting there. He repeated his instructions to follow the Range Rover, and Max, too, agreed.

Running back to the Range Rover, Harry felt, for the first time, a small, deeply unwelcome ripple of sympathy for his terrible adversary. Yes, these two people *were* all that had mattered at the end to Vova and Julian. What was left of the mad vanity and murderous cruelty of their schizophrenic lives was only one pure emotion: love.

Carol drove them to the nearest lay-by, with the two limos in convoy. They were now at least a mile away from Raxall. They would be safe, or as safe as they could be, especially as there was practically no wind in the early-morning air.

Soon, the sun would rise, and the horizon would fill with the armada of vehicles and helicopters that Robinson and his masters must already have despatched.

And then, as he opened the door, the sky filled once more with the apocalyptic light that Vladimir Voldrev and Julian Smythe had made their own. Seconds later, the terrifying blast made him stagger and cling on to the door of the car. Where Raxall Manor had stood rose a mushroom cloud rising towards the heavens. The patches of forest nearby blazed furiously and the atomic winds flattened signposts, hedgerows and glasshouses. Fragments of timber flew through the air as if borne by a tornado.

For the second time in less than twenty-four hours, this demented criminal had destroyed all trace of a palace that had been a mark of his status, power and global reach. Like the Caribbean chateau, it had simply ceased to exist, leaving behind only the angry gusts of atomic detonation: the last will and testament of Julian Smythe and Vladimir Voldrev.

# 38

Harry felt her hand on his shoulder, awakening him from his reverie.

'Hey,' Iris said. 'You'll get cold outside. Come back in and have another drink. Robinson has started to do impressions. They're terrible. You don't want to miss it.'

Harry laughed. Iris could always make him laugh, and it always felt good. He had stepped outside the Lamb because the atmosphere inside the pub of celebration, conviviality and relief was making him fretful. He knew he should be joining in, knocking back the beers with his team and all the well-wishers from the Yard. But his mind was still racing.

'I know,' he said. 'It's just . . . I keep thinking we could have stopped him earlier. Him. Them. Voldrev-Smythe.'

She was serious with him now. 'Nobody could have stopped it sooner. He said it himself. Without you, he might have carried on. He *would* have carried on, but you were smart enough to give him the final showdown his sick ego needed. You saved a lot of lives, Harry. There are people at home with their families tonight, still breathing, because you ended it all.'

'I hope so. I'm not sure. At least the rest of the uranium is back in safe hands. Maybe they'll keep a closer eye on that shit now.'

In both envelopes had been identical letters addressed to him, giving the precise location for the final device: the Stepney dump. But *of course*, Harry had thought. The symmetry of it. The great showman would just love the circular drama of *that* bloody finale.

After he briefed Robinson, Carol was despatched with Counter Terrorism (SO15) to disarm the fourth bomb. She had made the request, and, this time, he felt he could not deny her the chance.

They had listened to her reports in the situation room and watched the live feed from a drone hovering above the dump. There were four officers on the scene, including Carol, all weighed down by explosive-ordnance-disposal suits – as if that would make the slightest difference if the device was triggered.

'Gold,' she said over the comms. 'This is Blue Team. Approaching the package now.'

On the screen, he and Robinson – flanked by the Met's top brass and an unidentified adviser from Number Ten – watched Carol and another officer approach what looked like an old-fashioned beatbox. On an ordinary day, you wouldn't even have noticed it, thought Harry. *'Things aren't always what they seem.'* Too right.

The drone feed zoomed in on the box. It was not the mess of wires and circuitry he had expected. He watched Carol and the EOD sergeant examine its surface and confer quietly.

'This is strange.'

*Oh Christ*, he thought. *Not another riddle. Not another maze in which they might all get lost.*

He spoke into the comms panel. 'Blue, this is Taylor. Say again. Strange how?'

'Gold – it's strange because it looks so – so simple. It's a bloody kindergarten switch, this one. Basic training model.'

He could see the accompanying sergeant nodding.

'Blue – we hear you. Can you tell us more?'

'There's a single wire. Cut that – and it should deactivate.

Simple as that. Weirdly simple. Unlike our man. Where's the catch?'

Harry looked at Robinson, who was pale and drawn. 'Roger that, Blue. I hear what you say. Do you want to withdraw? Scope it out further with the drone.'

He could see Carol thinking, probably as deeply as she had ever thought in her life.

'That's a negative, Gold. I see what he's doing here. It's over. Unless we leave it, of course. In which case—'

Silence reigned in the situation room.

'Request go-ahead to proceed, Gold,' said Carol.

Harry's mouth was dry. 'Roger that, Blue – stand by.'

The call was not his to make. That had been made very clear. Not his, not Robinson's, not even the Met Commissioner's. Sir Muhammad sat silently at the table, his fingers pressed into his temples. The order to proceed – or not, as the case may be – would come from the Prime Minister, who was monitoring the operation from Chequers in consultation with the Home Secretary.

He watched the Downing Street adviser – another tall, spindly toff – speaking quietly into his secure mobile. Harry felt himself age as the conversation carried on. He thought of Carol in the field. And of John.

'That's a "go" from the PM,' said the young man, nodding a little too imperiously for Harry's taste.

He cleared his throat. 'Blue – clear to go. Proceed at will.'

'Roger that, Gold,' said Carol. 'Wish us luck.'

The sergeant handed her the cutters – the most basic tools of his trade – and Carol took them in her gloved right hand.

'Proceeding,' she said.

The zoom on the drone was now as tight as it could get, the image a little fuzzier. They could see her hands as she carefully placed the lone wire between the blades of the cutter.

She paused for what seemed an age – but was only a few seconds. 'Cutting now.'

And then his mind was suddenly ablaze with images: the flashing lights at the Cube, the chateau on Elena, the slashed throats of the Devereux gang, the rage of Ramirez, the images of death from Barbados, the wasteland of the Manchester towpath, the crazy dual life of Voldrev-Smythe unravelling in clouds of death and mayhem.

'All clear.' Carol's voice lifted him out of the whirlpool of his thoughts. 'Gold – I repeat, device deactivated.'

An audible sigh of relief coursed through the situation room. And then a round of applause.

The Commissioner shook hands with Robinson and Harry. And then was handed a phone by the adviser, doubtless to be congratulated on all the fine work he had personally done to spare the British mainland a third atomic explosion in less than a week.

'Congratulations, Blue Team,' said Harry. 'Get back to the Yard. Drinks are on me.'

Later, when he and Carol talked it through, he saw that they had reached exactly the same conclusion. There was no mystery, really. The fourth device was never meant to detonate – as long as the envelopes were handed over. That was the script. That was the twist in the tale.

As for the remaining uranium, there was also a location for that. Which was why Eaton Square had been evacuated and cordoned off for much of the previous day, as an MoD specialist unit extracted the original metal case from Julian Smythe's walk-in wardrobe where it had been left, with a bottle of Dom Perignon thoughtfully placed at its side and a monogrammed compliments slip.

The envelopes also contained instructions that would enable Emilia Stepanov and Max Sherwood – half-siblings, who somehow shared two fathers – to access one billion dollars apiece lodged in Swiss bank accounts, and an additional sum of cryptocurrencies that was harder to value. In short letters, their respective fathers – the same person, of course – had admonished them to put the money to wise and peaceful use and to forgive them for the terrible lives they had led.

Harry had assumed that neither child would ever see a dime of the money. Wrongly, it seemed. Robinson, who had whisked daughter and son off to a secure location after the handover, had broken the news to him the following day that the orders from the very top were: leave well be.

'You're joking,' Harry said when they were back at the Yard. 'You have to be *kidding*, Bill. That's drug money. Blood money.'

'I know, Harry,' said his boss. 'It stinks. Though the kids are clean. They've no involvement in anything criminal as far as we can see. They check out, pure as the driven snow. He seems to have kept them away from the family business.'

'You really buy the idea that neither of them knew why their father – Julian or Vova – was quite so rich? Or that they never heard the rumours?'

Robinson stretched back. 'Christ, I don't know, Harry. They're kids. Who knows what they knew? Who knows what they wanted to know? They've both led bloody protected lives, I can tell you. Away from the action. Not known in any capacity to law enforcement. Boarding schools, separate homes, housekeepers. The closest thing to innocence in this whole deplorable world.'

'But we can't just be letting children inherit the proceeds of crime. Billions of dollars. And what do you mean "leave well be"?'

'I mean that it's going to take a bloody long time to clear

up this mess. Did you know that the United Kingdom just became the second nation ever to have been attacked twice by nuclear weapons? Us and Japan. Sharing top honours. Barbados gets the bronze for its single explosion.'

'You think this is funny?'

'Not really. I'm just being realistic. Come on, Harry. Think it through. Do you really believe that our political masters are going to admit that *one man* managed to fool the entire world's security services for several decades, using a dual identity? And – to add to the insult – had the nerve to get hold of a significant quantity of uranium-235 that, somewhere along the line, had been misplaced by a bunch of clowns? In what world does that version of events ever appear on the front pages?'

'When you and I tell the media. That's when. When we tell the truth.'

Robinson stood up. 'I agree, we could try. But I promise you this: we'd be locked up immediately on grounds of national security. D-notices all round. Our names dragged through the mud, lies drip-fed to the press and social media, the whole idea laughed out of court.'

'So, who's getting the blame for the bombs, then?'

'It will be blamed officially on a rogue team of select terrorists, most of whom are already in custody at classified locations. Kept vague, for reasons of national security. And – one thing Voldrev-Smythe would have liked – it'll be used by governments all over the world as a cautionary tale about nuclear smuggling.'

'So they can grab lots of anti-terrorist powers for themselves? Shred a few more civil liberties?'

'Maybe. But maybe not. Maybe this will be a wake-up call. Who knows?'

'Do you really *believe* that crap, Bill? Really? Don't you just feel sick to the pit of your stomach?'

'Of course!' he snapped. 'It makes my skin creep. But I'll tell you this: there's also a big part of me that's fucking glad Vladimir Voldrev and Julian Smythe will be denied their moment of public glory, they – he, whatever – craved so badly. I absolutely don't want that bastard to become some sort of historic figure. And he won't now. No books, or documentaries, or Netflix series, or T-shirts. For dishonourable reasons, I grant you. But it's the right outcome, by shitty means.'

'It's all wrong.'

'Yes, it is. And there's a whole lot of wrong at moments like this. Always. They come along very rarely and they force blokes like you and I to ask the only question that counts.'

'And what's that, Bill?'

'Are we willing to stomach the lies and the politics so we can carry on catching villains? Swallow hard and keep doing the job? So that we can say "fuck you" under our breath to our masters and then get on with what we know has to be done. Which, by the way, they *absolutely* want us to carry on doing, with a considerably enhanced budget, I might add. Big shake-up of the Yard coming up. And Harry?'

'Yeah?'

'Before you get all noble on me and flounce out of here with a moral nosebleed, remember this: there are fucking few people who can do what you did. What your team did. What we all did. This is the beginning of something new and very scary. You're the first senior copper anywhere to deal with this escalation in the criminal world. It's a game-changer. Are you really ready to walk away from it? Not to be around for next time? Because I'm not. You've got a lot to do, my son.'

'That's emotional blackmail, Bill. You can't do that.'

'Harry Taylor, my old mate. Don't you know, after all these years in the trenches together, that's pretty much *all* I do.'

Would he stay? That was what Harry had really stepped out of the pub to decide, he realised. How could he? How could he collude in the bullshit for a second longer? How could he honour his comrade, John Williams, and all the other innocent people slaughtered over the years by Voldrev and Smythe by swallowing a lie of this scale?

And yet, how could he walk away? Robinson was right about one thing: there was plenty of work to do. The international networks left behind by the two men – one man – had to be rolled up, and quickly. And the new map of the drug trade needed to be policed in the right way by people with experience. It had been a brush with history, and it wasn't over. Not really. Was he ready to leave the job unfinished just when it was starting?

And what, in the end, would he do instead? A forty-five-year-old copper who had seen two nuclear explosions up close. He couldn't pretend to be someone else, even if everyone else was lying. This was what he did, God help him. It was what he was. It was the job. It was the life.

'I keep thinking back to something Voldrev said on the island, Iris,' Harry said. 'He said that Russians try not to "chase death". That's what I feel I've been doing all this time. Chasing death.'

'Yeah,' she said softly, 'but you're still alive. And so am I. And you have work to do. And a life to lead.'

He looked at her. She smiled. 'You'll figure it out. You always do.' She kissed his cheek tenderly and went back inside.

He looked out at the empty street – the cars passing, the couples walking quickly through the cold and laughing – and thought about what she had said and the way she had kissed him. Then he opened the door and went to join her.

# Acknowledgements

I've always enjoyed reading thrillers and had the idea of writing one of my own for years – so I'm glad that life has finally allowed me the time to do it. This story is inspired by a true one I read in the paper about uranium being found by workmen on an East End dump. I am very grateful to my friend Matthew D'Ancona for all the support he gave in helping me to put it together. Matthew did a great deal of the research, but no doubt I've taken a few liberties for the sake of the story, and so any mistakes are down to me.

I also want to thank the team at Hodder & Stoughton, especially Rowena Webb, Nick Sayers, Morgan Springett, Olivia Robertshaw and Eleni Lawrence. Thanks too to my agent Caroline Michel.

And lastly, my love and thanks as ever to my wife Shakira.

## About the Author

Sir Michael Caine CBE has been Oscar-nominated six times, winning his first Academy Award for the 1986 film *Hannah and Her Sisters*. He has starred in over one hundred films, with critically acclaimed performances including his first major film role in *Zulu* in 1964, followed by films such as *The Ipcress File*, *Get Carter*, *Alfie*, *The Italian Job*, *Dirty Rotten Scoundrels*, *Educating Rita*, and the *Dark Knight* trilogy. More recent films have included *Harry Brown* and *King of Thieves*, while 2023 sees the release of *The Great Escaper* co-starring Glenda Jackson.

He was appointed a CBE in 1992 and knighted in 2000 in recognition of his contribution to cinema. In 2023 he celebrated his 90th birthday.

In 2018 his memoir *Blowing the Bloody Doors Off* was a *Sunday Times* top ten bestseller. *Deadly Game* is his first thriller.

Married to Shakira for more than fifty years, he has two daughters and three grandchildren, and lives in London.